THE
BRIDLED
GROOM

Also by J. S. Borthwick

Dude on Arrival
Bodies of Water
The Student Body
The Down East Murders
The Case of the Hook-Billed Kites

THE
BRIDLED
GROOM

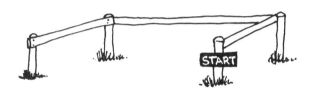

J. S. Borthwick

St. Martin's Press
New York

THE BRIDLED GROOM. *Copyright © 1994 by J. S. Borthwick. Text illustrations © 1993 by Willette Brown. All rights reserved. Printed in the United States of America. No part of this book may be used or reproduced in any manner whatsoever without written permission except in the case of brief quotations embodied in critical articles or reviews. For information, address St. Martin's Press, 175 Fifth Avenue, New York, N.Y. 10010.*

Design by Basha Zapatka

Library of Congress Cataloging-in-Publication Data

Borthwick, J. S.
    The bridled groom / J. S. Borthwick.
        p.   cm.
    ISBN 0-312-10435-9
    1. Deane, Sarah (Fictitious character)—Fiction. 2. McKenzie, Alex (Fictitious character)—Fiction. 3. Man-woman relationships—Maine—Fiction. 4. Women detectives—Maine— Fiction. 5. English teachers—Maine—Fiction. I. Title.
PS3552.O756B74 1994
813'.54—dc20   *93-42101*
                                                                              CIP

First Edition: March 1994

10 9 8 7 6 5 4 3 2 1

For Jet and The Griffin

A grateful nod to Alec Creighton for assistance with the details of nickel mining and other matters geological. And many thanks to Willette Brown and the staff at Hunter Hill Farm for help in designing the cross-country course and for discussions about farm layouts and general horse management. Also a thank you to Ida Anderson for a particularly macabre suggestion regarding the placement of a body. Finally, let me express my gratitude to my chief riding instructor and my companion of many years: my horse, Conky Noodle.

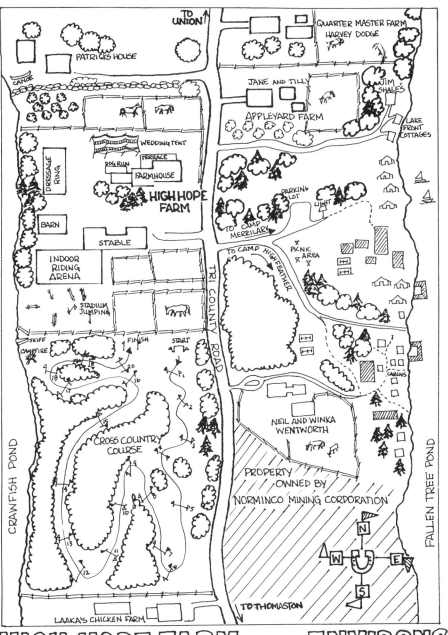

HIGH HOPE FARM AND ENVIRONS

Cast of Principal Characters

Sarah Deane—Teaching fellow at Bowmouth College

Alex McKenzie—Physician

Julia Clancy—Owner of High Hope Farm; aunt to Sarah and Jessica

Patrick O'Reilly—Stable Manager, High Hope Farm

Sean Conners—Stableman at High Hope Farm

Rafe Posner—Stableman at High Hope Farm

Jessica Jacoby—Cousin to Sarah Deane, niece to Julia Clancy

Colonel Harvey Dodge—Owner of Quartermaster Farm

Farney Thompson—Stableman at Quartermaster Farm

Tilly Martin—Co-owner of Appleyard Farm with Jane Zimmer

Jane Zimmer—Co-owner of Appleyard Farm with Tilly Martin

Winka Wentworth—Director, Camp Highfeather for Boys; wife of Neil

Neil Wentworth—Assistant Director, Camp Highfeather

Leah Pfeifer—Director, Camp Merrilark for Girls

Bradley Pfeifer—Assistant Director, Camp Merrilark, nephew to Leah Pfeifer

Tim Fournier—Farrier

Jim Shale—Geologist with Norminco Mining Corporation

Sergeant George Fitts—State Police CID

Mike Laaka—Sheriff's Deputy Investigator

Katie Waters—Deputy Sheriff

And assorted campers, neighbors, firemen, horses, dogs, and cats

THE BRUSH

ONE

I sing of Maypoles, Hock-carts, wassails, wakes, of bridegrooms, brides, and of their bridal cakes.

—Robert Herrick, "Hesperides
The Argument of his Book"

APRIL. Sunday. Wet and disagreeable. Mud. Rain to continue through the day.

It was well after eight o'clock in the morning when Julia Clancy, a sturdy gray-haired woman of advanced years, who, having assisted at morning chores—the feeding and watering of a large number of horses—decided that she had earned a second cup of coffee and a quiet hour with the morning paper. To this end, she squelched her way down the drive, crossed the road to the white plastic cylinder marked *Maine Sunday Telegram* that stood next to her mailbox, and reached for the large rolled periodical. Then, turning to leave, she was forced to jump back as a gray Wagoneer honking, jammed to a stop at her feet. The driver's window rolled down and her neighbor, Colonel Harvey Dodge, poked out his head, his cheerful face a full moon with a fringe of white hair.

"Hah, Julia. Good morning," called Harvey, smiling broadly. "I've been to church. I have been shriven. Or is it shrived?"

"Good for you, Harvey. I have not. And going to church hasn't improved your driving. You almost ran me down. Now

1

move along before someone rear ends you." And Julia ducked in front of his car and, as she recrossed the road, waved the colonel on with a flick of the wrist.

But Harvey lingered. "Shall I come in? Have coffee with you?"

"Certainly not, Harvey. I'm extremely busy. Every minute is taken care of." And Julia, thinking of peace with her Sunday paper, again gestured the colonel forward, turned her back, and marched toward her farmhouse.

This exchange of courtesies prevented Julia Clancy from examining her paper until she had settled in a comfortable chair and taken a life-giving draught of coffee. Now she shook the front page loose and on doing so brought forth a long unstamped white envelope that had been folded into the paper's midsection.

"Oh damnation," said Julia. She dropped the envelope to the floor as if it emitted a noxious odor, kicked it to one side, and addressed herself to the editorial section of the Sunday paper.

This attention to world news and opinion did not last.

"Damnation," said Julia again. She reached for the envelope, picking it up between thumb and forefinger. The same as the first two. Her name cut out, letter by letter, from a glossy magazine. JULIA CLANCY—HIGH HOPE FARM. No complete address because this letter had been hand-delivered, inserted into the fold of the newspaper, while the previous two had been mailed in self-stamped envelopes with Julia's name and address in cut-out letters and numbers: 3285 TRI-COUNTY ROAD, UNION, MAINE.

Julia, with an expression that suggested she was confronting a venomous snake, tore off the envelope's end and extracted a sheet of paper. A now familiar-looking sheet on whose surface was pasted a set of clipped-out letters. The letters, like those of previous messages, were arranged to spell out a mangled nursery rhyme adapted to fit the recipient: Julia. This one was short and to the point: Ding dong bell, / Pussy's in the well. / Julia Clancy go to hell.

With a snort of annoyance, Julia stuffed the offending piece of paper into her khaki corduroy breeches and picked up her newspaper. But her pleasure in it was gone, her coffee had cooled, and looking out the window she noticed that the early morning drizzle had changed to a more settled and determined rain.

With the hope of redeeming the day—or at least the morning—Julia rose to her feet. She felt the need of doing something positive and, fortunately, she had the very thing at hand. A wedding reception. There was nothing like a wedding reception to keep one distracted, especially since the happy event was to take place at her own beloved farm in honor of her favorite niece, Sarah Douglas Deane, and her husband-to-be, Alex McKenzie, Julia's own physician and arthritis counselor.

Julia stumped to the door, grabbed her olive drab slicker from a hook, wrenched the door open and, head bent against the rising wind and rain, made her way to her car. Sarah and Alex would have hot coffee. They might have a slice of toast or a pancake for their old aunt. And they might have an idea about the three pieces of disagreeable mail. She gunned her all-purpose vehicle, a battered Dodge Ram, out of the drive and turned toward the Camden hills and the house of the bride- and groom-to-be.

And indeed a wedding was in the works. The bride—although she might have bristled at the word—was Sarah Douglas Deane, a twenty-eight-year-old woman who labored as an underpaid teaching fellow and doctoral candidate in English—nineteenth-century fiction—at Bowmouth College, an elderly institution of higher learning wedged into the foothills of Camden, Maine.

The groom, Alexander Sinclair McKenzie, plied his trade—medicine—at the Mary Starbox Memorial Hospital and at Bowmouth Medical School—one of the many graduate arms of Bowmouth College, which like its more illustrious cousin, Dartmouth, hid its university status under the title of "college"—being, as Sarah remarked, yet another academic wolf in sheep's clothing.

This wedding had been long debated and delayed, not only from spasms of bridal uncertainty but also from the conflicting work schedules of the two parties. To many the wedding seemed to have been purposely put off by the happy pair in order to outwit and generally irritate hovering relatives. Now, however, a date was set for the third week of June.

Sarah Deane and Alex McKenzie approached the coming ceremony unencumbered by previous marital baggage and with several useful years of living together under their belt. This last fact alone made them aware that cohabitation only whets the wedding appetite of concerned family members—particularly those in the grandparent generation. These long-in-the-tooth relatives could hardly wait to count china, number silver spoons, drag formal costumes out of mothballs, plan trips to pricier dress shops, and spend long evenings going over lists of unheard-of cousins once removed. The communications fall-out from these activities had for some weeks kept local post offices busy, telephone lines crackling, and answering machine tapes clogged.

On this particular rainy Sunday morning, Sarah and Alex were for once together at the breakfast table. Alex was not on call and Sarah had corrected three quarters of her student papers on *Middlemarch*, so that both were free to sort through an accumulation of telephone messages, mail, notes, memos, and lists.

Alex picked through the litter and produced an oversized postcard featuring a green-tinted androgynous nude leaping across a desert landscape. "It's from my cousin Giddy," he announced. "She'll be able to make the wedding after all and she wants to bring her new boyfriend—that art student called the Gorilla."

Sarah pushed her orange juice aside and grabbed the card and grinned. "He's the one who got hold of your father's old golf clubs for that student sculpture exhibit at the art institute."

Alex groaned. "That guy. I remember. He sprayed the bag and clubs with silver paint and entered the thing under the title 'Capitalist Toy—from the collection of Professor John McKenzie, Harvard University.' If the Gorilla turns up at the wedding my father will throttle him on the spot."

"Well," said Sarah, "I thought it was quite effective. The public loves to hate anything tagged Harvard." She opened a pink envelope and pulled out a pink and silver folder. "Oh God, it's from something called Bridal Bouquet Catering: 'We at Bridal Bouquet can make your VERY SPECIAL day one that will live forever in your dreams.'" She looked up. "More like nightmare if we don't get a handle on this wedding."

"Scrap Bridal Bouquet," said Alex, reaching across the table, and tearing the pink paper in half. This act he followed by discarding in fast succession an invitation from Horse & Carriage to hire a team of Belgian horses and a replica stagecoach in which to drive to the wedding and an offer from Bridal Bed & Breakfast to make that "First Night a Night to Remember."

"Like the *Titanic*?" asked Sarah. "Okay, what's next?"

"Music," said Alex. "My mother called last night and said that it's crucial at the reception because if there isn't music and dancing, guests drink too much and start insulting each other."

"She has a point," Sarah admitted. "My mother hopes we won't just have rock because half our relatives can barely totter into a foxtrot or a waltz. I told her I've nailed a music group called the Fore and Aft. Rock, soul, folk, country, plus Big Band for the Waltzing Matildas." Here she ruffled through the papers on the table and brought out a piece of yellow lined paper. "Aunt Julia," she said. "She wants a conference about reception details. Says she's allergic to answering machines and is sure we're home when she calls but won't answer the phone."

"She's right," said Alex. "And we won't answer this morning either. We need extreme quiet. I love Julia, but . . ."

"She's tough to take before breakfast," finished Sarah. "But Alex, she's the presiding spirit, the fairy godmother of the reception. And think of the work she's facing. A horse farm needs organizing with all that stuff around, tractors and pieces of fencing and hay and straw underfoot, not to mention horse manure."

"Is it too late to divert the whole business? Have the reception somewhere else?" asked Alex, who in the interest of breakfast had taken up a position by the waffle iron.

"Alex, she's been living for this—as much as she could live for something unconnected with horses. You know our parents have tried to derail her and were trampled in the process. She wants to have the reception. And to pay for it. No argument. We're the closest thing she has to children. So what if the wind is in the wrong direction? Horses are a lot less smelly than pigs."

"We weren't expecting to have the reception at a pig farm," said Alex. He extracted a waffle with difficulty from the grid and presented Sarah with the slightly damaged product.

"Anyway," said Sarah, dousing the waffle with maple syrup, "let her get on with it. I only said we didn't want the cake in the shape of Secretariat."

"And hope she won't serve oats and hay," said Alex, joining her at the table with a blackened waffle on his plate.

"She might," said Sarah thickly through a mouthful. She chewed hard, considered for a moment, and put down her fork. "I think you've found a substitute for Harris tweed."

"Don't bite the hand that feeds and don't change the subject," said Alex. "We're talking about managing your aunt with a minimum of damage to all concerned."

At which the kitchen door swung open, banged against the wall, and swung back. Julia had arrived.

"It's raining," she announced unnecessarily, "and who's talking about managing me?" Julia shook herself out of her slicker and made for an empty chair at the kitchen table.

Sarah looked up and sighed. Then smiled. Julia Clancy in her shapeless corduroy breeches, her rubber Wellingtons, with her stubby body and her short-cropped gray hair, always reminded her niece of an elderly terrier—one of the scrappy Scottish varieties.

"We're talking about managing you, beloved Aunt. We don't want you to work yourself into a decline and never ride again."

"If I didn't work, I would decline. What's that you're eating? Carpet slippers? Alex, give me one. I'm starved and it doesn't matter how it tastes. I've been up for ages with morning chores because Patrick, my rod and my staff, went to early mass, and Rafe Posner, my other rod, came in late. Is that coffee over there?"

Sarah pushed aside the wedding clutter, produced a mug of coffee while Julia wrestled with a new-made waffle. For a few moments she chewed and drank. Then heaved a sigh of satisfaction.

"Now I feel more human. At least as human as it's possible for a female who's almost seventy and has spent the last three hours in a stable." She turned to Sarah and fixed her with a reproachful frown. "Sarah—and Alex—I'm here in person because I can't get past that dreadful answering machine of yours with that canned message about being busy. I need decisions and I need advice. Something rather annoying has been going on. No"—this as both Sarah and Alex paused in mid-waffle—"first the reception. I need input. The guest list. How many? Because of the food. Just let me know the awful total and if you want maids and bartenders or just family slaves."

"The farm," murmured Sarah. "There's so much to do."

"I suppose you're fidgeting about the manure. Don't worry. I've got people to clean up around the stables and make everything look like Virginia or Kentucky. I think the horses out in the pasture will look picturesque so when people get tired of milling around in a hot tent they can wander on down to the stable. The cake's all taken care of. Tilly Martin has promised to make the whole thing even if it has to be the size of a refrigerator."

Alex looked up. "Tilly? You mean that wacky blonde librarian on the farm near you? Appletree something."

"Appleyard Farm," said Julia. "Sarah knows her. Tilly lives with Jane Zimmer. They retired together after putting the Kennebunkport library on its ear with readings on the women's movement. Tilly is a bit mad, but she makes divine cakes and does things with herbs and potions. I'm very fond of her." Here Julia paused and then took a deep breath. "But here's what's bothering me. Someone wants me to leave the farm. Get out. I've been getting mysterious messages."

Sarah looked up. "Messages? What sort of messages?"

"Stupid ones. Jumbled-up nursery rhymes. I've brought one to show you. I think it's that mine. You know that new copper or cobalt or nickel mine company that's trying to move in on Tri-County Road? Almost across from my farm. Everyone's in a lather about it and wondering whether we farm people will sell out. I know that Harvey Dodge has had calls from real estate people, and a geologist from the mine people has called on Tilly and Jane. But someone seems to want my farm in particular. That seems to be the point."

"No name?" put in Alex. "No signature?"

"Anonymous, cut-out letters, like a kidnapping ransom note."

"Someone thinks your farm has copper and nickel?" asked Sarah.

"Or cobalt. Possibly. Though why, I can't think. I've never had the soil tested. Nor will I. As long as there's breath in this old body it's going to stay a horse farm. Norminco is the name, meaning, I suppose, Northern Mine Company. Their people have been sneaking around, trying to buy up—or lease—the shore property around Fallen Tree Pond. Taking core samples. Can you imagine what a mine will do to the Union Valley Hunt?"

"Yes," said Sarah. "All those horses and hounds crashing into a mine crater. What did Oscar Wilde say about fox hunts, the unspeakable in pursuit of the uneatable?"

"Oscar Wilde didn't hunt," said Julia. "Besides, we don't chase foxes, it's a drag hunt. The hounds follow a scent. My point is that even though I'm hanging on, I know everyone's on edge. It will be the end of an era with just a few farms left like little islands in the middle of big-time mining industry."

"Sic semper agricolae," said Alex.

"Agricola, agricolae, feminine farmer," said Julia. "Very odd, I've always thought. Perhaps the Romans were more enlightened about gender roles than we've given them credit for. But now read this." And Julia pushed herself away from the table, reached into her breeches pocket, and extracted a rather crumpled sheet of paper.

"Ding dong bell / Pussy's in the well," began Sarah.

"Yes, yes," interrupted Julia, "I've read it."

"Are the other two like this?"

"The same idea. The first started out 'Ladybird, ladybird / Fly away home / Your farm is on fire / Your horses are gone.' Some crank, I thought, so I just put it away. The next began 'Julia Clancy sat on a wall / Julia Clancy had a great fall' like the Humpty-Dumpty nursery rhyme. The last two used my name, so it's no mistake. Feeble efforts, except the scissor work, which is quite careful."

"Don't you think the police should know?" said Sarah.

Julia let out a sigh and put down her coffee mug. "No. Not now, anyway. It's just, well, annoying. But I suppose with everyone in a frenzy about the mine, messages like these aren't that unusual."

"Has anyone else around had them?"

"I haven't asked," said Julia, looking troubled. "After all, they may be from one of my own neighbors. For now I thought I'd just tell you two." She pocketed the note and rose, made for the door, then paused. "Get busy with your lists. I have to let the caterer know something. Weddings are a dime a dozen in June."

"Aunt Julia certainly has a way with words," said Sarah as the door slammed behind her departing aunt. She returned to the table, stacked the plates, gathered the coffee mugs, dumped them with a clatter into the ancient white enamel sink—their farmhouse was old—and sat down again at the table. "So what do you think," she asked, "about those so-called nursery rhymes?"

"Nothing yet. Distasteful but harmless."

Sarah nodded agreement and then spread the wedding papers in front of her. "Damn, why can't we get control over this thing?" She indicated several sheets of paper covered with names and addresses. "Aunt Julia wants to know how many. How about just the family?"

Alex looked up and frowned. "Make that families. They're multiplying like hamsters. Sisters having twins, sisters with new live-in boyfriends or girlfriends, brothers with new live-in girlfriends or boyfriends, aunts and uncles remarrying. Not to mention Giddy and the Gorilla."

"The immediate family. Not once-removed uncles and aunts and cousins and their new boy- and girlfriends."

"Wait until you try to cut some of them. It's not just family. Your Grandmother Douglas, for instance. She's handed in the list of the whole parish of St. Paul's–by-the-Sea in Camden as well as the rector, his assistant, plus the entire choir and assorted beadles and vergers and grave diggers."

"I know," said Sarah. "Grandmother Douglas is something else. And she thinks I'm going to be married in her church."

"Are we? Aren't we?"

"Damn," said Sarah again. "I don't know. Why not be married right here in our kitchen? I love our kitchen. Or I will when we get it painted." She turned and looked over at the walls, which were covered in a stained and faded rose-trellis paper. The kitchen-cum-dining-room was a space unchanged since its previous farmer-owner had had it "modernized" in 1924.

"Perhaps," Sarah added, "the garden. Or by the pine trees."

"We haven't got a garden," Alex reminded her. "Just crabgrass and pine trees. I suppose, Sarah, my love, you think we can just float hand in hand through our weeds to the squeal of a bagpipe playing 'Road to the Isles.' "

"Something like that," admitted Sarah.

"Then say I love you and I do. Like *Brigadoon.* Listen, major family occasions like weddings grow. They divide, metastasize."

"Like fungi? With spores?"

"More like bacteria. Or a virus. And the simple wedding is an oxymoron. Wherever you have it."

Sarah gave a violent shove to the assembled papers and watched them fan out over the floor with a certain grim satisfaction. "Let's take a walk. Patsy needs a run." Here she indicated a full-grown Irish wolfhound who, snoring softly, stretched his hairy length by the kitchen door. "Yes, I know it's raining. We have to do something normal unconnected with getting married; it's only the first week in April and this wedding—or circus—isn't until June. So let's get out and get some good wet air into our lungs."

"And all these guests? Or guests-to-be?"

"Later. Right now I'm not going to worry about who is going to come unglued because we didn't ask Aunt Phyllis, who's a kleptomaniac, or dear old Uncle Freddie, who's into wife abuse."

"Have you an Aunt Phyllis and an Uncle Freddie?"

"Probably." And Sarah stood up, reached for a slicker, attached Patsy to a dog leash, and headed for the door. "Come on. We'll make a stand. A simple wedding." She flung open the kitchen door and let in a sheet of blowing rain over the threshold. "Simple," she repeated.

By six o'clock that evening Sarah and Alex returned to the problem of a simple wedding and reception for hundreds of indispensable relatives and friends.

Alex walked to the refrigerator and removed two cold bottles of Heineken beer, handed Sarah hers, sat down, and raised a bottle. "Look over those names again," he said, nodding at the strewn papers now rumpled from the passage to and fro of Patsy. "Friends who've stood by in thick and thin. Your best buddy, Mary Donelli. She promised you an Italian wedding. Her husband, Amos Larkin, is on your doctoral committee. And there's your brother, Tony, who says his girlfriend, Andrea, will be out on parole by June."

"Oh God," said Sarah. For a long minute she stared at the papers. Then she scooped them up and wafted them into the air. "Let it snow, let it snow. Let it happen. Go with the flow. What the hell, we only live once. Maybe marry only once."

"We hope," said Alex. "Let's count and give Julia the total. Then we can infest the home of Mary and Amos. We'll see if they can produce an Italian wedding reception with a Scottish flavor."

"It's already been done," said Sarah. *"Lucia di Lammermoor.* The result was a little scary, though I must say it would be different." She stood up, walked to the window, and looked out across the field, where the roof of the Donelli-Larkin farmhouse could be made out across the rising pasture. "Poor Lucia went bananas after her wedding, so let's play it straight."

"Impossible. Mary Donelli has fierce Italian ideas and my mother's never played anything straight in her life. I wasn't joking when I said bagpipes."

Sarah grimaced. "Okay, here's how it'll be. Win one, lose one. The wedding here. Our own kitchen, backyard, wherever. Small. Our own thing. The reception? Whatever Aunt Julia wants. The works. An omnium gatherum. Italian. Scottish. Bagpipes. The Loch Ness Monster. *Lucia di Lammermoor* on horseback. The ghost of Elvis. Dracula. Madam Butterfly. Horses, dogs, cats, relatives unto the third and fourth generation."

"That's the spirit," said Alex. "Go for broke."

"No problem," said Sarah. "We will be. And so, I'm afraid, will Aunt Julia."

THE LOG

TWO

SEVERAL weeks later Alex met Sarah for a quick lunch at the cafeteria of the Mary Starbox Memorial Hospital. Sarah was between classes and Alex joined her after morning rounds.

Strangers watching the couple settle themselves at a small table, watching their gestures and arguments, might have come to the conclusion that the two were in some way related. Both were dark-haired, dark-eyed, and both showed a certain intensity in what they said and did. But, as friends pointed out, Alex masked his emotions with a pretense of calm reasonableness—very suitable in a physician practicing internal medicine. He kept his voice low, considered and analyzed and worked off tensions by skiing, sailing, and through the distractions of bird watching.

Sarah lived more on the edge of things, moved by urgencies, and a sympathetic imagination—this latter quality useful to the teacher and student of literature. And while Alex was strongly built, the sharp planes of his face and the brace of his shoulders suggesting mass, she was of a more birdlike construction, her body, elbows, and knees giving the impression—a false one—

that they were breakable; her thin face, her high cheekbones, her short dark spiky hair suggested someone ready for action, someone impatient. A tendency to plunge into troubled waters while more prudent friends—Alex frequently was one of these—stood on the shore and counseled discretion.

Now they settled themselves at a corner table, each with a plate of the day's specialty, that strange dish American chop suey. It was not an item tasty enough to interfere with the ongoing wedding debate.

"The trick," said Sarah, "is to delegate. Let our families have the ball. We can make a few executive decisions and go back to work. Of course, Grandmother Douglas is going on about the service, so if we don't check her now we'll have the Episcopal equivalent of the Vatican in charge. I'm trusting Aunt Julia can handle Grandma. It's her mother, after all. Stone wall meets stone wall. Two mighty fortresses."

Here Sarah spooned a quantity of chop suey into her mouth, chewed, and then laid down her fork. "How do they make this stuff? And why does all our food lately taste like something to wear? I suppose," she added thoughtfully, "that masterminding the reception is keeping Julia young. After all, she can't do the competitive horse scene anymore. But, poor dear, she's had another of those odd nursery rhyme messages. Something about 'Sing a song of sixpence' and Julia flying away. It's rather sinister, but she's still refusing to tell the police. Do you really think they're coming from someone connected with that Norminco mine?"

"I'll bet other landowners abutting the proposed mine site will be getting messages, maybe even heavy-breathing telephone calls or big cash offers, and some will be selling out. Julia'd better give in and have her land checked for minerals." Alex reached for the slab of apple pie beside his plate. "So what have we decided?"

"We've decided to give the family its head except for Grandmother Douglas. As for me, I won't come up for air until classes and exams are over." And Sarah rolled her napkin, smoothed her skirt, picked up her briefcase, leaned over to give Alex a passing glance of a kiss, and left the cafeteria at a trot.

Thus it was that Sarah and Alex through the month of April and well into early May endured like struggling swimmers, barely keeping abreast of incoming tides and strong currents. Occasionally they put their heads up into the world to say "no" or "yes" loudly to family movers and shakers and then ducked thankfully back into the flood of their work.

And the wedding plans like a mighty rock on a steep slope rolled forward, gathering accretions. Flowers were chosen, music practiced—Alex's brother, Angus, an aspiring trumpet player, wrestled with selections from Copland's *Appalachian Spring;* a menu of appropriate Italian foods was submitted to Julia Clancy by Sarah's friend Mary Donelli; and Father Smythe, the rector of St. Paul's–by-the-Sea, was tormented by messages from Mrs. Anthony Douglas, grandmother of the bride, and by ensuing vetoes from the granddaughter. And through it all, Julia Clancy prepared, planned, and created a reception that as time went by began to suggest a cross between a hunt breakfast and a hunt ball.

Julia Clancy, daughter of the above Grandmother Douglas, exemplified one of the two rules about children of strong-minded parents. These offspring either turn into human doormats, living lives of service and yes-saying, or they develop formidable personalities of their own. Julia was of the latter breed.

In the sixties she and her now-dead husband, Irish Tom Clancy, had bought High Hope Farm on a ridge in the town of Union, Maine, and from there had dealt with matters pertaining to the horse—riding, teaching, schooling, breeding, combined training. Now, although under siege by widowhood, old age, and an encroaching nickel mine, Julia, with the help of staunch farm manager Patrick O'Reilly and other horse types, tried to carry on with a full schedule. Children still came to be bellowed at about their hands, their heels, their seat. Horses arrived green and left tractable and trained, with the Julia Clancy seal of approval. Mares foaled, foals grew to yearlings, were eventually broken to saddle and bit, and went forth to the local equestrian marts. But of late, even with the help of Patrick, Julia was feeling the weight of years. She needed more help. Fewer horses. Not so many lessons. After the reception was over she would take stock. Cut back. Sell, reduce, retrench, and look to a diminished future.

And consider, for the hundredth time, the offered hand and heart of her neighbor and fellow rival in the show world, Colonel (Ret.) Harvey Dickerson Dodge.

The hand she could use. The heart she wasn't so sure of. His was not the sort of heart upon which most marriages are founded. Harvey Dodge had the heart of a nursemaid. A nanny. He cared, he advised, he scolded, he fussed. Fussed about horses, property lines, barns, fences, the mine. And fussed about Julia.

So what's my problem? Julia asked herself. At my age a nursemaid is probably just what I need. She added up Harvey Dodge's virtues. He cares about my farm as well as his own. Especially since Tom died. He comes over with advice, helps mend fences and stalls. He's finished four needlepoint pillows in my stable colors for me—Harvey was an ardent needle-pointer—and he's a good conversationalist. For Julia, of course, this meant that Harvey Dodge could talk pleasantly about such things as the management of colic, laminitis, strangles, and Potomac Horse Fever—subjects irrestible to the horse owner.

And, thought Julia with a slight start, there he is now. She looked out her kitchen window and saw the gray Wagoneer belonging to Colonel Dodge pull up by the side entrance to the stable courtyard.

Just as if he owned the place, thought Julia with a certain irritation. She picked up a saddle she had been cleaning, opened the door, and made her way down the path to the stable.

"Hello, Harvey."

"Julia, my dear." Harvey Dodge extended a hand—or as it

seemed to Julia, a paw—to take the saddle. This courtesy she refused, reminding him that she was not yet ready for a nursing home and was still able to carry her own tack.

Julia was right about the paw. Harvey Dodge was built rather like a large bear. Round-shouldered, grizzled hair, a mustache of bushy proportions, rather tubby as to shape, hirsute as to limbs, he wasn't exactly the sort of colonel one could picture confronting a Sioux uprising, facing the British at Princeton, or the Afghans at the Khyber Pass. The fact was that Harvey Dodge had spent his army time worrying about supplies, containers, and shipping schedules. Lately, to Julia's sometime annoyance, Harvey Dodge had transferred his caretaking energies to Julia and her farm.

And here he was again, and even though Harvey saw Julia almost daily he treated each meeting as an occasion for solicitude. "Julia, how are you? A little pale, I think. Iron deficiency. I have a wonderful tonic. With beta-carotene. Just for people our age." Harvey smiled his motherly smile. His conversation was often larded with mixed-up adages, maxims, and after several drinks with recitations of school-learned poetry. He knew every verse of the "Destruction of Sennacharib" and great chunks of Tennyson.

Julia ignored Harvey's comments. From long familiarity they floated by like falling leaves, unsought but not harmful.

Colonel Dodge went on, his voice serious, "A town meeting tonight. These Norminco people are making a presentation."

Julia shifted the weight of the saddle. "Let me put this back in the tack room," she said. And then over her shoulder, "A lot of good another meeting will do. We can rage and stamp and there will probably be a mine. Or several mines."

Colonel Dodge followed Julia down the gravel path into the stable, past the stalls to the tack room.

Julia settled the saddle on a rack and turned to her friend. "One mine leads to two mines. Three mines. The geologists are already sneaking around. Drilling. I've heard that Tilly Martin and Jane Zimmer over at Appleyard Farm had a man the other day in their north pasture. The whole area may turn into one big pit."

"Great heavens," said Harvey Dodge, who never gave in to strong language before the ladies.

"The trouble is," said Julia, throwing herself into an ancient brown leather chair whose stuffing exuded from various seams, "the trouble is that the whole area needs a mine."

Harvey looked puzzled. "Needs?"

"Needs. Like money. Cash. Livings. Harvey, you don't live in the real world. You're too used to going to the army PX and getting everything at discount. Lord above, we're in the middle of a recession. This whole area is up for grabs. A few cow and horse operations, a few summer cottages can't compete with what a mine can do for the community. Jobs and a steady income. They say that Norminco will spend between thirty and forty million developing the project. Even so, I won't sell. No nickel mine can take away sixty acres of pasture. We'll put earmuffs on the horses and go on."

"Of course, Julia."

"I was hoping for the EPA. Get the EPA to stop it. But Norminco is promising a hundred ways to—in their words—minimize the impact. Fill in holes, recycle the water, regulate water acidity. Anyway, I'm afraid that economics will win out."

Colonel Dodge looked past Julia seeming to inspect a dusty line of show ribbons and a series of shelves holding tarnished silverware representing past triumphs of High Hope Farm. In particular, his eye was drawn to impressive pieces won by the sixteen-hand gray gelding Mickey Mantle, on whom Julia had ridden for fourteen years and beaten the pants off Colonel Harvey Dodge and his succession of Quartermaster Farm beasts.

He turned away from the display and took a deep breath. "Julia, what I came over to say, again, is that I think you'd better marry me and let me worry about this mining business. Or help you worry. We'll face the mining people together."

"No," said Julia, as she had so often before. "Thank you, but no. I'm not giving up High Hope. Cut back, yes, but not give up. It's my whole life."

Harvey again extended his paw, which he now rested heavily on Julia's shoulder. "Been thinking it over. I'd be willing to sell Quartermaster. To a farmer I hope, not Norminco. Come here with you. Live at High Hope. Bring my horses over. Join forces. Face the enemy together. Shoulder to shoulder."

In an automatic reaction Julia lifted Harvey's hand from her own shoulder. But she was shaken. This was new. Up till now the proposal went with a plan for Julia to sell her property and move into the colonel's Quartermaster Farm down the road. She had to gather her wits and fend off this new idea with due acknowledgment of what must be a great personal sacrifice.

She made the appropriate noises. Said thanks again, was touched, hoped they'd always be friends, relied upon his help and advice, but no.

"Think it over, Julia," said the colonel. "We're both getting on." He drew a breath and looked down at Julia with a sentimental eye. " 'But at my back I always hear / Time's winged chariot hurrying near.' "

"You don't have to remind me," said Julia. "Even in poetry."

"Companionship. Help through old age."

"You on your farm visiting me. Me on my farm visiting you."

"Julia," said the colonel, with something like exasperation, "it would be a perfect match. Think it over. I'll go now and check the rails on your west paddock and tonight I'll come round for a drink." And Colonel Dodge took his burly tweed-covered self—it was cool for May—out of the tack room.

Julia watched him go with something almost like regret. But she reminded herself: a caretaking person like Harvey allied to a take-charge person like herself was a recipe for strife.

Further, the use by Harvey Dodge of the expression "perfect match" did something to Julia's spine. It stiffened it. A perfect match was exactly what Julia had had. With Tom Clancy. A marriage made in horse heaven. No matter that the High Hope breeding program had produced only foals, and that the middle-aged lovers themselves had brought forth no young Clancy riders; it was in Julia's mind the perfect match. The only perfect match. No room for another. And yet . . .

A sound at the tack room door. Her niece Sarah Deane stood on the threshold. "May I come on in?" she asked.

"Sarah, good. I'm sitting here lost in nostalgia. Wanting Tom and being offered Harvey. Do you think I'm wrong? After all, a couple of old goats like us . . ."

"Not goats," corrected Sarah. "Old campaigners."

"But," said Julia, "I don't love the man, although I suppose it would be a perfectly practical alliance."

"Are you saying Harvey Dodge isn't sexy?" asked Sarah.

Julia smiled. "I've never thought of Harvey and sex in the same breath. He was married to Phyllis, of course, and had those two girls, but I never could picture him between the sheets. Phyllis's sheets. Or my sheets. I've always thought of him as a very kind neighbor. But not sexy. More like a nice gelding."

"I know what it is," said Sarah. "It's High Hope Farm. You couldn't give it up."

"But that's the odd thing. He suddenly offered to sell Quartermaster and move in here. I was quite taken aback. Naturally, I didn't say yes, but I was rattled. I admit it."

"That *is* a switch. Do you think he knows something? They haven't found gold on your farm, have they? Or nickel or copper?"

"No. Nor will I let anyone dig for it. Not even if someone told me I was sitting on plutonium. I've the finest grazing for miles around. I have what I want. Everything. Except life everlasting in a stable with Tom. In a heaven with horses."

"Harvey Dodge might think you have everything *he* wants. He hasn't the spread you do. You can't tell about men who act like nannies. After all, those anonymous messages were made out of nursery rhymes. Harvey Dodge is always spouting poetry."

"But not nursery rhymes. If he has a nefarious purpose I can't imagine it. He adores Quartermaster Farm. It's plain old-fashioned sacrifice. He wants to share our old age." Julia sighed a sigh that came from the soles of her mud-caked farm boots. "Enough of that. Now, Sarah, what of the reception?"

"You tell me," said Sarah. "Is it going to be a hunt ball and the place filled with red coats?"

"Pink," said Julia. "Pink coats. They may look red but they're called pink. The redcoats were the British. Against the embattled farmer. The shot heard round the world. One of Harvey's favorite poems. And it's not so far out. All of us around are embattled farmers. We might consider getting up a militia."

"No, Aunt Julia. After the wedding you can run amok. Lie down across the road, chain yourself to the mine office. But now we need you out of jail. Change of subject." Sarah fished in her jeans pocket and came up with a cream-colored card with green printing. "I'm taking some reception invitations around by hand. COME AND CELEBRATE AT HIGH HOPE FARM. SATURDAY, JUNE EIGHTEENTH. FOUR O'CLOCK. Right to the point. Nothing about a wedding reception so no one need feel he has to send presents. I'm going to see Mike Laaka's family and then Tilly and Jane. I've heard Tilly is off on one of her flights from reality and Jane is being protective."

"Tilly," said Julia, "is usually on a flight from something. Or toward something. Probably on a broom. The only time she's really sane is when she's cooking, working in the garden, or sorting books. But since you're going over, ask what that Norminco geologist was doing in their pasture. What he said. And are they going over to the enemy."

"Aunt Julia, I will not snoop on your neighbors. My mind is on a wedding. On my uncorrected papers and student exams. On what to do about Giddy and the Gorilla. And on Alex. Not necessarily in that order." And Sarah marched out of the tack room.

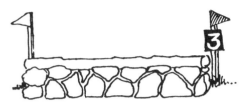

THE STONE WALL

THREE

THE Laaka family lived on a small farm—white clapboard house, attached barn, chicken house, and tractor shed—at the end of Julia Clancy's southern pasture. The Laakas were animal lovers who, because their house was set on a rise of ground, could view Julia's horses without the trouble and cost of maintaining their own. Instead the Laakas concentrated on poultry, as testified to by the sign FRESH EGGS that stood at the foot of their entrance road.

Sarah was welcomed, offered coffee and a tour of the latest hatching of Plymouth Rock chicks—both of which she declined pleading schoolwork—and she handed over the invitation.

"You don't want moldy old folk like us," said Alice Laaka.

"Yes we do. You and Fred. And Mike and his current girlfriend, whoever she is. Alex and I want all the Laakas. In those two awful murder cases last year, Mike practically lived with us. And Alex grew up with Mike. Alex says they were both terrors."

Alice Laaka smiled, a little grimly. "Terrors isn't the half of it. And imagine, they've both turned out respectable."

Respectable was perhaps too strong a word, Sarah thought. Alex, as both an internist and one of the county's medical examiners, certainly appeared respectable, but his past contained many examples of unconventional action. And Mike Laaka, busy Knox County Deputy Sheriff Investigator, had his own unorthodox moments, among which was satisfying his passion for Thoroughbred racing and so spending a certain amount of clandestine time on the phone to arrange off-track betting. However, Sarah was not one to disturb a fond parent's picture of the two men.

Ready to depart she shook hands, adding, "Now I'm going over to Appleyard Farm with an invitation for Tilly and Jane."

Alice Laaka's pleasant face darkened. "Tilly's on a new kick. She's gone in for the stars and wants to buy Julia's farm."

Sarah stopped abruptly at the door. "Is she the one sending funny messages? Aunt Julia's been getting some peculiar mail. Rhymes telling her to leave the farm."

"I'm afraid I don't know what Tilly would do. Or not do," said Alice. "She's always been a little weird. But Sarah, if it is Tilly, she may switch to something else. She's never been what you call steady in her interests, except for her garden and her cooking. Last year she bottled some awful stuff made out of ginger and oak leaves that she called a youth tonic and two months later went into weaving dog fur. From Jane's Siberian husky. She knitted up some awful neck warmers out of it. I got one for Christmas."

Sarah thanked Alice for the information and climbed back into her car, turned, and headed up Tri-County Road in the direction of Appleyard Farm, home to Tilly Martin and Jane Zimmer.

This piece of land sat only a quarter of a mile north up the road, catty-corner to High Hope Farm, its eastern boundary lying along the shore of Fallen Tree Pond. The farm, made up of a series of rather dilapidated buildings painted in a now fading red, had been named when the orchard of apple trees had been a going item, and the two women on its purchase ten years before had seen no reason to change the title.

As Alex had remembered, Tilly Martin and Jane had been librarians in their professional life. Militant librarians, a term that may seem a contradiction in terms—librarians generally being considered by the public as a soft-spoken and careful breed.

Not so Tilly and Jane. In their librarian personae they voiced disapproval of certain best-selling authors, sneered at Ernest Hemingway, and kept photographs of strong-minded women such as Amy Bloomer, George Sand, Susan B. Anthony, and Betty Freidan on the wall facing the check-out desk. In short, they rocked the library boat in the small southern Maine town of Kennebunkport. So much so that there was a cry of relief among the town's conservatives when the two women at age forty-five retired early and settled down on Appleyard Farm to tend Welsh cobs and Siberian huskies (Jane) and corgis and a vegetable and herb garden (Tilly). Unencumbered by family—it was widely believed that strong-minded Jane had "put down" a husband and Tilly had no visible relatives—they lived frugally on a tiny income, struggling to keep their heads above water, but always doing so in apparent harmony.

They were busy—busy working, digging, plowing, seeding, all to little avail. The farm lay along a ledge; the orchard had ceased to bear anything but misshapen wormy apples; the pasturage was sparse and rocky—a real hardscrabble affair—and at the end of their first ten years they were down to one Siberian husky, one elderly Welsh cob, and three corgis. It was generally agreed at the start of their adventure that, since Tilly was unpredictable, Jane's broad shoulders and firm square hands would hold the show together—quite literally keeping her hand on the plow. So Jane toiled, and Tilly tended the garden and did the cooking with the genius of a born witch and in her spare time gyrated on the edge of things, took up arcane causes, and sponsored obscure projects. The locals called them Frilly Tilly and Plain Jane, at which Tilly laughed and said they were right on the money.

"I do feel frilly a lot of the time," Tilly said. She had golden-from-the-bottle curls, preferred yellow sweats, and was given to warbling sentimental war songs like "Lili Marlene" while working in her garden. Plain Jane sported woolen knickers or khaki drill, wore her salt-and-pepper hair in a modified chop, and rode with the Union Valley Hunt on her remaining horse, an old Welsh cob mare named Lily Glendower. Tilly followed by car with brandy.

Sarah thought they both added a great deal to the neighborhood and wished she could have spent time visiting.

At the sight of Sarah crawling out from the wheel of her old VW bug, now in its seventeenth year and on its third engine, both Tilly and Jane ran forward, followed by three barking corgis and the gray-and-white Siberian, named Tikka, who made Sarah welcome with a series of whooping *wurra wurra* noises.

"Guess what!" cried Tilly.

"We've been offered bags of money," said Jane. "For the whole place. Or fewer bags for a lease. Norminco says we're adjacent to the nickel deposit. Even that the deposit may extend to our land."

"You've accepted?" said Sarah in a shocked voice.

"Well, no," said Tilly. "But it's shaken us."

"Because we are a little desperate for money," admitted Jane. "Never mind, we resisted. I finally threw the geologist out."

"Not until after he'd finished the core samples," said Tilly. "He was quite nice. But a Gemini, and you never know which way a Gemini will turn. But I'm upset about the minerals. They can be dangerous. Cobalt, for instance. Toxic. They can send emanations."

"Tilly's gone a bit soft," said Jane. She looked at her companion with affection. "Real bats in her belfry."

"Yes," said Tilly, shaking her curls. "I like it that way."

Sarah extended the two invitations. "You've both got to come. Don't say no. We can't have a party without you."

Jane opened her envelope, turned it over to see if it bore the Crane imprint, found it did not, pursed her lips, and extracted the card proper and read it.

"Splendid," she said. "We'll be there with bells on. Or at least Tilly will have bells. And probably crossed garters as well. But you may have to persuade her, because she's not speaking to Julia. She called her just now and Julia was very cross."

"I'm sorry, Tilly," said Sarah, "but Aunt Julia's been upset. She's had some notes telling her to leave the farm, so if you talked about selling she might have hung up." As Sarah said this she watched Tilly to see if there was any change of expression, but Tilly looked not so much self-conscious as determined.

"She ignored my warnings," said Tilly. "All the signs."

"What Tilly means," said Jane, "is that Julia doesn't believe in the stars. Well, neither do I, but it makes Tilly happy if we take advice. When to put on the storm windows, when to put in the tomatoes. I'm Leo and Tilly is Scorpio."

"And Julia," said Tilly, "wouldn't you know, she's Taurus. Taurus people need tact and firmness."

"But Tilly," said Jane, "hasn't much tact. She's fey. Fey people are quite different."

"I depend on the stars," said Tilly. "They stay put. You know what Keats called them: 'still steadfast, still unchangeable.' "

Sarah sneaked a look at her watch and found she had ten minutes to spare for the stars. "What advice was it Aunt Julia didn't take?" she asked.

Tilly sighed. "I checked. The stars and Julia's horoscope. I threw the runes and I laid out five rows of cards and did a five-card triple shift into a pentagon. It was perfectly clear."

"What was?" said Sarah.

"Julia. To marry Colonel Dodge. Before the harvest moon."

"But," protested Sarah, "Aunt Julia doesn't want to marry Colonel Dodge."

"Want! Want! Wanting has nothing to do with it," said Tilly, her cheeks now quite pink with excitement. "Not only must she marry Colonel Dodge, she must promise to marry him by Midsummer's Eve. And she must move into his Quartermaster Farm before the harvest moon. Although actually it would be better if she moved by the August high tides."

"And if she doesn't?" asked Sarah, greatly amused.

Tilly's face set, her hands folded tightly together, and her eyes shifted to the horizon. "If the Widow Clancy does not marry Colonel Dodge, then there will be blood on the moon, blood against the sun, blood soaking on the new-mown hay." For a moment she stood unmoving, then her face crumpled and her hands fluttered.

"There, there, Tilly," said Jane. She took hold of one of Tilly's agitated hands. "This is one of her excited days," she explained to Sarah, who, rather appalled, had backed up a few steps. And to Tilly, "Now dear, get a grip."

And Tilly got a grip. She freed her hands and spoke quietly, rationally, as if explaining a simple arithmetic problem to a child.

"You see," said Tilly, "it's time to rotate. I knew that when that geology fellow came here wanting to dig. It was another sign. We must rotate each a quarter turn."

"Rotate? Rotate where?" said Sarah, who felt she'd walked in on the last part of a badly made sci-fi film.

"A quarter turn," repeated Tilly. "Julia rotates to Quartermaster Farm, we rotate to High Hope Farm because we can't stay here. The emanations. Later on the Wentworths at Camp Highfeather down the road may rotate to the Laakas' and the Laakas to the Wentworths'. The timing isn't quite as important as our move. Camp Merrilark may have to rotate as well. That part hasn't come clear. But it will all be perfectly simple."

"As mud," said Jane, and she reached again for her friend's hand and patted it.

"Jane will become a believer," said Tilly. "Through love."

"Where will Colonel Dodge go?" asked Sarah. "I mean after Aunt Julia has moved—or rotated—into his farm?"

"He will stay put. Because of marriage," said Tilly. "He will become one with Julia, who will already have rotated."

"I see," said Sarah. She leaned forward and gave Tilly and then Jane a hasty kiss. "I do hope you can *both* come," she said. "Even if Aunt Julia isn't paying attention to the stars."

"It's not a laughing matter," said Tilly with reproach.

Sarah settled herself in the driver's seat and then on impulse leaned out the window. "I've heard a rumor that one of the local libraries wants volunteer help. Tilly, did you ever work as children's librarian down in Kennebunkport?"

"I filled in sometimes," said Tilly. "And I read to the pre-school children every Friday afternoon."

"All the old favorites?" asked Sarah.

"You mean Goldilocks and Red Riding Hood and nursery rhymes?" said Tilly. "Of course. So did Jane. She used to act out some of the Grimm fairy tales, didn't you, Jane?"

"Quite a specialty of mine," said Jane. "But neither of us has any time to volunteer. Not this spring. We have enough to do to keep this place going, plant the garden, feed the animals."

"I just thought I'd ask," said Sarah, glad that she hadn't been pinned down for more details. "But one more question. What will you do, Tilly, if Julia won't marry Colonel Dodge and rotate?"

Tilly didn't hesitate. "Steps," she said. "I shall take steps.

"Tilly's over the edge," said Sarah to Alex when he came home at five that evening. "Gone absolutely balmy. She's into the stars. Plus runes. Probably tea leaves and tarot."

"So are a lot of people," observed Alex. "Perfectly normal people. Crystal balls, casting entrails. Man does not live by bread alone."

"Tilly certainly doesn't," said Sarah. "And listen to this," and she told him of Tilly's umbrage over Julia's refusal to marry and "rotate."

"That *is* loopy," admitted Alex. "Maybe we should give her a turban and a tent at the reception."

"As Tilly said, it isn't a laughing matter. She may refuse to come to the reception at all. And I tried them out on nursery rhymes. Indirectly. They've both worked in the children's library. Jane's specialty was Grimm."

"I'll bet she could freeze blood and chatter teeth," said Alex. "Those happy tales of dismembered dwarfs and toads and snakes coming out of the mouth of the wicked stepmother. But working in a children's library doesn't prove anything. Everyone knows nursery rhymes. By osmosis. I can recite a dozen at the drop of a hat. As for Tilly, trust Jane to keep her in line. A strong woman of infinite sense. Feet on the ground." He swiveled around. "Isn't that the telephone?"

But Sarah had already gone to answer. She came back looking upset. "Aunt Julia."

"What's happened? Is she hurt?" This always seemed a possibility when an older woman persisted against all advice in riding horses.

"Not Aunt Julia. One of her men. A stable helper. Sean Conners. A bad fall. He's stuck. Fell partway through the hayloft floor. They've called the rescue squad, but I said you'd go anyway. Aunt Julia's really upset."

"Okay," said Alex. "Come on." He strode toward the door and jerked it open.

Sarah followed at a run and climbed into the front seat of the newly purchased Ford Bronco. "You don't suppose," she said, "that Tilly's been at work?"

"What do you mean?"

"Talking like Cassandra. Blood on the moon. *And* blood on the new-mown hay. Julia said the accident was in the hayloft."

Alex shoved into first gear and gunned the engine. "Tilly's read too damn many Gothic novels. Julia will straighten her out."

"Unless Tilly tries to straighten out Aunt Julia first."

"But farms are absolute traps, something's always happening," complained Alex as he and Sarah sped toward the town of Union, which lay in a hollow some four miles short of High Hope Farm.

Sarah, balancing herself as Alex swung the Bronco into a hard right turn onto Route 90, thought the same could be said about certain impatient physicians at the wheel of a new vehicle. But she held her peace as they bounded up and down the hills and thought only of how lucky it was that Aunt Julia herself hadn't plunged through a broken hayloft plank. If it had to be someone, better a sturdy young man than a sixty-eight-year-old woman.

But Alex was still on the subject of farms. "All those hay bales balanced on top of each other, tractors, manure spreaders, electrical wires, sawdust. It's a wonder any farm owner—or the farm—lasts more than five years."

"You haven't even mentioned thousand-pound horses who wear metal shoes and buck and kick and trample people," Sarah added.

"Horses," said Alex, "are the least of the problem. They're interesting, useful, fun to ride, and very decorative. What bothers me is Julia in charge of machinery. Machinery and tools. Horses, yes. Machinery, no. Julia is death on machines. She hasn't a mechanical bone in her body."

"And yet she can put a bridle together faster than greased lightning and fix saddles and reins," said Sarah. "Besides, this hayloft accident wasn't a mechanical thing, just a loose board."

"Which means that farm maintenance is too much for her now. She's understaffed."

"I know," said Sarah. The Bronco roared down Route 17, and the Camden Hills rose and fell behind them in a soft green-brown blur. Hanging on to the door handle, Sarah shook her head. "What you're really saying, Alex, is that Aunt Julia had better marry Harvey Dodge and have a built-in handy man. But I think he's crowding her. She has Patrick and the other helpers, and she's still thinking of Uncle Tom."

Alex nodded and swung the wheel around and shot up the Tri-County Road, and in ten minutes they whirled with a spatter of gravel and dirt into Julia's stable parking lot.

"Alex, good God," said Julia, emerging in a disheveled condition from a side door. "What if there had been someone unloading a horse from a trailer, you coming in like a locomotive."

"But there wasn't," said Alex. "Besides, I'm on an emergency call. What's up?"

"The ambulance is here, thank heavens," said Julia, waving toward a barn by the end of the stable.

And sure enough there was the boxy end of the white-and-orange vehicle protruding close by the barn door.

"Right now they're working to free his leg," said Julia, her voice strangely high and breathless. "It's Sean Conners. Patrick's nephew."

"Can't they just saw the board and free his leg?" asked Sarah, climbing down from the front seat.

"That's the problem," said Julia. "Sean slipped, the loose board he was standing on shifted, his leg went through, and a great long sliver of wood went into his thigh. Alex, go up and see if you can help. They're trying to free him without wiggling the splinter. He's in horrible pain, as pale as a ghost, so I'm afraid he's losing blood or is in shock."

"Or both," said Alex grimly. He climbed out of the car and made his way rapidly to the door, entered, and disappeared.

"What can I do?" asked Sarah.

"You can help," said Julia, "by going in and shooing out all the bystanders. Especially Tilly. Jane is on the rescue squad, of course, but Tilly is hanging around and making noises like a banshee. Something about the planets and it was all foretold."

Sarah grimaced. She'd had enough of Tilly for one day, but duty was duty and this was an emergency.

"Take Tilly right up to the farmhouse out of our hair," ordered Julia. "The Laakas are both here—Fred's helping to move the hay so they can bring Conners down on the stretcher. Alice Laaka can go with you and help make coffee. The Wentworths from Highfeather are working with Harvey Dodge to put the horses in their stalls and give them their hay and fresh water."

Sarah did as she was told. She walked quickly over to the indicated barn, a large structure for the storage of hay, sawdust, and odd farm machinery that stood at a distance from the stable proper and found Tilly inside, standing below the ladder to the loft. She was calling to unseen persons. From above Sarah's head came a low groaning.

Sarah took hold of Tilly by the sleeve of her yellow sweatshirt and pulled.

Tilly whirled about, saw Sarah, and without pausing said, "See, what did I tell you, Sarah? The planets are disturbed. But no one listens. I've even warned Sean Conners about rotating. I tell you, I may have to take the whole thing into my own hands."

"What we're going to take into our own hands is coffee-making," said Sarah. "Lots of coffee for all these people. Come on and help me. We can't do any good here."

Tilly showed signs of resistance, but just then Jane Zimmer assisted by a short man in overalls came in with a stretcher, which they hoisted to the hayloft. Hands from above grabbed at the stretcher and it vanished from sight. There followed heavy shifting noises, feet shuffling, and a loud sustained wrenching cry.

"Please, Tilly," said Sarah urgently. "They're going to be bringing him down. We're in the way."

And somehow, by pushing Tilly in the small of her back, Sarah managed to move her to the open door, nudge her forward and out.

But Tilly proved stubborn. She took three steps forward and rooted herself just beyond the open ambulance doors.

Sarah left to find reinforcements, discovered Alice Laaka, recruited her. They returned to the ambulance and Tilly in time to see Sean Conners wrapped like a mummy in a blanket lying on the stretcher, ready to be loaded into the ambulance.

But just as Sean was about to disappear, some adjustment in the tilt of the stretcher was made necessary and he raised his head slightly, caught sight of Tilly standing by the ambulance.

"You there," he shouted. "You bitch, you goddamn bitch. You and your crazy ideas. Telling me something was going to happen. Bitch." With that Sean let his head drop back to the stretcher, and he was lifted into position and slipped into the ambulance interior, followed by Fred Laaka and Alex. The doors closed, the driver jumped into the front seat, the motor roared into life, the red lights began blinking, and as the ambulance mounted to the top of the drive and turned north, the siren began its high-pitched *queeep, queeep, wheeeeee, wheeeeee,* the sound rising and falling and finally fading into the soft evening noises of frogs and a faraway passing car.

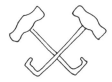

THE OLD MILL

FOUR

IT was a subdued group of helpers who came straggling into Julia's farmhouse for coffee, the groans and accusations of the injured Sean Conners still ringing in their ears.

Mercifully, thought Sarah, Jane Zimmer had taken Tilly home, explaining that her friend was upset but that she'd be quite herself tomorrow.

"Which self?" said Sarah to Julia, who was cutting large uneven hunks of banana bread to pass around the circle of neighbors.

"I certainly wish," said Julia, "that her this week's obsession wasn't moving into my farm. Of course, it may explain those nursery rhymes, although I must say I thought Tilly had better taste than to write such trash."

"It may not be Tilly," said Sarah, "so don't jump the gun and accuse her. Right now she's saying you have to marry Colonel Dodge by the August high tides and go and live at Quartermaster Farm. Or else. She apparently doesn't know that he's done a switch and wants to move into High Hope Farm."

"Blast Tilly. I hope she's not going to scare Harvey. Even

though he looks like a bear, he's not terribly brave. The army knew what it was doing when they put him in charge of supplies. And I like Tilly. So generous. Always bringing something she baked. Biscuits, this banana bread. Deep down she has a heart of gold."

"Or nickel and copper," suggested Sarah. "How about crazy like a fox? Sell Appleyard Farm for what they claim are bags of money and move—make that rotate—over here. Stay in the same neighborhood and enjoy your sixty acres."

"Sarah," said Julia severely, "you have a sick mind. You've been mixed up in one too many nasty affairs. Tilly may be eccentric to the point of dementia, she may be cutting out mean little nursery rhymes, but she hasn't a subtle scheming hair on her head." Here Julia craned her neck in the direction of a tall red-haired man wearing horn rims and a tall, blonde, carefully coifed woman in a blue denim wrap skirt. "Now there is a couple who have an entire wardrobe of schemes. I almost wish Neil and Winka hadn't shown up. They always make me feel like scum. As if I lived in a thatched hut. Just because they're so spic and span and glowing with indecent health is no reason to go about making the neighbors feel like low-grade peasants."

"Not fair, Aunt Julia," said Sarah. "Neil and Winka helped Patrick in the barn and now Winka's passing the coffee. And of course they seem healthy to you. They're thirty years younger and run a boys' summer camp. I think you're jealous."

"Stuff and nonsense. They're here helping because it's the right thing to do, not from any overflow of human kindness. They're both snobs. Look, he and Winka are over there tittering over my slipcovers."

Sarah looked over at Neil and his wife, Winifred—both transplanted Brits, she regrettably called Winka since babyhood. The couple, still crisply dressed despite recent exertions, were standing talking, drinking coffee, next to a club chair draped in an Indian bedspread, as were most of Julia's chairs and sofas. A saddle sat athwart one arm of the chair and even at a distance, Sarah could see a large red patch covered the other arm.

Aunt Julia's house was what a charitable person might call

"lived in." Bridles hung from lamps, and saddles in need of cleaning balanced on arms of chairs. Threadbare oriental carpets were covered here and there with hooked rugs or simply remnants—these to cover the mistakes of generations of English setters, the most recent two representatives of which were draped languidly along a sofa. Decoration—such as it was—amounted to a series of hunting prints showing riders in the act of being thrown, having fallen, or being about to fall from their horses. A raucous parrot named Joe hopped about in a huge cylindrical cage by the front window; cats were everywhere.

Aunt Julia was still fulminating on the subject of the Wentworths. "I've even heard," she said bitterly, "that they've allowed the Norminco mine people to take core samples in their fields. It's probably because Neil and Winka are planning to sneak off, leaving us in the middle of a mine pit after having sold out for a great sack of cash."

"They won't leave, they run Camp Highfeather. Winka inherited it from her grandfather; it's sacred. Besides, you have that farm in Maryland," said Sarah. "And the one in Ireland. You could escape."

"Not anymore I can't," said Julia. "I've sold out. Cutting back. As of last week this farm is it. Money is very tight, so what I have left goes here. Fencing, new stalls, feed. And the best wedding reception for my dear niece Sarah. I will never spend good money on things like slipcovers and designer clothes."

"Certainly, Aunt Julia," said Sarah, thinking it was time to change the subject. Her aunt always overreacted to someone else's interest in decorator houses and high-style clothes. And, Sarah had to admit, there were times when the farmhouse's interior dilapidation plus Julia's ragbag attire—this evening featuring a particularly moth-eaten pullover—perhaps went too far in the other direction. She searched around for a new subject. "Where was Rafe Posner tonight? You could have used another helping hand. I thought he was full-time now, working with the horses."

Julia gave an exasperated shrug like that of a parent over an erring but beloved son. "Oh, Rafe. I let him off again this afternoon. A concert in Bangor. His music is important to him. He gets restless because he's not a nine-to-five type. Quite different from Sean Conners. A free spirit. But very, very kind."

"Can you really afford a free spirit, no matter how kind?"

"I just have this feeling about Rafe. That he'll always watch over everything here. He loves the animals. Granted, he does march to a different drummer."

"He and Tilly would make a nice pair," said Sarah. And then, looking about the room, "Who's that over there talking to Mike Laaka? That man in the checked shirt and jeans."

"Total stranger," said Julia. "I just issued a blanket invitation to everyone who came over and helped and he turned up. I think his name is James something. Or John. With a *J* anyway."

"He looks pleasant," said Sarah. "At least he's smiling and laughing. He's even got Mike looking agreeable, which is tough to do if Mike's just finished a long day at work." She put down her coffee cup. "I'll go over and check him out."

"You do that. As I've said, once a snoop, always a snoop."

"No," said Sarah. "Neighborly spirit."

"Fiddlestick," said Julia. "That neighborly spirit has almost done you in. Several times. Never mind. Go and find out."

Mike—a tall white-blond man with broad cheekbones, blue eyes, and a sunburned face—greeted Sarah with a hearty slap on the back. "Might have known if there was trouble in River City, Professor Deane would be hovering."

"Not professor, Mike. Just teaching fellow. An academic appendage. And Sean Conners just had an accident. That board's probably been loose for years." She looked over at the tall stranger with the green checked shirt. Thin, big hands, stooped shoulders, brown eyes, with a lean face and a flop of brown hair over the forehead. "Introduce me, Deputy Laaka."

"I can't," said Mike. "Except he's called Jim. Just met him myself ten minutes ago. Jim, this is Sarah Deane, niece to your hostess, Julia Clancy."

The man grinned. "Hello, I'm Jim Shale. One of those names. You know, name is fate."

"You do something with shale?" asked Sarah.

"Shale, silt, iron, copper, nickel, cobalt . . . you name it."

"Geologist!" exclaimed Sarah.

"You've got it," said Jim Shale.

"That mine," said Mike. "Norminco. You work for Norminco."

"Not this minute," said Jim. "Now I'm eating banana bread and drinking good coffee and meeting my new neighbors."

"Neighbors?" said Sarah. "But you're with Norminco."

"Right," said Jim. "A neighbor and with Norminco."

"Why," demanded Mike in a belligerent voice, "didn't you say so? People here are pretty upset about the mine idea."

"I've found that out. No Welcome Wagon around," said Jim. "Lot of people hate Norminco. Which we expected. We're the enemy within."

"You sure are," said Mike. "How did you get into this house, anyway?"

"Invited," said Jim. "Like the rest of you. As a neighbor. As a helper in the recent rescue event."

"But," objected Sarah, "how can you be a neighbor? Norminco hasn't bought any land yet, has it? No one that I know has sold out. Aunt Julia would have told me."

"Whoa," said Jim. He looked untouched by the change in atmosphere, but his tone was a shade less amiable. "I'm not standing here in this living room trying to screw anyone out of land. Right now I'm Jim Shale, the neighbor who came over to help. I've rented a cabin on the Appleyard Farm boundary line. Right on Fallen Tree Pond. I was driving home and heard the commotion, saw the ambulance, stopped to see if there was anything I could do. Thought maybe it was a horse accident. End of story."

"You've rented a cabin?" Sarah said.

"Please," said Jim. "I'm not trying to infiltrate the neighborhood, I'm trying to be a neighbor. I've an option to buy the cabin. Winterize it. Live in it. Enjoy it."

"With no ulterior motive?" asked Sarah.

"Come on," said Mike. "You can't make us believe that

you've chosen a cabin on Fallen Tree Pond because you love the view. Or think having a mine next door is healthy."

"My motives—since I seem to have to explain them—are as follows. First, I do love the view. I've always wanted to live on a lake—or a pond, as you people in Maine call it. Second, I thought if I lived smack next to the site, it might show that I had confidence the mine wouldn't total the environment, wouldn't change the pH of the lake, wouldn't scare the wildlife out, and when the mine was finished, we would clean up our act, fill in and replant. Besides, I'm a bird-watcher. I don't want to be a part of anything that scares away the birds."

"A mine isn't exactly a sanctuary," said Sarah.

"What's this about birds?" It was Alex, back from the hospital.

"Never mind birds," said Sarah. "How is Sean Conners?"

At which point Julia rushed up and repeated the question.

"He's doing pretty well considering what a nasty wound it was," said Alex. "They've loaded him with antibiotics, tetanus booster, a painkiller, and will probably give him some blood. He lost quite a bit when that big splinter went shooting into his leg."

Alex turned to Julia and to Colonel Dodge, who had joined the group. "As far as working on the farm, I'm afraid Sean will be out of it as a stableman for a while."

Harvey Dodge nodded. "I've been thinking about that. Julia, you'll be a man short with only Patrick and Rafe Posner, and he seems to be a fly-by-night. So I'll send Farney over to you for the duration."

Julia protested. "Farney? Farney Thompson? But you need Farney. He runs your place."

"No," said the colonel. "I still have old Ben Carter. We're down to four horses, and I have no riding school to take up my time. I can spare Farney. He's crazy about your farm—likes the layout better than mine—and he gets along with Patrick."

Julia gave in. "I can only say thanks. I was wondering how I'd manage." Then turning away from the colonel and seeing Jim

Shale standing with the group, she said, "Welcome, whoever you are. And who are you?"

"A bird-watcher from Norminco," said Sarah.

"Your new neighbor," said Mike Laaka.

"Glad to know you, Mrs. Clancy," said Jim.

Alex, perceiving currents and undertows, spoke up. "You're a bird-watcher?" he asked.

"Among his other interests," said Sarah.

Jim smiled, a bit ruefully. "I'm afraid I'm the specter at the feast. I do bird-watch. I contribute to wildlife organizations. And I'm a field geologist working with Norminco. I came in from Idaho five weeks ago."

Mike Laaka smiled a grim smile. "If someone finds you floating in Fallen Tree Pond among the lily pads, well, I won't be surprised, because, seriously, there's a lot of raw feeling in the area."

"Mike is overdoing it," said Sarah, "but this is a rural area."

"We love our farms, our lives here," said Julia. "So, though I'm very grateful for your help tonight, I hope you'll be packing up and going back where you came from."

"He's rented a cabin down by the water," said Mike. "That doesn't sound like he's thinking of leaving town."

"I'm not," said Jim. And he went on to tell Julia his reasons for renting the lakeside cabin.

Julia was silent. Then she shook her head. "I'm afraid it won't do. You're the enemy. You can't have it both ways—our friendly neighbor and a mine developer."

Jim walked up to a small wall table, moved a tin of saddle soap to one side, and placed his coffee cup carefully down next to the soap. "Well, that's that," he said. "So, thanks again."

He nodded briefly to the little group, turned and strode to the hall, pulled open the door, and disappeared into the night.

"Good riddance," said Julia loudly.

But Sarah was now having qualms. "We weren't even barely polite," she said. "Or decent. And he did try to sound reasonable."

"Reasonable-sounding people are dangerous," said Mike. "I know. The state prison is full of them."

"From what I've just heard," said Alex, "none of you could be accused of being in the least reasonable. Or open-minded."

"There are times," said Julia firmly, "when it is a serious mistake being open-minded."

During this exchange the general babble and movement of the remaining members of the rescue party had quieted and all heads had turned to watch Jim Shale's departure. Then the clamor grew and Julia moved from person to person letting them know that the notorious Norminco in the person of one Jim Shale had been in their midst. Sarah, listening on the fringes, felt that the general opinion seemed to be that the geologist had come into the farmhouse like some sort of Masque of the Red Death and had partaken of hospitality under false pretenses.

"Imagine the nerve," said Julia. "He must know that we're all working tooth and claw to get rid of him and all his works."

"Tooth and claw is a good word for it," said Sarah. She was feeling more and more uneasy about her role in the confrontation. "Aunt Julia almost snatched the food out of his mouth. The man was perfectly polite. And we were rude."

"Are you saying we should snuggle up and make friends," said Mike Laaka. "Just because he's moved in down the road."

"A little common humanity wouldn't hurt," returned Sarah.

Mike reached for another slab of banana bread, balanced it on his hand, and turned on Sarah. "You're quibbling, probably because you have a warm and loving heart."

"A man," put in Julia, "who makes his career with a company that plans to blast holes in a rural community against that community's wishes can't be forgiven because he comes around to help in an accident."

"You wouldn't call that a mitigating circumstance?" asked Alex.

"My mind," said Julia "is not fouled by nit-picking. Yes, he helped out. Perhaps he thought this was a way of infiltrating the neighborhood. Then the next time he knocked on my door, I'd have to say, 'Goodness, here's Jim Shale, the helper in our time of need.' And Mike, something you should know, something all of you should know"—here Julia raised her voice and looked out at the people still remaining, the Wentworths, Harvey Dodge, and Mike Laaka's parents—"I've been receiving some disagreeable little poems made out of cut-out letters. Someone wants to move me off my farm, so I'm saying right now, in public, that it won't work. Spread the word. Julia Clancy isn't going anywhere."

With this announcement there was a general stir and Julia found herself surrounded. "That's all I'm going to say. Fair warning, that's what I'm giving. I have my idea about possible suspects and Norminco is certainly one of them. No, Mike, no more details. You can't have the poems. Not now." This as Mike Laaka brought out a small notebook and looked ready to deal with Julia in his official capacity.

Sarah looked across at the grandfather clock at the end of the room. "All right, Aunt Julia, you've stirred everyone up, so if they stay here all night it's your own fault. But it's time for me to go home and correct some papers. How about you, Alex?"

"Agreed," said Alex. "Home it is."

Sarah kissed her aunt, waved good-bye to the rest, and with Alex behind her escaped into the night.

"Well, Julia opened a can of worms," said Alex as they sped home across a darkened landscape. "Now everyone will be watching mailboxes for cut-out messages."

"Aunt Julia could no more sit on that sort of news than she could fly," said Sarah. "So okay, maybe someone will be flushed out of the woodwork. As for Norminco, well, it's hard to be decent and sensible. We're all up in arms about the mine and in comes—what did he call himself—the 'enemy within.' "

"He's got a sense of humor about it anyway," said Alex.

"And a lot of good it's going to do him. Though," she added, "I suppose we could listen to what he has to say in defense of the whole damn project."

"We could," said Alex, "but we probably won't."

"So what can anyone do? Julia's not exactly on target when she says everyone is against the project. I'm sure there *are* people who want to make some money selling off a summer cottage or an unprofitable farm. And there's a shortage of jobs in the county."

"Wait and see what the town wants. And the state. Votes, meetings, referendums, hearings."

Sarah closed her eyes and pictured a denuded Fallen Tree Pond entirely surrounded by mine machinery, shafts, pits, and pyramids of tailings. A few dusty songbirds, a single remaining pair of loons tottering about on the gravel. Aunt Julia standing at the gate of her farm with a shotgun. The Laaka family departing in their pickup truck like latterday refugees from the Dust Bowl. Tilly and Jane with bundles of books and leashes of corgis and Tikka the Siberian husky in a wagon, pulled down the road by the mare, Lily Glendower. Colonel Dodge manning a machine gun from Quartermaster Farm. Neil and Winka Wentworth loading Highfeather campers onto a school bus and hoisting sacks of cash onto the roof rack. She took a long breath, shook herself, and opened her eyes, seeing ahead the dark rise of the Camden Hills, a sprinkling of stars, a rising crescent moon.

"You and I don't vote in Julia's township," Alex reminded her. "And besides . . ."

"Besides," Sarah finished, "it's a beautiful night, which we should enjoy while we can. We're both overextended. I've got to be completely selfish until after my teaching's over."

"And I had three hospital admissions this afternoon, so I'll have to go back to the hospital tonight and see how they're doing. And I want to look in on Sean Conners."

Sarah looked up. "Poor Sean. That leg must hurt like holy hell. But what on earth was that business about Tilly? Sean calling her a bitch. Tilly's really harmless, even if batty. But she did say she'd warned Sean. You don't suppose she came over and said it was foretold that she and Jane were moving in? And that he, Sean, would be out of a job?"

"God knows. Conners was half crazy with pain. He may not

even have recognized Tilly. Thought she was someone else. Someone he was out to get. Julia told me he has a temper."

"Yes, but he's supposed to be terrific with horses. Well, I'm sorry for him, but right now, as I've said, it's work time. And that means that Jim Shale and all his works are on a back burner."

"Correct," said Alex, swinging into the entrance of Sawmill Road toward their own farmhouse, at which nothing was farmed and little grown, as the owners had previously noted, except weeds, stray evergreen seedlings, and alder thickets.

Sarah woke early the next morning—a Wednesday—to the ringing of the telephone. Alex, groggy, reached over, said hello, and then said, "No, I haven't." Then, "I'm sure he'll turn up" and "Not to worry." A listening pause, then, "At least you've got Farney."

Sarah sat up, leaned over and examined the table clock-radio. Five past six. "Was that Aunt Julia?"

"The Widow Clancy. In another snit. Her stable helper, Rafe Posner, hasn't shown up yet. He was due at five this morning to start morning chores."

"Well, it's only six, for heaven's sake. I know Rafe. Gentle. Sort of sweet. Always singing around the place."

"Which is beside the point. Julia is very edgy about this. After Sean Conners yesterday she's overreacting. But she says Rafe is something of a loose foot, a bit of a drifter."

"So maybe he's drifted somewhere else."

But Alex was already in the bathroom, the shower sounding.

Sarah considered the missing Rafe Posner. With stable manager Patrick O'Reilly's increasing age, Rafe and Sean Conners did most of the heavy work around Julia's farm, and of the two men, Rafe was the favored. Long of limb, fair of hair, Rafe was a lean giant of a man who preferred playing the guitar and singing to working, but he had a touch with animals. Julia often praised his ability to soothe a fractious horse and admired his ability to relate to the children who came for riding lessons. "A real Hans Christian Andersen, always telling them stories," said Julia.

Alex came out of the shower, rubbing his hair into dark tufts. "Are you going over to see Julia? Calm her down?"

"I can't. I simply can't. She'll have to muddle along and make do with Harvey Dodge and Farney and Patrick. I've three classes today and my exams to put together. There's no time for any extracurricular activity."

Alex agreed. The penalty for taking a ten-day wedding trip meant being on call every weekend and taking on the patients of other vacationing physicians, plus functioning as one of the county medical examiners in cases of unattended deaths.

The end result of the preoccupation of the future bride and groom was that not only could they not fling themselves into Julia Clancy's farm problems, but they had to let the wedding reception continue to take its own course. Which it did.

Sarah's parents from New Hampshire, Frances and Roland Deane, she a landscape designer, he an architect, began a series of telephone calls to assorted members of Alex's family. These took root and brought forth more calls on subjects as varied as the question of whether allergic guests at the reception would begin to wheeze because of the proximity to hay and horses and was the rehearsal dinner black tie, any tie, or no tie at all?

"What's this about ties?" asked Sarah, meeting Alex accidentally on the Bowmouth campus.

"Not to worry," said Alex. "I told my mother that anything goes except perhaps total nudity—and maybe even that's okay."

Sarah agreed and said that she'd run into Julia at the Shop N' Save supermarket, who'd reported that Rafe Posner had drifted back and Farney was a treasure, that Conners was still out of it, and Tilly had been found in the farmhouse measuring Julia's living room for curtains. Julia had ushered her out and told Tilly in no uncertain terms that regardless of what the heavenly bodies advised, she, Julia, was staying put.

"Tilly does have a nerve," observed Alex. And then he added,

"Come on over to the hospital cafeteria for lunch. You don't want to faint from hunger in front of your students." He stood back from her and gave her a critical once-over. "Even though I see you every night, it isn't until I run into you in the wide-open spaces that I really look at you. You're peaked and pinched."

"And palely loitering? Except I can't loiter. That's the trouble. I can't even remember to have lunch."

"Today you will," said Alex firmly. "Lunch with all the trimmings."

Alex was right. Tunafish salad, potato chips, and banana cream pie put Sarah in a better frame of mind.

"You're right," she told Alex. "Bulk without taste is what I needed. And by Thursday the semester ends, my grades will be in, and I can join the human race. Even think about the Norminco mine and how to rescue Aunt Julia from the clutches of Jim Shale."

"Jim Shale is very small potatoes. Don't waste your time shooting the messenger. It's the Norminco bigwigs you've got to think of. And you have no clout. Nor do I."

"Never mind. After next Friday I can wrestle alligators and move mountains. Get a handle on this wedding."

"Did Julia say anything else? Any more nursery rhymes, and is she softening toward the colonel?"

"No to both. As for Harvey, she has the best of it now. Keeps her independence and still has Harvey as her visiting swain. Noble Colonel Dodge. But I suspect nobility. It still wouldn't surprise me if he had designs."

"He does. On Julia," Alex said.

"He'd make a good villain because he doesn't look the part. Noble villains are best—they're really more interesting than the Don Giovannis. Or Iago. Iago bores me stiff."

"Is that what you tell your students?"

"No. I suggest that he's a marvelously interesting foil for poor trusting Othello. If a villain is needed, I vote for Colonel Dodge. And he has that lovely deep voice. If we were in an opera he'd sing basso."

As Sarah departed, hauling her bulging briefcase, Alex watched her with concern. At the rate she was going he would be marrying a wraith who might well star in an opera, an Italian-Scottish one.

THE HAY WAGON

FIVE

ON the following Monday, May the sixteeenth, ruffled feathers had been smoothed, troubled waters had subsided, the mail contained no disturbing cut-out nursery rhymes, and Julia Clancy presided for twenty-four hours over a peaceable kingdom. It's the way the world ought to be, she told herself that evening after the last horse was in its stall, the last flake of hay tossed, the grain distributed, the water buckets freshly filled. She made her way to the farmhouse and entered the front parlor. The old upright piano seemed to beckon and Julia found herself walking over and sitting down at the keyboard. Often in moments of stress she found solace by thumping away at martial tunes. Tonight so mellow was her mood that she played through a Chopin nocturne and a Beethoven sonata without her jaw tightening and her blood pressure rising.

Tuesday, however, was a different story. On Tuesday Colonel Harvey Dodge, during one of his frequent visits to High Hope Farm, discovered Tilly Martin standing by the kitchen door matching paint samples to the clapboards of Julia's farmhouse. He took her inside and administered herbal tea while Julia called Jane and discussed counseling.

On Tuesday afternoon, Sean Conners, white-faced and limping, showed up for work and was given the light job of cleaning tack. Harvey Dodge took one look at Sean and decreed that Farney should stay on for a while. Julia reluctantly agreed.

"He does look awful," she said. "I think they let him out too soon."

"I'd keep an eye on him," warned Harvey Dodge.

"Oh dear, I hope he hasn't been drinking. I don't think I'll ask him about swearing at Tilly because Jane thinks Tilly told him that he'd be out of a job when she and Jane moved in over here. Tilly is becoming a genuine nuisance."

On Wednesday, Julia awoke to the fact it was now the eighteenth of May and that her annual Preakness party was coming off on Saturday. Barely recovered from her Kentucky Derby party, the Preakness party now seemed more a burden than the pleasure it had once been. She and Tom had begun the "Triple Crown" parties thirty years ago, but now, going it alone, the whole affair had lost its luster. All that drinking and loud talking, the drawing of horses, the shouting during the race, and then people hanging around too late after the race was over. Next year I'll cancel the whole business, she told herself.

Resigned, Julia reached for the telephone and dialed the florist to arrange for black-eyed Susans, the decorative touch appropriate for the Preakness. Flowers ordered, Julia turned to matters at the farm. In an hour she'd be taking the beginner riding class and the very idea of dealing with a noisy group of ten- and eleven-year-olds was enough to cause an immediate onset of chronic fatigue syndrome.

Wednesday ended finally in a town meeting held to confront the fact of an encroaching nickel mine. At this session nothing was proved but that the townspeople were united in hating change, in loathing of all things pertaining to mining, in expressing a deep love of Fallen Tree Pond, its remaining wildlife as well as its motorboat and water ski opportunities. At the same time many of the citizenry referred to the recession in plaintive terms and expressed the wish to have more jobs open up in the area. The Norminco representative in the person of Jim Shale had been shouted down before he had delivered himself of more than a sentence or so. Julia, numb from sitting on a metal folding chair, left early, saying loudly to Jane Zimmer that it was a plague on all their houses and to please keep a closer watch on Tilly.

"I do try," said Jane. "And I hope by next week she'll have moved on. It's time to plant the rest of our garden and that usually keeps her out of trouble."

"Let's hope she behaves herself at my Preakness party," said Julia, "and not act like she owns the place."

With that Julia drove home, spent a redeeming hour at the piano attacking Grieg, and then crept thankfully into bed.

On Thursday morning Alex caught up with Sarah outside Malcolm Adam Hall, the English department's center of operations.

Sarah fell on his neck. Then detached herself, shook herself like a dog emerging from water, and said, "Bless you and keep you, Alexander McKenzie, the semester's over. I don't think I've had a human moment in months—except for Aunt Julia's events. And you, the hospital's been eating you alive."

"I'm off tonight. We'll celebrate. You can bless me again."

"Okay by me," said Sarah. "I never want to see another book. Or student. Or classroom."

"Right," said Alex, grinning down at her.

"At least not until September."

Alex disappeared into his medical routine and Sarah suddenly found herself in an entirely alien state of freedom. No matter that next week brought exams to prepare and correct for her undergraduate classes; today the chains were lifted. But the release was too sudden. For a moment she stood stupidly staring at a bulletin board covered with notes about graduate seminars, rides needed, and a plea for a lost dog. After studying these without comprehension, Sarah went into the ladies room and sluiced her face and arms with cold water. She thought, I'm decompressing, just like a deep-sea diver. She wandered back into the hall and looked out the window toward the central campus. Trees in leaf, clusters of tulips around dark plots of garden, lilacs almost in bloom, and a blue sky with not the wisp of a cloud anywhere.

So to hell with academe. Sarah took off down the stairs, ran to her car, slammed the door, and spun away out of the parking lot. What she needed was country air. Aunt Julia's farm. Anybody's farm. Go out into the world and flex muscles. Regain health. Climb a tree, a hilltop. Swim across Fallen Tree Pond. Anything.

The first hilltop she came to after leaving the Union town center featured Harvey Dodge's Quartermaster Farm, an incongruous plaster and timber faintly Tudor assemblage with arches, trefoils, and leaded windows, quite out of place in the New England countryside of extended white farmhouses and shingled or clapboarded barns. Sarah remembered hearing years ago that the countryside had buzzed at this break with local architecture, but Harvey Dodge's wife, Phyllis, had wanted echoes of her family house in an Ohio suburb and had prevailed.

She slowed along the highway and pulled up on the lefthand verge by one of the colonel's outlying pastures and surveyed the scene. Beyond on a rise of ground the cluster of four horses was grazing. In the middle distance the farm buildings and the house. Below the buildings, more pasture and the woods, and seen through a swath cut through the trees, the blue-gray sheen of Fallen Tree Pond. There, Sarah knew, the colonel kept his small lakeside cottage. But as she looked about this familiar pastoral scene, Sarah had a sense of something not quite right. At first she was unable to put this impression into words; it had something to do with a disturbance in line, in symmetry.

What was it? She turned off her ignition and left the car. It was the fence. The fence standing not more than ten feet away. Harvey Dodge had chosen for his pastures a dark brown stained board fencing rather than the more usual—at least in that part of Maine—post and rail.

But the stain was fading; some of the boards had split and had been replaced with unstained, unmatching planks. And on one post Sarah saw a crack had been tied together with wire. This from a horse owner, to whom wire was anathema. Sarah walked over and ran her hand around the mend. Perfectly smooth. No harm to horse or man. But unsightly.

She returned to her car and considered. Was Harvey Dodge becoming careless about appearances? Sarah took a second look at the farmhouse itself. The same sense of shabbiness. The lawn needed cutting, the bordering hedges and yews were unkempt, the gravel driveway rutted and potholed. Obviously the remaining helper, old Carter, wasn't up to extensive maintenance.

Yet this was the home of Colonel Tidy. Colonel Housewife. And what had he been doing, since obviously he wasn't caring for his beloved (formerly beloved?) Quartermaster Farm? Answer: He was at Aunt Julia's farm, mending and tending and fixing and maintaining and lending his number-one man, Farney, to help.

Why? Sarah remembered that she had cast the colonel in the role of a villain, someone hankering after secret mineral deposits that might be under Julia's pastures. Someone planning to move in on the Widow Clancy, marry her and her farm. Or perhaps it was all too romantic. Had Julia changed her mind and was keeping the good news a secret? Sarah's nose had been to the grindstone for so long that there might have been developments of which she was unaware. Another match made in horse heaven. Tom Clancy, not forgotten, but fading away.

Sarah started her car. She decided that Quartermaster Farm was not where she wanted her country air, not with its faint sense of decay and loss. Nor Appleyard Farm with its resident seeress, Tilly Martin. So on to Aunt Julia.

Arriving by the farmhouse door Sarah drew a blank. No Aunt Julia. She made her way down to the stable and looked in. There stood Harvey Dodge's gift to the farm, the invaluable Farney Thompson, his back to her, brushing a bay horse on cross-ties.

Farney was obviously a man in love with what he was doing. For a minute Sarah stayed and watched him work with the curry comb, the brush, the sponge, the cloth, all resulting in the animal he was tending looking like burnished satin.

She was glad that Farney was working out. He certainly wasn't much to look at, thin with pale sparse hair, no chin to speak of and with a prominent Adam's apple. If she hadn't known better, hadn't seen him at work, she would have put him down as a salesman of poor-quality vacuum cleaners. But appearances to the contrary there had never been—except for Patrick himself and the not-so-reliable Rafe Posner—a better, kinder man around animals.

"Hello, Sarah Deane," called Farney. "You want your Aunt Julia? She's off in the north pasture with Patrick."

"Thanks," said Sarah. Then she added, "The one you're brushing now, he looks great."

"*He* is a mare," said Farney, but he smiled. "You didn't recognize her. Lollipop, one of those western numbers you helped rescue last Christmas at the ranch. She's going great. She'll make a jumper yet."

"Good," said Sarah, remembering Lollipop as one of the most recalcitrant beasts she'd ever come across. But to Sarah most horses had major faults—the chief of which was always that they were horses. Large, untrustworthy, hooved animals. She edged a little closer and was rewarded with a velvet muzzle thrust toward her and a soft nicker.

"She wants a handout," said Farney. "Mrs. Clancy's spoiling her rotten. But her attitude's improving. Last month she'd have taken the shirt off your back. Lay her ears back and kick the bejeezus out of anyone around. Now she's settling in."

Sarah backed up a few feet, said she was glad Lollipop was settling in, and that she was going to look for Aunt Julia.

She took herself off, walked out through a pathway between paddocks, made it to the north pasture, and came upon her aunt and Patrick walking toward her, Julia leading a large gray pony.

"Hooray, Sarah," called Aunt Julia. "School's out."

"I feel loose as a goose," said Sarah.

"And I've the very thing for loose people. This is Whiskers. A Connemara cross. Perfect lamb."

"That's nice," said Sarah warily.

"For you, Sarah," said Patrick. "Mrs. Clancy, she's got this idea in her head and you're the one'll be paying for it. Paying by the seat of your pants, I'd say."

Patrick was a short, tough man with arms and face made entirely of leather, ears like flaps, and a wide mouth splitting his face in two. He spoke in the soft rhythms of Erin with an overlay of the Maine throaty staccato, and he spoke pretty much whatever he pleased. Long in service to Tom and Julia Clancy, Patrick was the engine that kept High Hope Farm moving. He maintained the fiction of employer-employee by calling her "Mrs. Clancy," but his was an equal voice in all matters pertaining to stable management.

Julia was going on about the gray pony. "We thought you needed something different to take your mind off Bowmouth College. Patrick and I knew Whiskers would be perfect."

"Oh, he's a grand pony," said Patrick. "Just the thing for a beginner like you, Sarah."

"Hold it, you two," said Sarah. "I'm in a state of delight and I'd hate to ruin it by climbing on that horse."

"Whiskers is just a pony, fourteen two-hands," said Patrick.

"Enough spunk but completely bomb-proof," said Julia.

"Bomb-proof?" said Sarah. "Are you planning to test Whiskers with a bomb?"

Bangity, bangity, bang! Bang! As if in answer to Sarah's question, a blast, two blasts, three blasts, four blasts racketed from the direction of the farmhouse. Then a great spattering sound and the distant tinkle of shattered glass.

And at first bang, Whiskers snorted, reared, jerked the lead from Julia's hand, whirled, and took off across the pasture.

"Holy Jesus and Mary," breathed Patrick.

"My horses," cried Julia.

"I'll see if I can catch the buggers. See if there's a car." And Patrick took off at a run.

"Patrick," called Julia. "Come back. It's dangerous. You're too old to run. So am I."

"I'm not too old," said Sarah.

"Don't be a fool," said Julia, grabbing Sarah by her shirt-sleeve. "The shooting may not be over. Patrick, come back!" But it was too late. Patrick was up and away.

"Oh lord, he'll give himself a heart attack or be shot." And then, "My animals. My horses, my dogs. The cats."

Sarah took charge. "Let's walk quietly toward the stable yard, away from the farmhouse," she said. She indicated the knoll in the middle of the pasture. "We'll go behind that and be covered from the road. The shots must have come from there."

Julia trembling, her face pale, let Sarah walk her on an oblique path that led on a roundabout route to the enclosed stable yard. There they found Patrick, purple in the face, panting and shaking in anger. "No one here. The bloody bastards got away."

"The animals?" puffed Julia.

"Nothing hit as far as I can tell. Most of the horses were out in their paddocks and a real blessing it was." Patrick pointed toward the farmhouse, which stood at the top of the rise. "That's what was shot," he said. "Right into Sarah's car. And your little greenhouse." He gestured toward a glass-outcropping at the side of the farmhouse where Julia massed her indoor plants.

"Cats? The dogs?"

"Let's go up and call 'em," said Patrick, "and we'll see."

Ten minutes later the two English setters, Tucker and Belle, were discovered hiding under the farmhouse porch, unharmed but shivering with fear. Gradually six cats manifested themselves from various nooks and corners of porch and barn.

And Farney at a run. White-faced, wide-eyed. Followed by long-legged Rafe Posner.

"My God, Mrs. Clancy," shouted Farney. "What in hell was that? You okay? I was out in the west pasture turning out Lolli-pop."

"And I was bringing in Duffie," said Rafe. "Duffie went pure crazy." He gestured toward the nearest stable paddock. "All the horses went crazy."

"But they're all right," said Julia, voice shaking.

"Far as I know," said Farney. "That girl, Jessica, the one you've taken on for the summer, she'd just finished lunging Joker. Soon as I heard the shots I checked around. No shots came down toward the stable. None of the outbuildings. Just the farmhouse."

"And my car," said Sarah.

Julia shook her head slowly. "Whoever it was, well, they weren't out to get the animals." She took a long heaving breath. "They were out to get me. Or my farmhouse. Or . . ." She paused.

"Or me . . ." said Sarah.

Patrick finished the sentence. "Or the whole lot of us."

There was a pause. A long pause, a pause in which the breathing air felt as thick and heavy as a blanket. Patrick's remark seemed to have summed up the situation with direct and chilling brevity. Then Farney and Patrick took off for a roadside search hoping to find evidence left by the recent visitors. "See if we can find shotgun shells or tire marks," said Patrick. "Or some fool kid hiding in the bushes," said Farney.

But Rafe Posner lingered and Sarah had time to study Aunt Julia's other stable hand. Lanky with the sort of limbs that suggest folding tables and chairs. A long chin, light feathery hair, a long brow and disconcertingly dark eyes overhung by brooding dark eyebrows, a thin crooked slice of a mouth. Hands as big as plates, feet like bread loaves.

Now he was soothing Julia. "Not to worry, Mrs. Clancy. Shoot-ups, they happen to everyone around here. Bunch of crazies. We'll keep our eye out. Someone probably thought you were the new mine headquarters. Those Norminco guys."

"Thank you, Rafe," said Aunt Julia. "Now please go and check out the paddocks. Make sure none of the horses banged each other when they started running around." And Julia called the setters to her and began to stroke their heads with trembling hands.

Sarah had to admit that as a method of decompressing from the stress of teaching there was nothing quite so effective as gunfire. She forgot everything connected with Bowmouth College as she helped calm the dogs and then joined Julia in an inspection of the greenhouse, their feet crunching on the shards of glass.

Julia picked up a jasmine plant lying disembowled next to a shattered earthenware pot and gave an audible sniff, her face bunched in misery. "Sarah, it's happening again. I'm being pursued. Remember last Christmas at the ranch. Me being squirted, mud in the coffee, horses stolen."

"As you would say, Aunt Julia," said Sarah robustly, "stuff and utter nonsense. And as Jane would say to Tilly, get a grip. That ranch business involved politics, a takeover, and you were the one who stole the horses. This is something else entirely. Random vandalism probably. You know how some guys go around shooting mailboxes, tearing down road signs. This farm is a conspicuous facility. And the greenhouse, well, it's a natural target."

"The farm has never been shot at before," objected Julia. "Besides," she added, "there was Sean Conners falling through the hayloft floor, and the cut-out poems."

"But Aunt Julia," Sarah objected. "Sean Conners was an accident. Regrettable but understandable."

"Not understandable to me," retorted Julia, her distress now shifting gears into solid anger. She turned around and started toward the stable and met Patrick and Farney walking toward her.

"We've searched about, looked along the bushes on the road, in the drainage ditch, but no empty shells," said Patrick. "You'd better be calling the police. They'll do a proper job of it."

"I don't want the police," said Julia. "They'll go around unfastening gates and letting horses out, getting kicked. Sarah says it's just random vandalism."

"Sarah also says call the police," said Sarah. "Patrick's right. If you don't, I will. Or Patrick will, won't you, Patrick?"

Patrick grinned, a tough tense grin. "That I will."

For a moment Julia stood firm, then her shoulders sagged and she blew a whistle of air. "All right," she said. "But Patrick, and you, Farney, watch them. I don't trust a policeman on a farm as far as I can throw one. They're all town boys. Or fishermen."

"We can call the sheriff's office, too," said Sarah. "Find Mike Laaka. He's your neighbor."

"Well, if it's Mike," said Julia. "Mike is different."

Patrick nodded. "Good idea. Now I'm off to find that Whiskers pony. He'll still be having the lead shank clipped to his halter and I don't want him tripping on it."

Julia nodded and allowed herself to be led by Sarah into the farmhouse kitchen. To the telephone.

Fifteen minutes later four troopers from the state police and Mike Laaka of the sheriff's office had arrived. These were now prowling about the perimeter of the farm, taking measurements, picking up detritus and photographing the damaged greenhouse and Sarah's former windshield.

"Well, Aunt Julia," said Sarah, thinking to move her aunt's mind off the depressing scene, "I can't go anywhere, not until the police have gone over my car. That means you've got to give me lunch. We can talk about the wedding reception."

It was a happy thought. Julia bustled into the kitchen and began heating up soup and assembling the makings of sandwiches. And asking appropriate wedding questions.

"A dress, you have a wedding dress?"

"Cream-colored thing with a high collar that belonged to a great-aunt. Lace bits here and there. Everything else is on course. Grandmother Douglas is fighting to keep the service recognizably Christian and Alex's mother has two pipers lined up."

"I've brought the caterer to heel, your friend Mary Donelli is instructing him on Italian cuisine, and Rafe will fill in on the guitar when your music group is resting. And the whole farm will be spic and span." But with that sentiment, Julia became agitated and returned to topic A. "My poor greenhouse," she mourned. "Someone shooting at High Hope Farm. We've always tried to be good citizens. Do you think it's those Norminco people? Trying to frighten me into leasing my mineral rights? If I have mineral rights, which I doubt. Because those nursery rhymes haven't sent me packing."

"No," said Sarah sharply. "I don't think it's the mine people sending messages. Can you imagine a large mining corporation writing sinister nursery rhymes? Cutting out little letters? And the company wouldn't hire thugs with shotguns. Norminco is a well-known outfit. I've asked around at college about them. As mine operations go they have a fairly decent reputation."

"Reputations and outward appearances," said Julia, "mean very little. Don't tell me that reputable companies haven't hired thugs before this and used unorthodox methods to get what they want."

Sarah put down her sandwich. "The time has come for you to show me those little cut-out messages and then we will turn them over to the police. Dig them out and let's have a look."

Julia walked to her kitchen desk—operation central for the farm—opened a drawer, and produced four envelopes, three with postmarks and stamps, the other with the address only.

"Do you think I need gloves?" said Sarah. "I mean, how about fingerprints? Does paper hold fingerprints?"

Julia went to another drawer and brought forth a pair of surgical gloves. "I use them for cleaning," she explained.

Sarah pulled on the gloves, extracted the messages from the envelopes, and lined them up. "That's the first one," said Julia, indicating a paper by Sarah's elbow. "It's the 'Ladybird, ladybird, fly away home' one."

It didn't take much time. The messages were simple-minded to the point of idiocy, but the idea was clear: Julia was to move out.

Sarah laid the second message flat and read: "Julia Clancy sat on a wall / Julia Clancy had a great fall / And all of her horses and all of her men / Couldn't put Julia together again."

"About a C minus," said Sarah. "What's next?"

"It's the one I brought over to read to you. Ding dong bell, Julia Clancy go to hell."

Sarah turned to the remaining poem, which Julia had designated as the latest received: "Sing a song of sixpence / A pocket full of rye / Julia Clancy leave your farm / Fly away or die." "That's the nastiest of all," she said. "The police may want to put a watch on your mail. I think you've been much too relaxed about all these. Anyway, here's Mike now, so you can hand them over."

But Mike had something else on his mind. "We're trying to check your property. We've found a few old empty shotgun shells, but nothing else. Julia, have you thought about an alarm system?"

"I've never had to," said Julia unhappily.

"Mightn't be a bad idea," said Mike. "In view of this affair. But," he added, "right now we're thinking it's just your average case of wildies out on a shooting spree. It's called 'summer fun' at the sheriff's office. A sort of reaction to tourism."

"But," protested Julia, "I'm not a tourist. I've been here forty years."

"That's what you think," said Mike. "You're from away. Born in Massachusetts. And Tom Clancy, an Irishman. Someone from 'away' is fair game; I don't care if you came to Maine when you were two weeks old. And horse farms like yours are seen as elite. It's okay to have a couple of backyard horses behind an electric fence and show at the local fairground. But you, Julia Clancy . . ."

"I know what's coming," murmured Julia.

"You, Julia Clancy," repeated Mike, getting into it, "you're big time, at least in this part of Maine. Sixty acres, pastures and paddocks like they're going out of style. And Thoroughbreds, those fancy European horses, warm-bloods, Trakehners, Hanoverians."

"My, my, Mike," said Julia, "you have been paying attention."

"I love horses," said Mike. "They're my favorite animals, even the fancy ones. But Julia, you may be paying the price of being different. As in expensive and different. And from away."

"Wait up, Mike," said Sarah, who had been listening to Mike with attention. She knew from Mike of old: There was always an edge of animosity toward what Mike called the "rich and fa- mous." He was a local man, born and bred, and had seen what he called "outsiders" move in, buy up land, saw his family un- able to handle new taxes on waterfront property and move to their present site on the land next to Julia's south pasture. Mike, without approving, could understand an attack on Julia's farm, could understand resentment of the have-nots for the haves.

None of which Sarah could say. Mike was a solid friend, had grown up with Alex, whom he forgave for making triple his own salary. But Mike still kept a needle out, ready to stick it to the deserving rich if it proved necessary. Now Sarah felt a need to defend her aunt. "Mike, Aunt Julia isn't your average wealthy target. She works with the 4-H groups, the Pony Club, and has riding clinics for the local kids, the summer camps. She's ac- cepted."

Mike shrugged, then turned to Julia and smiled. "Don't let this get you down. Like I said, it's maybe just some dudes all liquored-up and looking for a target. Nothing personal at all."

"Thank you, Mike," said Julia. "Tonight I'm going to ask Alex and Sarah to come over. And the other close neighbors. We'll talk about security. A sort of farm-watch thing. Will you come?"

"Sure," said Mike. "Will you invite the Norminco people?"

"Certainly not," said Julia. "They may be part of the problem. And Mike, Sarah thinks you ought to see these." Julia turned to the kitchen table and pointed out the four cut-out messages.

Mike nodded, his expression impassive. He reached for a paper towel, wrapped it around the collection, turned, opened the door, and rejoined the police search party.

Toward four o'clock the day, which had begun with soft breezes and a sun-filled sky, resolved itself into the sort of af- ternoon that reminded inhabitants of the frozen North that May can be glorious. The wind dropped to the merest whisper of a zephyr, the sun remained benign, and the temperature settled itself at a delightful seventy degrees with not a blackfly in sight.

All of which should have restored Aunt Julia to partial optimism. Her animals were unharmed and were quietly grazing in their appointed pastures. To add to her pleasure she could see the three new foals trotting on their long knobby legs beside their dams in a near paddock. And the signs of the recent disturbance were fading. Patrick and Farney had swept up the broken glass and two men in overalls were that very moment affixing new panes to the greenhouse frame. Sarah's VW bug had been towed away, and after certain telephone negotiations she was now the temporary owner of a rental Subaru.

Still Julia brooded. "I feel violated," she said. "It's like being mugged. The same feeling I had once in Boston when I was knocked down and my handbag grabbed."

"Cheer up," said Sarah. "At least with Sean Conners back you won't be so shorthanded."

Julia started. "Sean!" she exclaimed. "Sean Conners? Where is he? Where was he during the shooting? Oh my heavens, you don't suppose . . ." She jumped to her feet, upsetting a glass of iced tea that spread and dribbled onto the floor.

"Sean Conners," she repeated and then, stepping over the puddle of tea, started for the door, opened it, and almost running headed toward the stable yard.

Sarah followed, caught up with her, pulled her sleeve and brought her aunt to a walk.

"Easy, Aunt Julia. You've had enough excitement and running around for one day. One more minute won't matter. Sean has probably gone home. He was still pretty much under the weather."

Sean Conners was not in the stable. The bridles and girths he had been cleaning were neatly hung up on their racks in the tack room, the saddle soap replaced on the shelf, and the sponges rinsed and laid out beside the sink in the washroom.

"Where is everyone?" demanded Julia. "Patrick, Farney, Rafe? And Jessica?"

"Jessica who?" asked Sarah, because she had not yet identified this member of the High Hope Farm crew.

"Jessica Jacoby. For heaven's sake, your own cousin Jessica.

She's fourteen now and I've taken her on for the summer. She bicycles over every morning. Helps with the riding program and the mucking out. Never mind Jessica. She's all right, I saw her this afternoon in the riding ring with Rafe. What I want to know is, where is Sean Conners? It's almost time to bring in the horses."

And as if in answer to a summons, Patrick leading Whiskers, Farney with Lollipop, Rafe with Plum Duff, and Jessica leading Copper came in one after the other with their charges and disposed of them in their proper stalls.

"Sean Conners," called Julia. "Patrick, where is Sean?"

Patrick looked puzzled. "Now you mention it, I haven't seen hide nor hair of the boy since before noon."

"Not since before the shooting," put in Farney, coming over to Julia. "He'd finished the tack cleaning and I was doing up Lollipop. I didn't pay attention to him. I think he went outside."

"Jessie, come here a minute," said Julia to the tall, sandy-haired girl who was hanging a halter on a hook by Copper's stall.

Jessica Jacoby came forward. She had straight features, a firm mouth, her hair pulled tightly behind. Broad shoulders for a fourteen-year-old, competent hands, long legs encased in tan breeches, her feet in rubber boots. Sarah, looking at her cousin and thinking of her own soft muscles, felt diminished. Perhaps more time spent on her bicycle. Running with Patsy up hills, training for the local marathon.

Busy with these ruminations Sarah, after her first call of "Hi, Jessie," missed the beginning of the interrogation of Jessica on the subject of the missing Conners. Jessie was just saying, ". . . so after the shooting Sean went off to check on the fences. Look for broken rails. He said he couldn't do anything heavy so he might as well go over the fencing."

"What direction?" said Patrick.

"Hey, I didn't notice," said Jessica. "Like I'd just finished cooling out Joker in the ring."

"All right," said Julia. "I'll tour the whole blessed property. All sixty acres, if necessary."

"Aunt Julia," protested Sarah, "you can't do the whole place."

"We'll split into three groups," said Patrick, taking charge. "Jessica, Rafe, and Farney take the south pastures and the stable paddocks. I'll take the west pastures. Sarah, you do the north side, and your aunt can walk along the road on the east side." And Patrick strode off toward the west pasture and the lowering sun.

Aunt Julia, Sarah saw with amusement, nodded with something like docility, and started for the east pastures while Sarah herself trudged forth to the north perimeter, walking awkwardly in her sneakers, squelching through muddy swales, jumping a small brook, and fending off a little nervously the attentions of two nosy yearlings.

As she picked her way across paddock and pasture she wondered why her Aunt Julia could ever want Harvey Dodge when Patrick took care of her so nicely. Though probably not, Sarah told herself, in the manner of D. H. Lawrence's groom. Did Julia want that sort of consolation? Of course, life as well as literature was replete with accounts of steamy sessions in which the lady of the manor rolled in the hay with her groom, but somehow Patrick didn't fit the part. He had a wife, children, and grandchildren, and by all accounts was a devoted husband, going home every night to the house Julia had given him at the northwest corner of High Hope Farm.

Then, mindful of duty, Sarah gave up—at least for the present—on her aunt's potential as an elderly Lady Chatterley. She hiked over to the northeast corner of the pasture that lay along the main road and worked her way west toward Patrick's small cape and barn and the gate that gave him access to Julia's acres.

The north pasture was contained in part by a crumbling stone wall that snaked along Julia's property line. On Patrick's side a dirt access road to his house ran along the stone wall and was shaded by a line of ancient apple trees—relatives no doubt to those opposite at Tilly and Jane's Appleyard Farm. On Julia's side of the wall ran a post-and-rail fence with here and there an occasional tree giving shade.

But no Sean Conners. Sarah dutifully inspected the heavy grass by the fence, climbed at intervals over the stone wall, scuffed about under the apple trees for the presence or absence of the missing Sean. She hoped fervently that this was not going to be one of those episodes involving a body. She and Alex had bumped into several bodies and she wished no more of it. If Sean turned up, she wanted him alive. Perhaps, being still weak and tired-out from his exertions, he was taking advantage of the beautiful day and having a long outdoor nap.

Sarah climbed, walked, stumbled on. Then, just as she had decided that the final hundred yards of the northern run of fencing were empty, she saw him.

Sean. Sean Conners leaning against a post. Slumped against a post underneath a long overreaching apple tree limb. His head tilted down, his chin resting against his collar.

Sarah took a step, two steps nearer, feeling her heart like a hammer stroke in her chest. Another step and she saw the inhale of a breath making a hollow in Sean's cheek. Then the exhale. A heavy exhale with a slight snore that parted his lips in a blubbery sound.

Alive. Thank God, alive. Napping as she had hoped. Sleeping the afternoon away.

She hesitated, wondering whether to wake him first and then shout to the other searchers or to slip back quietly with the news and let the poor man finish his nap. She decided on waking him. After all, it was now well past five; the air, although still warm, would inevitably begin to chill—not a good thing for a man just out of the hospital.

She walked forward and touched Sean on his shoulder, and, receiving no response, gave it a slight push. This action resulted in a slight alteration of the man's position, causing the head to loll to one side and fall farther forward. And then Sarah saw it: A tangle of wet hair and dark sticky material just above the top of the hairline. And between the cheekbone and the ear a dried irregular crimson line that ran from the jawline to the neck and spread into a damp patch on the blue work-shirt collar.

Sean Conners was not lying there taking a refreshing nap. He was unconscious.

THE SNAKE

SIX

SARAH took an involuntary step backward and then stopped. Sean Conners was alive. Alive but hurt. Hit on the head, attacked. Whatever. She had to act. CPR? No, that was for breathing. Help? Get help? Yes. Sarah took off shouting, down the pasture, tripping on hummocks, stumbling into hoofprints.

And help came. It usually does. Sooner, or sometimes, regrettably, later. In this case, almost immediately. Sarah, waving her arms and yelling, was spotted by Farney and in a matter of minutes Patrick in the farm pickup came rocketing along the north pasture access road that led to his own house.

By the time Patrick arrived, Sean had come to, groaned, rubbed his head, groaned again, and tried to stand up. This effort proved unsuccessful and Patrick was there in time to catch him as he slumped back to the ground.

Then the rescue squad—"Makin' a habit of this, ain't you?"— loaded Sean Conners into the ambulance for his second trip to Penobscot Bay Regional Hospital.

"Really," said Julia, flinging herself into a lawn chair on the back terrace of the farmhouse, "really we are jinxed."

Sarah, who had produced tea and toast for her wilting relative, corrected her. "If anyone is jinxed, it's poor Sean. It looks like someone has it in for him. Maybe he's involved in something he shouldn't be."

"It's because of Patrick," sighed Julia. "He came to me about Sean. Patrick has a sister in Boston and her son Sean was hanging around with a group who seemed to specialize in car theft. Well, Sean had grown up on a horse farm so I told Patrick I'd give him a trial."

"Car theft!" exclaimed Sarah, for this seemed to be the nub of the story.

"Nothing of the sort since he's come here—as far as I know. He found a room in Rockland, comes here on a motorcycle, and has been a pretty steady worker ever since. He and Rafe do the hard riding. Both Patrick and I are too old to be thrown by young horses—we'd splinter into bits. But Sean isn't very successful with people; he's one of those animals-only types."

"You don't suppose one of his Boston friends has been looking him up," said Sarah.

"I don't suppose anything," said Julia wearily. "I just want it to stop. Poems, accidents, gunshots."

At which juncture Patrick appeared at the edge of the terrace. He was holding aloft a length of tree limb.

"From the apple tree," he explained. "Near where you found Sean. I think it's got blood and hair on it."

"Someone hit him with a branch!" exclaimed Julia.

"More like he whacked himself," said Patrick. "The limb of that tree hangs way over into High Hope Farm's pasture and it was at about Sean's eye level. My guess is he ran right into it."

"But that's crazy," said Julia. "Anyone would see a branch coming at them."

"I mean," said Patrick, "he sat on a horse and ran into it."

"What do you mean? He wasn't riding," said Julia.

"Ah, there now, you don't know these young fellows," said Patrick. "What Sean likes to do—I've seen it a dozen times—when he's off in the pasture, he jumps on a horse bareback and has some fun riding around. To change the routine. Lots of times when he's gone to fetch a horse from the pasture, he'll ride him to the gate bareback. No harm to it unless he fools around with the mares and their foals, or with the young horses."

"Are you saying he hopped on one of the horses in the north pasture and rode into an apple tree? With that bad leg of his?"

"Even so, he might have been riding and the horse spooked—maybe at the gunfire—took off, ran to the end of the field, away from the noise, and he didn't duck in time. Seems likely."

"Well," said Julia, "have you tried out the story on Sean? Is he conscious enough to answer?"

"I asked before he left in the ambulance, but he's got a sort of amnesia for the whole accident. That kind of blow on the head can do it."

"What I'm thinking," said Julia severely, "is that Sean is extraordinarily accident-prone. I'm not sure I want him back."

Patrick waited, regarded his employer with a serious look, and then shrugged. "Think it over, please, Mrs. Clancy. One more chance'd be fair enough. The lad's behaved himself so far, and falling through the hayloft, it wasn't his fault."

Sarah watched her aunt's face, her tightened lips, her frown showing clearly that her disapproval was at war with her devotion to, her dependence on, Patrick. And, as Sarah might have predicted, Patrick had his way.

"All right," said Julia. "One more chance. But lay down the law. No more bareback. He's to lead the horses in. On foot."

"I'll tell him," said Patrick, "and now it's time to water and grain the horses. It's coming on for six o'clock."

"So, does that settle it?" said Sarah when Patrick had left.

"No, it does not," said Julia. "If Sean was too weak to do regular chores, why was he hopping on a horse? But never mind that. We have our meeting coming up. A select group. Mike Laaka, Alex, you, Harvey Dodge, the Wentworths. And Jane. Pray heaven Tilly is busy tonight. The only occult power I'll grant her is an extrasensory perception about situations where she can cause trouble."

"Maybe it's Tilly's dance night. I'll drop over there and see if I can find out."

But a conference with Jane, cornered by her chicken house, yielded the information that Tilly, who was busy setting up a loom in the attic, had canceled her dance classes "for the duration."

"The duration of what?" demanded Sarah.

"Well, you know, the whole thing," said Jane. "This rotation business. I haven't seen her quite so taken with an idea since that time four years ago when she discovered Martha Graham. That led to the dancing classes, but now she says she's too busy. The loom, I gather, is part of the rotation scheme."

"Jane, don't you think—" Sarah began.

"Of course," Jane interrupted. "She's going too far. It's time for another appointment with her therapist, but Dr. Glover has fallen out of favor. Dr. Glover, she's a Virgo. Virgos apparently give out too many medications. So I'll have to stir around and see if I can find someone acceptable. Sagittarius or Libra. It's not everyone who can be on Tillie's wavelength."

"Lord, I hope not."

"I'm crossing my fingers that her loom will distract her. She's planning what she calls a 'web of destiny.' "

"Whose destiny?" asked Sarah, but even as she said it she knew the answer. "Never mind," she told Jane, "I can guess that one. A web all woven with hanks of hair and jawbones and dead newts and pieces of Aunt Julia's shoelaces."

"Everyone's shoelaces," said Jane. "She's not leaving anyone out—in the neighborhood, that is."

"A true universalist," murmured Sarah and took her leave.

That evening, as Alex and Sarah debarked on Julia's driveway preparatory to the meeting, Sarah asked Alex's opinion on the influence of planets. "I mean, I do know Leos who think they're kings—or queens—and Geminis who can't make up their minds, and Aunt Julia's a Taurus, stubborn to the core."

Alex gave a noise that sounded like a cross between a snort and a humph and started for the porch stairs.

"But there's moon madness," persisted Sarah. "Dogs howling, people dancing in the street, and I read somewhere that there are more homicides during a full moon."

"Because they see better," said Alex, holding the door open. "More light on the target. Listen, my darling, there's enough going on at this farm without astral influences. I refuse to allow Tilly or her machinations room in my brain."

"I'm glad you didn't go into psychiatry," said Sarah as they moved toward Julia Clancy's brightly lit front parlor.

"That's two of us," said Alex. "I have enough trouble with mutant viruses and resistant bacteria without adding moon madness."

"Ah, there you are," said Julia Clancy, looking up from a pad of paper. "Sarah, sit over by me. Alex, there's room on that settee. I chose the front parlor," she explained, "because all this Victorian furniture is so blessedly uncomfortable. We'll have to think, pay attention instead of dozing off. Oh, hello Mike, sit over there"—this as the deputy sheriff edged into the room and looked with disapproval on the motley collection of horsehair stuffed settees, chairs, and love seats.

But even hard furniture could not bring the group to focus on the beginning of a plan. Julia, after she had placed the last of the neighborhood guests—Tilly and Jane—in a far corner of the room, told Sarah in a loud whisper that if any sort of agreement was reached she would be very much surprised.

She was not surprised. The neighbors agreed only to disagree. The idea of a watch association was rejected as being too complicated and made up of people—themselves—who could never settle on one plan. The only consensus reached was a general horror over random shotgun attacks.

Harvey Dodge was solicitous and pledged more time at High Hope Farm, the Laakas offered spot day checks, Neil and Winka Wentworth offered their services as mounted patrols—when they could spare the time from Camp Highfeather—"never on weekends and perhaps not on Monday or Friday" murmured Winka. Jane Zimmer suggested trip wires and a Doberman, and Tilly, who had sat silent throughout the session, her eyes wandering first to the furniture then to the lighting fixtures, came to and said that there was no point in talking since no one would be in the same place next year and she personally would see to it that all access to High Hope Farm was stopped by a stone wall with broken glass on its top.

"That will teach the barbarians," said Tilly, leaning forward, cheeks crimson with excitement. "Jane and I will not allow vandalism and gunfire, and you, Julia, will be quite safe at Quartermaster Farm with Colonel Dodge. However, I don't feel that Jane's suggestion of the Doberman is quite sound because it's generally thought that Rottweilers are considered better guard dogs. Julia, for the interim, until we all rotate, you could look into a Rottweiler."

At which Julia said through clenched teeth that she was quite happy with English setters but thank you, Tilly, for sharing.

Then Jane Zimmer rose from her chair, pulled Tilly unceremoniously to her feet, and expressed fatigue. "We're with you, Julia, in whatever you decide," she said. "Or if," she added more realistically, "you decide nothing, we're still with you."

At which Tilly twisted in Jane's grip, turned her head, and beamed a beatific smile on the assembled company. "All of you remember, it's love that makes the world go round. We can overcome noxious emanations beneath our feet with the aid of the planets. Reach out to Julia Clancy and prepare. Prepare to rotate."

And then Tilly, still smiling, was dragged bodily from the room by the strong arm of Jane Zimmer.

For a moment there was total silence in the front parlor. The Laaka seniors then shifted uncomfortably in their chairs, muttered that it was getting on, and with a reassuring touch on Julia's arm slipped out into the evening.

Neil Wentworth recovered speech first. "Well, I'm fond of Tilly—she's one of a kind—but she needs help. Directly. Tomorrow morning at the latest. But now we can get on with it. All right, Julia, what do you propose? You're the reason we're here. Not that shotgun blasts spattering the neighborhood aren't a worry to all of us."

Neil was one of those graceful human beings who manage to look comfortable even when seated, as he was, on a piano stool. Now he pulled out a small notebook from an inner pocket, poised a pencil, and waited. He was perhaps forty-five with intense blue eyes, jutting chin, dark copper hair, and with the lean look so beloved by the photographers of Ralph Lauren clothes. He was, Sarah thought, a decorative and informed addition to the company. As assistant director of the Highfeather Camp for boys he was everything a parent could want as a role model—intelligent with a light touch, urbane, and well read. And Highfeather had a reputation of being efficiently run and was popular. Sarah herself had enjoyed discussing books—even Joyce and T. S. Eliot—with Neil, something she could not do with Aunt Julia. Or even Alex, whose leisure reading tended more to the spy and adventure story.

And there was Winka, too, sitting next to him, her fair hair wound into a knot at the nape of her neck, her eyes bent a little over a knit cable-stitch something she was working on, her fine long legs crossed and revealing a strong muscle development. Winka, besides her director duties at Camp Highfeather, played the flute, volunteered in the local schools, and organized Halloween costume parties for the community. Unlike Julia, who loathed anything smacking of beautiful people, Sarah could enjoy Neil and Winka, and if she had felt any emotion, it was one touched with the tincture of jealousy. The pair made her feel small, brittle, and insectlike.

She woke from these thoughts to realize that Julia was fulminating on the subject of emanations. "What did Tilly mean 'noxious emanations?' " she demanded. "Did she mean the smell in my barn? Her barn smells the same way."

Sarah stepped in. "I think she means the mine. Norminco. When I was over there just after Jim Shale had finished taking core samples she went on about the dangers of emanations. From whatever minerals they've got under their farm. I'd guess that's what started this rotation business."

"Aha!" said Neil. "Perhaps Tilly is being clever."

This idea was shot down, although Sarah remembered her own speculations on the subject—Tilly the fox.

Julia held up her hand and quieted the babble. "Tilly hasn't a calculating hair on her head. She's—what's the word—artless. Off the deep end, but artless. Now let's see if we can have a sensible talk without this palaver about Dobermans and Rottweilers and planets. I agree with Neil that Tilly needs immediate help. This rotation business might have been amusing but it could be dangerous if Tilly is going about telling my staff that they're going to lose their jobs."

"Get back to those emanations," put in Mike Laaka. "Do you want the Norminco subject off-limits?"

"Certainly not," said Julia. "Now all of you listen. I will be perfectly frank."

"When are you not?" murmured Sarah from her corner.

"Perfectly frank," repeated Julia. "My idea is that the mine is at the center of all—well, almost all—the things that have been happening at my farm. Those cut-out messages, the accidents, the gunshots. In the first place, everyone for miles around is in a fever about the mine coming."

"Or not coming," put in Mike.

"It's not even been voted on," said Sarah.

"Mike, Sarah, don't interrupt. Listen: Norminco has put perfectly normal people on edge. So what is happening? Here's how I see it. First you have the mine people like Jim Shale making offers, taking core samples in backyards. We're in the middle of an economic mess and these geologists are talking big money. And people who would normally hang onto their land for dear life are starting to think that jobs are more important than beautiful woods or a clean lake. The idea of money is beginning to change people. It's like an epidemic."

Here Neil Wentworth protested. "Whoa there, Julia. You're suggesting that someone having their soil tested by Norminco is out of line, money grubbing? My dear Julia, that's pure rot. I shall be perfectly frank, too."

Oh brother, thought Sarah. She looked at Alex, who grimaced.

"Neil and I," said Winka in the clear clipped tones of the BBC, "are practical people. We want to know everything about our property. Our land, which includes our Highfeather Camp, lies along the southern edge of the proposed mine site and, of course, our camp children come first . . ."

"Oh for heaven's sake, Winka, cut it short," said Neil in a voice that had a decided edge. "What she's trying to tell you is that we've had our land tested, surveyed, sampled, the whole bit, just to find out what's down there. As simple as that. We don't plan to sell now, but it's possible that we might. If conditions become unbearable. For the camp, for comfortable living. Dust, heavy machinery, noise. All that sort of thing."

"That's what I was going to say, Neil," said Winka.

"What they're both saying," Mike whispered to Alex, "is that they might want the cash."

"Mike," said Julia, "have you something for all of us?"

"My God, Julia Clancy, you sound like my third-grade teacher, Miss Dutton. She always said that. And sure, I'm thinking that quite a few property owners in these parts may be short of cash and will have their land tested."

"I won't," cried Aunt Julia, face flushed, hands turned into fists. "I won't be tested. And that's exactly why I am being targeted. By Norminco or persons unknown. Or," she said looking about the room, "enemies who call themselves friends."

"But Aunt Julia," protested Sarah. "That doesn't make sense. Do you think you're being hit because you won't be tested?"

"It's simple," said Julia with something like triumph. "I think someone may have already tested my property. Sneaking around my land with a shovel. Or a drill. Metal detector. Whatever they use. Taking samples. There's a lot of drilling around so I wouldn't have noticed any noise, not with sixty acres of land. Someone's after me, or rather after my farm. Someone thinks—or knows—I'm sitting on hunks of nickel or copper or gold."

"No one has mentioned gold," put in Mike.

"I wouldn't put it past them to have found gold," said Julia, now quite red in the face, her gray, bristly hair rumpled. "And this someone has decided to move me out. Scare the daylights out of me, send me letters, injure my staff, kill Sean Conners and probably Patrick, and then when my hair is completely white, my horses are lying dead in the field, why, they'll come in with an offer I can't refuse because I'll be having a nervous breakdown and will have lost my insurance and all my friends and my money and my house will be riddled with bullet holes." Here Julia paused for breath and Sarah reached over and took her aunt's hand.

"Aunt Julia, simmer down or Alex will add you to his list of hypertensive patients. And no one's been digging out in your fields . . . have they? Now have they?"

Aunt Julia, slumped back in her chair, breathing fast from her outburst, shook her head. "It's just a guess. An educated guess."

"Well," said Alex, "I don't know about the educated part, but it might be easy enough to prove. Have your people go over the whole place tomorrow. Look for signs of drilling. Check over the old records of the farm before you and Tom came here and see if anyone had dreams of mining. If you can't find anything, call in Norminco. Ask them to take some core samples. Then you'll know exactly what you've got and whether anyone has reason for taking an interest in your farm."

"Absolutely, Alex," said Neil. "We've had it done and it didn't hurt a bit. Then you know where you are."

Mike nodded. "Alex and Neil are right. If you find out that there's nothing under your pasture but good clay and granite, we can go back to saying that you're the victim of vandals and that Sean Conners should take out accident insurance."

But Julia brought her fist down on her knee. "You have not been listening. I don't want to know whether I have minerals. I'm not interested in selling my land. Period."

"But Aunt Julia," protested Sarah, "that's putting your head in the sand. How can you prove your idea? It doesn't have to be Norminco who does the testing for you. It could be some warm and fuzzy geologist who loves horses. Then if minerals turn up you can take it from there. Buy Dobermans, set up trip wires. Show whoever it is what a stubborn old coot he has to deal with."

"Or she," said Alex. "The contemporary world is no doubt filled with rapacious money-hungry female miners."

"Touché," said Sarah. "Male or female. Although statistics prove that the male propensity to violence . . ."

But Harvey Dodge had come to life. "Sarah, your aunt is not an old coot. Though stubborn, I'll grant. Tomorrow Farney and I and Patrick and the rest of the crew can go over the farm, see what we can find. And I think I should move in and keep a weather eye out. The guest room, the stable, the barn. To be on hand."

"Thank you," said Julia, "but I have Patrick just around the corner. And Farney and Rafe here at daybreak. And now it's my bedtime, so please all of you go home and put on your thinking caps about who has decided to ruin me." And Julia pulled herself stiffly to her feet, made a farewell gesture to the room at large, and made for the door.

That night, back home, after Sarah settled her dog Patsy beside the bed, after Alex had called in to the hospital about the state of two new admissions, the two compared notes about the evening's meeting.

Alex, climbing over Patsy and into bed, observed that Sarah had not properly described her aunt.

"Stubborn old coot doesn't even touch it," he said. "Has anyone ever made the Widow Clancy see reason?"

"I'd say only Patrick, her farrier, her vet, and sometimes, if she's in the mood, Harvey Dodge."

"Well, she wasn't in the mood tonight. What's the harm in finding out if the farm is sitting on a mineral deposit?"

"I think she'd feel contaminated somehow. Hell, I can't explain Aunt Julia. She's a tough New England lady made entirely of gristle. As for me, I'm voting for Tilly. If I can't have Colonel Dodge as the villain, I'll take Tilly."

"Tilly," said Alex, "is completely mad."

"Those noxious emanations may have affected her brain. But not as you think. Consider money. Appleyard Farm is on its last legs. Not moon madness or planetary influences. Money. Good old-fashioned money."

"Neither Tilly nor Jane Zimmer is money crazy."

Sarah wriggled down under the blanket; nights in Maine could still be chilly even in early June. She turned over and faced Alex. "How do you know? They may yearn for a better life, a new kitchen, a hot tub, a swimming pool. Travel to far places."

"I don't buy that. If you're looking for people who need money, there's half the county."

"Of course," said Sarah, "Harvey Dodge's place is falling apart, but since he's planning to move into High Hope Farm, why keep his own place up? He can sell out for big bucks and then start cashing in on Julia's minerals."

"Then why offer to go over her pastures for signs of drilling with Farney and *Patrick*. You can't tell me Farney and Harvey Dodge *and* Patrick and the High Hope staff are all in cahoots. Forget Harvey. And forget Tilly. This stargazing is just another of Tilly's tilts toward space travel."

"Even so," said Sarah, "I think I'll make another visit. I've only two exams to give tomorrow. See if I can get a handle on what kicked Tilly off. Was it Jim Shale's drilling?"

Alex yawned. "If you want a villain, try Sean Conners. He's trouble."

"No, he's another victim. Maybe one of his nasty friends in Boston is after him." Sarah returned to her favorite suspect. "Harvey Dodge. You don't suppose he's been proposing marriage all these years just to get his mitts on High Hope Farm? Mike told me that everyone's known for years about mineral deposits near Fallen Tree Pond. Julia's farm may have been tested ages ago."

"I told Julia to do some deed searches."

But Sarah was in full flight. "Harvey gets around. He probably has his ear to the financial world. And the army is filled with spies. The Corps of Engineers probably has records."

"Settle down, Sarah," said Alex. "Until a few weeks ago Harvey was asking Julia to go and live at his Quartermaster Farm. Wanting her to sell High Hope and move in with him. Harvey is devoted. Like a hound dog. He's been her slave and nursemaid for years. Come to my arms, or at least go to your own pillow and go to sleep. It's past eleven."

But Sarah remained sitting, hands clasped around her knees. "There's something sinister about faithful friends. Of course, there are the Wentworths. They're so gorgeous and such inspiring camp directors that there must be something criminal about them. But I still go for Harvey and Tilly."

Alex raised his head off the pillow. "If you think Harvey's busy trying to destroy Julia's farm operation with scare tactics *and* marry her *and* move in and *live* on that same destroyed farm, you have rocks in your head."

Sarah slid down under the covers into Alex's arms. "Rocks in my head, maybe," she murmured, "but rocks full of nickel, cobalt, and copper."

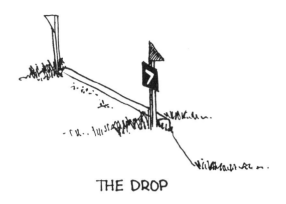

THE DROP

SEVEN

BUT the next day, Friday, academic duties intruded and Sarah's plan to visit Tilly and Jane had to be put on hold. After giving her freshman classes their exams she was asked at noon to act as monitor for a professor who had better things to do than sit for two hours while students toiled over their blue books. And since a mere teaching fellow must defer to a high-profile tenured faculty person, this request took care of her early afternoon. Later, when returning the finished exams to the English office, she was met by her old friend Assistant Professor Mary Donelli—Mary, who was in charge of the Italian flavor of the wedding. Mary, who appeared unfrazzled by exam week, her person wrapped in a red shirt and blue pants, her dark hair tied with a red band, her brown eyes cheerful.

"Hello, Mary, how do you stay looking so put together?" said Sarah, dumping the blue books on the desk of the secretary. "That old buzzard Pengallon made me monitor his twelve o'-clock."

"Come on, we'll grab a sandwich together," said Mary. "We can talk about my appearance as your matron of honor. Walking down the stable aisle holding a bouquet of new-mown hay."

"Not the stable. In our kitchen or out on our so-called lawn. You can carry viper's bugloss and daisy fleabane."

'I'm going to get special dispensation from Our Lady of Good Hope to be your mainstay."

"Will they let you?" asked Sarah. "I don't want to upset the powers above and have you involved in heretical ceremonies."

"Not to worry," said Mary. "The church likes to reach out."

"I thought," said Sarah, "you could wear what you wanted. Alex will have his brother, Angus, who will probably be in torn jeans. No procession. We'll just straggle in and out."

"A simple frock for me," said Mary. "Perhaps a gray stuff dress with a white cap, a fichu, and an artfully designed scarlet *A* on the breast. In the literary tradition, you know."

But before Sarah could answer, Arlene, the English office secretary, poked her head out of her office. "Telephone call for you this morning, Sarah. Julia Clancy. Call her when you're free."

"Crikey," said Sarah, "what now?"

But Julia was unharmed. "Sarah," said Julia. "I'll bet you're thinking of ducking out of my Preakness party tomorrow. Well, you can't. I want you to slide among the guests and drop the subject of the Norminco mine into the conversation. Everyone will be drinking up a storm so they'll all be—what's your Grandmother Douglas's expression?—*elevated*. Elevated if not absolutely looped, so tongues will be loose and truth may out. Or at least some truth."

At this Sarah began to protest, but Julia cut her off.

"Having you at the party—not drinking, of course—is a marvelous idea. No one will pay the least attention to you. All that experience you've had with murder shouldn't be wasted. And now I've a dressage lesson to give. See you tomorrow. And Alex, too, although Alex isn't subtle. He's much too honest. Good-bye, dear."

"You have a nice day," shouted Sarah into the phone, but the line was dead. She turned back to Mary.

"Damn. Aunt Julia's setting me up for a house spy. Want to come and creep around, too? Be a co-spy?"

"No way," said Mary. "But I have heard through the grapevine that your Aunt Julia is under siege. You can fill my ear with poison during lunch."

They made their way to Dizzy's Diner—a popular fixture constructed from an elderly boxcar marked Boston & Maine that sat on a ledge with a distant view of Rockport Harbor. Here, jammed into a booth, sustaining life with grilled-cheese sandwiches, Sarah filled Mary in on recent events at High Hope Farm.

"It's not as if Aunt Julia provoked any of this beyond just being Julia," she finished.

"So she won't have her land tested," said Mary.

"Mule-headed woman," said Sarah. "But it's very human. Like not going to the doctor because you're afraid of what they're going to find. Julia doesn't want to know that there are minerals underfoot because then she might have to consider moving. She said that money is tight, so if she sold out she'd have extra funds to care for even more horses, have more help—which she needs at her age—and in general be more comfortable."

"So you don't blame her for playing ostrich?"

"No," sighed Sarah, "I don't. I sympathize. High Hope Farm is more than a place. It's her past and what's left of her future. We might just as well talk about chopping off one of her legs."

"And you'll put on a false nose and go sniffing about at her party?"

"I guess. Oh lord, look at the time. Now I've got to do all those things I was supposed to do two hours ago. I was going to visit Tilly and Jane, but that will have to wait. Poor Tilly, she's really over the edge. And damn it again. There's Saturday shot. Sure you won't come and help? After all, you're my matron of honor. No? A fine no-good terrible lousy friend you are." And Sarah slapped down a five-dollar bill on the check, grabbed her briefcase, and headed out.

Mary watched her retreating form and shook her head. "That

person," she told the approaching waitress, "is a dangerous international spy who is presently disguised as a faculty member of a well-known college. Next time don't bring her a sandwich, bring her fried toadstools."

Julia Clancy, much distracted by recent events, had made only a minimal effort at party preparations. She had telephoned a local restaurant for a number of food items, hot and cold, and had called on Harvey Dodge to come early and mastermind the drinks. Efforts at decor went no further than stuffing the black-eyed Susans into jugs and dusting the screen of the television set.

By three o'clock the farmhouse was packed, drinks went round, and by three-thirty the names of the horses had been drawn from a hat. By quarter of four the tried-and-true horse people had settled down for the duration in front of the television screen to watch interviews with trainers, film clips of early efforts by the entries, and the ever-changing odds. However, there were other guests whose attention wasn't grabbed by the goings-on in Maryland, and these wandered about the farm, making visits to the stables and paddocks to check out the new foals or perhaps venture into Julia's overgrown garden and point out what a pity it was that she hadn't done more in the way of spring landscaping.

One focus of the outside crowd was Winka and Neil Wentworth's ancient but refurbished Land Rover. Julia, going out to greet her guests, had examined this object briefly and sniffed. "So like them. Making the point that everything British is better. And they won't give an inch on nomenclature. They insist on lift, not elevator, trainers not sneakers, and biscuits for cookies, and now listen to Neil going on about the boot and the bonnet."

"We all have our little ways, and Uncle Tom never gave an inch either. He always sounded as if he'd just made it over from the County Clare," Sarah had reminded her aunt. Now, at almost four o'clock, she had drawn the name of a horse from a hat, a long shot named appropriately Slewth after its daddy,

Seattle Slew. This ceremony over, Sarah went outside for fresh air and new faces. Eavesdropping among that noisy drinking crowd proved a lost cause. The name of Norminco had certainly cropped up, but it was so intermingled with talk of entries and racetrack conditions and local interests such as quality of feed, the spruce budworm, and the price of lobsters that sifting out the dross from the gold was hopeless.

Now Sarah leaned over the open bonnet of the Land Rover and made appreciative noises about the revealed engine while Neil pointed out features with a wrench he referred to as a spanner. Searching for an opening wedge, she asked him if he thought the possibility of a mine in the neighborhood would be a hazard to driving. Flagmen sneaking about and all that blasting.

"Everything around is a hazard," said Neil, stroking an object that might or might not have been the distributor cap. "I mean," he went on, "just look at the Tri-County Road. Absolutely rotten surface. But, of course, all those lorries loaded with stone ought to shake it up, make it worse."

"So you'll move," said Sarah, "if the mine really goes in."

"What a dreadful bother that would be. It would cost the earth. And Highfeather Camp, it's Winka's whole life, you know."

Neil raised a sleek copper head from the bowels of the Land Rover, pushed his glasses back on his nose, and looked seriously at Sarah. "Yes, we can move. Relocate. Even Highfeather can be moved. But what about Julia? Julia isn't growing younger, it's all really too much for her. Winka's concerned because she's *very* fond of Julia. As am I. She reminds me of my Aunt Cecily, who wouldn't give in until they found her facedown under a ladder. She'd been trying to clean her eaves. Do your best to persuade Julia to think about the future. I'm not saying she should give in to these goings-on, but perhaps in the long run discretion is the better part of valor. And Harvey will welcome her with open arms. Oh hallo, Tommy"—this to an approaching young man holding a tall amber-colored drink. "Come to see my pride and joy? Mind what I've said, Sarah.

Winka and I *care* for Julia. If she wants to stay put, we're behind her. If she decides to sell, I'm sure she'd get a fair price.' And Neil returned to the interior of the Land Rover.

Sarah looked at her watch. Ten minutes to four. Post time for the Preakness wasn't until 4:20. Time for more outside rambling. Little knots of people stood here and there, beyond the stable, above the pastures. The whole scene, the paint colors of spring clothes, the bright reds, the blues, the yellows, the grass greens all seemed to Sarah like one of those old-fashioned toy farms with wooden horses and wooden barns and little bottle-shaped humans with jointed arms sticking out at the sides. With no particular plan in mind she climbed up past the back terrace and surveyed the rising landscape of the northeast pasture—site of Sean Conners' recent concussion. She could see the roof of Patrick's house, the row of apple trees that marched along the stone wall—all now in a cloud of white blossoms—and the glossy backs and swishing tails of the grazing horses. Then she turned her attention back to the stable and saw that the knots of people had broken up and were making their way back to the farmhouse. Among them she recognized Harvey Dodge and Mike Laaka's parents walking with Patrick. Mike himself, she decided, being the racing fanatic that he was, would have been glued all afternoon to the tube.

Then, just as she was about to join the stream, she heard the dogs begin. Barking coming from the other side of the house. Sarah turned. Aunt Julia, deciding sensibly that fifty-odd guests, tables of food and drink, and two English setters would not mix, had confined them to the fenced run that extended from the back door around to the old sunroom built off the rear of the house.

Now the dogs were jumping up against the wire, barking their heads off, and she saw that the sunroom door was ajar and a blue-shirted figure was disappearing into the interior.

Sarah followed.

Sean. Sean Conners.

Sean being greeted by the setters as an old friend. Sean who was so good with animals. But not so good with people.

He was pale, his black hair sticking out of the side of his head bandages, and he moved slowly, awkwardly, a cane in his hand. A cane Sarah recognized as once belonging to Uncle Tom, now used by Aunt Julia when her arthritis became unmanageable. It was an impressive affair, a great knobby blackthorn cane.

Sarah came up beside him and said she was glad he was out of the hospital. In time for the Preakness.

Sean smiled. A slight twisting of the lips, made with an effort, but a smile. "Mrs. Clancy called at the hospital, found I was going to be released this noon, and said I was to come to the party. She gave me the loan of the cane. She wants to know what happened when I got hit, but I can't remember a damn thing."

"Were you riding?" asked Sarah. It seemed the crucial question.

"Don't know. Don't think so because my leg was still chewed up after falling through the hayloft. Seems more likely that I'd have been sitting down. Taking a nap. But I can't remember."

"Well, I'm sorry," was all that Sarah could think of to say. She didn't think she should challenge him about riding bareback or taking naps when he was presumably employed to do something useful. Nor did she want to prolong the conversation, not really taking to the man. But then she certainly hadn't seen him at his best lately.

They stood together irresolutely, Conners apparently hesitating about joining the Preakness throng—a ghost at the feast, Sarah thought, if ever there was one. She, too, was in no hurry to pack herself into the front parlor. The back sunroom was a pleasant place, shabby, with a threadbare carpet of oriental design, dilapidated chintz-covered armchairs, a dollhouse, bookshelves crammed with old mystery stories and children's books, many from Julia's own childhood.

Sarah could have spent the rest of the day happily in this room, but she was on assignment, and since Sean, seeming reluctant to take the plunge, still lingered at the door, she put on a bright smile and said that they should go in or they'd miss the race.

Conners said something unintelligible, but he opened the sunroom door to the hall and Sarah led the way toward the sounds of voices and general jollity.

The front parlor was a sea of heads, all at different elevations depending on whether the rest of the body was sitting or standing. Sarah inserted herself into a corner by the window, next to Jane Zimmer. And where was Tilly? Up to no good, Sarah was sure.

But suddenly the babble of voices subsided, drinks were lowered, and there was a general craning of necks toward the television screen. A bugle sounded. Or was it a horn? wondered Sarah. A post horn, a hunting horn, a flügelhorn? "The horses," announced ABC's Jim McKay from the center of the screen, "are coming onto the track."

In apparent response to this announcement, the horses came onto the track, Julia planted herself at the piano and hit the opening bars of "O Maryland, My Maryland," and the tune was taken up by the guests, several deviant voices being lifted in "Tannenbaum, O Tannenbaum," while one lone female soprano sang "O Christmas Tree, O Christmas Tree" an octave above the rest.

Sarah, squinting, tried to make out Slewth. There he was, number six, and she discovered that she was even feeling a mild frisson of excitement. Then the horses were loaded into the gate, the gate clanged open, and they were off. A blur of horses, the quarter mile, the half mile, the far turn; horses weaving, bobbing, falling back, coming off the pace, charging up from the middle—and it was over.

A photo finish, a general relaxation of shoulders, a reaching for drinks, but still everyone glued to the screen. Slewth and something called Devil's Delight had finished nose to nose. The winner was flashed on the screen. Devil's Delight. By a whisker. And with this announcement Sarah found Alex next to her looking smug. "I drew Devil's Delight. Let's find something to drink, racing makes me very thirsty. Where's the bar?"

Sarah pointed at the crowded dining room and followed Alex, who headed for the drink table. She herself moved about, filling her plate with bits of smoked fish and a rolled affair with a mushroom sauce. For a few minutes she was joined by her cousin Jessica, who appeared to have at least eight pounds of food heaped on her plate. "It's pretty awesome stuff," she said, cramming a shrimp between slices of cheese and biting down.

Sarah shuddered and, abandoning her plate, pushed past the broad back of Mrs. Laaka, elbowed between Jane and Harvey Dodge, who appeared to be toasting each other, and made her way through the churning guests to the open door and out onto the long side porch that stretched almost the length of the southern side of the farmhouse. Julia, in her Preakness finery—a red paisley with jet beads—stood next to Neil Wentworth and Patrick O'Reilly—and was shaking hands vigorously with a man Sarah recognized as the assistant postmaster. Then, turning to Patrick, Julia seemed about to indicate something interesting on the lawn that sloped to the stable yard when Patrick, following her hand, stiffened, stared, and then shouted.

"Jesus Glory be to Heaven, what in hell is that?" And without another word Patrick strode off the porch, straight ahead toward where a grass terrace gave way to a strip planted with a row of pear trees.

"What, what?" Julia started after Patrick, stopped, gave a choking gasp, her hand coming up to her mouth.

"What is it?" demanded Sarah. But then she saw.

Hanging from a lower limb of one of the middle pear trees was Brandy Boy. Brandy Boy, Julia's old rocking horse, gray-dappled paint, a real horsehair mane and tail, a real leather saddle and bridle. Brandy Boy, the beginning of Julia's love affair with the horse, kept as an honored object always in the back sunroom for young visitors along with the dollhouse and the books.

And now Brandy Boy hung, hung by what Sarah recognized was a braided lead line that circled his painted neck, ran over a lower branch and was tied with a half-knot.

Sarah seeing and hearing Patrick and Julia's reaction had expected the worst: bodies, dismembered parts, a dismembered horse's head à la *The Godfather*. Now she exhaled thankfully. A joke. A not very funny joke. Perhaps strung up by some disgruntled guest. Sarah walked up to Julia.

"Someone's joke. Someone whose horse came in last."

But Patrick had gone up to the pear tree, had stooped, and now held up a cane. A knobby thick blackthorn cane. This he picked up and presented to Julia Clancy. "And is this," he said quietly, "a part of the joke?"

"Sean Conners' cane," Sarah said aloud. Then silently corrected herself. The cane Sean was using. Uncle Tom's cane . . .

But Julia pushed the cane aside and stood riveted by the sight of the hanging rocking horse. "That is foul, absolutely foul," she said. "Someone is threatening my horses."

"Nonsense," said Sarah stoutly, with more conviction than she felt. "It's a stupid joke. Someone who didn't have Devil's Delight to win."

But Julia was not to be deflected. "It's obscene," she said. And then to Patrick, "Get it down, please. Right now."

And Patrick, dropping the cane, walked over and tugged at the half-knot, the knot released, and the rocking horse came down into Patrick's waiting arms. He carried it to where Julia stood.

"It wasn't tied very firmly," observed Sarah. "Must have been a quick job."

"A perfectly good knot it was," said Patrick, setting the horse down beside Julia. "A regular quick-release knot." He ran a hand over the painted rump. "I don't think it's had any damage, Mrs. Clancy."

"Thanks be for that," said Julia. "Now please take him back to the sunroom where he belongs and then find Rafe and Jessica and check out the horses. Make sure that there's nothing more to this than hanging a rocking horse to scare me, because I think . . ."

But Sarah interrupted. "Why would someone hanging up a rocking horse use a quick-release knot? Wouldn't they want it to stay up there? I mean, why go to all the work of hoisting it up if someone could just give one little pull?"

"For heaven's sake, Sarah," said Julia impatiently. "The knot doesn't matter. It's a common useful knot. That's not the point. Don't clutter up your mind. Ah, Mike"—this to Mike Laaka, who apparently, alerted to untoward goings-on, had hurried out and stood watching as Patrick bore Brandy Boy around the backside of the house toward the sunroom door.

"Mike, it's more of the same. Frightening Old Lady Clancy. Can't you put your shoulder to the wheel and give the sheriff's department a goose?" said Julia, wildly mixing metaphors.

Mike shrugged. "If I call in and say that someone's strung up an old rocking horse, they'll laugh me out of the department."

"Then call the state police. Call George Fitts. Sarah, wasn't George Fitts working on that case last summer, the one with you and that man with the jellyfish?"

"Yes," said Sarah. "But that was a homicide. This is a wooden rocking horse. In perfectly good shape."

Julia stamped her foot. "I need help," she said loudly.

"I'm here," said a deep voice. And there was Harvey Dodge. Tweedy, solid, friendly Harvey Dodge. "You need a drink, Julia," said Harvey, and he handed her a tumbler of dark fluid. "Good Irish whiskey for what ails you."

"My rocking horse," said Julia. She lifted the glass and took a long sip and swallowed.

"Only one thing, Mrs. Clancy," said Patrick, now returned. He picked up the blackthorn walking stick and leaned it against the tree. "Sean told me when he came to my house for lunch that you gave him the loan of the thing because he was still tottery on his legs. So where's the lad now? Where's he gone off to?"

"Oh gracious, Patrick," said Julia impatiently. "I don't know. I haven't laid eyes on him since I went to the hospital this morning with the cane. I told him that bygones would be bygones and not to ride the horses bareback in the pasture."

"I was in the sunroom with him," put in Sarah. "He followed me into the house. Or," she added uncertainly, "I think he did. I didn't look back. Maybe he got cold feet and went back out."

"Well, I didn't see him," said Julia.

"And I didn't see him. Not a hair of him," said Patrick.

"Nor I," said Mike Laaka.

"It's a wonder anybody saw anybody else," said Sarah. "It was a mob scene. Everyone fastened to the TV screen. I only remember the person mashed up against me. Jane Zimmer."

"It's perfectly clear about Sean Conners," said Julia. "He decided he didn't like the crowd, didn't need the cane, and took off. Probably to some bar in Rockland. Which is all right, since the doctors told him not to report for work until Wednesday."

"You don't suppose," said Harvey Dodge thoughtfully, "that he strung up the rocking horse?"

Julia brightened. "You know, that's just the sort of thing he'd do. He's the practical-joke type. Doing things with water buckets. I suppose he might think this was amusing. Or a gesture."

"A gesture," said Sarah. "What kind of gesture?"

Julia frowned. "Well, you know. A sort of finger in your eye. Things on the farm have been a little hard on Sean lately."

"So, Julia, let's leave it at that," said Harvey Dodge. "You've got guests with their hands out. All the winning tickets."

But Julia lingered, thoughtful. "I've changed my mind. I wish it was as easy as saying Sean was responsible," she said. "But dragging the rocking horse out of the sunroom down to the pear trees, finding a lead line, tying it up—it all seems too elaborate for Sean with his sore leg. I see him wanting to thumb his nose at us, but not going to that trouble. Much more his style to write a dirty word on the bulletin board, or get drunk at some bar and bad-mouth the lot of us."

"I think Colonel Dodge is right," conceded Sarah. "Leave it for now. Later on try to find Sean and ask him. If he didn't do it, well, then you can think of something else."

"Thank you, Sarah," said Harvey Dodge. "Exactly my sentiments. Come on back into the house, Julia dear. You're still the hostess." He extended an arm, and Julia, suddenly docile, accepted it, and the pair made for the farmhouse.

But Sarah stayed outside. She walked slowly down to the pear tree from which the rocking horse had so recently dangled. The grass was trampled somewhat and the lead line lay snakelike by the foot of the tree. It was a green rope made of some tightly braided cotton material with a snap on one end. Sarah picked it up, dismissing at the same time the idea of fingerprints—after all, Patrick had touched it, and so had everyone on the farm at some time or other because these were used to lead the horses in and out of their pastures. Sarah stuffed the lead into the pocket of her skirt and saw that she had been joined.

"Hello," said Alex. "Stealing equipment?"

"Just being a responsible tidy person," said Sarah and described the scene just past. "I think Aunt Julia believes this is just one more scare tactic."

"But you don't?"

"I don't know what to think. For instance, where *is* Sean Conners? I mean, why bother to come to the party if you're just going to leave it in the middle of the big event and disappear?"

"A reasonable question," admitted Alex.

"And," went on Sarah, "whoever strung up Brandy Boy must have missed the race. It would take more than a minute to drag the rocking horse out of the sunroom and around here, not counting dashing down to the stable for a lead line, dashing back, and stringing up the horse. With a release knot."

"Whoever it was," said Alex, "may have had the lead line in his pocket and been counting on the fact that the whole crowd was watching television. The race only lasts a minute and a bit, but most people watch the post parade. That allows about ten minutes. Fifteen at the outside. Anyway you slice it, the person would have to be quick about the hanging business to be sure of not being caught."

"And there's the walking stick," said Sarah, pointing. "If Sean Conners did the job, then he wasn't as feeble as he looked, didn't really need the stick, so he dropped it and took off after he'd strung up the horse. Or took off even if he didn't string it up. And if that's true, he fooled me. He looked awful. Sickbed pallor, bandages, unsteady. Not a bit sure of himself."

"I think maybe this is all much ado about a stupid joke," said Alex. "No one's hurt and we can wait until Sean turns up to see if he's involved. We have other things to think of and . . ." Alex broke off in midsentence in response to a loud scraping and bumping behind them. He swiveled about, then pointed. "Tilly Martin. For God's sake what does she think she's doing?"

Sarah turned and stared. From behind the farmhouse came Tilly Martin. Tilly pulling one large gray-dappled rocking horse, an object most recently seen hanging from the lower limb of a pear tree. Tilly had Brandy Boy's reins over his head and was hauling the horse along, but because of the rockers it was literally an up-and-down job, the rockers catching, then slewing to the right or the left. As Sarah and Alex watched unbelieving, Tilly reached a point opposite the side door. Here she stopped, adjusted Brandy Boy's position so that he faced across the road in a northeasterly direction, and, patting the animal's painted rump, straighted up and smiled. Triumphant. Then she saw Alex and Sarah. An amazed audience of two.

"Tilly, what . . ." began Sarah.

But Tilly, puffing a bit from her exertions, joined them. "There now," she said. "Back in place. After all my work, I found Brandy Boy right back in the sunroom."

"But what— Why? I don't understand," Sarah fumbled ahead. "Tilly, have you been moving that horse around? You've scared Aunt Julia half to death. She thinks someone is after her horses."

Tilly looked complacent. She ran her hand over her blond curls and made a minor adjustment in her flowered skirt. "It's all part of the big picture," she said. "You can lead a horse to water but you can't make him drink. In this case, Julia to drink. So the mountain has come to Mohammed, so to speak."

"Tilly, Tilly," interrupted Sarah. "Take it easy."

"Sarah, listen. The rocking horse is a token. Or a totem. Brandy Boy points the way. He is the horse incarnate. He points to Quartermaster Farm, future residence of Julia Douglas Clancy. And Colonel Harvey Dodge. Bride and groom." Tilly paused and smiled at Alex and Sarah, a radiant, totally mad smile. "You could have a double wedding, Sarah. You could give each other away. And Jane and I will move in here only after the wedding because I know Julia has worked so hard on the reception that it would be a pity to deprive her, but soon, soon, she must fold her tent, fold her hands, fold up and . . . Alex, where are you going?"

This to Alex, who had turned and was now heading for the farmhouse door. "I'm going to get Jane. Stay right there with Sarah. Don't move an inch."

"Very well," said Tilly, nodding agreeably. "Such a nice man, your Alex. I don't as a rule care for men. The species, you know. Or are they a subspecies? A subset? Never mind. You see, it all came to me in a flash when I went out by way of the sunroom. Brandy Boy would do the trick. This shall be a sign unto you, I said. So I grabbed him by the bridle and hauled him out and pointed him . . ."

"Wait, wait," said Sarah, taking hold of this last piece of information as would a drowning person who found solid ground under her feet. "Wait up, Tilly. You hung the horse, didn't you? On the branch of the pear tree. As a sign?"

At this interesting moment Alex and Jane appeared and Jane took hold.

"Now, now, Tilly, all excited? Too much race party, I expect," said Jane robustly. "So it's time to go home. Devil's Delight was first. By a nose. Alex has told me about the rocking horse and so we'll let Alex put him back where he belongs because Julia is very busy with her guests. Tilly, put that down. Now, I say." This to Tilly, who had again clutched Brandy Boy's bridle.

And Jane took hold of Tilly by the shoulders, detached her hand, pushed the rocking horse to one side, and began to march her friend down the driveway toward Tri-County Road.

"But wait," called Sarah. "Tilly, Tilly, did you hang Brandy Boy? On the pear tree. Up by the neck?"

Tilly twisted about, partially loosening Jane's grasp. "Goodness, no. Why would I do that? I don't hang horses. Brandy Boy is a sign. I told you."

"Come on, Tilly," said Jane in a loud voice, and the two vanished down the road in the direction of Appleyard Farm.

"Oh Lord," said Sarah.

"Perfectly simple," said Alex. "Tilly, who is now balmy as a bat—Jane is taking her right now to the psychiatric wing of the hospital—Tilly lugged the rocking horse over, left it in the driveway, and Sean Conners strung it up for the hell of it. Case finished. Done. Over. Trivia."

"Not trivia," said Sarah stubbornly, "but I don't know what else to call it. I'm having vibrations. Or is it emanations?"

"Wait until Sean Conners surfaces," said Alex.

But Sean Conners did not surface. Not that Saturday, nor Monday, nor yet Tuesday. And Wednesday, the day of his planned return, came and went likewise without Sean. Telephone calls were made by Julia, by Patrick, finally by Mike Laaka on behalf of the sheriff's department, but all to no avail. Sean had disappeared, gone into thinnest air. His landlady claimed that he had not returned the Saturday of the Preakness, his parents in Boston had not heard from him, several drinking buddies, rounded up from surrounding towns, had not seen him.

On Thursday, the twenty-sixth of May, Mike Laaka, coming over on his lunch break, reluctantly began to consider the possibility of something untoward. "Okay," he said. "Tell Patrick as Sean's nearest available relative to file a Missing Persons with the state police. Maybe he just took off; he's the sort. The worst-case scenario is that someone's been after him and maybe finally got him. That shotgun blast could have been meant for him. If he wasn't riding bareback, maybe that tree branch was involved. I checked with Patrick, but the branch was burned. But stop worrying."

"I can't stop, and I do worry," said Julia tartly, "but it doesn't seem to have done a blessed bit of good."

"It's out of your hands now. I've turned those cut-out poems over to the state police to play with. Don't talk about them to anyone. And call my dad if you're short of help. He can give you a hand. Run the tractor, bring down the hay."

"No," said Julia. "I don't want your father disappearing, and besides, Harvey Dodge has sent Farney over for the duration, and he practically lives here himself. Farney loves my tractor—it's newer than Harvey's and has all those attachments. And Jane Zimmer has offered to come over. Even Winka Wentworth came this morning saying she'd help out. I let them all get on with it. Such neighborly devotion and probably, as Sarah thinks, part of a deep plot to take over the place."

"I think," Mike reminded her, "that you should concentrate on the future. Your Belmont party's coming up."

Julia heaved an enormous sigh, "Lord, yes, and I wish I could cancel it, but everyone's been invited for ages, for years. And then there's the wedding reception, which should be a joy if I can just keep my head above water because time is getting short."

This opinion was shared with an increasing sense of urgency by the two principal players. Families began what Alex called a feeding frenzy and surging process—sisters, brothers, aunts and uncles by phone and by mail began showing signs that travel, even from distances as far away as Santa Fe, Montreal, Houston, Calgary, Edinburgh, and Helsinki, was not beyond them.

"Where," groaned Sarah, "will we put them all?" They were sitting together on a Saturday evening a week after the Preakness at their kitchen table. The table was covered with a chart of available bed-and-breakfasts and a list of acceptances and regrets.

"We don't have to worry," Alex reminded her. "That's what parents are for. My mother is commandeering bedrooms and your mother will get in the act when they come in from New Hampshire."

"And then there's the reception," said Sarah. "Poor Aunt Julia is still gyrating. She's sure that Sean Conners is a dismembered corpse hidden in the hayloft."

"Well, at least Tilly is under wraps."

"I'm sorry about Tilly, stuck there in the psychiatric ward."

"I went to see her yesterday," said Alex. "After rounds. She's having a ball. Reading everyone's palm, calling on Athene and

Isis and Hecate, predicting and prognosticating. Says she's drawing up plans for remodeling High Hope Farm."

"Then she's no better."

"Much calmer. Jane seems to think she's coming down and it's just a matter of time until she'll be discharged."

At which remark the telephone began to ring. "We'll take turns," said Sarah. "You first."

The calls all had to do with a sudden anxiety on the part of relatives to come up with a suitable wedding present; it was as if a mass family telepathy had taken place. The first from Alex's mother, Elspeth, wondering if they'd like Cousin Edith's silver tea tray if she could get rid of the tarnish. Then it was Julia Clancy herself about a pair of brass andirons. "Do you have a fireplace?" she asked. And then, "Even if you don't now, you will someday."

"Julia didn't even mention Sean Conners or Norminco, which is hopeful," said Sarah, putting the telephone down. "And she says that Grandmother Douglas is giving us that oil painting in her dining room. The one with the sheep and the storm coming up."

This call was followed by three others involving a footstool, an umbrella stand with a dragon motif, and a set of silver nut picks found at an auction by Sarah's cousin.

And then Julia again. Anxiety had returned. Would they be coming to the Belmont party?

"Cripes," said Sarah, hanging up. "I said yes, but I feel it's like taking passage on the *Lusitania*. Cross your fingers that the party goes off without a single toy being hung or the dollhouse going up in flames."

"Or Julia herself disappearing," put in Alex.

"That," said Sarah, "would be a profound relief."

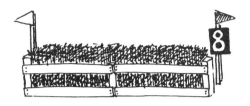

THE HEDGE

EIGHT

JULIA Clancy did not disappear, and the period following the vanishing of Sean Conners through Julia's Belmont Stakes party on June eleventh and thence to the wedding of Sarah Douglas Deane to Alexander Sinclair McKenzie one week later on June the eighteenth, was long remembered by the participants in the above events as a stretch of unexpected tranquility.

True, Sean did not reappear for work at High Hope Farm. However this was held to be something of a blessing, what with the trouble the young man had seemed to attract like a magnet. And, as Mike Laaka put it, no body had been found in a ditch, no corpse had surfaced on Fallen Tree Pond or washed up along the coast, no ransom notes had appeared, no sodden shoes, bloody shirts, hanks of hair, teeth, detached limbs, or bags of lime had turned up in odd corners. Nor had the state police's inspection of Julia's cut-out messages yet yielded anything beyond the fact that the letters were taken from *Newsweek* magazine, a source available to anyone. But Mike added, further lab tests pended.

The major blessing of this halcyon period was that High Hope Farm was vexed no further. Primroses blossomed, tulips shot up and bloomed, dropped their petals, the lilacs by the farmhouse came out and were followed by purple, pink, and cream lupine, orange day lilies, and budding delphinium, monk's hood and early phlox. But no shotgun blasts, no hayloft accidents. No poetic cut-outs by mail or by hand. Even Norminco kept a low profile, its spokesman, Jim Shale, simply appearing at local meetings and pleading for love and understanding and describing in glowing terms not only the mine owners' affection for a pristine environment, but also the economic benefits a mining operation could bestow on a rural community.

"I suppose," said Julia to Sarah and Alex, who had stopped in Sunday before the wedding to consult on final reception arrangements, "this Jim Shale does convince some people. He sounds so damn sincere. Anyway, my land appears clean. Harvey says he and Farney and Patrick have looked for drill holes and haven't found a thing. And nothing happened during my Belmont party."

This was so. The race crowd had come, mingled, drawn horses, and the women present had had the pleasure of seeing a long-shot filly—Alydarling—win by a neck.

"Aunt Julia seems to have recovered her starch," Sarah said later to Alex as they drove home from High Hope Farm along a winding scenic route through the blueberry hills and barrens of Appleton. Then as they neared the turnoff toward Saw Mill Road and their new-old house, Sarah added, "I'm the one losing starch. Those ten million guests, Grandmother Douglas. The Gorilla. My new shoes. Brother Tony and girlfriend Andrea out on parole. Do you suppose she'll try to lift the silver?"—this because the beautiful Andrea had been implicated in a complicated jewel scam. "And," she added, "I've heard that Tilly's out of the hospital."

"Out and under the stern eye of Jane. Somewhat stable. Word has it that she's taking an interest in royalty."

"That's a switch. What sort of royalty?"

"Queens, mostly. The British royals in particular, but I gather Queen Beatrix of Holland and Queen Noor of Jordan also figure. Apparently she wants to make High Hope Farm ready for Princess Di and the kids. As a sort of refuge."

"You call that somewhat stable?" demanded Sarah.

"Her astrology and rotation obsessions are slightly diluted by this new interest. And she still has to report in to the psychiatric unit for counseling sessions twice a week."

"Well, setting Tilly and the royals aside, the point is that I'm feeling exactly like the Admiral in *Pinafore* with his sisters and his cousins which he reckons up by dozens."

"And his aunts," finished Alex.

Sarah twisted around in her seat and looked at Alex, seeing in the late afternoon light all the hard angles of his face, his dark, deep-set eyes, straight dark hair, that chin, his piratical eyebrows. "You always remind me of a highwayman," she said. "Okay, last chance. We can skip the whole scene. You can saddle up a black stallion and ride off into the night, your cape flying behind you, your dagger thrust into your boot, me hanging on behind the saddle, the hood of my cloak pulled over my fair flowing locks, the hue and cry of the wedding guests, the cheers of the villagers sounding behind us."

"Have you thought that you could support me by writing Gothic novels?" said Alex, pulling the Bronco into the long bumpy dirt driveway, twisting the wheel hard around a granite boulder, and coming to rest beside the back entrance of their elderly and noticeably sagging house. "And," he added, "your locks, my sweet, are short dark brown bristles and you haven't taken Julia up on that offer of riding lessons. I don't want to elope with anyone who can't hang on to the back of the saddle."

"So much for romance," said Sarah. "Are you sure we can't take Patsy to Nova Scotia?" This as the huge gray dog bounded out toward them.

"Perfectly sure. Down Patsy, I said DOWN." Alex fended off Patsy's attentions with a push and shook his head sternly. "An

Irish wolfhound has no place on our trip. Mary Donelli will take him—she has before. She loves Patsy. Okay, let's brace ourselves. Wrestle this wedding to the floor. Six days and counting."

Six days in mid-June with perfect weather, with a welcome decrease in the number of blackflies, with soft zephyrs and long days and short nights; these days sped by, and before Sarah and Alex knew what they were about, bagpipes droned along the drive to the house on Sawmill Road, the wedding guests assembled, the trumpet sounded, the rites were performed, and the celebrants took off for High Hope Farm and the reception of what Sarah and Alex had begun to think of as the entire population of the county.

"Feel different, feel married?" asked Alex, as the Bronco bounded along Tri-County Road, Sarah in the vanilla high-collared sprigged muslin, Alex in his new gray suit.

"I suppose I should feel a sort of mystical transformation," said Sarah, "but except for feeling odd about being in a long dress in broad daylight, it hasn't hit me. But the music was lovely. And the big jugs of lupine looked wonderful. They made me want a real garden."

"Mary looked elegant," said Alex.

"Yes, I loved her dress. Crimson is her color."

"And the service," prompted Alex. "The Reverend Cynthia Lamb."

"Terrific. Said it was only her third wedding and she handled it like a pro, didn't choke up on Yeats or John Donne and did Saint Matthew to the manner born. It all sounded quite proper, but I can't remember a word except that I've probably promised something I'll regret. And so have you."

"Never," said Alex, leaning over and kissing her to the great hazard of his steering. "And your great-aunt's dress is elegant. *Fin de siècle.*"

"Which *siècle?*"

"Any *siècle.* And here's High Hope Farm, so let's eat, drink, tread a measure, cut a cake, and be off for Nova Scotia.

This they did, and when urged later to recall the reception in detail neither Alex nor Sarah could come up with more than a kaleidoscope. There was the music: inside the tent something for all ages, and sweetly sounding from the lawn and terrace Rafe Posner on his guitar giving out with an Irish-Scottish-Italian mix, he seated cross-legged, his long fair hair neatly tied in a ponytail. And Uncle Alfred's toast in French, Alex's mother, Elspeth McKenzie, dancing in a Scottish reel, Sarah's brother Tony looking like Bugsy Siegel in a white suit, and Tony's lady, the toothsome and felonious Andrea, in a thin layer of mauve chiffon, tripping about with a champagne glass held high. Jane Zimmer, sturdy in blue linen with Tilly Martin, she in yellow organdy ruffles talking of royal weddings at Westminster, and front and center in a wingchair surveying the scene, Sarah's ninety-year-old Grandmother Douglas in gray silk with her stick and cushion. For the rest it was guests whirling and turning and blending into constantly changing patterns of color and noise.

And then it was time for Nova Scotia. Sarah flung her flowers from the porch steps and nailed Alex's cousin Giddy Lester on the ear. Then mothers, fathers, friends, relatives, including Julia Clancy, an unfamiliar figure in garnet taffeta, and Colonel Harvey Dodge in blazer and flannels, all hurled rice at the bride and groom, who spun out of the driveway and headed north.

But only so far north. The Maine climate must never be taken for granted. The god of weather, having dispensed sun and warmth with such great generosity during the week and through the wedding itself, now turned his other cheek. Rain, mist, fog. Dense pea-soup fog. Fog of the sort that forces drivers to creep along trying to measure distance between the yellow middle line and what might or might not be the side of the road. Fog that causes persons in boats to fumble about, to blow horns, to scowl at radar and depth finders—if they have such equipment—and if they do not, to drift helplessly onto invisible ledges and rocks.

It caused persons just married to give up the Blue Hill Inn, where they had sent a fifty-dollar deposit for a night's rest, and end up in a Lower Slobovia–type B & B just off Route 1 only thirty miles north of High Hope Farm.

Its continued presence the following Sunday—wedding plus one—caused the happy couple to miss passage on the Blue Nose Ferry and to fetch up south of Bar Harbor in a state of frustration. Now they sat in Elmo's Diner over a late breakfast of pancakes and bacon and read in a Sunday paper the week's weather forecast for the North. The operative words were *fog* and *more fog.*

"But the ferry *will* run, won't it?" said Sarah, draining her cup of tea and dribbling more from the pot into her cup.

"I suppose so," said Alex. "What bothers me is that the fog is spread from here to Labrador and we won't be able to see a thing. It will be like traveling in a wet sponge."

Sarah nodded. "I agree, and I've been thinking. We're not absolutely fastened into this Nova Scotia idea, and we haven't made any reservations. Maybe the fog's burned off in southern Maine. Or western Maine. Why not try for the mountains? A little cabin somewhere on a lake. We could rent a canoe and swim. Go into reverse gear."

For a minute Alex stared out the diner window at the fog-shrouded parking lot. "Okay," he said with decision. "Let's do just that. But first let me call home and get a weather rundown. See about southern and western fog. I want to make sure the stuff is burning off. No point in just heading into space without a complete long-range report." He put down his napkin and shoved his coffee cup away. "There's a pay phone just outside," he said. "I'll be right back."

But he wasn't.

Sarah sipped her now lukewarm tea and waited. And waited. Then, feeling somewhat irritated, pulled a paperback mystery—*The Corpse by the Creek*—out of her raincoat pocket. Alex was probably talking over the wedding, who was there, which cousin was not speaking to which other cousin, who fell into the cake, why Uncle Barnard had canceled at the last minute and why second Cousin Freda, who had not been invited, had come anyway. All the delicious details of the reception that

Sarah might have enjoyed discussing if she had been invited to participate. Why hadn't Alex called her? She opened the mystery and glared at the opening sentence.

"The body was covered by moldering leaves and earth; covered so completely that only one arm protruded. One arm and one hand. One disintegrating arm and hand . . ."

And Alex returned. But did not sit down. He bent over Sarah with a frown and a defeated air. "Hell," said Alex.

Sarah looked up. "Fog?" she asked. "Fog everywhere? Even in New Hampshire? Or Vermont? The whole bloody country?"

"No," said Alex. "Fog's pretty much burned off back home. Not fog. Worse."

"Worse, how worse? Someone's sick? Hurt? Who? Someone in the family? Aunt Julia? Grandmother Douglas? Patsy?"

"No. None of those. But it's a body."

"What!"

"A body. A corpse. At the farm. High Hope Farm."

Sarah swallowed, bit her lip, closed her book. "Sean Conners?" she said.

"Try again," said Alex. Then sitting down heavily, "Not Sean Conners. Farney."

Sarah stared at Alex unbelieving. "Farney!"

"Yes, Farney. Farney Thompson. They found him this morning. About two hours ago. All hell's broken loose at the farm."

"What? I don't understand. Did he have an accident? A heart attack? And where on the farm? What happened?"

"I don't have all the details, but I gather he was found down in the stable in that little annex next to the tack room; it's a space used mostly for storage. Anyway, if Farney died there yesterday, no one went into the room and found him; I suppose the stable helpers were busy feeding the horses, doing chores, and there was no reason to look into the annex."

"But you haven't said . . ."

"They're not sure what happened. It was a hanging. Well, sort of a hanging. A bridle was involved. That's all I know. For now."

"You're saying you'll know more soon because you'll be

there—we'll be there—back on the farm. Both of us going back. Right?"

"That's what I'm saying. I talked to Julia, who was being brave and saying that we mustn't cut our trip short, but Mike Laaka said yes, we must. The state police are in charge and not calling it suicide. They want to talk to us and all the wedding guests."

Sarah let out a long breath. "Oh good God." And then, "Poor, poor Farney. I did like him. He was so kind and gentle. Harvey Dodge's right-hand man and such a help to Aunt Julia. But do the police think he died during the wedding?"

"They don't know yet when he died. And Rafe Posner hasn't turned up for work this morning. Anyway, the police need to talk to us and I think Julia could use some more family support."

Sarah nodded slowly. "Yes, I'm sure she could. We do have to get back. As soon as possible."

Alex lifted his coffee cup, found the coffee cold, and signaled the waitress. "One for the road," he said with a grim smile.

"Okay, drink your coffee and settle the breakfast bill," said Sarah. "I'll pack our things. We can be back at the farm in under three hours."

They made it back in two hours and forty minutes and found the parking lot of High Hope Farm filled with an assortment of vehicles, including, besides a number of unmarked cars, an ambulance and squad cars from the sheriff's department and the Maine State Police.

Mike Laaka welcomed them from the farmhouse porch steps. "You can thank that fog," he said, "because otherwise we'd be dragging you back from the ferry landing in Nova Scotia. Come on in and comfort Julia. The state police are on deck—George Fitts again—couldn't forget old George, could you? Well, George wants you to start thinking about the reception. When and where you last saw Farney. Our men are busy rounding up wedding reception guests. Three of them are already out of state."

"Lucky they," said Alex.

"We'll find them," said Mike firmly. "The arm of the law is long and has sharp claws."

"But," said Sarah, zeroing in on what she felt must be the main point, "are you really talking murder? Not a sudden heart attack? Or suicide? Or an accident?"

"As far as we can tell—without a final pathology report—the man was asphyxiated."

"By a bridle?" demanded Sarah. "And," she went on, "if it was a bridle, well, why couldn't he have hung himself with it—those long reins. Though why Farney would hang himself . . ."

"Wait and see," said Mike. "Maybe the reins were used, maybe they weren't—the lab reports will tell. But the bridle, well, it was in place when we found him."

"What do you mean 'in place'?" demanded Alex.

"In place," repeated Mike. "Like he was a horse. Over his head, fastened, the bit . . ."

"Oh no," said Sarah, a wave of nausea flooding over her.

"Yeah, I'm afraid so," said Mike. "Snaffle bit in his mouth. Alex, go on down to the stable and see the pathologist. You're the official medical examiner for these parts, although we did bring in a pathologist from Augusta. They haven't taken the body away. Sarah, I'm sorry about the details, but you asked."

"So am I sorry," said Sarah. "And I'll go in and see Aunt Julia." She began to move toward the kitchen door of the house and then turned. "Farney Thompson, he was with Harvey Dodge for years. Practically all his life. I never remember Colonel Dodge without Farney somewhere around. How is Harvey taking it?"

Mike shook his head. "I'd say he's shook, real shook. Devastated, I guess, is the word. Like you said, Farney has been his stableman almost forever. That man Carter he has is fairly recent. Harvey and Julia have been comforting each other, but now he's gone to his place to start calling Farney's family—they're all out of state. In Vermont."

Sarah made her way to the kitchen, seeing on the back porch cartons of empty champagne glasses and a laundry bag filled to overflowing with tablecloths and napkins. The reception was only yesterday afternoon and it feels like it happened last summer, she thought. Happened to someone else. For a moment Sarah stared at the champagne glasses as if she had never seen such things before, and then, shaking herself, made for the kitchen.

She found Julia in the kitchen, dressed in her oldest slacks and a faded blue work shirt, and beating a sticky mass of yellow in a large bowl. Julia's face was red and puckered, her lip trembled, her gray hair looked like a briar patch, and when she saw Sarah she put down her beater and threw her arms around her niece.

"Thank heavens, Sarah. Now I feel better. Having you and Alex here. I was making cornbread to distract myself. And I know it's horribly selfish to want to drag you back from your trip, but . . ."

Sarah interrupted her. "The police dragged us back, not you, and besides, we would have come back anyway. Do you want to tell me about it or shall I help you get lunch?"

"I'll tell you. It was dreadful. I found him. All by myself. Rafe Posner didn't turn up this morning—too much champagne yesterday, I suppose. Anyway, I was looking for some old saddle pads."

Sarah interrupted again. "Wait up. I'll make us some tea, and we can sit down right here at the table. And then you can get it all out and maybe feel a little bit better."

And Julia did get it all out. From her usual early-morning trip to the lower stable, not finding Rafe at work, having to cope with the early feeding herself, Patrick having gone to early mass. Measuring the grain, the bran, the vitamin supplements, and lastly the search for the saddle pads.

"He was propped in the corner and that awful bridle was fastened around his head, the bit in his mouth and his eyes open and bulging, and he, his skin, was almost dark blue. Oh, it was absolutely horrible."

* * *

It was indeed horrible, concluded Alex, examining the late Farney Thompson, still propped in the corner, still the object of
the photography lab's efforts, still a subject for measurements
by a yellow-shirted man moving about the room with a tape
calling out to a colleague distances to and from the body.

Part of Alex's brain told him that this bridled corpse was one
of the most repulsive things he had ever looked at; the other
part watched coolly, saw the pathologist—one Johnny Cuszak,
assistant chief medical examiner from Augusta—slip the head-
stall from around Farney's head, the cavesson from across his
face, unfasten the throat latch that lay under Farney's chin, and
then, forcing the mouth open—some rigor being still present—
remove the snaffle bit from the mouth, the metal clanking
slightly against Farney's teeth. Saw Johnny Cuszak hold the entire bridle up against the window, shrug, and slip the whole affair into a waiting paper bag. This operation was followed by
the placement of Farney on the stretcher, the pulling of the
gray blanket over the rigid body, and the departure.

Alex turned to Dr. Cuszak. "Hello, Johnny. When did you get
here?"

"Only about an hour ago," said Johnny, a short stout man
with a bushy head of gray hair and an equally bushy gray beard.
"I had another job down by the quarry near the cement plant.
Man on a bicycle went in last night."

"And Farney here?"

"Farney Thompson?" Johnny rolled the name around his
tongue. "Thought his name was Barney Thompson. Wrote Barney on the tag. Have to change it. Well, as you could see, rigor is
passing off. First of all, he's got a bump on his head. Sizable
bump, but it may be incidental to death. Did you see his neck?
Discolored, indentations front and back, small abrasions—all
look like strangling. Death by asphyxiation I'd say, but can't be
sure. Bridle was probably an afterthought. Decoration. I don't
think you can strangle someone with a bit in his mouth, but you
never can tell. Nothing surprises me. I've seen someone hung
with a bra. A man hung with a bra. Suicide, it was."

"So when do you think? Time of death?"

"Don't rush me, Alex. Contents of the stomach, digestion, temperature in this room, all that jazz. Come on over to the hospital. I'll be doing the post this afternoon."

"I suppose I'm wondering if it happened yesterday afternoon."

"Could have," said Johnny, peeling off his gloves. "Or early evening. Why, were you around?"

"Me and a hundred others," said Alex. "We had a wedding reception here. Music, dancing, champagne, the whole bit."

"Don't say," said Johnny Cuszak. "That ought to give the police a run for their money. Whose wedding? Who was the happy couple? Are they still around?"

"Yes," said Alex, "they are. Or rather, they've come back. I'm one-half of the happy couple, and my wife, Sarah, is up there at the house trying to cheer up her Aunt Julia, who gave the happy couple the reception."

"Well for God's sake, ain't that something," said Dr. Cuszak. "A wedding and a murder. That's a first. For me anyway."

"And," said Alex, "for us it is also a first."

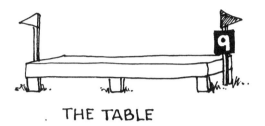

THE TABLE

NINE

THE Sunday after the wedding, the following Monday, Tuesday, and Wednesday, passed for the friends of High Hope Farm in a blur of arriving and departing police cars, the giving of statements with the promise of longer interrogations to follow, the pursuit of the wedding guests, some of whom had indeed returned to their native hearths, and the closing-off of the stable area to all but the persons who tended the horses. There was also a beating of the local bush to find not only the missing Sean Conners, but the now delinquent Rafe Posner, it being variously assumed that Rafe was unsteady by nature and, frightened by events, had drifted off somewhere as he had done in the past, or that he—along with Sean Conners—was lying murdered in some distant corner of Julia Clancy's property. Or even that Rafe—with or without Sean—having strangled Farney for reasons unknown, had taken himself off.

All this constabulary activity took place in an atmosphere tainted by the announcement that Farney Thompson's death was no accident; that Farney had sustained a head injury—the severity of which had not yet been determined but sufficient to cause unconsciousness but probably not death—and that subsequently Farney had been strangled by a length of narrow leather material, and afterward festooned with a bridle—purpose of this uncertain.

And this depressing stretch of time from Sunday noon until the Wednesday of June twenty-second found the bride and groom checked into a windswept motel on Route 1 not only because their own house had been torn apart for installation of new plumbing, new floors, and new supportive beams, but also in the interest of having some moments of peace unblighted by a homicide investigation.

It was unanimously agreed by those involved that the arrival at High Hope Farm of Detective Sergeant George Fitts of the Maine State Police CID had a glacial effect on all present. This was something Sarah could have predicted. She had tried hard during previous encounters with George to imagine him away from scenes-of-the-crime, at festive events—the Fourth of July, Christmas-tree trimming, birthdays, Bar Mitzvahs, Hanukkah candle lighting, but her mental pictures could never overcome the fact that George's presence seemed to act like that of a male snow maiden, chilling and killing his companions. Even during a criminal investigation at those rare moments of domestic comfort, George could appear and people would put down their sandwiches, their coffee, their whiskey, and reach for sweaters.

George, in Sarah's opinion, was totally bloodless. Smooth-faced, smooth-headed—bald as a lightbulb—thin, ageless, immaculate in ironed shirt and trousers even in the most desperate of situations—pale eyes with wire-rimmed spectacles, with a voice like the smoke from dry ice, George probed and countered and manipulated. Sarah, on her first encounter with him, had pointed out to Alex that Sergeant Fitts had the rare ability of making everyone about him feel as guilty as hell.

Now George on this Wednesday, like some noxious effluvium, filtered into Julia's usually friendly kitchen—a kitchen of comfortable chairs, bright curtains, and nesting cats—and Sarah could feel the frost.

"Mrs. Clancy," said George, "please stay right here, if you will. I want to go over the whole reception. From the beginning. And Sarah, if you'll wait out in the dining room, I'll take you and Alex together." George was free to use Sarah's first name, since this was the third time that they had met over what novels referred to as "incidents of foul play."

"And," said George, as Sarah rose obediently from the kitchen table, "congratulations to you and Alex."

"Congratulations?" said Sarah blankly. "You mean on Farney Thompson's body turning up in the stable?" It was all she could think of—such was the effect of Sergeant Fitts.

"No, no," said George. "Your wedding. Congratulations."

"Oh," said Sarah. "I'd forgotten. I mean with everything happening. Yes, we were married. It was a lovely wedding. Up to Sunday. Thank you, George." And Sarah fled the room.

"You're welcome," said George to the closing door. He turned to Julia. "Now Mrs. Clancy, beginning with Saturday. We'll go over past events later, those two stable workers who are missing, those other incidents. But for now, let's stick to the day of the wedding reception. The people you saw, the time you saw them. How the day went." And George took out his spiral notebook and placed a small tape recorder on the table.

"You have no objection, have you?"

"Yes . . . I mean no," said Julia weakly. She loathed tape recorders but felt that George might take a refusal as an admission that she herself had strangled Farney.

"Good," said George. "Now, I've heard that Farney Thompson has been coming over every morning to help you with the farmwork."

"Yes," said Julia. "Farney was a great help here."

"And he came over the day of the wedding?"

"Yes, as usual. Though things weren't as usual. I wanted the whole place to be extra clean, the horses turned out early, everything spit-spot because you know the guests—well, you can't bottle everyone up in a tent the whole time. Some were sure to walk out and look around. It was a beautiful day until the fog came in."

"And Colonel Dodge? Did he come with Farney?"

"No. Harvey came over at about ten. To help with anything I needed. He's an old friend."

"Very thoughtful." George picked up his pen and let the phrase hang in the air just long enough for Julia to start thinking that now he was considering Harvey as an evil presence. "All right," he said. "Suppose you go on and describe the day. Chronologically, if you can, though that may be difficult. Time sequences on busy days are hard to track."

As if I were senile, said Julia to herself. Feeling the need for comfort she reached over to a nearby chair and pulled to her lap Charlie, a large orange tabby cat, stroked its head, and then took a deep breath. "Fortunately," she said to George Fitts, "I have a very good memory. And I'm observant."

"Good," said George. "Not many people are."

But Julia found, as she plunged in, that the day, its sequence of events, the comings and goings, the phone calls, the caterer's arrival, the appearance of the bartenders, the straggling in of various relatives and guests from their appointed houses, inns, or bed-and-breakfasts, had all combined in her head to form a timeless collage. Her memory was a total mess.

"I'm sorry," she said helplessly as she finished a muddled account of her departure for the wedding luncheon.

"No problem," said George. "We'll be confirming everything. It will come together. Was Farney at the luncheon? I see it was held at the East Wind Inn at Port Clyde."

"Yes, yes it was. But only family and out-of-town guests, of which there were far too many. Why Alex's cousins from Alberta felt . . ."

"Mrs. Clancy," said George, "please. Farney—if he wasn't with you in Port Clyde, where was he?"

"Probably having his own lunch at Colonel Dodge's farm. He lives there, you know."

"Describe every instance that you can remember seeing him through the afternoon."

Julia sighed, took a long breath, and began. Farney instructing the car park people, Farney refusing to let Jane Zimmer leave her car by the front door. Farney holding a glass of champagne, saying he was going to check on the dogs, they were barking. Farney watching the dancing, looking at the cake but leaving for the stable before the cake was cut. The back view of Farney, his jacket now off and slung over his shoulder, making his way down the path toward the stable. Farney no more seen.

"Until this morning," prompted George.

"Until this morning," Julia repeated in a dull voice.

"How about interactions you observed between Farney and other persons. Arguments. Any person off alone with him."

"Oh my gracious, Sergeant Fitts, I haven't any idea. I saw him in the reception line. He kissed Sarah. And I saw him talking to Harvey Dodge and Patrick O'Reilly. And Winka Wentworth had him off by the window pointing at something in the pasture. I suppose she saw something wrong with the fencing, she's that sort. And oh, Tilly Martin was walking about with a piece of cake on a plate saying it was for Farney because he missed seeing it cut."

George looked up. "So did Tilly Martin take the cake down to the stable?"

"I don't know," said Julia. "But I did see her later holding an empty plate."

"I have talked with Tilly Martin," said George, making it sound as if he'd been exposed to an ambulatory case of influenza.

"Yes, well, she's been a bit confused lately."

"She claims she and Jane Zimmer are moving over here, taking over this farm. Keeping it in custody for"—here George flipped his notebook back a few pages, frowned, and said in a disapproving voice—"in custody for Queen Elizabeth and her family."

"Oh Tilly, what are we going to do with you?" exclaimed Julia.

"She sounded quite definite," observed George. "About moving in anyway. By the end of the summer, she said."

"Oh Lord above," said Julia crossly. "If Tilly doesn't stop this nonsense she's going to be found with a bridle in her mouth, and it won't be a snaffle, it'll be a curb bit."

"Is that a threat, Mrs. Clancy?" said George mildly.

Julia subsided. "No, of course not, but Tilly is . . . well, she has these ideas about the stars being crossed. But she did bake the most wonderful wedding cake. Four tiers. Sugar daffodils."

"I can see that a Tilly Martin could complicate things," said George. "But go on. What else? Nothing is too small, too trivial." And George gave Julia his wintry smile.

Julia nodded, and making no more attempt at coherence, allowed herself free rein: The melting block of ice for the champagne, the tent pole with a crack, the musicians playing "Mac the Knife" twice, Tilly Martin saying she had switched from Elizabeth Taylor's Passion to Yardley's Eau de Cologne because it was by appointment to Her Majesty. Giddy's friend the Gorilla with a beer bottle in his hand, and beer wasn't being served. And Sarah dancing with her father, then dancing with Alex's father, Professor Angus McKenzie, who, from what Julia had overheard, was speaking Old English—his area of interest. And Alex dancing with Sarah's mother before the cake was cut. Neil Wentworth helping pass the cake plates, Sarah's father giving a toast. Other toasts. Harvey Dodge saying he wanted fresh air, the tent was heating up. Rafe Posner out on the lawn playing "Greensleeves." And "Cockles and Mussels." "I went out and took Rafe a piece of cake and a glass of champagne."

"Hold up," commanded George, writing busily in his notebook. "Colonel Dodge went out. Down to the lower stable?"

"He left, but I didn't actually see where he went. And that's about it. My feet were hurting, so I took off my shoes after the cake, and Sarah danced once more with Alex and went upstairs. I remember looking out and seeing that it had gone quite gray, a fog was coming in, and I thought, Oh dear, I hope they make it to the ferry. Then Sarah came down with Mary Donelli and absolutely hurled her flowers at Giddy Lester, Alex's cousin, and got her in the head. And Giddy pulled some of the flowers out and pelted someone else. And then we all got rice and threw it at the car."

"Farney wasn't with you? Throwing rice?"

"He may have been, but I didn't see him. I wasn't surprised because I thought he'd gone to feed and water the horses."

"Who else threw rice?"

"Rice and tapioca. I found out that Tilly Martin had passed out boxes of tapioca earlier. It's supposed to have special properties. Honestly, that woman. But you want to know who was there. Well, I saw Mr. and Mrs. Laaka, Mike Laaka, and Patrick O'Reilly, my stable manager. And Giddy, of course, and Leah Pfeifer of Camp Merrilark. Lots of others, but that's all I remember because I had my mother to think about. She's ninety and very frail, and it was time she went home."

"So neither Neil Wentworth nor this Winka person—"

"Winifred Wentworth. She's called Winka."

"Mr. and Mrs. Wentworth, Colonel Dodge, Tilly Martin, Jane Zimmer, or Rafe Posner—you didn't notice any of these throwing rice?"

"That doesn't mean they weren't there, and I may have seen Neil Wentworth coming from the lavatory after the rice throwing. But, Sergeant, it had been such a long day. I was done in and there were still the late chores. Night checks, hay and water for the horses. Weddings mean nothing to horses. And I only had Patrick and Jessica to help. I remember feeling disappointed that Farney—who had been so helpful—and Rafe Posner had skipped out."

"And none of these late chores took you into the annex room?"

"As I've already told you." Julia folded her hands over Charlie, the orange cat in her lap, who, apparently resenting this attention, rose, arched its back, gave a hiss in the direction of Sergeant Fitts, and noiselessly sprang to a kitchen counter.

George stood up abruptly and offered a hand and Julia reluctantly accepted it, telling Sarah later that George's hand made her feel she was helped up by a dead haddock.

"That, Mrs. Clancy," said George, "will do for now. Please send in Sarah Deane and Alex McKenzie."

The bride and groom thus summoned to the presence found

George putting on his windbreaker. The fog had sent the temperature down into the fifties. "I think," he said, "that we can talk while I take a quick tour of the farm. I haven't had a proper chance to look the place over. We'll be talking to you several times, but now I only want to get a general idea of what you remember." George walked to the back kitchen door and held it open.

Escorted to the outer world and along the sloping gravel path to the stable area, Sarah explained that she had no clear memory of the reception. Just snips and bits and sound bites.

"My mind was all going round and round," she complained. "It's like a kaleidoscope, everything bright and whirling and regrouping. I remember dancing with all sorts of people, Alex, my brother, my father, Alex's father, who was reciting 'The Seafarer' in Old English to me, which was very flattering but I didn't understand a word. The trouble was that I told him once I'd done two semesters of Old English in graduate school. And I saw Tilly Martin stick her finger into the bottom edge of the frosting before we'd cut the cake, which is very like Tilly. But after all, she'd made it, so maybe she was quality testing. Jane gave her hand a little slap and pulled her away. And I saw Aunt Julia slip her shoes off after we cut the cake. Poor thing, she usually lives in sneakers or boots. And I remember seeing my brother Tony kissing Andrea—that's his girl—and I heard Mary Donelli asking Alex's mother when to throw the rice. And the orchestra playing 'Lucy in the Sky with Diamonds' at the same time the piper was cranking up with 'Road to the Isles.' Just odd, disconnected things, nothing significant. The whole reception really went bing, bing, bang, and then we took off. Ten or fifteen minutes after six, I think. Alex was in a hurry to leave, weren't you, Alex?"

Alex nodded. "I saw the fog coming in and thought we'd better get a move on. We had reservations at the Blue Hill Inn and a ferry to catch the next morning."

"None of which took place," said Sarah. They had reached the stable entrance and she turned to George. "Do you want to go in or just walk around?"

"Around if you please. I want to check the entrances. How many. Where located." Here George pulled out his pad and made a swift sketch of a rectangular building and began making *X*'s at suitable places. "Go on," he said. "I'm listening. Alex, what do you remember about the reception?"

And Alex, who had a clinician's eye for detail, led George from their arrival at the wedding itself to the reception line, the nature and taste of the eatables (strong on seafood and mushrooms), the make of champagne (domestic), the eclectic program of music with something for everyone. He remembered many of the guests who danced and gave toasts, but not Farney.

"Not even once?" asked George. "Not at the beginning?"

"Yes, once. In the reception line. One thing I've noticed about big groups—you remember not who *is* there but who *isn't*. I don't remember seeing Farney after that one time."

"You, Sarah?" said George. "You didn't mention Farney."

"Going through the reception," said Sarah. "He kissed me, which I think was awfully nice of him, but I don't remember him during the dancing. Just the back of him walking toward the stable before we cut the cake. He had his jacket off."

"When you threw your bouquet? When all that rice was thrown at you? When you drove away? When there were large numbers of people close to you?"

They both denied seeing Farney at these occasions. Nor Colonel Dodge. Nor Mrs. Laaka, nor Winka and Neil Wentworth. Nor Rafe Posner.

"But that doesn't mean they weren't there," said Sarah. "There was a crowd and we were in motion. Throw the flowers at Giddy, kiss parents and relatives and Grandmother Douglas, and duck out. I wasn't taking notes."

"We moved fast," said Alex. "I ran interference and we got away with only a pound of rice down our necks."

"Okay, hold it for now," said George. He put one foot on the lower rail of the yearling paddock, and, while Sarah and Alex watched the six young horses bucking and snorting and running and stopping suddenly, George began writing in his note-book, a long line of neat pothooks, lines, and slashes—the George Fitts shorthand system, as Sarah had once been told.

"Is that it?" asked Sarah. "May we go now?"

"Yes," said George. "But not away. I'll spend the rest of the afternoon walking the farm perimeter. Please stay where we can reach you. No wedding trips to the Bahamas."

"Is that a joke?" said Sarah.

"No," said George. "I've had people take off for the Bahamas or farther when they're needed for an investigation."

"Well, we can't go home," Sarah told him. "We're stuck in the Seascape Motel out on Route One. Our own house is being re-vamped. Rewired, replumbed. It's not livable."

"Well then," said George, "I'll note you as being at the Sea-scape. Though it would be more convenient to have you closer."

"Perhaps," said Sarah with heavy sarcasm, "we should stay right here on the farm. To be completely convenient."

"That," said George, closing his notebook, "is an excellent idea. I'll speak to Mrs. Clancy about it."

"I was kidding," said Sarah. "We can't stay here."

"Of course you can," returned George. "A large farm like this."

"Aunt Julia wouldn't stand for it; she loves her privacy," said Sarah, grasping at a straw—and a very weak straw it was. Julia had often offered them both bed and board.

It was all arranged in a minute. Escorted back into the farm-house kitchen they were greatly welcomed. Julia, worried face smoothed, went upstairs to see about towels and blankets.

"Damn you, George Fitts, that motel was our wedding trip," said Sarah as she watched Aunt Julia disappear around the landing.

"Not anymore it isn't," said George. He ran his finger down a file card and stopped midway. "The Wentworths," he said.

"Our wedding trip," repeated Sarah.

"Later," said George. "You can take a very nice trip in July or August. Relax then. Nobody relaxes in the middle of a homicide. And you two are directly in the middle. Crucial. And there's an advantage to having you at the farm. As I've remarked in the past, you are not totally unobservant. Although I urge you, Sarah, to forget about any solo efforts."

At which juncture the kitchen door banged open and Mike Laaka in his role as sheriff's deputy investigator stalked into the room. His fair hair was ruffled; his rolled sleeves and the bits of hay and straw clinging to his person suggested that he had been rooting about in the stable area.

"Good," said Mike. "The two chief suspects are here. Are you holding them, George?"

"In a way," said George. "They'll be staying here at the farm. On tap. Now wait a minute, Mike"—as Mike gave signs of moving on—"I want to ask a couple of questions. The Wentworths? Tell me about them. They live almost opposite your parents, so you must be familiar with the couple."

"Both the Wentworths stick in my craw, but maybe that's just the accent and the uptilted noses. Whenever I try for normal conversation with Neil I end up with a lecture on the poor quality of American cars, tractors, and government. To give the devils their due, they run a good summer camp. Highfeather. For boys. Down on Fallen Tree Pond. Winka inherited the place from an uncle and the kids seem to have a good time. Come over here for their riding lessons, which Winka and Neil help Julia teach."

"How about you, Sarah? And you, Alex? It's obvious that the deputy here doesn't care for the Wentworths," said George.

"Well," said Alex, "I went to Camp Highfeather. Back in the old days when Winka's Uncle Horace was running it, and, judging from the camp bulletins I get, the place is thriving."

"They are rather posh," put in Sarah. "But they seem to have warm hearts. They always speak kindly to the peasants. Actually, I do rather like them, but they drive Aunt Julia up the wall. She can't bear people with beautiful clothes, beautiful things—except horses and fences and saddles."

"Sarah," said George reprovingly. "That's just sentiment and prejudice and hearsay. Can you give me something like facts?"

"I can't think of anything interesting about the Wentworths that you haven't been told. Besides having their land tested by Norminco. That they think it's practical to know what's under the sod. But that doesn't make them unusual, because I hear that lots of the neighbors are doing the same."

"Ah," said George, making a note. Then he looked at his watch and turned to Mike Laaka. "I have to meet with the forensic people again. Go on with this line of questions and I'll get back to you later." And George took two brisk steps, snapped open the door, and was gone.

"Okay," said Mike. "We can chat outside. I have to check the crew working the south pasture."

"We were just outside with George," protested Sarah. "It's cold and clammy."

"The sun's coming out; it'll heat up fast. The thing is," Mike went on as the three headed up the drive and turned in the direction of the south pasture, "do you know anything substantive about the Wentworths? Something we might not know? After all, I don't move in their social circle and I haven't visited Highfeather camp." Mike in his turn pulled out a notebook and waited.

"Aunt Julia really knows them," said Sarah.

"She'll have her turn," said Mike. "We'll cross-fertilize her answers with yours and everyone else's. Come on, walk faster both of you. The wedding must have destroyed your muscles."

And Mike surged ahead at a lope and then halted to speak to two uniformed deputies, who were huddled over the edge of the southern roadside pasture fence. One man appeared to be straining grass through some sort of net and the other was sorting, tagging, and bagging a pile of oddments, such as a broken Pepsi bottle, a whole Bud Light can, several Styrofoam cups, a McDonald's wrapper, and a rusty-looking horseshoe with nails sticking out of its edge.

Resuming the walk, Mike turned to Alex. "To your knowledge, have the Wentworths mentioned selling their property, or leasing it, to Norminco? If the test drilling turns up something?"

"Neil talked about the expense, the bother to them if the

mine goes through," said Sarah. "But he said if they had to move the camp, they would, because it was Winka's whole life."

"Did he suggest buying Julia's place?" asked Mike.

"Not in so many words, though it seemed to me that the idea was hanging in the air," said Sarah.

"The Tilly Martin idea? Rotation," said Mike.

"Not exactly," said Sarah. "The planets weren't involved. It was a perfectly rational discussion. Neil went on about Aunt Julia's being aged and creaky and that her farm is too much for her. The conversation struck me as a bit self-serving."

"Who's being prejudiced now?" said Mike. "All is fair in love and real estate. Besides, face it—High Hope Farm *is* too much for one sixty-eight-year-old lady whose workforce keeps disappearing. Do you think either of the Wentworths could have been cutting up paper letters and mailing messages?"

Sarah paused and considered. Then shook her head. "Not those messages. They were mindless. A little scary perhaps, but inane. I think Neil at least would come up with something classier."

"The mine may fit in," said Alex. "Sarah has this idea—and it may not be entirely wild—that the mineral deposits, the ledge that holds them, may extend, even widen, through High Hope Farm."

"Because," said Sarah, "there does seem to be a kind of local gold rush going on in Julia's direction."

"Nickel," said Mike. "Copper, cobalt, trace minerals."

"A rush," repeated Sarah. "Even if the Wentworths haven't exactly offered for the farm, Tilly Martin's going on about it, and Harvey Dodge seems ready to give up his place and move in with Julia. You don't have to be a genius to think that someone must have leaked something about her property. Maybe even sneaked in and taken core samples, even if no one can find holes. Or used a metal detector. Come on, Mike, isn't there some way you can find out if this has actually happened? I mean, why on earth does half of Tri-County Road want to move Aunt Julia out?"

Mike, who was walking briskly ahead down the long gray weathered post-and-rail fence that enclosed the south pasture, turned back, stopped, and leaning against a post shook his head. "Two, maybe three households, don't equal what you call half of Tri-County Road, but I'll talk to one of those Norminco people and see if I can line up one of the state geologists to take a look at her farm. If Julia will allow it."

"She won't," said Sarah. "She's dug her feet in."

"I gather," said Mike, "from some of my not-so-secret sources that the mine people are in a cooperative mood. They want to win hearts and minds."

"The point is," said Alex, "would Julia Clancy's land be part of the grand scheme? Are there good goods under her pastures?"

"That's it," said Sarah. "Because then everything falls into place. All those nasty attacks are meant to drive Aunt Julia—if not out of her mind—at least off her farm."

"Not that simple," said Mike. "You can't lump all those incidents into one basket. Not to mention Rafe Posner and Sean Conners. Find those two guys and you might have some answers."

"So what have you got?" asked Alex. "Is it one problem with one answer, or ten separate problems with ten answers."

"I can count," said Mike, "and when I do, I come up with more than ten. Think of the people in this area who are hurting financially and might want to get hold of sixty acres with mineral deposits under them. And that doesn't take into consideration speculators, investors, big-business types, who are probably hovering out of sight behind the bushes. And," he went on, warming to the subject, "there's Camp Merrilark on the north side of Camp Highfeather. Highfeather isn't the only summer camp around. Merrilark is as close to the action as Highfeather. Both camps might want to relocate over at High Hope Farm. Crawfish Pond fronts on Julia's woods. Perfect camp site. Actually room for two camps."

"Of course, there's Merrilark," exclaimed Sarah. "It's a wonderful place. I went there and so did my mother and Aunt Julia. You're absolutely right. Both camps are threatened."

"You see," said Mike. "And think of those lakeside cottages. It isn't just Tilly and Jane and the colonel and Lord and Lady Wentworth. It's half the frigging county who might want to go somewhere else. To a nearby farm with land and a waterfront. Having sold out for big bucks. Or perhaps move to this same farm, find minerals, and sell that, too, for more big bucks."

For a moment Alex and Sarah and Mike stared at each other, the truth of Mike's remark only too evident. Then Sarah gave herself a quick mental shake. "We have to start somewhere," she said. "Mike, see if you can find any geological records of Julia's land. As for me, I think it's time for some social work. First a supportive visit to Appleyard Farm. Poor dears, George Fitts will come marching over and scare them to death. Or scare Tilly anyway."

"I think," said Mike grinning, "considering Sarah's past activities in the crime world, the sight of her in their front yard would scare them more than George. "Everyone knows she attracts homicide like flies to flypaper."

"Ease up, Mike," said Alex. "Let Sarah go off and make her visit. After all, she is a lot less intimidating than George Fitts and his damned notebook. Or you in your present capacity. Both of you could throw Tilly into a monumental relapse."

"I'll make sure Jane's around," said Sarah. "Poor woman, she's hardly left Tilly's side in days. Lately she's had no life of her own." She turned to Alex. "Would you like to come? Make a housecall? Though of course a man, any man . . ."

"Thanks, Sarah," said Alex, "but you go along and do woman things. We men will stay together and work on our bonding."

"Actually, the bonding will have to wait," said Mike. "The pathology lab's come through with some reports on the murder. We're due at the hospital. And Sarah"—this as Sarah started toward the road—"think about this: If you wanted to move Julia off her farm by a series of violent incidents and the murder of a helper, would you advertise your interest by saying she should consider moving as Neil Wentworth did, or try and marry its owner as the colonel did, or 'rotate' onto the farm as Tilly Martin keeps saying? Wouldn't you lie low and be very quiet about your interest?"

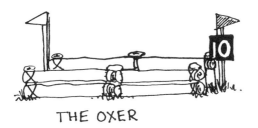

THE OXER

TEN

SARAH, frowning for a moment, watched Alex and Mike make their way back across the south pasture toward the farmhouse. Okay, Mike, one for you, she thought. Why would a murderer conduct a terrorist campaign and at the same time advertise an interest in taking over the place? Unless it was a double ploy. Go public about wanting Julia to move and so be judged innocent.

Marching along the road toward Appleyard Farm, she tried to think of those of Julia's neighbors who—so far—showed no interest in buying her farm. Mike Laaka and his family. Patrick O'Reilly. Jane Zimmer. Dear old Mrs. Pfeifer of Camp Merrilark. All solid citizens and longtime friends. So how about Sean Conners, should he be alive and hiding? Ditto Rafe Posner. Neither man by word or deed had ever suggested he was interested in owning the farm. Or any farm. But Rafe seemed to have taken a particular and personal interest in Julia and her animals.

Sarah, arriving at the entrance to Appleyard Farm, made her way under the fully leafed maple trees that lined the road and kept the passage shady and cool. Blessed coolness, for the temperature—after repression by fog—had begun to rise into the eighties.

On her right, beyond the trees, she saw a long narrow stretch of plowed earth and there was Jane Zimmer bumping along on her tractor. Jane saw Sarah, brought the tractor to a halt, and waved. And Sarah, as she waved back, remembered saying that Jane had no life of her own. Not true. Jane on such a tractor that clawed and ripped through the earth was, while seated there, her own person. Queen of the road—or at least of the field.

Jane jumped down, exclaiming about Sarah's return from her wedding trip, and in a matter of minutes both were settled in basket chairs on the screen porch enjoying chicken sandwiches and lemonade, Jane having correctly deduced that Sarah had not had lunch.

"Tilly ate early," said Jane. "She's out on the croquet lawn."

"Jane, I didn't mean to drag you from your tractor."

"I was just chugging about. Trying to clear stones. See if we can grow a crop on it. How they can tax our property at almost the same rate as Neil and Winka Wentworth's is beyond me. I suppose it's because we have frontage on Fallen Tree Pond. But to be honest, being in the field is a way of getting away from Tilly. I love her, but peaceful cohabitation these days takes some doing."

Sarah smiled sympathetically. "Still trying to rotate?"

"Yes, and I don't know whether the addition of the royal family is making it better or worse. The stream will dry up eventually, so right now I buy her copies of *Majesty* magazine and she's happy. And how could I leave her moldering away in the hospital in the middle of summer?"

"And so far this has been quite a summer," said Sarah.

"Yes, yes, I know," said Jane. "Your wedding was wonderful and Farney's death so tragic. One of the good people. And Harvey Dodge. He and Farney Thompson have been together for years."

Sarah went to the point. "Jane, have you any ideas about what's going on?"

Jane frowned and then nodded. "Motive. Motive, that's where I'd begin. Who has an interest in moving Julia out? Besides Tilly. But have you thought about Camp Merrilark? And Camp Highfeather? Both are threatened by the mine."

"Although directors of summer camps don't quite fit the terrorist profile," said Sarah. "Especially someone like Leah Pfeifer. I think it's wonderful that she's still running Merrilark. She was at the wedding reception and looked as strong as ever."

"Well, she won't step down. As stubborn as Julia."

"I went there. Four years. Horribly homesick and had a wonderful time. I learned to paddle the war canoe."

"Leah Pfeifer probably still paddles a war canoe. And if she thought her beloved Merrilark was going to be turned into a nickel mine she might take steps."

"What sort of steps?"

"Go see her and judge for yourself. She has her nephew now, Brad Pfeifer, as co-director. Brad is someone I'd never want to cross, and I'll bet he's talking tough to the Norminco people. He's secretary of the group opposing it."

"I guess I didn't want to think about Merrilark," admitted Sarah. "Only Highfeather and Aunt Julia's other neighbors."

"You'll have a chance to study both camps in action because they send their campers to High Hope Farm for riding. Winka and Neil Wentworth help teach along with Julia. The advanced riders usually take part in Julia's big event."

"What big event?"

"Sarah, where *have* you been all these years?"

"Teaching. Studying. Doing my master's. Up to my ears. Not living in Aunt Julia's pocket. Although now"—here Sarah sighed deeply—"I—I mean we, Alex and I—are in her pocket. We have to stay at the farm until the police have finished—or until our own house is renovated. So, what event?"

"Combined training. Dressage, cross-country, stadium jumping. The first weekend in July. The whole neighborhood goes."

"But she won't have it now. Not with the murder."

"It's Julia's big moment. Even a strangling won't stop it."

Sarah stiffened. "How do you know Farney was strangled?"

Jane put her lemonade glass down with a thump. "Lord, Sarah, you sound just like a bad mystery novel. Trap the librarian into admitting what no one but the murderer could have known—that the victim was strangled. And that he was wearing a bridle. But everyone knows. Everyone for miles around knew within ten minutes of Julia's finding Farney. Julia called the police, Patrick, Harvey Dodge, Mike Laaka, me, the Wentworths, everyone. And now, Sarah, I've got to check on the hens. Go say hello to Tilly but don't excite her." Jane stood up, brushed a crumb from her blue jeans, and opened the screen door and paused. "If you need another suspicious character, consider Jim Shale." And Jane strode out into the sunlight and moved off in the direction of the henhouse.

Sarah stayed in her chair. Before confronting Tilly she needed a moment to pull her thoughts in line. Okay, consider Camp Merrilark as well as Camp Highfeather. After all, stranger things in the annals of education had happened, and, probably, there languished at that very moment in some maximum security prison a few errant directors of summer camps.

As for Jim Shale, the notion of Mr. Norminco himself as a suspect was acceptable. But how to bring him into a setting where casual conversation might yield something to the point? Things had not been exactly cordial between the geologist and the community on their first and last encounter. Well, she'd have to shift gears and apologize on her own behalf at least.

But now for Tilly. Sarah made her way around the back of the farmhouse to a patch of rough grass optimistically called the croquet lawn.

Tilly was bent over her mallet, three balls about her, a red, a blue, a black. Tilly's round face was creased, her plump body tense with concentration. Sarah hesitated. A voice—Alex? George Fitts? Mike Laaka?—some inner voice was telling her to hold it, butt out. Back off. Sarah, long practiced in not listening to such cautions, closed her ears.

"Tilly," she called. "Hi, Tilly. I dropped by to say hello. I'm glad you're out of the hospital."

Tilly put down her mallet and walked over to Sarah. Today she wore what must have been once a summer print dress—patterns of violets and leaves sprinkled over its surface. But much washing had faded and shrunk the garment so it ended well above her plump knees. She indicated a faded canvas butterfly chair. "Sarah, sit down while I finish. I'm playing three balls, but one of them's poison, so I may eliminate all of me by the next turn."

Sarah sat as instructed and watched while Tilly stroked and sent away and wicketed herself against herself. Finally the black ball broke loose and in seven successful shots hit the stake, and Tilly laid down her mallet.

"You won?" asked Sarah. It seemed the right thing to say.

"As black I won. As blue I came in second. As red playing poison I came in dead last. Well now, Sarah. The bride comes visiting. Blessed be the bride the sun shines upon—or did shine upon. Isn't that the old saying?"

"What about the fog? The bride whom the fog catches."

"It didn't catch you and Alex. It caught Farney Thompson and Julia Clancy's farm. As I warned. Sarah, you know I warned."

Sarah nodded yes, Tilly had certainly warned. Had she thought that Farney might be a victim? Did that surprise her?"

Tilly turned and pulled over a second butterfly chair, sank into it, looking rather, Sarah thought, like a large variegated cabbage coming to rest in a bowl.

Tilly laid a finger across her lips. "Mum's the word," she whispered. She leaned forward in a conspiratorial way. "Jane doesn't like me to talk about it. Says it upsets me. I say it upsets her. I'm used to it."

"Used to it!" exclaimed Sarah. "Used to people being strangled with bridles?"

"No dear, used to life. And death. You know, in the midst of life we are in death. One generation passeth away, and another generation cometh. *Après moi le déluge.* Do not ask for whom the bell tolls. Librarians see it all."

Sarah tried to adjust her features into a mask of placid acceptance. She couldn't quite decide whether Tilly was addled beyond recall or was a brainy eccentric given to spasms of unreason who, like some academics she knew, jumped from insight to insight, without giving anyone enough clues to make the trip along with them. After all, she supposed, librarians do see it all—in books—at a rather large remove from the actual grit and gore of outside life. Sarah settled for the safe remark.

"I suppose librarians do get a dose . . . all the books that come across the counter. From Abacus and Alphabet to Zen and Zanzibar."

"Zanzibar to Zen," corrected Tilly. "And I mourn for Farney. One of the good men. Responsible, never shouted, knew his job. Wonderful with animals. His passing is a grief to us all. My heart goes out to Harvey Dodge. A real loss."

Sarah swallowed. Suddenly Tilly was back making appropriate remarks. Perhaps now was the time, now that Tilly seemed taken by a brief fit of sanity.

"Farney was such a help to Aunt Julia," Sarah said, by way of beginning. "And I wish I'd seen him at the reception, but it was such a circus, the music, the dancing—well, except for the reception line, I missed him completely."

"I saw Farney," said Tilly. "I spent quality time with him and I cut him a piece of cake, but then he disappeared. I wouldn't want it to get back to Julia, but she is—or was—using Farney far too much. Harvey Dodge's own place is going to wrack and ruin. I told Harvey he should have kept Farney at his own place and let Julia face reality. Then she might have accepted his proposal. They are well suited and should be quite happy at Quartermaster Farm."

Sarah tried to lay hold of some part of this flow. The significant part. "Farney," she said. "You cut him a piece of cake. But did he eat it? Did you see him after we'd taken off for Nova Scotia? Down in the stable?"

"Not *in* the stable," Tilly corrected. "I saw him going *down* to the stable. Jane was ahead of him with someone in a big hat. In a pink dress. Winka Wentworth, I think. And there was Farney going to meet his destiny. A rendezvous with death. You remember that poem, very popular after the first World War. 'I have a rendezvous with death at some disputed barricade when spring comes round with rustling shade.' But I suppose it was inevitable."

Sarah sat up abruptly—difficult in a butterfly chair, but she was startled. "Inevitable? Why inevitable? Had anyone been threatening Farney? No one hated Farney, did they?"

"No, but he was one of Julia's props. Along with Rafe Posner and Sean Conners. Knock the props out and where are you—or where is Julia? Alone and quite unable to handle the farm operation. It's all part of the whole. Yin-yang."

Sarah stared at Tilly. Except for the yin-yang tag she sounded as efficient and coldly sensible as George Fitts himself. Sarah took a deep breath and returned to square one. "So you didn't see Farney after he took off for the stable?"

"No, unless he was one of those people going down to look at the horses. People who don't know that if they pat the wrong horse they may end up without a shirt on their backs. That animal of Julia's—about five years ago, that paint mare Tessa, she got hold of my blouse with her teeth and ripped it right off. Left me standing in my bra. And now, Sarah, I must walk the dogs. Don't you think it's a twist of fate that I have corgis? Pembroke corgis. Just like the queen and princess royal. They'll be right at home."

Sarah couldn't resist. "At home where?"

"At High Hope Farm, of course. Where else?"

Sarah stumped away from Appleyard Farm and along the heated black asphalt of the Tri-County Road feeling as if she had wandered into the Red Queen's croquet party—all the scene had needed was Tilly to be wielding a flamingo at a hedgehog. In fact, on reflection, she decided that the *Looking Glass* event, compared to the working of Tilly's mind, was a model of sobriety and sense.

And had she learned anything beyond the fact that Tilly seemed to think that Farney should have been working at Harvey Dodge's farm rather than propping up Aunt Julia's maimed operation? And that Jane and Winka Wentworth had been two of the multitudes visiting the stable area. Sarah looked at her watch. Two forty-five. Not enough time to visit two camps, so start with one—the Wentworths and Highfeather. Turn up at their house at four o'clock because arriving then at the house of any native of the British Isles meant tea for the guest, even an uninvited guest. Then, in the warm mood induced by tea, sandwiches, and cake, a trip down to admire Camp Highfeather. Tomorrow Merrilark and a social hour with Jim Shale.

By the time Sarah reached the stable entrance at High Hope Farm these schemes were neatly in place in her head. There she discovered Alex sitting at the wheel of the Bronco staring into space. She marched over and banged on the door.

"Wake up. Rise and shine." She opened the door and climbed into the passenger seat. "Hey, Alex, you're back."

Alex jerked his head around, pushed his hair back, and smiled. A reluctant smile. "Yes, I'm back. Was just sitting here wool-gathering. Out of it. Post-pathology syndrome."

"Oh, of course. Well, did you learn something?"

"I'd like to forget the whole business. Just sit here and look out on the wholesome scene of Julia Clancy's east paddock, where that gray gelding is trying to kick the bejeezus out of that big chestnut. Animal aggression is much healthier than the human variety. At least at the moment I think so."

"Ten minutes into 'National Geographic' or 'Wild America' watching owls grab rabbits or lions gnaw zebras and you'd change your mind."

"I wouldn't change it; it would just confirm my feelings about human predators—the worst of the lot."

"You're depressed. So am I. Or disoriented. Out of joint. I can't believe there was a wedding yesterday. It seems like a play we went to. Only Farney being dead seems real. Isn't that awful?"

"Awful," agreed Alex, climbing down from the car. "And I'm

always depressed after one of these exhilarating sessions with the pathologist. I suppose it's harder if you know the victim, know that he was in good health, died without reason. If I lose a patient to a disease, well, it's not pleasant, but I usually know why it happened. Just—oh hell."

"We all knew Farney. It's hard to think of Colonel Dodge's place—or Aunt Julia's for that matter—without Farney around."

Alex nodded. "I loathe seeing decent people end up feet-first on the autopsy table. Their parts being sent around to path labs. Actually, I don't like finding indecent people on the table. Anyway, as far as the autopsy went, a few peculiar things turned up, but not all the lab tests are in. We can talk it over later."

"Yes, after tea with the Wentworths."

"I'm not having tea with the Wentworths. I don't have tea."

"They may offer sherry. Or even a beer."

"I can have a beer right here, then have dinner somewhere with you. Then go for a walk. Hand in hand in the twilight."

"After the Wentworths' we can plan a call on Jim Shale."

"I think I'll go back to the hospital and stay there."

"We can't just sit around being depressed. We've got to see Jim Shale. See him in an everyday setting. Like neighbors."

"I don't want to see Jim Shale at all."

"You will," said Sarah. "The idea will grow on you. You'll be stuffed with teatime goodies by the Wentworths—they have wonderful black currant cake—and you'll be happy to make plans to see Jim Shale. And plan a Camp Merrilark visit."

"Negative."

"That's what we can't be," said Sarah. "Come on, Alex. Upward and onward. To save Aunt Julia. Avenge Farney Thompson. Help George clear up this mess. He can't have cozy teas with Neil and Winka or have a powwow at Camp Merrilark. We've an inside track and we've got to use it."

"Did anyone ever tell you you're an overachiever?"

Sarah gave Alex a reluctant smile. "No, I meddle. I poke my nose into things. I stumble around and ask stupid questions.

But every now and then I hook onto something out of sync. Accidentally. Every now and then it works out. I learn something."

"So do I," said Alex. "Usually something I regret."

As they walked up toward the farmhouse they saw that not only was the farm infested with the usual number of police vehicles, but that a large green van with "Festive Occasions" inscribed on its side had arrived. Apparently police permission had been given and the wedding reception was being dismantled. The bride and groom, moving to the safety of the kitchen steps, watched as a troop of men and women in coveralls burdened with folding tables, tent poles, and rolled-up canvas began packing them into the open maw of the van. This process was watched by two men in sports shirts and dark trousers—obviously members of George Fitts's observation brigade.

"I said it was just a play and now they're taking down the set," said Sarah. "What was it? A tragedy, I suppose. The tragedy of Farney Thompson. Black comedy for us, with Tilly doing a cameo."

"We're only in to the second act," remarked Alex. "Lots of walk-ons and spear carriers still around." He pointed past the stable, and Sarah saw that other members of George's team had spread themselves to the paddocks and the pastures. And intermixed with the police, as Jane Zimmer had predicted, a crew of unknowns in preparation for the coming combined training event were creating a sinister-looking log obstacle near a small brook. In contrast to these goings-on, the farmhouse seemed a peaceful refuge. Alex and Sarah retreated to the kitchen and Alex indicated the clock. "Almost four. Let's get this tea scene over and done with."

Sarah ran upstairs to change, scraped a comb through her hair, came down, and held out a hand. "I'm ready."

At which Julia herself appeared in a disheveled condition at the kitchen door. "Where have you two been? Up to no good, I suppose." She advanced into the room and sank wearily into a chair. "We still have stalls to muck out and the horses to do and now this." Julia sighed heavily and shook her head.

"What do you mean?" said Sarah, alarmed.

"Another cut-out message. By mail. But different this time. I've turned it over to Mike."

"How different?" asked Alex.

"Tennyson. 'Half a league, half a league onward. / Hers is not to reason why; hers is but to move or die.' "

"That *is* different," admitted Sarah. "Certainly not Mother Goose. Though I found the nursery approach pretty disgusting."

Julia shrugged. "I agree. What does the original poem matter? As they say, it's the sentiment that counts." She closed her eyes for a moment and then appeared to brace herself. "Never mind. The police are in charge now. So where are you off to?"

"Tea. The Wentworths'," said Alex.

"I wasn't invited."

"Nor were we," said Sarah. "But we will be. It's all in your interest, Aunt Julia. We're trying to cover some ground that the police can't. Making social visits. Follow up your theory about people wanting your property for mineral development."

"Go," said Julia. "Go, but not with my blessing. I'm beginning to remember the trouble you caused at the ranch last Christmas."

"And I," said Sarah, "remember how Alex and I saved you from ending up in an Arizona canyon. Now take it easy and we'll come back around five-thirty and help with the chores."

"We will?" said Alex as they drove off. "How about the dinner and evening delights?"

"I've got it worked out. Tea, then stable chores. Then a late dinner over candlelight. We can plan a trip to Nova Scotia."

"A novel idea." Alex turned the Bronco into the wide gravel sweep and stopped by the front door of a classic Greek Revival farmhouse, its white paint fresh, red geraniums in pots by the door, a brass knocker in the shape of a fox head on the dark green door. Alex took a deep breath and lifted the brass ring and let it fall heavily against the brass plate.

"You know," said Sarah as they waited, "that new poem, *The*

Charge of the Light Brigade takeoff—it suggests Harvey Dodge. He's always reciting odd bits of poetry."

"Or Tilly," said Alex. "She sings war songs. 'Lili Marlene,' 'All Quiet Along the Potomac.' "

"Hush," said Sarah. "Here they come. Neil and Winka won't be happy to see us, but they're too polite to say so."

This proved to be the case.

And, sitting in the library on upholstered chairs covered in a handsome blue pattern, a late-afternoon breeze coming from open French doors, amid the delicate clatter of Royal Doulton teacups, it seemed almost profane to raise the subject of murder.

At the mention of Farney's death both Winka and Neil expressed regret. "Such a fine man," said Winka. "Imagine—strangled with a pony bridle. I mean, how obscene."

"Indecent," said Neil. "Absolutely indecent. Nauseating. And poor Julia. Yes, she's a tough lady, but my word."

Winka, sounding like a hospice worker, took up the strain. "Sarah, Alex, we want to be perfectly honest with you. Up front as you Americans say. We worry about Julia . . ." She turned large brown eyes to Neil, who was examining a piece of black currant cake on his plate. "Don't we worry, Neil?" she prompted.

Neil seemed to recover his composure. "Of course we worry. Perfectly honest worry. No deep, dark motives."

"Right," said Winka. "And we also worry about the effect the mine will have on our place, on Camp Highfeather. And yes, if Julia decided to sell, we'd be interested in her farm. But we don't want to pressure Julia by an offer. She'd think we've been trying to give her the push by terrorizing her. Julia can be suspicious."

"And who could blame her?" said Neil.

"Let's say," went on Winka, "that we're just two concerned citizens. Julia is almost seventy and she's lost Rafe Posner and Sean Conners." Here Winka appeared to wrestle with herself, and then she put her teacup down into its saucer. "All right, this is what I'm trying to say. If—only if—Julia thinks about selling, do you suppose she might give us first refusal? There, I've said it and I feel like some sort of criminal, but if I, if Neil and I, can't be honest with our neighbors . . ."

Winka ground to a halt and took another gulp of tea, and Neil picked up the strain. But not without a frown at his wife. "Winka's only saying that High Hope Farm seems to have become a tremendous burden for your aunt."

Sarah put down her teacup with such a clank that if it had been anything but fine bone china it would have shattered on the spot. "Aunt Julia doesn't think of the farm as a 'burden,' " she said. "Not even with everything that's happened."

"She probably thinks of the whole thing as a sort of ghastly challenge," said Alex. "To me she's never seemed stronger, more determined to go on." (Or more pigheaded he finished to himself.)

"Now Sarah, Alex," said Neil in a soothing voice. "Let's give it a rest. All in good time. See how the summer goes."

Sarah looked at Alex and repressed a frown. She found herself increasingly irritated by this toss and catch game. Such concern for dear Julia. Shit, she said to herself. Then, bracing herself against the back of a Queen Anne chair, fixing her eyes on an opposite portrait of a dark-visaged man who looked like Captain Hook, she asked, "If you sold your farm, would it be to Norminco?"

There was an imperceptible pause and then Neil smiled warmly. "Of course not. Not without consulting the neighbors. And now, would you both like a tour of the camp? We have a new canoe dock, and the tennis courts have been completely resurfaced."

At which suggestion Sarah expressed great eagerness. "I have a nephew," she said. "Cooper. Cooper is crazy about animals, especially snakes. I told his mother I'd look for a camp. He lives in California." Sarah rose to her feet and moved toward the door.

"Where in California?" asked Alex in a conversational tone.

"San Francisco," said Sarah firmly. "With a view of the Bay Bridge." She measured the distance between her foot and

Alex's ankle and decided she wouldn't be able to land an effective kick.

So it was Camp Highfeather time. Sarah and Alex admired the cabins, the lodge with its banners and photographs of sailboat skippers, its tennis tournament winners, its riding team.

"Since 1902," said Winka proudly. "My great-great Uncle Horace started it with fifteen campers and it's been in the family ever since. I inherited it five years ago, and we decided to move to the States and make a go of it."

"That's right," said Neil. "And now she's legal. An American citizen. Last year. She decided to do the thing properly. Winka looks forward to the camp session all winter."

"I certainly do," said Winka. "My finger is in every pie. I teach a Red Cross swimming course and beginning riders at Julia's. Neil does the advanced riders and the sailing."

"Winka," said Neil—and again Sarah thought she could detect an edge in his voice—"is the motor that runs the place. Her Uncle Horace would be pleased. I'm simply comic relief."

Sarah smiled and praised, then said it was time to leave, thank you for tea, such a well-run camp, and yes, she would love a catalog for her nephew, Cooper.

"So," said Sarah as they drove home, "have we been snowed by two terrorists? That business about being perfectly honest?"

"Snow job or not," said Alex, "it's been a useful visit."

"You mean going on about poor Aunt Julia and wanting to make her old age a happy one by being ready to buy High Hope. Garbage."

"Not garbage. They came out in the open about wanting Julia's farm. And that Winka's doing great-great Uncle Horace proud."

"Did you see that they subscribe to *Newsweek*? Mike said those nursery rhymes came from *Newsweek*. And that bird picture in the library. Découpage. Winka's, probably. Done with little scissors."

"The good colonel does needlepoint," said Alex. "And everyone for miles around owns scissors." He swung the Bronco into

Julia's stable parking area, turned off the ignition, and twisted around to face Sarah. "Okay, let's get these chores of Julia's done with all possible speed. Bust our butts off. Because, Sarah, love of my life, I intend to salvage something of the day."

"All right. I'll put off seeing Jim Shale until tomorrow."

"Tomorrow or next month; he's not going to tell you a blessed thing. Company business is company business. Not yours."

"It won't hurt to try a little softening."

"The police will be getting into the mining business, so your softening up Jim Shale will be a waste of time."

"It's never a waste of time to try and know your neighbor better. Lighten up, Alex."

Chores meant that Patrick and Julia and Cousin Jessica brought in the horses from their various pastures and paddocks, and turned them into their stalls. Sarah and Alex followed behind, helping where possible, tossing hay, filling water buckets, distributing grain.

During a moment's respite Sarah asked her aunt about the upcoming event. "Why are the police letting you go on with it?"

"George Fitts is in favor of it. He thinks it should go on, that it might bring some of the nonsense out in the open."

"Nonsense like murder?" asked Sarah.

"Including murder. George is going to keep the farm under surveillance during that entire weekend. He's even dug up several state police members who have horses and have done competitive riding. We'll insert them in the entries. And he's arranging to have Mike Laaka prowl about in boots and breeches looking like a rider. After all, even if I wanted to I couldn't really cancel the thing unless the police wanted me to. The course has been sent in to the Maine Combined Training Association, I have a pile of entries, the tent will go up next week."

"Tent? Another tent?"

"For horses. Temporary stabling for visiting riders. Thank heaven for Jane Zimmer and Harvey. They're going to come over on a regular basis. And Neil. And Winka. They'll bring their tractors or use mine. Perhaps I've been a little hard on the Wentworths."

"Go right ahead," said Sarah, "and be hard on the Wentworths. They're tough. And is Harvey still courting you? As well as protecting you?"

"Yes," said Julia. "I think he just goes on as a matter of habit. An object in motion, you know." Here Julia stopped and frowned at a hanging blanket rack. "Oh dear . . ."

"What's wrong?" said Sarah, alarmed.

"I seem to be short of some things. Coolers."

"Coolers? You mean to keep ice in?"

Julia shook her head impatiently. "Not for ice. For horses. To cool out a horse gradually after it's been exercised. It's a wool blanket. And I'm missing at least two." Here Julia bent over the rack and began counting folds. Then she turned to a wooden box, opened the lid, rummaged about and straightened. "Besides the coolers, I'm missing a rain sheet. That's a kind of poncho for a horse. Drat it. It's all those police and plainclothes men. Or that vagrant or tramp I saw over by Crawfish Pond yesterday."

"What vagrant or tramp?" exclaimed Sarah. "For God's sake, Aunt Julia, you've never mentioned a vagrant or a tramp."

"Oh, it's probably one of the Medlock boys. They both go through my pasture to fish in Crawfish Pond. If it isn't a vagrant, it's likely the police. You can't tell me that at least one of them isn't light-fingered. I'll have to take a complete inventory. I thought yesterday I was missing a bucket. And a garden shovel."

Sarah considered the matter. "Losing a few blankets and tools," she said, "doesn't seem in the same class as gunfire and murder. But report everything—the tramp, the missing things—to George. And Aunt Julia, please be careful."

"But I am. Patrick and I do the stable rounds every evening around ten, and we have lights at the corners of every building. Just like a prison camp. And with all there is to do getting ready for the event, I can't keep looking over my shoulder. We're working double-time on the cross-country course because I've changed it since last year. A new gallop by the beach with a coop."

But Sarah was not interested in the finer points of cross-country layouts. She straightened up, wiped her hands on the knees of her jeans, and announced that she was finished. "The beasts are fed and the only sound I can hear is munching."

"Such a wonderful sound," said Julia with a dreamy look on her face. "There's not a nicer moment in life than sitting in your barn listening to the buckets rattling and the horses chewing."

"To each his own," said Sarah. "Alex and I are going out for dinner to pretend we're a newly married couple." And suiting action to words, she opened the stable door, went outside, and found Alex drinking water from a hose.

"Come on," she said. "We'll wash up, have a peaceful dinner, and then moonlight madness. We can take Patsy. I rescued him from Mary's. He can stand guard and not let a policeman near us."

But this was not to be. Showered and clothed in light cotton, they were confronted at the point of departure by Mike Laaka—he in freshly ironed slacks and a crisp, short-sleeved shirt.

"I suppose," said Mike, "that you thought you had plans. Dinner for two? Wrong. Dinner for three." He pointed to the open door of his old Chevy Blazer.

"No," said Alex.

"Yes," said Mike. "I'm supposed to go over some lab details with you, Alex, and tell you both about a couple of oddball findings, so you may as well eat with me because otherwise you'll go hungry. Patsy is welcome to ride along."

Sarah rolled her eyes and looked heavenward, Alex shrugged, and Mike grinned. "Come on," he said. "It won't be glamorous but it serves food. Cap'n Mac's Seafood Place. In Thomaston."

"I wanted candles and a view of the water," said Sarah.

"We all have our dreams," said Mike. "Cap'n Mac has candles. And a view of the harbor. Now let's move it."

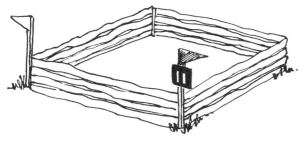

THE PIG STYE

ELEVEN

THE three were shown into a booth overhung by a herring net-ting embellished with dried sea urchins, starfish, lobster claws, and other such ocean relics, with a view of Thomaston harbor and a number of moored boats. Thus settled, Mike pulled out his notebook.

"Hope this won't diminish appetites," he said. "I'll keep it basic. Postmortem results as you know showed asphyxiation."

"As in strangle," said Sarah. She looked out over the water and thought, Why in hell am I doing this? Sitting here. About to be told everything I don't want to know about throttling some-one as nice as Farney Thompson. Then she saw Mike looking at her inquiringly. "Would you like to go out on deck and swat mosquitoes until I finish the details?"

Sarah swallowed. "No. Go ahead. But let me order a rum something. Make me think I'm having fun."

Drinks ordered and served, Mike smoothed his notebook open. "Like Sarah said, strangled."

"By the bridle?" asked Alex. "The reins?"

"No," said Mike. "Not the reins on that bridle. That bridle

was for decoration." Mike dipped a bread stick into a crock of cheese, twirled it about, and bore it laden to his mouth. "Cap'n Mac's is turning trendy. Cheese and bread sticks yet. It'll be smoked trout and quiche next."

Sarah reached over and grabbed both of Mike's hands. "You stop it. Explain yourself and get the details over so we can at least eat dinner. If it wasn't reins, what was it?"

"Other reins," said Mike. "Long leather reins. They left a definite indentation mark, oil from the leather-cleaning process, a few microscopic fragments of leather. Curb reins. Narrow curb reins. Curb reins are thinner than snaffle reins. They're used with the wider snaffle rein on a bridle that uses a curb bit together with a snaffle bit—the point being that you can strangle more efficiently with a narrow curb rein than with the wider snaffle rein."

"But why put the bridle on Farney?" exploded Sarah.

"You weren't listening. Decoration. Black humor. If I wanted maximum shock effect, I'd put on a bridle that fitted his face. I wouldn't have time to make adjustments on the regular horse-size bridles. There wasn't time for fiddling around. I mean, jeezus, there was a goddamn wedding reception going on, people all over the place. Even if the body was stashed in that annex room where no one goes, someone might have come snooping."

"So what kind of bridle fits humans?" demanded Sarah.

"None of them, since horses don't have round human skulls, but the one on Farney came pretty close. A small-pony bridle. And Julia has only one small-pony bridle because she only has one small pony—about eleven hands. Fuzzy chestnut thing called Gingersnap. The three other ponies are big ones and take larger bridles."

"You're saying the murderer went for a custom fit?" said Alex.

"I'm saying the murderer not only knew where the extra reins are hung—those not attached to a bridle—but knew where the little-pony's bridle was. Julia told us that she keeps that one hung on a rack in the grain room because her students were always grabbing it by mistake and trying to force it on a larger horse."

"Conclusion," announced Alex. "Murderer knew the barn, knew where equipment was kept. That shortens up the time needed. Instrument of death right at hand."

"Hell," said Mike, "like I've told George, everyone for miles knew their way around that stable. Julia has these big open-house things once a year. Lots of farms do that. And she has schooling shows for her students and local riders. Not to mention this big combined training event, when horse people and their buddies are knee-deep all over the place."

"Okay, okay," said Alex. "You've made the point. It's always an open door at High Hope Farm."

"Right. Every day. Nothing locked-up. People drift in and out. Girlfriends, boyfriends, students, salesmen, the feed delivery guys. Sawdust. Hay. People looking to buy a horse. Or sell one. Have one trained. And in the summer, campers from Merrilark and Highfeather. Christ, anyone planning a strangulation with reins would have an easy time of it. No need for special research."

Here Mike waved his menu in the air and was rewarded by a two-hundred-pound waiter who said his name was Don. That the specials were beef kabobs and blackened Cajun swordfish—"Told you they've gone upscale," said Mike, going for the swordfish. He waited until Alex had put in for the beef, Sarah for crab, and then said there was another item that had the lab people riled up.

"Like?" said Alex.

"Like Farney was bopped on the head before he was strangled. Stunned, maybe knocked out. Big occipital lump. Small amount of bruising over the ear.

"Bopped? With what?" demanded Sarah.

"Don't know. Sort of peculiar. The injury is consistent with the sort done by a patrolman's nightstick coming down on a skull. Smooth hard wood. Trouble is, Julia denies owning a nightstick."

"Broom handle?" suggested Alex. "Rake handle?"

"Broom handle, manure-fork handle, anything like that is too light for this sort of damage. We need a nightstick. And something else. A chain."

"Farney was chained?" exclaimed Sarah.

"Wait up," said Mike. He turned and welcomed his salad and assisted with the rotation of the bread basket. He buttered a piece of French bread, held it ready, and said again, "Yeah, a chain. A chain pattern that's tough to decipher. The marks run across the side of one cheek and neck. Doesn't make sense to the lab people. Why a chain? Why fancy up a straightforward business? Whack Farney a couple of times with the nightstick, he slumps, goes down. Whatever. Then reach for the reins you've got in your pocket, throw 'em around the throat, twist, pull, and that's it. Murder accomplished. No need for chains."

"Mystery weapon," said Alex. "I suppose you've searched the whole barn?"

"Practically vacuumed it. Every damn blanket, saddle, salt brick, stirrup, whip, crop, hard hat, boot, spur, you name it, we've seen it. No nightsticks. No cute little chains."

"Wait," said Sarah. "There are chains on some of the lead lines. Or lead shanks. I watched Aunt Julia bring in a horse with a chain around its nose. She said it was for control."

"Okay, that's about the only chain candidate of the right length, but it's attached to a long line—canvas or cotton or leather. At what point does the murderer start swinging a lead shank? Before he knocks him out with the nightstick? But why? He'd just put his victim on alert. Or after Farney's hit with the nightstick, to leave a chain mark for the hell of it? That's crazy. Listen, that chain is a real bitch. It doesn't fit in. Time is short and this guy is fooling around with a chain?"

"Here's dinner," said Sarah. "Let's cool it on the lab stuff." She accepted her crab in a little brown earthenware dish and put a tentative fork in its center.

"Okay by me," said Mike, spearing a piece of swordfish that looked to Sarah like someone's boot heel. "But do me a favor. If on your trips to the barn you see an oddball chain and a nightstick together or separate, give a yell. All right, the next item of the evening," announced Mike, "is Sean Conners."

"He's turned up!" exclaimed Sarah.

"No," said Mike. "Still a missing person. I should have said Sean's accident in the hayloft. It wasn't."

Alex put down his fork. "Not an accident? Someone pushed him?"

"No," said Mike. "Not pushed. A board loosened. We found nails pried. Bent over. Fairly new nails. Not rotten boards. Nobody went over the loft when it happened because it was supposed to be an accident. Before Julia became target numero uno in Knox County. Point is, someone was out for Sean from the start."

"But anyone could have fallen through that hole," said Sarah.

"Wrong," said Mike. "Patrick and Julia don't go up there. Rafe Posner has a thing about heights, and Jessica hadn't started work then. The Sean Conners stuff may not have anything to do with killing Farney, but it's an interesting sidelight."

For a few moments the dinner party proceeded with the matter of eating, each silently considering the possible fate of Sean Conners. Then Sarah decided that cold minerals went better with dinner than either a battered Sean or a strangled Farney. "That nickel mine. Have the police found out which properties Norminco has bought? Or leased? Or where they've been drilling?"

"You kidding?" said Mike. "Those mine corporations are like Swiss bank accounts. No one says nuthin'. No lease details, no sales info, no saying where the deposit starts or ends."

"But with a murder next door?"

"If we can come up with a real connection, not some flabby motivation crap like some people can't stand the idea of all that drilling near their property so they're going to shove Julia out on the street, well, maybe we can pry open Norminco's files. But speaking of mines, has Julia told you that George says there are no signs of core drilling on her land?"

"I suppose," said Sarah, feeling deflated, "that we shouldn't be surprised. It would be hard to sneak around her farm with tons of drilling equipment and keep it a secret. All that noise."

"Do you think," said Alex, "that the mine operation will really go through?"

"Yeah. Yeah I do," said Mike. "I've this gut feeling that the county can't sit on a huge nickel deposit until the end of time. Maybe we won't get a mine by Fallen Tree Pond next month or even next year. Maybe not in ten years, but people use nickel. They use cobalt. They use copper. More and more they use the stuff. You think all those wilderness types are going to give up on refrigeration, telephones, computers, fax machines, stainless-steel gadgets? Electronics? Me, I'm as bad as the rest. A hypocrite. I don't want that damn Norminco across the road from my parents' little three acres, but I want my technological goodies like everyone else. We should all go back to oxcarts and communicating by tom-tom."

"It's so complicated," said Sarah sadly, thinking of their new bathroom, the washing machine and dryer, the heavy-duty electric line going into their renovated house.

"Okay, if you want to feel better go ahead and swallow the Norminco sales pitch, how they want to help, not hurt. Soft talk, smoothy lawyers. Listen to Jim Shale. He's one of the best things Norminco has going for it because he looks and sounds like Jimmy Stewart in *It's a Wonderful Life*. Mr. Rural America."

Alex looked up from the dissection of his beef kabob. "The whole mess is a sort of odd couple. The murder, the attack on Julia's property, those incidents—they're personal. Very focused. Dangerous stuff, but limited to one private farm. And the mine is this great thing spreading like some sort of octopus into everyone's life. The two things don't go together. A huge mining corporation and all its machinations, its spokesmen and lawyers, its lobbying power, and one little old lady in riding boots."

"Motivation, motivation," said Sarah.

"Motivation all by its lonesome," said Mike, "never won a ball game. Go find someone in the act of cutting out letters and pasting cute little messages. Get a search warrant for all the houses along Tri-County Road and look for a recently fired shotgun—which is probably at the bottom of Fallen Tree Pond by now. Or go find a nightstick and a length of chain in that stable or in the Wentworths' Jacuzzi or Harvey Dodge's oven or in Tilly Martin's underwear. Under Camp Merrilark's totem pole. It may lead us to who. Then maybe to why."

But Sarah wasn't listening. She'd put down her fork and had angled her head slightly toward a small table on the other side of the room. A table with a single figure bent over a menu. "I've just seen Mr. Rural America," she said.

"Who?" said Alex.

"Jimmy Stewart. Or his clone. Jim Shale. Same initials, as a matter of fact. I'm going to raid his table."

"Hey, Sarah," said Mike. "Jim Shale has talked to us—we're the police—but he won't to you. Despises the lot of you. He tried to be nice, get to know all the friendly folk along Tri-County Road, and all he got was lip and the back of your hand. My hand. Everyone's hand. Julia threw him out of her house when he'd come to help after Sean hurt himself. He's reported that Brad Pfeifer, of Camp Merrilark, set a collie on him. Only person decent to him was Tilly Martin, and she's gone crazy as a bedbug."

Sarah put down her napkin. "I shall see what an abject apology and a sympathetic ear can do."

"Jim Shale," said Mike, "is no dummy. He'll know you're trying to pump him. Maybe try and lay a murder in Norminco's lap."

"Well, I am going to pump him," said Sarah, rising from the table. "But not tonight. Tonight it's mea culpa. Mea maxima culpa. Sackcloth and ashes."

"Stop her," said Mike to Alex. "We're having this nice intimate dinner."

"I don't stop Sarah. I wait around hoping not to pick up too many pieces. What's the line? 'They also serve who only stand and wait.' "

"I thought that was about faithful dogs."

"Faithful dogs, the poet Milton, and Alexander McKenzie."

But Sarah did not stay long enough in the vicinity of Jim Shale's dinner table to try the patience of a faithful dog. Alex and Mike watched the approach, Jim Shale putting down his napkin and standing politely, Sarah extending her hand, Sarah indicating he should sit down, he refusing—a negative shake of the head—thus making it impossible for Sarah to join him and begin her reach-out program. For several minutes the rear view of Sarah—her tense posture, feet together, hands clasping each other—indicated little progress in the matter of warm conversational give-and-take, and then she was back at her own table.

She pulled up her chair and shook her head. "I struck out."

"We noticed," said Alex.

"After apologizing, me being completely humble, he just stood there waiting for me to leave. Finally I asked if he'd like to come over for drinks tomorrow. For better understanding all around. He said he'd let me know. He certainly wasn't doing his Jimmy Stewart act. More like Clint Eastwood."

"This," said Alex, standing up, "has been a long day's journey into you-know-what. Let's skip coffee and dessert. I'm beat. How about home—or at least the home of the Widow Clancy. And a walk with Patsy and Sarah in the gloaming. Without you, Mike, old buddy."

This proved an acceptable idea and the drive along the Tri-County Road to High Hope Farm was a healing experience. Patsy slumbered peacefully in the rear seat, his head on Sarah's lap. The temperature had fallen into the sixties and the mild southwest wind had switched to cooling northwest. A quarter moon was rising, so Sarah could almost make out the dark blur of the woods against the rim of fields, the shadowy outlines of scattered farmhouses, whose windows showed as little squares of yellow light, and once even the soft shape of an owl cruising low across a meadow.

"Nights like this are pure magic," she said as the car climbed over a rise and swooped down and over a black-as-ink brook that ran under a stone bridge.

No one answered, Mike and Alex both seeming—however

briefly—under a peaceful spell. Sarah let her eyes half close, her mind float, and in this almost dream state she saw them. Saw them without understanding. Campfires. Or watch fires. Each separate fire sparkling, twinkling in the far distance in a long crescent by the western edge of the road. How does it go? she thought sleepily, 'I've seen Him in the watch fires of a hundred circling camps; they have builded Him an altar in the evening dews and damps . . .'

"Jeezus Christ, what'n hell is that?" Mike stamped on the brake, Alex braced himself, and Sarah was jerked awake by the sudden tightening of her seatbelt.

"Fire!" she shouted. "Fires all along the field. Almost by High Hope Farm."

"Not almost," said Alex. "*At* High Hope Farm."

A collective gasp, and Mike gunned his Blazer, wheeled around a curve tires screaming, shot up over the next rise, down, and then Alex let out his breath.

"Okay. Not exactly *at* High Hope Farm—at least not the farmhouse itself. Nor the stables."

"Thank God," said Sarah, who had a horrible image of Aunt Julia burned to a crisp while trying to haul maddened horses out of their stalls.

The fires blazed at intervals, forming something of an irregular curve—Sarah's circling camps—and as the truck careened down the hill past the Wentworth property on the right and up toward the left-hand post-and-rail margins of High Hope Farm, Sarah could now see that the fires marked at intervals the starting section of the cross-country course. The jumps were on fire.

Jump after jump. First, the brush fence, flames and sparks shooting up and blowing in the breeze, then flames licking the length of a fixed log hurdle, then a smaller smoldering grass fire at the foot of a stone wall. A hay wagon jump crackling merrily. And, because the cross-country finish line was close to the starting box, the last three fences of the course were ablaze: barrels arranged as a fence pouring black smoke into the night sky, then a twin fire at an in-and-out, and the last jump, another brush, hissing and sparking.

And in the midst of it all, the fire departments of Knox County. Hoses, running figures, whirling lights. The state police. The town police. The sheriff's department. Two ambulances. And undoubtedly the members of the rescue squad.

And Aunt Julia, Tilly Martin, Jane Zimmer, Neil and Winka Wentworth—these last two rather dressy—had they been having a formal dinner party?—and Colonel Harvey Dodge, rolled sleeves, the tails of his shirt half out—had he been going to bed?—and the Laaka family all in nightdress, Mike's mother with a long gray braid down her back. And running to and fro with buckets and brooms, what appeared to be the entire counselor and senior camper population of camps Merrilark and Highfeather.

Sarah caught up to Harvey Dodge, who was beating with a broom at the flames around the side of the brush jump. She grabbed his arm. "Ambulances," she yelled. "Who's hurt?"

He twisted around, his round face smeared by perspiration mixed with soot. "No one. A precaution. Just in case." And he resumed his beating. The fire on the brush fence seemed to have spent itself and now smoldered and flickered while giving off small popping noises.

Sarah raced back toward the barn and collided with Julia herself. Julia, who was staggering forward with a bucket of water. "Sarah. Thank heavens, we need all the hands we can get. Find a broom, dip it in the water, and start beating the brush around the jumps. We can't have this thing start a ground fire and escape. This damn wind."

"The horses," said Sarah.

"Still all right. No danger. Not yet. No fires near the paddocks or the stable. Thank the dear Lord. But my fences. My jumps. My beautiful cross-country course." And Julia, with a half growl and half sob, plunked the water bucket down and was immediately surrounded by a broom crew. They dipped, soaked a minute, and raced back to the fires. And Sarah did the same, seeing from time to time Patrick, and Patrick's wife, Alex and Mike, Jane Zimmer in constant motion, Winka Wentworth whacking the ground with a broom, Neil pounding by with a filled bucket, and Jim Shale—Jim Shale!—and the others running back and forth in a blackened condition. And all the time the fire hoses from four engines arched their heavy streams over the fires and wove them back and forth, drenching the flames and soaking the ground.

And then it was over. By midnight the Union fire chief said that they'd licked the bugger and the police and arson squad could start sifting through the rubble to see if they could come up with some evidence of why the fire had started.

"Maybe some nutso counselor or kid from one of those summer camps," said a fireman.

"It must have been set," said the chief, one Pete Lurvey, a solid-looking man with a soot-smeared face. "I mean, what the hell, those jumps are way apart. Some joker woulda had to go around to each one and fix it up. Or used a fuse. Must've been set on fire after dark, when everyone is indoors for the night. Didn't see anyone sneaking around tonight, did you, Mrs. Clancy?" This to Julia, who with her broom upright in her hand and her blackened face and smeared shirt looked to Sarah's eyes like some prehistoric female warrior.

"No one. Not tonight," said Julia. "Colonel Dodge had a drink with me before dinner and went home. You could ask him."

"How about after dinner?" prompted Pete Lurvey.

"After dinner—around eight—Jane Zimmer and Tilly Martin came over with some cookies Tilly had made and some radishes from their garden, and the three corgis got loose."

"The what?" said Chief Lurvey.

"Tilly's corgis. Dogs. Herding dogs. It was quite hectic. Tilly must have have left their truck door open. I called the neighbors to be on the lookout and then we all went looking. Patrick finally caught the dogs trying to herd the yearlings in the north paddock—the yearlings stay outside with a run-in shelter."

"Nothing else? No flashlight?" said Chief Lurvey. "No one striking a match? A cigarette butt, a cigar? No one behind trees?"

"No. Patrick and I did night check—hay and water for the horses—and then I went up to my bedroom. I try to get to bed early. I was undressing and then I looked out my bedroom window. I saw the fires. Three fires and then another. By the time I made it to the telephone there were five. By the time I ran outside and met Patrick the whole starting fence sequence and the three finishing jumps were going. But I never saw anyone. It's as if they started by themselves."

"No, they didn't start by themselves," said a voice. Neil Wentworth. Neil, usually so spruce, now smoke-smeared, his white shirt torn from shoulder to waist. He walked up to the chief and held a blackened rag to his face. "Smell that," he demanded. "Paraffin. You call it kerosene. Soaked in kerosene. Winka found it and brought it to me. Julia, someone's out to ruin your cross-country course."

But Chief Lurvey had seized the rag and given a shout. In minutes police with flashlights were circulating about the cross-country fences, shouting, holding up pieces of cloth, collecting them in bags.

Julia, in an infinitely weary voice, said she was going to bed. "Enough is enough. Thank you, Neil. Thank you, Chief. Thank you everyone." She peered into the darkness at the diminished crowd, some still holding their brooms, others beginning to haul buckets back toward the stable.

Sarah and Alex joined her on the trudge to the farmhouse.

"I suppose," said Julia bitterly, "I should hire professional guards."

"For what it's worth, you have an army guarding you now," Sarah reminded her. "The police, Mike Laaka, your neighbors. Harvey Dodge practically lives here, the Wentworths are in and out, and Jane and Tilly are in gear. What more can you do?"

"I know, I know," said Julia. She stood for a moment at the kitchen door, turned and looked back to the policemen, now reduced to tiny specks of moving lights. "Everyone pitched in. That Jim Shale, too. Oh dear, how can I dislike people who are always rescuing me? But you know, this isn't an armed camp. Even with half the neighborhood and the police on watch, anyone can come through the pastures and the woods, even across Crawfish Pond in a boat. It would take the National Guard to patrol sixty acres. Maybe it's our mysterious stranger starting the fires. The one I told you about. The one I thought might be a Medlock boy because I really don't believe in mysterious strangers."

Here Sarah almost leaped into the air. "Good God, look there! You may not believe in them, but look." She pointed along the ridge by the stable, where a shaft of light spread out from the light fixed to the stable roof. A blurred pyramidal shape stood illuminated on a small rise on the west side of the stable. It stood perfectly motionless and then with a sweep of draperies floated off the little hill and disappeared.

"All right," said Alex. "Let's go after it. Now. We might just nail him. Or she or it. Come on. We can slip into the woods very quietly and look around."

"*You* can slip after it," said Julia. "Be my guest. Because I have had it. I'm going to bed. I will get some sleep and then I will plan. I will fortify, recruit, defend, and bear arms. If we have a Canterville ghost or a headless horseman or some vampire on the property, Alex and Sarah, it's all yours. Find it. But don't you or the police disturb the horses or leave the pasture gates open or I will personally nail your scalps to my stable wall." And Julia wrenched open the door to the house and vanished.

"I think she's coming apart," said Sarah. "Not that I blame her. I'm surprised she's even able to walk in a straight line."

"All we need," said Alex grimly, "is Julia stalking about with a shotgun."

"So are you going to sound the general alarm?" asked Sarah. "About that shape person. When Aunt Julia first told me about seeing someone I thought if it wasn't one of the Medlock boys then she was hallucinating. Imagining banshees."

"No general alarm. No search party. Quiet does it. If we alert the police, we'll scare it off. Too many escape hatches on sixty acres. Besides, the police are busy with legitimate work. I'll find Mike Laaka and have a look around. If it's not a local kid going swimming, maybe it's someone looking for a free camp-site. How about it? You want in? We could use Patsy to track."

"I'm not sure Irish wolfhounds track anything but wolves, but take him along. I'm like Julia. I've had it. I'm going to hole up for six solid hours. You take Mike and Patsy and report to me in the morning."

"It seems strange," said Alex thoughtfully, "that I ever once considered the practice of medicine a demanding occupation."

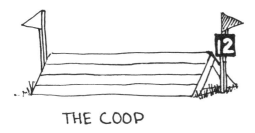

THE COOP

TWELVE

SARAH had pitched into Aunt Julia's four-poster guest room bed like a fallen tree and hadn't moved until morning. Or until Patsy reared up from his cushion on the floor, planted two front paws on the blanket, laid a bearded head on her pillow, and began a vigorous washing of her chin. And then turned his attentions to Alex.

Alex rose protesting out of the bedclothes. "No peace. The great part of our wedding trip was going to be waking up without a tongue on my neck."

"A sign of love," said Sarah. "But what about last night," she went on. "Did Patsy track or pick up a scent?"

"No and yes. No, we didn't find Julia's ghost, but that's not surprising, what with the woods and the big spread of pastures. And it was pretty dark. And yes, Patsy picked up the scent of a large porcupine and it took every ounce of muscle to hold him. He wanted to swallow the thing whole."

"Patsy still needs a little obedience work," said Sarah, smiling down at the gray, whiskered face.

"Patsy," said Alex, "needs marine barracks."

Sarah pushed the dog to the floor and sat up. "Two things. First, I am worried about Julia. She may end up at the psychiatric center with Tilly. Second, have you considered that Sean Conners or Rafe Posner might be our mysterious stranger?"

"Of course. Mike and I talked about it. But why? Unless, of course, one or both are behind the whole destruction and murder scheme. If Farney caught Conners or Rafe doing something nasty and so he had to be eliminated."

"Okay, but why the other accidents? Why that ghastly business with the bridle? That doesn't sound like Sean. He's more the sledgehammer type. And though Rafe is a bit flaky, he never struck me as someone into macabre jokes. Let alone murder."

"Mike says the police are still on alert for both men. New England and beyond. And don't worry too much about Julia's state of mind. She's a female constructed of tough natural fiber. Like All Bran or goat hair. She takes out her misery on the piano and on all comers. Come on, it's past seven. I'll bet Julia is down in the kitchen making someone's life miserable."

This proved an exaggeration. Principally because Julia, looking only slightly worse for wear, was alone at the large round table, papers and notebooks spread wide, a telephone at her elbow. The English setters, Tucker and Belle, were curled by her feet; the orange cat, Charlie, sat on the telephone book and washed his ears by licking first a front paw and then hooking it around the ear in a circular motion. The scene was both purposeful and domestic.

"Command central," said Sarah as they came into the room, Patsy behind them, his nails clicking on the bare wooden floor. The setters raised their heads, snuffed, and lowered them down without interest. Patsy was an old acquaintance.

"You had better believe it," said Julia. "The coffee's over there, the juice is in the fridge, and the muffins are in the oven. I got up at five and made them. You know I always cook something when I'm in a muddle. And everyone has been marvelous about the fire; the phone's been ringing off the hook. Also I have an idea. A plan for you, Sarah."

"I, too, have a plan for myself," said Sarah. "A plan made with considerable gritting of my teeth."

"Not to be outdone, I also have a plan," said Alex. "One that has absolutely nothing to do with High Hope Farm."

"Splendid," said Julia, picking up a pencil and pulling a chart toward her. "Let's hear yours first."

"A simple medical plan," said Alex. "I ran into the doctor who's taking my patients yesterday. He's up to his ears and said that since I didn't seem to be in Nova Scotia, how would I like to do a little part-time labor. See some of my own patients. I said that I was living in an atmosphere of assault, murder, arson, and rampant vandalism, and seeing patients sounded like a rest cure."

"Curiously enough," said Sarah, "that works into my plan."

Julia, who had been making erasures on her chart, looked up. "Having Alex gainfully employed doesn't distress me. Sarah, would you like to speak your piece?"

"As follows," said Sarah. "I'm going to take riding lessons. With great reluctance. Against my better judgment." She waited while Alex settled his eyebrows—Sarah, after a heavy fall last Christmas at a ranch, had often remarked that anyone sitting atop a thousand-pound animal who could be spooked by a fluttering newspaper was expressing a need to end it all. Julia, however, to no one's surprise, nodded her entire approval.

Sarah pointed out the window toward the stable parking lot—this, besides the usual number of horse trailers, was packed with vehicles. "See there," she said. "The police, the homicide people, the arson squad, all making everyone nervous. If we're going to find anything that the police can't because—well, because they're police—we have to be ordinary citizens going about ordinary lives. Aunt Julia isn't ordinary. She's the victim, the target. She and the farm. And if I wandered down to the stable asking questions, I'd be one more snoop. But if I'm a legitimate beginning rider with a schedule of lessons, I'll be part of the woodwork. Especially if I help with the chores. Aunt Julia needs extra hands, so I'm ready to sign on and keep my ears open. I can handle a wheelbarrow and a fork. I know manure when I see it. I can fill a water bucket and pass out hay. Okay, Aunt Julia? Am I hired? Can you use a beginner in one of your classes?"

Julia looked pleased. She reached over and patted her niece's hands and said in the tone of a missionary whose heathen friend has just seen the light, "Well done, Sarah. I'll sign you up. I knew you'd come round. Horses make such a difference. And the exercise will do wonders for you. Your posture, your muscle tone."

"Falling off that horse called Pokey did wonders for me. I was stiff and bruised for a week."

"Never look back," said Julia. "And your plan is my plan for exactly the same reasons. If you work with the stable crew and take lessons, you will be part of the farm. You can listen and look about. We'll start today. Nine o'clock. I'll give you half an hour on the lunge line and then see if you can join the ten o'clock beginners class. Walk, trot. Nothing demanding."

Sarah took a deep breath and exhaled. "So be it."

"And," Julia continued, "as I said, everyone's pitching in. The Maine Combined Training Association has rallied round. We're going to rebuild all the fences, rake over the footing between jumps, and be ready to go as scheduled. Volunteers have called. Highfeather and Merrilark will send counselors and the campers. We'll get to work as soon as the arson squad has finished."

"Great," said Sarah. She walked over to the oven, extracted a tin of muffins, set it on the table on a pot holder, gingerly removed one, and began a careful spreading of strawberry jam.

"What about those rags that were found last night?" said Alex.

"Thank heavens for Neil—though I never thought I'd be saying that," said Julia. "Why, if he hadn't found the rags, whoever set the fires might have picked them all up."

"Unlikely," said Sarah with her mouth full. "Too many firemen and police looking. And besides, Neil said Winka found them."

"So thank heavens for Winka. And even Tilly pitched in, although I've asked myself if Jane can watch Tilly every minute. I've been wondering if Tilly with her delusions isn't up for a spot of arson. The trouble is that I've identified the rags. A few didn't burn completely. They're mine. My rags. I have a basket in the stable filled with old towels to use as rub rags, or to clean tack. All anyone had to do was slip into the stable, grab an armful, and wait until it was almost dark and everyone was indoors. Or wait until we were all racing around in the north pasture chasing after those damned corgis."

"Is your kerosene available for the taking?" asked Sarah.

"The police wanted to know that. I keep kerosene tins in the tool room in the storage barn. Right in plain sight, along with some lanterns. For power outages. And a kerosene tin is certainly missing."

"Go back to Tilly," said Sarah. "Do you seriously think she's organized enough to steal the rags and the kerosene, wait until nighttime, let the corgis out, pack the rags around the jumps, set fire, and move out and rejoin the corgi hunt? Help put out the fire and go back home and fold her hands and read *Majesty*?"

Julia shrugged. "She's piling obsession—or delusion, whatever it is—on top of obsession. This morning she phoned to say she's inviting the Morris Dancers to come in honor of the queen's visit."

Alex put down his coffee cup and pushed away from the table. "Julia," he said. "I think if the Morris Dancers appeared, no one would even notice." He turned to Sarah. "I'm off to the hospital. Listen to your aunt and keep your head up and your heels down."

Alex departed and Julia began pulling on her barn boots, ancient high-laced leather objects. "I've got to go around with the insurance people," she said. "If arson is proved they may not pay me. For all they know I might have set the fire myself. I mean, those rags were *my* towels, the kerosene was probably *my* kerosene."

Sarah was silent for a minute, trying to think of how to word her next suggestion. "Aunt Julia, have you ever seriously tried to sort out the people? Take Winka and Neil Wentworth. They seem very interested in your farm, and Camp Highfeather will certainly be in the soup if the mine goes in. I suppose you could say the same about Camp Merrilark, but they haven't gone public about it. Or take Colonel Dodge."

Julia gave a sort of snorting huff and bounced to her feet. "Harvey! Harvey Dodge? That's impossible. The Wentworths I'll be willing to consider, but I've known Harvey all my life. Are you suggesting that Harvey murdered Farney Thompson, his old faithful friend Farney, just so that I'd be shorthanded and let him move over here?"

"Murderers have killed faithful friends before this," said Sarah stubbornly.

"Pooh. Absolute pooh. Sarah, as an investigator you leave a lot to be desired. Forget about Harvey. He's been my right arm—he and poor Farney—ever since this whole mess started."

And that, Sarah said to herself, as she watched Aunt Julia stamp out of the house, is exactly right. Harvey Dodge had indeed been Julia's right arm since the beginning. Morning, noon, and night, there was Harvey. Sarah peered out the kitchen window and saw two of her suspects walking toward the house. The colonel side by side with Jane Zimmer—Jane, another right arm.

The screen door flapped open and the two helpers came into the room. "Sarah, good," said Harvey Dodge. "We need a pow-wow. Jane and I have been talking. We want to air an idea."

Sarah nodded and reached for the coffeepot. To herself she queried with a sort of sickening rush, So what about both of them? Not supporting the farm, destroying it. In together. Both needing money, both farms run-down. A deadly duo. Aloud she said, "I've just been thinking of you. How helpful you've both been. Julia's right arms. Here's coffee and Julia's muffins."

But coffee with Julia's "two right arms" did nothing to bolster Sarah's suspicions. Both presented themselves as staunch allies against chaos and ruin. With Julia thick and thin. In spite of dungeon, fire, and sword. Practically until death did them part. And well it might, thought Sarah gloomily.

Unable to shake the assertions of faith and loyalty and grave concern, Sarah moved the subject to the Wentworths. And hit pay dirt. Well, if not pay dirt, eager interest and boiling suspicion.

Colonel Dodge, his ruddy round face troubled, said, "Yes, it's the idea we want to share with you. I hate to think ill of my neighbors, a couple who work with young people. But Jane and I have been talking and we feel that Neil lacks, Winka lacks—how can I say it?—openness. I have a sense of things being suppressed. And I never feel I can drop in on them and be sure I'm welcome."

Sarah privately thought that Harvey's propensity for "dropping in" might account for a certain coolness, but she simply turned to Jane and said, "You agree?"

"Yes, in a way," said Jane. "I do feel that Winka's courtesy and Neil's little jokes and remarks are really ways of playing cards close to the chest."

"Playing what cards?" demanded Sarah.

This question opened up a deluge of speculation on the subject of the mine. That Neil and Winka had had their land test-drilled and were now floating the idea that High Hope Farm would be a possible substitute for their own property. "Winka said as much to me last night after the fire," said Jane.

"When Julia's at her most vulnerable," said Colonel Dodge.

"Her farm in shambles," said Jane. "Absolute shambles."

Sarah gathered the coffee cups, agreed that things could be better, and did they have anything else in mind that morning?

"Work," said Jane. "I'm leaving my tractor right here and Patrick and I are going out on the cross-country course. Winka and Neil were here at dawn taking away burned brush and debris. Very helpful, although, as I said, I doubt their motives. I hope the police are keeping an eye on them."

"The local horse people are turning up this noon," said Harvey. "After the insurance men and the police finish. Put the whole course back together. Build new fences."

"I'm surprised Julia isn't canceling," said Jane.

"Well, she isn't," said Sarah. "And the police are letting it go on. Aunt Julia's mad as a hornet and it's full-speed ahead." Then, as the visitors rose to leave, she added that she, Sarah, in spite of previous qualms, was about to embrace a riding career. Or at least a riding experience.

"After all, Alex and I are staying here. I'm on vacation and since all that riding I did in Arizona, well, I thought it might be fun to go on." A blatant lie, she thought, if ever there was one.

But Jane and Harvey Dodge showed no surprise, and even mild approbation because, after all, like Julia, they probably couldn't imagine life sustained without an intimate relation with a horse.

Only five minutes passed between the exit of suspects one and two and the arrival of suspect number three. Neil Wentworth. And such a perfect suspect, Sarah told herself, as she watched his progress toward the porch steps. So smooth, charming, humorous. Weren't these qualities all part of the lethal personality?

Neil stepped through the door. A different Neil, wearing the oldest of faded shirts, mended jeans, worn boots. His red hair, usually sleek and brushed, was on end, his face streaked—as it had been last night—with dust and soot. And because of this obvious work costume and his dirty face he looked disappointingly honest.

But Sarah, ushering him in and offering coffee, reminded herself about appearances.

"Thank God for caffeine," said Neil, displacing the cat Charlie and sinking gratefully down in Julia's wicker chair. "I think we're making progress in spite of the police. They're going through every load of burned stuff as if they expected to find at least five bodies."

"I suppose they have to," said Sarah, pouring herself a second cup and passing the muffins to Neil. All for a good cause, she told herself.

"Julia is amazing," said Neil. "Hanging on like a tiger. I've told you about my Aunt Cecily, haven't I? Another tiger. They don't make women like that anymore. Well, yes, with the women's movement, I suppose they do. Julia Clancys emerging all over the place. Boediceas and Golda Meiers and Emmeline Pankhursts."

"You're good to come over and help," Sarah put in to keep the ball rolling. She had never seen Neil in quite such a relaxed mood.

"Least we could do," said Neil through his muffin.

"We?"

"Winka and I. Winka's out on the tractor now. She loves our tractor. She and Jane Zimmer would make a great tractor team." Here Neil glanced out the window, and as if to check on eavesdroppers lowered his voice and said, "But that's not why I'm here. I know that I'm not supposed to speak ill of my neighbors, but have you wondered about Harvey Dodge? He makes no bones about wanting to marry Julia, never has, but to give up Quartermaster Farm? Doesn't that strike anyone as extremely odd? I like Harvey, he's an old pussycat, though how the U.S. Army put up with him is beyond me. But you know pussycats. They can be rather stealthy. And they often get what they go after. And Jane, do you ever wonder about her? So protective of Tilly. And Appleyard Farm is absolutely on its uppers—I'm sure you know that—and so, I'm afraid, are those two women."

He put down his coffee cup, sighed, and rose to his feet. "Back to work. And Sarah, I'm sorry about yesterday at tea. Mentioning our interest in Julia's farm. Winka insisted I say something. Told her it was pretty tasteless, but when Winka digs her feet in, she's hard to resist. And you know all our efforts on the cross-country course are to help Julia. Only Julia."

Here he looked seriously at Sarah, and then getting only a frown as a reply, said, "I don't blame you. At tea yesterday. Rotten manners. But I did promise Winka." He paused, then shrugged. "No excuse. Sorry." And Neil turned and departed.

Sarah allowed herself a few moments' irritation. By Neil saying he felt their remarks about the farm inappropriate he had raised the subject again. Put it back on the table. But then he had seemed quite human. Genuinely embarrassed. What was he up to? Sarah rose from the table with no intention of removing the Wentworth name from her roster of suspects. Time for the riding lesson, the chores. And, after lunch, a visit to Camp Merrilark, where she would undoubtedly be adding the name of her old camp director, Mrs. Pfeifer, plus the nephew, Brad, to her list.

Dressed in her oldest jeans and a pair of laced work boots, Sarah presented herself for the nine o'clock lunge-line lesson. At ten o'clock she joined three twelve-year-old girls, Beth, Becky, and Louisa, for an hour of trotting torture while Julia bellowed "Up down, up down, watch your hands, sit up straight, watch your heels." Then at eleven in a state of soreness unparalleled, she crept down from the saddle and reported to her cousin Jessica for a lesson in stall cleaning.

Two hours later, the proper use of the manure fork, the loading of the wheelbarrow, the shoveling and distributing of sawdust having been practiced, Sarah reported back to the farmhouse kitchen for a late lunch with Julia and the returned Alex.

"Aunt Julia, I'm almost wiped out. How do you all do it? I won't have the strength to look around or ask questions. At least not today. Besides, I'm sure Patrick and Jessica think I'm a spy."

Julia approached with a ladle and a bowl. "Fish chowder. I had it frozen. Alex, yes, go right ahead and read *The Boston Globe*. It's filled with Red Sox news. And Sarah, of course someone will think you're a spy, but work hard, do extra stalls, clean tack, and you'll fit in. It will help if you fall off a few times during lessons."

"I will. It's just a question of how many times. So what's on for this afternoon? After our Camp Merrilark visit."

"The insurance people are pretty well finished. Arson is certain. Payment will be held up since I have to establish innocence. So do you and all of us, the High Hope Farm staff. And our neighbors."

"Speaking of neighbors," said Sarah, "I talked to Jane and Harvey this morning. They zeroed in on the Wentworths."

Alex looked up from the sports section. "For arson? For murder?"

"A general suspicion. Because of the mine and their interest in High Hope Farm. And as soon as they left in came Neil Wentworth to say he's suspicious of Jane and Harvey. For a while I thought he was quite human, but the feeling has passed off. He talked about Winka. Said she drives a mean tractor."

"Yes, and so does Jane. So do I. And I like Winka better on a tractor than off. They'll both work with Patrick on the course this week. And no one's found signs of our ghost. Patrick says it probably *was* one of the Medlocks. Or the Wilcox boy. The Wilcox boy is a little funny in the head and he likes to camp out in my woods and fish Crawfish Pond."

"Too many people around here are funny in the head," complained Sarah. "Sean Conners had a concussion, Rafe Posner's a flake, Tilly's weird, and now the Wilcox boy."

"Even thee and me," said Julia. "So off you go, and say hello to Leah Pfeifer for me. We were campers together. Green poplin bloomers and middy blouses. And now I see the farrier's truck has just driven in. Farm life goes on despite. We're having the horses trimmed and shod today."

After Julia had departed, Alex lifted his head from the sports section. "Must I visit Camp Merrilark?"

"I think we should go together, pool our impressions. Listen, I went to Merrilark, so did my mother, so did Aunt Julia. I'll chat up Mrs. Pfeifer. You be the chorus. Look around. Gather vibes."

Alex made the sound of a person in pain. "All right, we'll go and annoy more busy people, but we'll probably find George Fitts already there sitting at the camp fire skewering counselors and roasting the directors."

But Sarah was not listening. "I'll say I'm looking for a niece this time. And stop glowering. I don't want you scaring poor Mrs. Pfeifer. She was my camp director. And she was at our wedding reception, for God's sake."

"Sarah, I don't scare elderly women,"

"I know. Some of your best friends are women."

"My wife is one. And so are a large number of my patients."

"Probably because the women physicians' practices are full."

"Sarah, are you trying to have a fight? Because I'm not. Look, we're both on edge. No vacation, this damn business. I'll keep my lip buttoned and try not to glower, and I'll leave Mrs. Pfeifer to your tender mercies. Okay?"

"Okay," said Sarah, reaching for his hand. "Sorry. I'm over-reacting to everything. Maybe it's that riding lesson. Now, to coin an expression, let's hoof it out of here."

THE COFFIN

THIRTEEN

THE main entrances to Camp Merrilark, as well as to Camp Highfeather, lay almost directly across from High Hope Farm. Alex drove with caution down the sandy road that led to the fork dividing the properties of the two camps. Here a sign lettered in green paint announced Merrilark to the left; another in red indicated Highfeather branching to the right. Alex swung the Bronco to the left and continued jouncing down the road until the waters of Fallen Tree Pond came into sight beyond a row of white pines and a scattering of log buildings and tent tops.

Leaving their car in the camp lot they made their way toward a log building, which Sarah identified as the Merrilark Lodge. "Marvelous. It hasn't changed. Makes me feel about thirteen."

Alex slowed his steps. "What's our cover?"

"Our niece, Abigail. She'll be nine and collects lizards. Just like our nephew, Cooper. They're a lot alike."

At which a young man emerged from the lodge and introduced himself. Brad Pfeifer. He had a turned-up nose, freckles, a buzz haircut, and an impressive width of shoulder and depth of chest. He produced a catalog, hustled them forward and began pointing out the camp features.

Sarah having said that her niece, Abigail, was crazy about lizards, the emphasis of the tour was on wildlife, and the visitors were led through the nature hut and examined a pet salamander, a hornets' nest, and a cage with a dour-looking guinea pig. Then Sarah, thinking she had done enough in the role of a concerned aunt, pushed the subject of the Norminco mine into the arena.

Brad Pfeifer's cheerful face clouded.

"You must be anxious," said Sarah. "Your lovely waterfront. These woods. Such a marvelous natural setting."

At which Alex went to town. Recalled his own camp days. Talked about a boy's memories, what havoc would be played if the lake—Merrilark's own Fallen Tree Pond—was turned into a dredging pit. A mine with shafts and blastings. Piles of tailings. Wildlife frightened. Loons killed. No more Merrilark—or Highfeather—to shape children, give them lasting values.

And Brad Pfeifer melted like warm cheese. For a minute he looked out over the gray-blue shimmer of Fallen Tree Pond. Then he thumped his fist down on the guardrail—they were sitting in a row of wooden rockers that overlooked the waterfront—and almost shook with anger. His jaw thrust out, his faced seemed to darken, his brow bent, and Sarah could almost hear his teeth grind.

"We'll do something. We *are* doing something. We have a plan. Can't talk about it, but believe you me we're not going to let the Merrilark family down. You know that Mrs. Pfeifer is my aunt. Aunt Leah. I'm very fond of her and I've promised that Merrilark will go on."

Sarah and Alex both commended Brad for his strong-mindedness, Sarah adding that her Aunt Julia was also worried. And much harried. The murder, the fire. She wondered if Norminco might be behind the continuing events at her farm.

"Don't doubt it," said Brad Pfeifer. "Poor Julia Clancy, such a good neighbor. We'd be sorry to see her leave, but, of course, her age is against her. Norminco is the Evil Empire. The spoiler."

"Your whole way of life," said Sarah. "All your traditions."

"We laid it on a bit thick," said Alex, when after a heartfelt handshake they started toward Leah Pfeifer's office.

"Brad Pfeifer is beyond sense," said Sarah. "He's absolutely furious. So I've added suspect number four—or is it five?—to my list. He's going to do something. Or has done it. He has a plan. And he's another person who thinks Julia might hang it up."

"His plan may just be a petition to the town hall."

"Take a look at him. He's a physical type, built like a tank. No petitions for Brad Pfeifer. I'll bet on direct action. And I'll bet he might want to relocate. Say he thinks the mine has a fair chance of going through—why not plan ahead and move the camp across the road? Gobble up High Hope Farm. And he says what everyone's saying: She's too old to manage a big farm operation by herself. So if her helpers are knocked off, the place is vandalized, voilà. Brad and his aunt walk in and buy High Hope. Having sold out to Norminco. Maybe they're working with the Wentworths and Highfeather. A joint camp effort. I'll have to have a serious look at Aunt Julia's beach on Crawfish Pond. I remember going down to her shore and swimming when I was little. Mike said it would make a good camp site, didn't he?"

"You've got it all added up, haven't you?"

"So far all my suspects are neck and neck. Except Tilly. I don't see Tilly sustaining such a thorough system of destruction."

"I agree. Tilly is under the direct control of Aries under Scorpio and the dictates of the House of Windsor. Okay, let's go and fit your noose around Leah Pfeifer's neck."

Arrived at the log cabin office of Camp Merrilark they were warmly welcomed by the elderly woman sitting at a rolltop desk.

Mrs. Pfeifer, the director of Camp Merrilark, was, like Julia Clancy, in her late sixties but leaner, sparer, taller, with her still-brown hair in a knot at the back of her neck. She wore a sort of compromise camp costume of a green cotton divided skirt, a white blouse with the black tie of a senior counselor, and a pair of sporty white Reeboks. Sarah she welcomed, remembered her as having been hopeless at archery, and grew sentimental about the appearance of one of her old campers. A camper whose wedding reception she had just attended.

"I'm so sorry, Sarah dear, that I had to leave so soon, even before the cake was cut, though Julia saved me a piece. Camp duties, you know."

The visit was a short one, Leah Pfeifer being much occupied with dealing with three homesick twelve-year-olds—"The older the camper, the worse the homesickness," she announced.

After saying good-bye and climbing the path back to the parking lot, Sarah remarked that from an investigatory point of view this last visit was hardly an unqualified success. Mrs. Eff, as she was affectionately called by fond old campers—and "that effing Mrs. Eff" by some not so fond counselors—had been hard to divert. The director kept returning to old times, old girls, and how night air could contribute to useful lives (Merrilark clung to the use of tents). The mention of the Norminco mine had brought pursed lips, reference to her nephew Brad, and the mention of her lawyer.

"Are you going to fight it in court, Mrs. Eff?" asked Sarah.

"Certainly I am," said Leah Pfeifer. "In and out of court."

"Aunt Julia's worried, too," Sarah had pointed out.

"Well she might. I'm putting myself into the hands of Providence. And my lawyer. Never you mind, Sarah dear. Merrilark will survive. Brad and I are determined. And now, I have to meet with the waterfront counselors. About our new windsurfing boards this year. Unsafe in my opinion, but we must move with the times. Give Julia my love. We'll be seeing her Friday. The two camps are joining in an orienteering session on her property. Because of the compasses."

"What did she mean about compasses?" asked Sarah as they drove back to High Hope Farm.

"Orienteering. It's sort of an exercise in finding your way according to compass directions," said Alex.

"I'll ask Aunt Julia later," said Sarah. "And," she added as Alex swung the Bronco into the driveway of High Hope Farm, "now it's back to work. Toil and trouble." She climbed down and made her way reluctantly to the stable, back to dirty water buckets, bales of hay, and large and frightening horses.

Sarah's assignment in the stable did nothing for her sense of well-being. With every joint protesting, she wobbled about with water buckets, separating bales of hay into package-sized flakes ready for stall distribution and collecting dirty saddle pads for the laundry. All these duties were made more difficult by the presence of horses standing in the stable aisles on cross-ties. The farrier was still at work, and some of the horses seemed to resent his attentions in the matter of rasping, trimming, nailing, and clenching. This resentment took the form of pawing the ground, breaking the restraining cross-ties, and in some cases of backing and rearing.

Now the farrier, one Tim Fournier, was trying to calm Julia's large bay gelding, Plum Duff—known as Duffie—and as Duffie yanked his head about and pawed, Tim stopped Sarah as she scuttled by with an empty bucket. He needed a hand. Sarah's hand.

"I'll have to get a twitch on this guy," he said. "You can hold it for me. Duffie's being a monster."

"Twitch?" said Sarah. "I'm new here. What's a twitch?"

"Never mind. Just hold the thing and don't let go." With that Tim picked up an implement that looked to Sarah's eyes like an object from a medieval torture chamber: a smooth heavy wooden rod with a metal band and chain at one end. This chain Tim took and slipped over the soft velvet nose of Duffie and twisted suddenly until part of the muzzle was bunched and circled by the chain like a large piece of bubble gum. Keeping the chain taut, he handed the stick end to Sarah. "Don't loosen up, okay? Don't let go."

"But," spluttered Sarah, "doesn't it hurt?"

"Not if he keeps still," said Tim cheerfully. "That's the point.

He stands still and it doesn't hurt. Good work," this as Sarah turned the chain, keeping it tight.

"How horrible," she exclaimed.

"Hell, you *are* new. We always twitch the bad actors. You don't want to get stepped on, do you? Or kicked?"

"No," said Sarah with feeling, "I do not."

"So hang in there," said Tim, running his hand down Duffie's foreleg, lifting the hoof and examining the metal horseshoe preparatory to its removal.

And Sarah hung on, perspiration running down the sides of her face, Duffie rolling his eyes, Tim in his leather apron working away with rasp and hammer and shoe.

And then, her first spasms of revulsion receding, Sarah looked at the object in her hands. A stick. A wooden stick, rounded and smooth like a policeman's nightstick. A truncheon. With a metal band at one end. And a chain. A chain fastened to the end of the stick. A twitch. Something presumably no well-run stable was without. What had Mike said: Go find a nightstick and a length of chain in that stable and it may lead us to the who. Maybe the why.

Sarah, more and more agitated, her hands sweating, managed to survive what seemed the endless process of pulling Duffie's old shoe, inspecting the state of Duffie's hoof and frog, paring the sole, trimming the hoof, rasping it smooth, sizing and fitting the new shoe, hammering the nails into the hoof, and finally clenching the nails.

And throughout the procedure, Sarah, gripping the end of the twitch for dear life, saw in an inward eye the approach from the rear to Farney Thompson, the twitch upraised, the heavy hardwood handle, metal end up, coming down on Farney's skull, Farney slumping to the ground, the twitch dropped. Kicked perhaps into some corner until it could be cleaned and put back. Then Farney strangled with the curb rein—this taken in advance of the attack and kept, perhaps, in the pocket of the murderer. Farney, now dead, being dragged quickly into the little annex room. Farney propped in the corner, and for that extra touch, Farney fitted with the pony bridle. Then the twitch retrieved, wiped clean with some handy sponge or cloth, the cloth or sponge pocketed or hidden. Stuffed into the trash bin, the daily manure pile, anywhere. The twitch then replaced. Then the guest—for surely the murderer was an invited reception guest—making haste back to scenes of celebration: champagne, dancing, general postnuptial merriment.

"Hey," said Tim's voice. "I said you can let go. Are you trying to paralyze Duffie's nose? And thanks. When you concentrate on a thing you really concentrate."

And Sarah, recalled to present time, blinked and released the chain; Duffie stamped, shook his great head, and was led off down the stable aisle.

By the time Tim had returned from putting Duffie away in his stall, Sarah had regrouped.

She held up the twitch. "Is it always here in the stable? Available?"

"Huh, what'd ya mean, *available?* Sure it's available." Tim grinned. "Is there something you want to twitch? Twitching turns you on, maybe?"

"No," said Sarah. "I just want to know where it's been all this time. I've never seen it before. Because I'm new here," she ended lamely, "and I have to know where everything is kept."

"You mean someone's been asking for the twitch?" said Tim in a regretful voice. "Okay, I might've known. My fault. Trouble is last time I used the thing I stowed it accidentally with the rest of my gear, hauled it off in my truck. Kept meaning to drop the twitch off and forgetting. I've had a lot of farm calls up the line, Lincolnville, Montville, Augusta, around up there, and I didn't get back this way until today."

"So you've had it all this time," said Sarah.

Tim nodded. "Like I said. When I got the call from High Hope Farm, I said, jeezus, that damn twitch. And I knew I probably had to twitch Duffie, so I'd remember to leave it here this time."

"When was it? What day," said Sarah slowly and clearly, "did you use the twitch at this farm? What day did you take it away with you by mistake?"

Tim, who had begun putting away the assorted tools of his

trade into their carrying box, looked up. "Hey, does it matter? It's back, isn't it? Come on, a big place like this must have twitches by the dozen." He picked up the box by its handle and straightened. "Anyway, thanks for your help."

"Wait up just a minute," said Sarah. "You see, because of what's been going on, with the police searching . . ." She fumbled forward, her hesitancy a direct function of the sure knowledge that Tim's immediate future was most certainly going to be messed up by the likes of George Fitts and Mike Laaka. "Farney Thompson's murder," she finished. "The police have been checking all the stable equipment, but I don't think they knew about this twitch. Or found one that looks like this."

Sarah lifted her hand, a hand the fingers of which were still fastened tight around the smooth wooden handle.

But Tim, not following where Sarah was trying to take him, still frowned. After all, a twitch, or a rasp or pliers—any of the usual stable tools—hardly fitted his idea of lethal weapons. But Farney's murder he did remember.

"Yeah, that was terrible," said Tim. "I've known Farney Thompson for years. I do all Colonel Dodge's horses. Farney was a hell of a nice guy. Damn shame. Some psycho musta got at him, because Farney wouldn't hurt a flea. Yeah, we had our differences. Farney never trusted me to shoe the colonel's horses without him hanging over my shoulder. We'd argue like hell sometimes. But he was a pretty square guy. Hard to think someone'd come along and do that to him."

"Listen," said Sarah a little desperately. "Can you hang in here for a while? I think someone's going to want to talk to you."

"About me taking the twitch? For Chrissake, I brought it back, didn't I? It was an accident. Haven't you ever walked away with something without meaning to? You've got twitches on the brain if you don't mind my saying so. And I can't hang around. Jane Zimmer's old mare's cast a shoe. I should be there now." And Tim strode off toward the side stable door, pushed it open, and disappeared.

And Sarah let him. After all, for the next hour he'd be within reach at Appleyard Farm. With a shudder of distaste, Sarah dropped the twitch on a heap of empty feedsacks and went to wash her hands. Wash them of the sweat and dirt from twisting Duffie's nose and, in a larger sense, like Lady Macbeth, wash off the invisible but still imaginable blood, the bits of hair, the microscopic shreds of skin.

Then, wrapping a paper towel around the twitch, holding it away from her body, Sarah walked up to the farmhouse kitchen door. And saw George Fitts's car parked next to Julia's Ford pickup.

She stopped dead. She wasn't ready for George. Not yet. She needed time. Ten minutes. Ten minutes off. Ten minutes for being outside on a beautiful late June afternoon. Ten minutes for being away from strangling and bashing the skull of good kind Farney Thompson with the handle of a twitch.

Carefully she laid the twitch in its paper towel wrapping by the side of the kitchen steps. Then she turned on her heel and strode fast, taking big steps, taking deep breaths, around to the back of the farmhouse. She climbed over the post-and-rail fence that surrounded the north pasture and up a small central knoll and sat down on an outcropping of granite at the top of the rise.

Yes, it was a beautiful time of day. A soft west wind, wisps of clouds, the sun low in the sky. Sarah wrapped her arms around her knees and tried to take in the whole stretched-out scene. See it. Taste it. Smell it. Store it all up as an anodyne to all the busy ugly things that would follow.

Ten minutes. She turned her head, taking in her immediate circle. The hawkweed was out: little yellow and red tops on thin stems stuck up out of clumps of grass and clover not yet cropped by the horses. And bunches of field daisies, their heads bobbing in the moving air. And beyond, on the road side of the fence, the pink and white and purple of wild phlox, the flat white yarrow, and tiny yellow dots of buttercups. In the middle distance moved the yearlings, brown, gray, bay, roan, heads down, nibbling, munching, tails swishing. Ahead to the north, almost a quarter mile beyond, stretched the long stone wall and fence that led to Patrick's house, the line of apple trees now in full leaf. And around to the west, below the dark lines of the wood, a glossy dark slice of water—Crawfish Pond.

Seven minutes, six, five, four, going, going, gone. One more big breath and on your feet. Up and at 'em. Act III. Aunt Julia, Alex. The new star, Tim Fournier. And George Fitts, maybe Mike Laaka, and God knew how many other disturbers of domestic comfort. Well, she was ready. Ten minutes of peace was worth a lot.

Sarah collected the wrapped twitch and holding it in front of her like a baton made her way into the kitchen. A conference. Around the table sat Aunt Julia, George Fitts with a notebook and a sheaf of printouts in front of him. And Alex. Alex obviously fresh from the shower, hair slicked back, a clean shirt, a bottle of Heineken in one hand. And Sarah, dropping the twitch to one side, was suddenly aware that she was filthy. Hair, hands, jeans, boots, a mess of dirt, hay wisps, standing there in a cloud of horse odor making her feel like the original Pig Pen.

"Sarah, you're a perfect fright," observed Julia, looking over her glasses. "Never mind. Sit down. George wants to bring us up to date. The wedding guests. What the police know so far."

Sarah pushed her damp hair from her forehead and scowled at her aunt. "I'm filthy in your service, my dear aunt. I'll wash my hands and face at the sink and join you. And George, you'll have to put up with me, because I've found something."

"All in good time," said Julia. "George has the floor."

"I'll get you a beer," said Alex, pushing away from the table. "Or iced tea."

"Iced tea, please," said Sarah. She walked to the sink, busied herself with soap, water, and towel, and returned to the table. She lifted the twitch in its wrapping, laid it with a thunk on George's notebook, and opened the paper towel. "George may have the floor," she said, "but I have a significant item. It's a twitch and it's been hiding out with Tim Fournier, the farrier. It's made of smooth wood, it has a chain and a metal band at one end, and it looks very much like a policeman's nightstick. And Tim right now is over at Tilly and Jane's shoeing a horse."

George took one hard look at the object before him and rose to his feet, strode to the telephone, dialed, asked for Tim, and put a single question to him. That single question was followed by a demand for his immediate presence in Julia Clancy's kitchen. Then he returned to the table, pushed the twitch in its wrapper to one side. "Tim Fournier," said George, "used the twitch the evening of the wedding reception and took it away by mistake—or intention—at that time. He returned it today. Mrs. Clancy, how many of these twitches do you have in your stable?"

Julia frowned, bit her lower lip, and considered. "I used to have three, but one disappeared years ago. So I have two left."

"Two!" exclaimed Sarah. "But the police searched all over for something like a nightstick. A wooden handle with a chain. They didn't find anything. Did the murderer take away the other one?"

"It's possible," said George. He turned to Julia. "Didn't you notice that two twitches were missing?"

"But they're not," said Julia. "Patrick used a twitch three days ago. On Ghengis. We were clipping him and he was misbehaving. But it was the other twitch."

"Other?" said George.

"The all-metal one, aluminum. It's a different shape at the top, like a triangle. With a double metal handle and a nylon line that wraps around it. It's the same principle; you fasten the horse's muzzle between the two metal poles and . . ."

But George was no longer listening. "You mean it isn't a wooden stick?"

"I'm trying to tell you," said Julia. "It's a different model. Not wood. No chain. It's kept in the storage barn."

"Good," said George, slapping his hand on his notebook, a gesture showing almost more emotion than the company had ever seen from him. "Then this twitch right here fits the bill. Completely. Sarah, thank you. You did keep your eyes open."

"Praise from George," murmured Sarah.

But George Fitts was not one to linger exchanging courtesies. "I'll call Forensics to pick it up. Even after all this time there's probably some residue the lab can pick up."

"But it's been used and wiped clean and handled by Tim and me and was mixed in with all Tim's tools," said Sarah.

"You'd be surprised what a good forensic lab can find," said George. "You might think the wooden handle is smooth, but there will be minute fissures, catchall places for blood cells, strands of hair, skin particles. And it's hard to clean a chain. Okay, while we wait for the farrier I'll give you all a rundown on the wedding guests and other people we've pretty much eliminated."

Alex put down his bottle of beer and looked at George. "Other people? Like the bride and groom and their nearest and dearest," suggested Alex.

"Certainly not," said George. "I said wedding guests."

Sarah eyed the sergeant with disgust. "George Fitts, do you mean after all this time—how many years is it?—that you can't eliminate Alex and Aunt Julia and me and our family? Come on, be real. Sometimes I think you swim around in a crime think tank and haven't the faintest idea of what everyday people do. That we get up in the morning and go to work and eat meals and go to bed and make love not war and never bash someone on the head or pull out a gun and blow someone away. Or strangle a friend with a pair of reins."

"I'm not suggesting that you or your family have taken to murder," said George mildly. "But I think that some of you may know more than you've told me. That you know some things you don't remember now or don't think are pertinent. That some of you have decided by yourself what's important and what isn't. I want it all. Every detail. The wedding reception and daily life. For instance, where were you today? I called the farm and one of my men said you and Alex had gone off down toward the two camps."

"We visited Merrilark," said Sarah. "I used to go there."

"Are you thinking of signing on again?" asked George. "Or did you decide to visit because you think that Brad Pfeifer and Mrs. Pfeifer have very good reasons for moving Aunt Julia elsewhere. And you thought you'd just see what they thought about the mine . . ."

Sarah looked at Alex, then at George. "That was," she admitted, "the general idea. Because I think that they'd both feel a lot easier with us than with you. The same goes for Camp Highfeather and the Wentworths."

"I grant your point," said George in a disapproving voice, "but please leave that sort of work to the police. I told you to keep your eyes open. And ears. Not to take to the field. The police aren't as stupid as you think. We all see that High Hope Farm and its Crawfish Pond frontage would make a fine summer camp. Or even two summer camps." George smiled his icy smile and spread out a sheaf of papers. "First, your wedding reception guests," he said.

Sarah, still smarting from being treated as a sort of junior Nancy Drew, closed her mouth tight, resolving not to say another word. Serve George right if she snatched the twitch away and gave it to some more deserving member of the force. She looked over at Alex, but he just gave a resigned lift of his shoulders. In fact, only Aunt Julia seemed interested in finding out which of the reception guests had been eliminated. She reached for the top sheet of names and had it removed quickly from her fingers by George. "Just listen," he said. "We've checked out everyone, including the out-of-town guests. Cleared the deck. Fortunately the guests tend to cross-reference themselves and account for each other. Most of them were at the cutting of the cake and the rice throwing and can vouch for quite a few of the others. The real mavericks—apart from Julia Clancy's immediate neighbors—are Giddy Lester—Alex's cousin—and someone called Edward Kemp."

"Who?" said Sarah, speaking in spite of her resolve.

"Edward Kemp. He's called the Gorilla. Apparently Mr. Kemp spent some time in the kitchen helping himself to trays of food and a six-pack of beer and the rest of the time chasing after Andrea Elder, the girlfriend of Tony Deane, Sarah's brother."

Alex looked up, interested. "Did the Gorilla catch Andrea?"

"No, Tony caught him. Sometime after Sarah and Alex had left for their trip. The two men had a fight in the storage barn behind the stable and Tony ended with a cut lip and Mr. Kemp with a slight concussion. Mr. Kemp passed out after that and remembers nothing until later—well after eight o'clock. Giddy found him under a bush and took him away in her car to the emergency room. He was evaluated, kept overnight, and then discharged. He does say—and this is interesting—that before he had the fight with Tony he saw a figure wrapped in a sort of sheet or blanket standing on a ridge in the west pasture. Of course, Mr. Kemp had been drinking, so it's quite possible he was literally seeing things. But he was quite specific. The figure in the sheet—it appeared to be a dark material—began walking to the south toward the woods. He says in his deposition he thought it was one of the guests in costume. Or from a religious group. Or Batman. He's not sure which."

"My ghost!" exclaimed Julia.

"The apparition," said Sarah. "After the fire. Standing there in a blanket."

"The one we didn't catch," said Alex.

THE HAY BALES

FOURTEEN

GEORGE Fitts made a threatening noise in his throat. "You see," he said. "You are holding out. Not one of you has mentioned apparitions or ghosts or someone in a blanket."

"Mike knew," said Alex. "I thought he'd tell you. We tried to chase it down, but it was too dark and we never saw it again."

"Patrick thought it was one of the Medlocks or the Wilcox boy camping out on my land," said Julia.

"Mike," said George, "sometimes forgets who he's working for. How many times have you seen this thing, Mrs. Clancy?"

"Only twice," said Julia. "Just a glimpse. But you know that some of the neighbors—the young boys, girls—do go down through the woods to fish or swim. Or have parties. I've found beer cans and remains of fires. I can't keep sixty acres untouched."

But George was not deflected. "What we have here," he said severely, "is a wild card. An unidentified person who seems interested in what's going on at the farm."

"Who wouldn't be interested?" put in Sarah. "It's been the wild west and an inner city rolled into one."

"Mrs. Clancy," said George, "are you missing anything from your stable? Or your farmhouse? A blanket, for instance?"

Julia bent her head, reached down for Charlie, lifted him to her lap, and began stroking along his spine. Then she raised her head and her face wore the expression of someone seeing a great light. "Yes, yes, of course. My stable blankets, the wool coolers. Rain sheets. A bucket and a shovel. I was complaining to Sarah."

"How about food?" said George.

"I don't know about food. With the wedding reception and everyone in and out and people eating at all hours of the day, well, I wouldn't have the slightest idea whether any food is missing."

For a minute George wrote in his notebook and then snapped it closed. "So," he said, "we have a person, or persons unknown, camping on your property. Or going through it. Possibly lifting equipment. Well, do any of you think the figure resembled either Sean Conners or Rafe Posner?"

But Julia, Sarah, and Alex shook their heads together. It had been too far away. The sighting too brief. The light too poor.

"It could have been anyone," said Sarah. "But not a child. It was fairly tall. Taller than I am."

Julia and Alex agreed, and Julia added that the Medlocks and the Wilcox boy, all above average height, had been using her property for years. "Not taking any blankets, as far as I know."

"That leaves out Tilly and Jane," said Sarah. "They're both quite short. And so is Mrs. Pfeifer and Mike's mother and father. But everyone else seems to fit."

"Including Sean and Rafe Posner," finished Alex.

"We'll go through the woods again," said George. "But the next time anyone sees a ghost, tell me. Not just Mike Laaka. *Me.*"

After another iron look at the group around the table, George picked out a second sheet from the paper collection on the table. "I haven't finished with Alex's cousin, Giddy Lester. Apparently there was another confrontation. Shortly after the cake cutting."

"Giddy's pretty outspoken," Alex put in.

"Then she met her match," said George. "Miss Lester said she went looking for the Gorilla—Edward Kemp—after the cake was cut and thought he might be down at the stable. It seems Mr. Kemp likes animals. The cake was cut at about five-twenty-five, which puts Giddy down at the stable at about quarter of six or so. There she saw Farney Thompson alive and well, brushing one of the horses."

"The confrontation?" Sarah said.

"It was with Mrs. Wentworth. She was urging guests to leave the stable. Not to pat the horses, not to offer them hay or lumps of sugar because someone might be hurt, that she was familiar with the stable because she taught campers at the High Hope facility."

"That's right," said Julia. "Winka and Neil both help teach the Highfeather and Merrilark campers."

"Was she out of line in sending people away from the stable?"

"No," said Julia. "That was proper. I didn't need a group of champagne-filled guests wandering around opening stall doors, having their feet stepped on, letting horses out. I'm surprised Farney and Patrick hadn't cleared the place themselves."

"Giddy Lester said that both men backed up Mrs. Wentworth. Patrick was measuring grain for the evening feedings, and he's told us Farney then went out into the arena to close the doors for the night and afterward left for the north pastures to check on the mares and foals. Miss Lester apparently told Mrs. Wentworth that she was in the stable looking for a friend and that she was more or less a member of the family. Mrs. Wentworth told her that, no matter, she should leave the stable and return to the reception. They had quite an argument and Mrs. Wentworth left in a temper. Walked off in the direction of the farm house and tent."

"Oh," said Sarah, who had just begun to see a noose being drawn about Winks Wentworth's beautiful neck and now felt she must add Alex's cousin, Giddy, to her list.

George, however, disposed of Giddy. "Miss Lester said she left the stable right after Mrs. Wentworth, joined several guests at the reception just before six o'clock, and started asking about Mr. Kemp. Guests confirm both the argument and Giddy's return."

"Did they confirm Winka Wentworth's return?" demanded Julia.

"She was seen in the tent at about six o'clock. Unfortunately, Alex and Sarah left the reception a little after six so we have all that going-away confusion with a crowd and the rice throwing. No certain confirmation for Mrs. Wentworth, Jane Zimmer, Tilly Martin, and Brad Pfeifer for the period just after six to about six-forty. Nor for Rafe Posner. However, Mrs. Clancy says she thinks she saw Neil Wentworth coming out of a lavatory after the rice-throwing."

"Which leaves Farney Thompson out in a pasture," said Alex.

"He obviously returned to the stable, but was never seen alive again," said George. "Patrick had finished his chores, left the stable, and returned to the reception in time to see Sarah and Alex drive off. He didn't go back to the stable. The reception was still in full swing. After all, June eighteenth was close to the longest day in the year and it was still light."

Julia looked apologetic. "And I forgot to tell you that the farrier had come that evening. Horses lose shoes all the time. It's just routine."

George removed his glasses, wiped the lenses with care, replaced them, and shook his head with regret. "One more thing no one has bothered to mention. This farrier, this Tim Fournier."

At which a knock on the door produced Tim Fournier himself. The farrier, looming large at the door, looked apologetically at his hands and at Julia. "I came right away," he said. "Soon as I finished that old mare of Jane Zimmer's."

"Never mind, Tim," said Julia. "Sarah's just as filthy as you are. Wash at the sink and come and sit down and I'll get you some coffee. Or a beer. Or anything. What would you like?"

Tim allowed that a beer would be welcome, and George

opened his notebook and fixed Tim with the George Fitts look. "When were you last doing a job at this farm?"

"Like I've said to Sarah here, it was a couple of days ago. Just checked my schedule. June eighteenth. Big wedding affair going on up at the house. I guess I got here some time after seven-thirty."

"And that's the evening you took the twitch away."

"Said it was a mistake. Just packed it away with my things."

"Was it clean?" demanded George.

Tim accepted his beer from Alex, took a long drink, touched his mouth with the back of his hand, and scowled at George. "The twitch? Sure it was clean. I mean, as clean as it ever is, which isn't saying much. I mean, it gets used a lot. The chain seems a little rusty. I think Julia needs a new one."

"And you found it where?"

"Where I always find it. On a rack with a bunch of halters."

"And Farney?"

"No Farney. No Patrick. No Mrs. Julia Clancy. Big noise up at that tent. Music, people making one hell of a racket. But the stable was empty and I knew I had a problem. I always have to twitch Lollipop when I shoe her. And I don't like that other single-hand aluminum twitch Patrick uses."

"Then how did you manage to twitch her and shoe her at the same time?" asked Julia.

"Easy," said Tim, grinning. "Just went outside and grabbed the first guest that I knew was familiar with horses. Turned out to be Tilly Martin. She was down at the south paddock, looking over the field. Watching for the sunset, I guess. Yeah, I know she's a little cracked and she doesn't like horses all that much, but she helped out. Said she was tired of all the noise up at the tent. Tilly's not a bad egg if you can get her to concentrate."

"No one," said George, "has come close to telling me the truth. Tilly never said she helped with the shoeing." Here he flipped back through his notebook and stabbed at a notation with his pen. "Tilly Martin left the reception at a little before nine with Jane Zimmer. Confirmed. No, thank you, Mrs. Clancy, I never take anything when I'm working."

This to Julia, who stood with a tray of cold beer, a bottle of Seagrams, a bottle of soda, and a bowl of ice.

"A Coke?" said Julia. "Chips? Doughnuts? Stale banana bread?"

"Nothing," said George. "I'm almost finished. Mr. Fournier, when did you return the twitch?"

Tim now looked thoroughly annoyed. "I've already told Sarah here."

"For the record," said George.

"This afternoon. Had to twitch Duffie. Sarah helped me. I brought it back this afternoon. And used it."

"And the rest is history," murmured Alex.

"Not yet," said George. "Wait for forensics." He stood up, patted his papers and folders into a neat rectangle, scooped them up, slipped them under his arm, dodged the reaching claw of Charlie, nodded to the company, and departed.

"Cold fish," said Tim as the sound of George's footsteps on the gravel faded. He finished his beer in three large swallows, rose to leave in his turn. "Thanks for the beer and sorry about keeping that damn twitch. What's the big deal, anyway?"

"To repeat what George said," answered Alex, "wait for the forensic lab. It may be a big deal, or no deal at all."

With the departure of Tim there was a moment of absolute silence. Julia, Charlie in her arms, sagged in her chair, Sarah slumped, and Alex picked up the front section of the local paper and bent over it.

Then Sarah pushed herself away from the table. "Shower," she announced. "Then food. We'll take you out, Aunt Julia. Alex, is this the night I was going to do something about Jim Shale? I'm losing all sense of time. And place."

Alex looked up. "Tomorrow, for God's sake. Enough is enough. We will not discuss murder or horses for the next twelve hours."

"At least not murder," said Julia. "I may mention horses."

Sarah stopped suddenly and turned. "You know," she said, "whoever has been at work here, killing, shooting, burning—well, no horses have been hurt."

"Knock on wood," said Julia sharply. "It's probably not for lack of trying. Think of Brandy Boy."

"That's a rocking horse," said Sarah. "A wooden rocking horse. A toy."

"Brandy Boy is a symbol. A threat of something to come."

"Not so far," said Sarah. "People, the farmhouse, your cross-country course have been hit, but no horses."

"You have a point," said Alex. "You mean a horse lover is involved. A farm destroyer who is also a horse lover."

"It's possible," said Sarah.

"But all the neighbors are horse lovers," said Julia.

"Not Tilly really," said Sarah. "Or Mrs. Pfeifer of Merrilark. Maybe not her nephew, Brad. Maybe not Jim Shale."

"That's four out of a crowd," said Alex.

Sarah persisted. "Not only a horse lover but someone who deals with horses and knows Julia's stable. Where the twitch is, where the pony bridle is, where extra curb reins are kept. Someone," said Sarah slowly, as if understanding for the first time, "someone who, when they hang a rocking horse from a tree, uses a release knot. The knot that you use to tie a horse. One pull and it's undone. Patrick showed me how today. Said it would become automatic."

"That still leaves half the neighborhood," said Julia crossly. "But I hope you're right about the horses. Go take your shower, Sarah, and we will indeed go out. We can talk about the price of hay. It keeps going up."

"Another fun evening," said Sarah, making for the stairs.

It was not a fun evening, but neither was it a total loss. Julia proved distractable, Alex was determined to keep things light, and Sarah made a conscious effort to push all matters disturbing her peace of mind below the conversational surface.

Nevertheless, sometime between dessert and coffee at Peter Ott's restaurant in Camden the forbidden subject reared its ugly head.

Julia kicked off. "I had another of those cut-up messages today. This morning. Mike Laaka brought it in from the mailbox. He wore gloves to open it and so did I when I was holding it. Imagine wearing gloves to read your own mail."

Sarah looked up from her work of turning a rum parfait into a swirl of brown sludge. "I thought they'd stopped coming. Is it another nursery rhyme?"

"No," said Julia. "And it's not from *The Charge of the Light Brigade* either. It's another takeoff from Harvey's repertoire."

"What!" exclaimed Sarah and Alex together.

"Well, I connect *The Light Brigade* with Harvey. He's always quoting old chestnuts. But this is one of his favorites. Changed of course, and not for the better. The police gave me a copy to keep." Here Julia fumbled about in her handbag and produced a folded sheet of paper. "If we had world enough and time / This slowness, Julia, were no crime / But always at your back I hear / Death's winged chariot hurrying near. Go, Julia, go."

Julia returned the paper to her handbag and shook her head. "Terrible, isn't it? The last bit sounds like a football cheer."

"Well," said Sarah, "it's certainly a quantum leap in literary merit from Humpty-Dumpty and *The Light Brigade*. Now it's Andrew Marvell. Next week, who knows—William Blake or Keats."

Julia put down her coffee cup. "Lord knows when Harvey recites the Marvell poem it's depressing enough in its original form, but this version makes my skin crawl."

Alex looked up from a last bite of cheesecake. "That's why it was sent, Julia. To make your skin crawl."

"What did Joe the fat boy say in *Pickwick*?" said Sarah. "I wants to make your flesh creep."

"Stop being literary," said Julia crossly. "I need advice, not Trivial Pursuit."

Sarah spooned up a portion of the now liquid parfait, swallowed it, and considered. "Well, Marvell's 'To His Coy Mistress' is a second departure. *The Charge of the Light Brigade* was the first. It isn't as if all the nursery rhymes have been used up. Whoever sent the first ones has hardly scratched the surface. There are lots of catastrophic choices left. 'London Bridge is Falling Down,' 'Jack and Jill,' 'Who Killed Cock Robin?' "

Alex looked up with new interest. "You're saying that the nursery-rhyme writer might not be the same person who sent *The Light Brigade* and the Andrew Marvell."

"That's right," said Sarah. "I mean, why switch? I know we've all probably thought that Tilly might be behind them, but I've heard that people in her mental state are obsessed with one idea and join new ideas to the first obsession. Tilly wants Aunt Julia's farm; she adds the British royal family to the stew and connects them to the ownership of Julia's farm. Why would she—if it is Tilly writing—switch poetry types?"

"So two people are sending me cut-up poems?" demanded Julia.

"Copycats," said Alex. "Common enough. Julia went public the evening after Sean had his accident. Said she'd been getting rewritten scraps of bad poetry telling her to leave the farm. But you never mentioned nursery rhymes per se, did you, Julia?"

Julia shook her head. "Only to Sarah and the police and you, Alex. And Mike. Not even Harvey."

"So it's possible someone else is getting into the act," said Sarah. "Someone who didn't know what the first rhymes were."

Alex nodded. "Harvey with his old favorites."

"Or," said Sarah, "someone deciding to pin it on Harvey. Everyone for miles around has heard him recite."

Julia groaned "Lord, Lord. Wheels within wheels. And I remember Harvey just before starting a cross-country event or at the beginning of a hunt. He'd wave over at me—we were always great rivals—and say, 'Ours is not to reason why, ours is but to do and die.' It was sort of his battle song."

"Someone imitating Harvey is interesting," said Alex. "I don't see Tilly doing it. She does her own thing and wouldn't stoop to copying someone else."

"Tilly," said Sarah, "is Tilly. Scary as that may be. Tilly would never try and be Harvey Dodge or anyone else unless it was someone out of this world. Hathor or Mary Queen of Scots. A reincarnation of someone with the right vibes is more her style."

"My style right now," said Julia, rolling her napkin into a ball and dumping it on her unfinished chocolate bread pudding, "is to go home, play the piano, and read. The trouble is I can't even read Dick Francis mysteries anymore because they hit too close to the bone—all those threatened horses. The only restful printed matter left is *The Chronicle of the Horse.* Things are under control in the *Chronicle.*

"And what sounds restful to you?" said Sarah to Alex as they prepared for bed that night.

"I have the Red Sox," said Alex. "A doubleheader tonight. I can catch the last game on the radio."

"Baseball won't cut it for me," said Sarah. "I want old-time distraction." She reached over to the guest room bookcase, ran her finger over the spines of a number of faded cloth covers, and stopped and pulled out a blue volume. "I've found it. Better than the Red Sox." She held up the book. "Better than a sleeping pill. *Pickwick Papers.* I'm looking forward to making my flesh crawl. Good nineteenth-century slow-moving flesh-crawling stuff."

Sarah rose that Friday morning with high praise for *The Pickwick Papers.* "The ultimate escape. Dingly Dell and Mr. Snodgrass and Sam Weller. But I suppose reality is lying in wait in the kitchen."

They found Julia peering out the window. She turned and indicated the parking lot. "I keep looking. Expecting Rafe Posner. It's as if I look hard enough for him, he'll turn up. Rafe was like that, you know. He'd go off sometimes without so much as a by-your-leave and then have some amazing excuse. He'd been asked to help out in a circus act; he'd been given a lift to the farm and the driver had taken him to Bangor instead; he'd rescued a wounded moose and had to find the game warden. A wonderful imagination. Sean Conners wasn't inventive. He'd just be late or miss a day because he'd been drunk the night before. Or his car broke down. Or he'd been in a fight and went to the emergency room. Well, so much for that. No Rafe—

no Sean—in the parking lot. But I still look every day. Alex, will you do the juice and coffee? I've made oatmeal."

Settled at the breakfast table, Julia doling out great dollups of oatmeal into blue bowls, Sarah asked about her riding program. "Not that I've recovered from the last lesson."

"Today I've put you in the campers' walk-trot class. After you finish a few stalls, that is. I'm going out after breakfast and go over the cross-country course. Just a week to pull this place together, although I suppose I should start with the kitchen."

Here Julia looked about the room with regret. A shaft of early morning sun lit a scene of dust and neglect. Dirty dishes in the sink. Last night's beer bottles on the counter. A box of the cats' Friskies up-ended on the floor, the remains being mouthed by the setters, Tucker and Belle. Fluffs of dog fur lay in the corners, the kitchen clock had stopped at two A.M., and fruit flies circled a basket of wrinkled grapes. One cat sat atop the refrigerator, another on a crumpled tea towel; a third had settled in a fruit bowl along with two dark bananas. Joe, the parrot, loose from his cage, honked and fretted on a shelf.

"Shall I help you in here this morning?" said Sarah, thinking of the world of Mr. Pickwick. Serving wenches, rosy-cheeked housemaids, jovial innkeepers, hard-working ostlers, all bustling about cleaning, making things bright and tidy.

"Lord no," said Julia. "Horses first. They can't muck out their own stalls, put themselves out to pasture. And I have the show entries to go over. I'll get to the kitchen sometime."

She rose, banged the double boiler down on the stove, and turned to face the breakfast table. "Even if I'm under siege, I've a big day ahead. Merrilark and Highfeather are coming over this afternoon for the orienteering and a cookout afterward. Once a year I make the property available to them. After that fiasco fifteen years ago. The police are allowing us to have it on the beach and will keep an eye on the High Hope people. Of course, the campers will love it—anything to do with murder and violence. Alex, will you be spending the whole day at the hospital?"

"A fair chunk of it," said Alex. "The good old summertime. A new stomach bug, and at least one in every three patients is sure he has Lyme disease."

"But you'll be back for dinner?" asked Sarah.

"Late afternoon if all goes well."

"Dinner is the cookout with the two camps," said Julia. "Patrick and I, Sarah and Jessica are invited. So is Harvey. He told me he's been trying to explain orienteering to Leah Pfeifer because she's never properly understood it. He loves to go on about compasses and trailblazing and pathfinding. He was an Eagle Scout." And Julia stood up, dumped her cereal bowl in the sink, took a last draught of coffee, and headed out the kitchen door.

"Eagle Scout," said Sarah to Alex. "Do they commit murder?"

"Probably as often as Sunday school teachers and choir directors, who seem to do it all the time. It's probably an occupational sideline."

"So we'd better leave Harvey Dodge on the list."

"Along with our neighborhood librarians, camp directors, and other civic-minded folk," said Alex. "Good-bye, I love you, especially in one piece, so stay on top of the horse and as George said, no more field trips. At least not without me."

"Wait," called Sarah as Alex moved to the door. "Do you know what Julia meant about a fiasco fifteen years ago? And tell me about orienteering. How do you do it?"

"I've got to go, so ask Julia. Or one of the Wentworths. Or the campers. Kids love to explain things to ignorant adults."

No truer statement, thought Sarah as she worked her way through her morning chores and riding lesson. In her mucking-out chores she was put under the supervision of that severest of critics, her Cousin Jessica, who fulminated on the subject of persons, like stupid adults, who leave stall doors open.

Sarah decided to turn the conversation to a more useful subject. "Mr. and Mrs. Wentworth spend a lot of time here during the riding lessons. Don't they keep an eye on what's going on?"

"You mean Winka and Neil," said Jessica. "They don't do any of the barn stuff, just the camper lessons. And some other kids.

You're signed up for our riding lesson. Walk-trot. Beginners. That's Winka. I'm not a beginner, but the pony I'm working on is green so I'm joining the class. Do you know how to post yet?"

Sarah admitted to a poor grasp of posting and Jessica promised to take her in charge. "But Winka will work you over. She's awesome, like a drill sergeant. I went to Camp Merrilark last year and she taught me here at High Hope. She wants the campers to be perfect—especially the Highfeather boys. Like they should be good enough for the Olympics or something. She's got Highfeather on the brain."

This was useful, thought Sarah later in the tack room as she tied the laces of her boots and put on her riding helmet. Winka as a fanatic. And what about Mr. Winka? Sarah caught up with Jessica. Was Neil Wentworth just like Winka Wentworth? A drill sergeant?

The question was taken up by another student called Wendy who wore a white Camp Merrilark T-shirt with the green pine tree logo. "Neil Wentworth is easy," said Wendy. "He teaches the advanced kids and you can get away with murder with him."

Another interesting comment, thought Sarah. Then, seeing Winka Wentworth looming, she joined the group, feeling with her five-foot-seven height like a female Gulliver among the ten- and eleven-year-old Lilliputians.

"Oh hello, Sarah," called Winka. She was in her working riding clothes, but the effect was splendid. Close-fitting olive drab breeches, glossy high field boots, a white polo shirt with the Highfeather logo—a canoe—woven in red. Her hair was smooth, her makeup in place, and her tall lean body looked ready for action. She reminded Sarah of some sort of high-achieving greyhound.

"Hope you don't mind being taught with kids," said Winka, walking over to check a girth on the fat little chestnut Shetland pony called Gingersnap—the pony whose bridle, Sarah remembered, had circled the head of Farney Thompson. Was the pony wearing *that* bridle? Or had a new one been purchased? Sarah shuddered and then realized that Winka was still talking.

"We're working on basics and Julia suggested you work out with our ten-thirty group for a while. You'll be riding Whiskers again. Clare will help you with the saddling."

Clare turned out to be another juvenile tyrant. The currying, the brushing, the hoof-picking, the settling of the saddle, the slipping on of the bridle had to be just so. "You really don't know anything, do you?" said Clare with a sigh. "Winka Wentworth wants us to do everything perfectly. All the camp kids are supposed to set an example."

"Do you?" asked Sarah.

"Not always," admitted Clare. "But she wants us to try. Mr. Wentworth, too, though he's not so strict." Clare took hold of the reins and began to lead Whiskers to the arena. "I suppose," she added, "if you run a camp you have to be pretty intense. Like Mrs. Pfeifer—Mrs. Eff—at our camp, she's into the camp-spirit stuff and worrying about someone drowning. Brad Pfeifer, he's sort of a tyrant about canoe tests. Okay, see if your girth is tight enough. Whiskers blows up like a balloon." Here Clare took hold of the girth and pulled it so tight Sarah was sure that Whiskers would explode. However nothing untoward happened beyond a malevolent rolling of the gray pony's left eye, and Sarah mounted safely.

She moved Whiskers cautiously into the arena behind Cousin Jessica, who was wrestling with a large buckskin pony called Cinnamon, who showed a great interest in going only sideways. After a warm-up period at a walk, Winka Wentworth called out to the group, "Trot, please. Up, down, watch your heels, sit up straight, up, down."

Sarah bopping along sedately in the trot had a chance to look over the scene. The arena was cavernous, with the light filtering in from translucent panels, and around and around like little clockwork figures rode the children, legs and arms pumping up and down, cheeks flushed with exertion, their faces half-hidden by their black velvet hard hats. They were all so serious, trying so hard, that Sarah decided they were concentrating on being examples.

The lesson went forward without incident. No shotgun

blasts, no bodies, no fires. No rider fell off, and what more could any student want? thought Sarah, climbing stiffly from Whiskers' back at the end of the lesson. Winka Wentworth had been firm, but also full of praise for the campers' progress.

Neil Wentworth, fresh from instruction in the outside ring, arrived to watch the unsaddling of Whiskers. It was Neil in his role of jester—a side of him Sarah hadn't often seen. He teased her about her attempts to put a halter on the pony, joked with a Highfeather camper named Nicholas about some incident at last night's campfire, and then sauntered off toward the arena.

"He's a kick," said Clare to Sarah. "You never know what he's going to say. I mean, he's not totally serious the whole time."

"Yeah," said Nicholas. "He sometimes lets us fool around and not do all the instruction stuff, like just go for a sail and not have to work on our tests and knots. But Mrs. Wentworth's different. Like, she's more serious. Sort of formal."

Sarah told herself that none of this information was new; but it did confirm her own impressions. Then under Clare's eye she was allowed to hose off Whiskers, scrape him dry, walk him about, and then put him out to pasture. By the time she returned, the last morning class had finished and Sarah started for the tack room to exchange her boots for sneakers. About to open the door she became aware of a sort of hissing going on within. Adult hissing. Adults who didn't want to be heard but who were so furious they couldn't control themselves. Sarah stopped, dropped her hand, and retreated one step. The voices were becoming increasingly clear.

"You bloody well won't," said the man's voice. Neil's, without a doubt.

"I bloody well will. It was my idea and I'll get on with it. And damn well do it my way." Voice of Winka.

"Christ, put a lid on it, will you? Keep your voice down."

"You're the one who's shouting. Too damn bad about you. I'm doing what I have to. What's the matter? Backbone unstuck?"

"Listen, listen." Voice of Neil lower, trying for control. "I know you've had the whole thing on your neck and I've tried to help. But enough is enough. Be sensible for once in your life. You're not God Almighty."

"Try and make me."

"Well sod you." This with a slam of something closing.

Sarah backed up, flattened herself against the wall of the wash rack area; the tack room door sprang open and a red-faced Neil Wentworth stalked out and headed for the arena. And Sarah turned and stepped inside the tack room. Winka was shoving boot trees into her riding boots. She looked up, and except for a certain pinched quality about her mouth, nothing seemed untoward.

"Sarah. You did pretty well today. Sorry I focus so much on the children, but I think you'll understand. It's important because these kids are really into their riding."

Sarah said yes and that she was looking forward to her next lesson. But now Winka was absorbed in sponging a bridle, so Sarah took off her helmet and trudged up the path toward the farmhouse, all the while trying to make sense of what she had overheard.

Fact. The Winka-Neil relationship had some very rough spots. And hadn't there been other moments of edginess? Fact two: Neil wanted Winka to stop something and she refused. Fact three: It was Winka's idea. Fact four: Winka had the whole thing on her neck—whatever the whole thing was. The camp perhaps? The camp the two girls said she had on the brain? Last fact: Winka said Neil lacked backbone.

Sarah mounted the kitchen porch steps ready to explore the Wentworth character with Aunt Julia and found Mike Laaka and her aunt in formation. Mike looked stern, Julia serious.

With them on the steps stood a sheriff's deputy, a small wiry blonde woman, recently appointed to hide in the scrub by the road and watch the mailbox for untoward deliveries, who now held out in gloved hand a pile of letters.

THE WAGON WHEELS

FIFTEEN

"MIKE, these are only copies," said the sheriff's deputy, whose name was Katie. Katie Waters. "I called the lab people on the field phone when the mail was delivered. They sent someone up, made the copies, and are going to start right in on the microscopic. They said it was okay for Mrs. Clancy to look at copies, but to be careful about wrinkling them because they don't want to keep making new copies. Money's tight." And with this Katie Waters departed to take up her station in the alder bushes behind the mailbox.

Julia subsided on the middle step of the back-porch stairs. "How very kind of Sergeant Fitts to let me see my mail. I suppose he's looked over my electric bill and the feed bill. And my social security check. My insurance invoice."

Mike, ignoring Julia's fit of self-pity, sat himself next to her on the step and gave his attention to the first of the two letters. "This sounds like a golden oldie," he announced.

> Under the wide and starry sky,
> Dig Julia's grave and let her lie.

Sad did she live and sadly die
And we laid her down with a will.

"One of Harvey's," said Julia miserably. "He says it's going to be his epitaph. Robert Louis Stevenson. You know, the poem that ends, 'home is the sailor, home from the sea, / And the hunter home from the hill.' "

"No, I don't know," said Mike, "but here's number two." He unfolded a second piece of copy paper and frowned. "Disgusting piece of junk."

"Let me see," said Sarah, reaching for the paper. She puzzled a moment and then nodded. "It's taken from a poem by James Leigh Hunt. 'Abou Ben Adhem.' It turns up in crossword puzzles." She read:

Julia Clancy, (may her farm disappear!)
Awoke one night from a dark dream of fear,
And saw in the moonlight from her room,
The body of her murdered groom.

"Garbage," said Mike. "Just a lot of garbage."

"New enemies," said Julia. "Two new enemies. They're multiplying like rabbits."

But Mike was reading a memo sent with the two copies. "Lab has finished a prelim on all the cutouts. The very first one, the ladybird-fly-away-home thing, was cut with short curved scissors, the next three nursery rhymes with long straight blades, *The Charge of the Light Brigade*, the Stevenson, and the 'Abou Ben Adhem' thing with short straight ones. More tests pending."

"Like rabbits," repeated Julia.

"But," protested Sarah, "it could be one person with three pairs of scissors. Lots of people have different kinds."

"I think you're stretching it," said Mike. "Three pairs of scissors and different sorts of poetry? I say we've got first a wise guy and then maybe a couple of copycats."

"But these last two messages are really nasty," said Sarah. "Graves and murdered grooms. Scare tactics."

"Yeah, I agree," said Mike. "Anyway, the first four were from *Newsweek*, but I'm hoping to hell that the lab can come up with some bit of exotic info telling us the new ones were cut out of an obscure rag like *Texas Agricultural News* or *Country Life in Old Cornwall* or *Gleanings from Bali*."

"What an imagination, Mike," said Sarah. "Maybe you're snipping out the letters yourself."

"I don't use scissors," said Mike. "Only knives. Revolvers. And automatic weapons." He rose from the table and headed to the door. "Take care. Orienteering this afternoon, right? The police will be as thick as maggots. Me, I think I'll do a little visiting. Trouble is, I don't have a search warrant to check out scissor inventories. But I can make casual calls. Hit the camp directors, Harvey Dodge, maybe Tilly and Jane. Start reciting how the cow jumped over the moon. Or say how this 'Abou Ben Adhem' is my favorite poem. See if anyone starts sweating." He reached over and touched Julia's shoulder. "All bad things come to an end, and I'd say this mess is about to come to a boil. Spill its guts, if you know what I mean." And Mike gathered Julia's letters, heaved himself up from the steps, and started down the path toward his car.

"Come to a boil, spill its guts," said Julia bitterly. "What a way to put it. I'm glad Mike never went into counseling the elderly. Now I feel worse than I did this morning, which is going some." Here a rustle behind the lilac bushes by the back shed caused her to crane her neck in that direction. "All right, whoever you are, come out. Friend or foe, get out of my lilacs."

It was Tilly Martin. Tilly in her yellow sweats, a band of striped ribbon pulling her hair back from her face, bits of twigs and small leaves clinging to her person. Tilly with a worried, uncharacteristically sober face.

"I saw that Mike Laaka was here and I waited until he left," she said. She paused uncertainly and then flopped down on the porch stairs. "I'm disturbed," she announced. "In my mind."

This was such an obvious truth that for a moment neither

Sarah nor Julia spoke. Then Julia smiled, stood up, and went over and patted Tilly's hand. "We're all disturbed, Tilly. In one way or another. Now how about some lunch? No one has had lunch."

"Lunch," repeated Tilly. "Yes, I brought my Thermos and sandwiches. For all of you. And my herbal cupcakes with the butter frosting. I do want to talk and I think if we just sit out here in the summer air things will be much clearer. Wait here a minute." And Tilly rose, slipped again behind the lilacs, and produced a wicker basket. "Jane dropped me off on her way to Rockland. She told me you'd be here because you probably don't dare leave the farm. So I said to myself let's just see if a picnic and a nice talk can make things more comfortable. For all of us."

"Well, a picnic certainly couldn't make us more uncomfortable than we already are," said Julia. "But why not on the back terrace? We can pretend we're civilized."

"What I mean," said Tilly when the three women had settled themselves in chairs on the brick terrace, "is that I'm depressed."

"You're depressed!" said Julia. "What about me? No one's trying to destroy Appleyard Farm. Or," she added, "move you out."

"Give Tilly a chance," murmured Sarah, turning an egg salad sandwich carefully in her hand. It seemed fresh and she took a tentative bite. Losing part of her mind apparently hadn't interfered with the provisioning section of Tilly's brain.

"Yes, give me a chance. Like the chance I gave you," said Tilly. "The chance of rotating. Going with your vital flow."

"Oh ye gods and little fishes," interrupted Julia, banging the top of a metal umbrella table with her fist "Stop that, Tilly. No more of the stars and garters and evil omens and portents. I'm sorry you're upset, but my good Lord . . ."

"Please, Aunt Julia," said Sarah in a louder and firmer voice. "Let Tilly say what she wants to say. Even if you don't agree. Let her talk."

And Julia subsided, grumbling.

Tilly took a large bite of her sandwich, chewed thoughtfully, and put it down on a paper plate. A plate Sarah was interested to see was decorated with the signs of the Zodiac.

"It's like this," said Tilly. "The royal family. The queen, Princess Di. All of them."

"Go on," said Sarah in what she hoped was a neutral voice, because the prospect of wallowing about in the trials of Britain's royals was not a happy one.

"I mean," said Tilly, "they aren't what I thought. They've been letting the side down. Not the queen, of course, but it's discouraging. And I'm not sure I want them to visit. So many of them fouling their nest—*fouling*, that's the only word for it. So I think I'll have to backtrack. Rescind the invitation."

Sarah looked up from the last bite of her egg sandwich. "You invited them? I mean really invited?"

Tilly looked hurt. "But how would they have known to come? Of course, I sent a proper invitation to Buckingham Palace."

"But Tilly," protested Sarah.

"Sarah," said Julia, "you're the one who said that Tilly should talk. Go on Tilly, but keep to the point."

Tilly's point, though much blunted, seemed to be that the royal family was no longer desired but that plans for Julia's removal from her farm were still on the table.

"But I seem to be having these black spells." Tilly sighed. "It's as if nothing was going to work out. Or happen. Ever. Never. Never. Never."

"Tilly, you sound like King Lear," said Julia sharply. "Prozac. That's what you need. A lot of my friends are on the stuff. Totally depressed and disoriented one minute, quite contented the next. Or Elavil. Or folic acid. Beta-carotene. Vitamin E. Something. You need to see your doctor again."

"Oh, I know, I know," said Tilly miserably. She slumped in her chair and put a distracted hand through her curls. "But I don't want a doctor. It's not chemical or mental. It's my aura. It's out of sorts. Weak. You know, if your aura is weak then outside influences try to impinge. And they have. It's that Norminco mine and the murder and Sean Conners being missing. And Rafe Posner. Rafe had a fine aura. Very positive, and now he's gone. I'm losing heart. Even though I've tried to fight back." Here Tilly turned her head into her shoulder and her whole body trembled.

Julia took Tilly's hand and began massaging it gently, but Sarah, feeling that an opportunity might be lost, said, quite sharply, "Tilly. Tilly, what do you mean, you had to fight back? How did you fight back?"

Tilly raised a puffy tear-streaked face. "Sticks and stones may break my bones but names will never hurt me."

"What?" said Julia and Sarah together.

"Never hurt me," repeated Tilly, her voice rising shrilly. "What I said. Exactly. Fight, no matter the cost. But it's got me down. Ah now, Julia. And Sarah." Here Tilly put on what in novels is called a brave face and tried a valiant little toss of her yellow curls. "You think I'm crazy. Don't deny it. Crazy as a loon. Or a bedbug. Nuttier than a fruitcake. But listen, I'm trying to put fear into you. Warn you. Because something is askew here and it's time you did something about it. Don't leave it to the police. Talk about auras—no policeman has a shred of one. Besides, life goes on—" here Tilly's voice became sober and sensible—"and the campers are coming. The Merrilark bus is turning in and I must pack up the lunch and go home and take care of the chickens." And Tilly stood up, smiled at Julia, who seemed to be trying to swallow her tongue, and made off at a trot, basket swinging and banging into her legs.

Sarah tried once more. "Tilly, Tilly," she called. "Come back. What are you going to do?"

Tilly, without pausing, twisted her head and called out, "Ask me no questions, I'll tell you no lies." And then, in a louder voice, "Sarah, you're seeing too much of the police. It's affecting your own aura. It's become extremely thin." And Tilly disappeared down the road in the direction of Appleyard Farm.

"Well, well," said Julia. She stood up, brushing crumbs from her denim trousers. "Well, well, well," she repeated.

"You sound as daft as Tilly," Sarah complained. "We don't

need two of you around the bend. Or three of us, since my aura is declining. But Tilly's right. The camps have just rolled in. There's the Highfeather bus."

Julia nodded. "So it is. I'd better go down. I try to keep an eye on the proceedings. Come and join us after you finish afternoon chores."

So Sarah, under Jessica's sharp eye, scrubbed buckets and swept the stable aisles until it was well after four o'clock.

"You're learning," Jessica told her. "Of course, you don't work as fast as Sean Conners or Rafe Posner did. Or Farney Thompson. But since they're gone or dead or something, well, you're better than no one."

"Thanks a lot," said Sarah, wiping a wet forehead. And then she remembered a question she had wanted to ask. Jessica might have the answer; she had been at Camp Merrilark last season.

"Why," asked Sarah, "do the campers have their orienteering game here at High Hope Farm? Why not at Merrilark? Or at Highfeather? The camps have plenty of property."

Jessica paused in the act of hanging up a handful of lead shanks. "I'm not sure," she said. "It's something about the compasses not working right on the camp property. Like they can't be trusted. I guess a long time ago the camps tried it on their own land and everything got totally screwed-up. Campers got lost and everyone sort of panicked and some kids had to be searched for. So they don't play it there anymore."

"But the compasses work all right on Aunt Julia's property?"

"Yeah. I guess so. They must work or the camps wouldn't do the orienteering here. Okay, we're finished. Patrick will do the feeding tonight, so we can go on down to the lake. There's usually a humongous barbecue and lots of cake and neat stuff."

"You don't play the orienteering game?" asked Sarah.

"Nah. That's for the camp kids. I've done it. Our team came in second place last year. Come on, it's almost five."

Sarah followed Jessica down through the pastures, cutting back and forth past the cross-country jumps, and as she hiked along her mind kept working over this new information. Compasses didn't work at Merrilark and Highfeather. They gave inaccurate readings. So inaccurate that some campers had lost their way. This must have been the fiasco referred to by Aunt Julia. And so ever after the orienteering had been held at High Hope Farm, where the compasses functioned correctly.

Why? Although Sarah had never taken a geology course, she had a general idea that certain minerals underfoot could throw off a compass. Throw it off so that north no longer read north, nor east, east. And so forth. Conclusion? Merrilark and Highfeather harbored minerals affecting compass reliability and High Hope Farm did not. Further conclusion? The interest expressed by Norminco in mineral deposits might be limited to the stretch of land owned by the Highfeather and Merrilark camps. And perhaps to other lands across Tri-County Road. Lands such as Quartermaster Farm and Appleyard Farm. But High Hope Farm must be pure. Innocent of a major mineral deposit. Virgin territory. Maybe.

Sarah said "Maybe" aloud and found herself stopped at one of Aunt Julia's evil-looking jumps: a double-log affair that forced a horse to jump from sunshine into gloom of woods. A challenge that any sensible horse, in Sarah's opinion, should absolutely refuse.

Okay. So maybe, just maybe, Aunt Julia's farm did not sit over anything but junk. Dirt and common garden-variety stone. So the big push to destroy High Hope Farm would have nothing to do with the presence of valuable mineral resources. Then why the terrorist campaign? Well, as Mike—was it Mike? was it Alex?—had suggested, perhaps someone wanted Julia's farm because it *didn't* have copper or nickel. Because they—he—she—could sell their valuable compass-disturbing property for big bucks to Norminco and buy for little bucks—High Hope now being devalued every day by untoward goings-on—because it was just a great piece of property with a lakefront. Property perfect for a camp. Merrilark and/or Highfeather. Perfect for a horse farm or an agricultural retirement farm. Tilly, Jane, and Harvey Dodge.

Sarah turned and began retracing her steps. She wasn't sure

what she was going to do, but at the very least a quick check on compass problems seemed in order. She and Alex had been going to try to see Jim Shale tomorrow for apologies and perhaps useful information. Well, tomorrow wouldn't do. Sarah reached the post-and-rail that ran along the farm perimeter and found herself walking toward a blue pickup truck that was pulled over on the edge of the road. Jim Shale. In the flesh. Jim Shale leaning out watching with binoculars the scattered groups of campers.

"Hey," called Sarah, running forward.

Jim Shale lowered his binoculars, took in Sarah's arrival at his truck door, and raised them again. Slowly, deliberately, he scanned the distant fields dotted here and there with little groups of campers holding papers and compasses. Then lowering the glasses he looked at Sarah.

"You wanted something?"

"Yes," said Sarah. "You. Some help. Right down your alley. Compasses and mineral deposits. Certain minerals throw compass directions off, don't they?"

"My impression," said Jim Shale, "was that none of you people had much of an interest in minerals, except to hope they'd go away. And Norminco with them. Correct?"

Sarah bit her lip with exasperation, but she—she and the whole neighborhood—had brought this on themselves. "Yes," she said. "You're right, but we still need you. We need information."

"Hold up," said Jim. "We? Who are we, exactly? The police? Your Aunt Julia? Farmers' alliance? Horse Lovers Anonymous?"

"We," said Sarah "is me. And Aunt Julia. I'm sure you've talked to the police, but no one's been able to see why Aunt Julia is being tormented. Farney murdered. The whole business. We thought it was because someone was drooling over her possible mineral deposits, but the camps do their orienteering here. On her land. Because the campers got lost once on their own land."

"The conclusion," said Jim Shale, "is obvious. Your Aunt Julia's land does not cause compass distortion."

"Meaning no copper and nickel? Or cobalt?"

"Nickel, copper, and cobalt alone don't cause deviations."

"Oh damn. Look, I'm sorry we've been rude. Alex and I wanted to have you over for a drink . . . or to go out. Talk it over."

"But now that you've cornered me here you won't have to. Fair enough. Look, Miss Deane. It is Miss Deane, isn't it?"

"Sarah."

"Okay. Sarah. To answer your question, cobalt, nickel, and copper are not magnetic, don't cause compass deviations, but some iron compounds, like magnetite and pyrrhotite, that often occur with these minerals do have magnetic properties. And now I have to go and help with the scoring, as I've promised."

Sarah frowned. "Wait up. Promised whom? Which camp?"

"I don't know. Had a message at my office. Would I go over and meet with both camps after supper—at Merrilark Lodge—and talk about orienteering. How to use a compass and follow a course. The Norminco people thought it was good PR, and since I have nothing against kids, I agreed. I'm invited to the cookout and now I have to go on down to the finish line and check the results and times."

Sarah protested. "I still don't see why they asked you. Not," she hastened to add, "that you couldn't help them a lot, but Brad Pfeifer and the Wentworths are big on that sort of thing. Aunt Julia says the camps do the orienteering every year."

"Brad Pfeifer was busy setting up a canoe trip, Mrs. Pfeifer wouldn't know a compass if it bit her, and the Wentworths have apparently been flat out starting the riding and waterfront activities. No counselors with any experience in mapping and compass use around, and the directors wanted the orienteering to start the camp session off with a bang. I'm a fill-in."

"Did Mrs. Wentworth do the inviting?"

"No idea. Just this message on my desk. Both camp directors

must have okayed me, since no one threw me out when I went down to give my lecture and demo."

"Was Brad Pfeifer there when you did?"

"Sarah, the Grand Inquisitor. Look, I said I have to go on down to the lake and check the teams as they come in. Tag along and I'll try to keep a civil tongue in my head and answer what I can. I'll also try to imagine that your motives are pure and you're not planning to wire my office or plant bombs in my truck." Here Jim Shale pushed open the truck door and emerged, binoculars in one hand. "Come on," he called to Sarah as he ducked under the rail of the pasture.

Sarah scrambled after him. "Wait up," she called. "What about Brad Pfeifer? Was he there when you lectured?"

Jim Shale—the possessor of very long legs—slowed his steps and turned. "Sort of. He came late. Stayed and glowered. Struck me as being none too happy about my being there but didn't say anything. One way or the other."

"The Wentworths?"

"Were cordial. As was the redoubtable Mrs. Eff. And the counselors. And the campers. No one shouted 'Environment polluter' at me. Called me a geologist from hell. All right, mind if I go ahead? I'm running late on this thing."

And Jim Shale, with his brown forelock hanging over his eyes, his lanky arms and legs pumping away, took off and left Sarah straggling in his rear.

But after a hundred yards or so she came to a halt on top of a rectangular expanse of green known to cross-country riders as the Table. This elevated patch offered a view of the southern part of Aunt Julia's property, and she could see here and there small figures running, stopping, turning, stopping again, bending over what must be maps, then running again. The afternoon was now well advanced and the trees, the bushes, the campers themselves made long dark shadows on the grass of the pasture. It was, thought Sarah, like an animated Flemish landscape. Or, more probably—considering recent events—like one of those allegorical settings of Breughel, or the Seven Deadly Sins landscapes of Bosch, in which envy, greed, sloth, pride, and their fellows sport on the greensward while retribution in the shape of the Grim Reaper hides himself in a dark cloud above their heads.

With these not very pleasant images in her head, Sarah plunged into the woods, picked up the cross-country trail, and found herself finally on the shores of Crawfish Pond and in the midst of an excited throng of campers and counselors.

Seeing that Alex had arrived and was helping with the barbecue, and Aunt Julia, Harvey Dodge, and Leah Pfeifer had settled into folding canvas chairs at the water's edge, Sarah joined her elders and for the next hour swatted mosquitoes and watched the tabulation of the scores, the forking out of the barbecued chicken pieces, the preparing of s'mores, and forgot all about Seven Deadly Sins and the perils of High Hope Farm. Forgot everything but watching in the failing evening light the blurred figures move to and fro beyond the campfire, listening to the rising young voices singing camp songs. Camp songs that seemed to be exactly the same ones her mother and father, and she, herself, remembered from camping days.

Forgot until Mrs. Eff, her brown hair fallen loose from its tidy knot, departed their group and then returned asking if her nephew Brad had returned. Had they seen him?

"Returned?" asked Julia in a disinterested voice. She had already told Sarah that she was tired; it was time to go home.

"Brad had to go back to camp," explained Mrs. Eff. "Back to Merrilark. One of our girls is in the infirmary. Nothing serious, a sore throat. But her parents wanted to call at eight-thirty and talk to one of us. He said he'd be right back. After all, he has to give out the rewards, the ribbons. He has the final results with him. It's at least twenty past nine and we have to get the campers to bed."

"Couldn't the Wentworths do it?" asked Sarah. "Call Merrilark and find out the scores and make the announcements?"

"No," said Mrs. Eff crossly. "It's Merrilark's time to be host, award the prizes. We do it in turn."

"Don't worry, Leah," said Julia. "Brad won't let you down."

"If he had to stay he should have sent someone back with the results," complained Mrs. Eff, and it was plain to Sarah, listening, that Mrs. Eff was as weary as Julia. Two elderly ladies wishing they were home by their own hearths.

"Should have sent a counselor," repeated Mrs. Eff. "Or one of the office staff. And now it's quite dark. And I don't even know which team won and we have to pack up."

"Well, your nephew *has* sent someone," interposed Sarah, pointing to the woods. And, as she said it, there came the bouncing beam of a flashlight, and a tall young woman wearing the black tie of the Merrilark counselor uniform came running, stumbling out of the trees and stopped.

"Mrs. Eff. Oh Mrs. Eff."

Mrs. Pfeifer sighed. "Lisa, you're always so dramatic. Just give me the results of the games and we can finish up here."

But Lisa, her shoulders heaving, her breath coming in gasps, shook her head. "I don't have the results. It's Brad. Something happened. He's on the ground. I think he's dead. The nurse called 911 and the ambulance. And sent me to tell you. You'd better come. It's his head. It's all caved in."

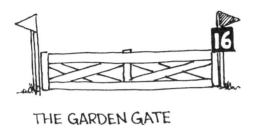

THE GARDEN GATE

SIXTEEN

LATER, remembering that evening, Sarah was able to marvel that children's camps were so ready for emergencies. No sooner had the news of Bradley Pfeifer's injury spread than the campers of Merrilark and Highfeather—in response to a command and a blast on a whistle—formed up by tents and cabins and began to make their way through the woods guided by flanking counselors and their flashlights. These miniature marching columns reminded Sarah, so lately contemplating scenes of Breughel and Bosch, of goblins on the move, many of the campers being less than four feet tall. As had happened before at such times, Sarah found her mind blanking out horror by concentrating on trivia. Goblins, for instance—small shifting figures lit by lanterns like tiny miners working their way through strange tree-marked tunnels. *The Princess and the Goblin, The Hobbit*, come to life. And all about were the trees, swales and meadows, the winding trails, so pleasant by sunlight, now so ominous by dark. Because Brad Pfeifer, robust and firm of step, had departed by dusk, by dark had lingered. By dark had been brought down. By person or persons unknown.

Sarah, her imagination busy with its avoidance tricks, heavy with goblins, now came to and saw that she had arrived at the fork dividing the two camps. After the news of Brad Pfeifer's accident, as if pushed by some starter button, she had followed Mike Laaka in a swift assault on the access road that led straight to the Tri-County Road and thence to the camp road itself. Passing on the way had come the Merrilark equipment van now loaded with the camp directors and Alex. Oddly, Sarah had no sense of police other than Mike; the forces of law and order manifested themselves only as figures with flashlights moving about in a seemingly random fashion, calling back and forth, all fitting parts of Sarah's nightmare scenario.

As for Julia Clancy, bundled aboard the camp van with Leah Pfeifer, she was trying hard to banish from her mind the uncharitable idea that this event—thank the dear Lord—was not an attack on High Hope Farm. That no man nor woman nor child nor beast connected with her farm had been hurt. This unworthy thought, however, Julia repressed, and as the van bumped its way up the dirt road and then sped toward the Merrilark entrance, she confined herself to sympathetic squeezes of Mrs. Eff's tightly fisted hands.

And Alex. After one long inhale of breath and the slow blowing out of air, he had simply put his mind and muscle into gear. No time to reason why or ask what; simply to get a move on and prepare for dealing with a stricken man if the ambulance had not yet arrived at Merrilark.

But it had. Not at Merrilark itself but at the camp parking lot. The van slammed to a stop and Alex jumped out, pushed forward through a small crowd of what must have been the residue of the Merrilark staff—kitchen workers, the nurse, two counselors.

The lamp below the parking lot sign sent a small round pool of light to the ground and, rather like a stage victim in some police opera, Brad Pfeifer lay facedown, sprawled, arms spread wide as if he were being frisked. But it was his head that demanded attention. A strangely misshapen head with a dark wet exudate oozing in patches and streaks in the blond buzz-cut hair.

The rescue team member who had been kneeling over the prostrate Brad straightened, saw Alex, and grimaced.

"Alive. Just. Vitals pretty loused-up. Air lines clear, though. Breathing. Sort of. Take a look. We'll run an IV, block the bleeding, and move him fast. The ER's been called and a neurosurgeon's on deck."

Alex nodded, knelt, reached, touched, and listened for a moment to a terrible snoring that bubbled out of the smashed head, and then stood up and began helping with the stretcher.

Sarah arrived just as the ambulance doors banged shut, and with police cars fore and aft, the ambulance, lights flashing, siren screaming, sped up the road and turned east toward the hospital.

She turned to see the camp emergency machinery still in motion. The Highfeather boys, with Winka Wentworth at their head and Neil at their tail, had disappeared toward their cabins, and now the Merrilark girls two by two shuffled away flanked by their shepherding counselors.

"It's as if they rehearsed all summer," said Sarah, back in Julia's kitchen, where the two women had sunk exhausted into the old wicker chairs. Julia had stayed long enough to see Leah Pfeifer and a counselor headed toward the hospital.

"They probably *have*," said Julia. "With all that's gone on at my farm the camps are probably ready for a nuclear meltdown. Poor Brad. Such a nice boy, even if he's a little headstrong. Since the Norminco people came to town, he's been spoiling for a fight."

"You mean," said Sarah, "he got the fight he's been spoiling for. Because of the mine? His opposition to it?"

The door banged open, slammed closed, and Mike Laaka and Deputy Katie Waters stood forth in the middle of the kitchen.

Julia raised a weary eye. "You," she said. "Never a moment alone without some policeman with a notebook."

"Katie has the notebook," said Mike, pulling up a chair to the kitchen table. He waved a lordly hand at Katie and beckoned her closer. "Hang in, Deputy Waters. Don't worry about making Julia and Sarah nervous. They're old hands at this. So Julia, how about it? Coffee and questions. Full-court press. We'll be working all night and you two are just the tip of the iceberg. You said Brad was spoiling for a fight. That was no fight; that was a direct attack. Assault. Battery. So we need statements. From the whole crowd at the cookout."

"He's still alive?" Sarah said. It seemed unbelievable. For a second she closed her eyes and saw again the battered head, the dark splotches of blood making patchwork of his short fair hair.

"Yeah, sort of," said Mike. "Fractured skull, as you can probably guess. Cross your fingers. We see some godawful injuries one day and a week later the guy's out washing his car. But if I had to bet I'd say if Brad makes it he'll need some recovery and rehab time. No more campfires this summer."

Julia, who had been busy about the coffee, returned with three steaming mugs. "It seems to me, Mike," she said, "that all I do is serve refreshments to the police. Now this business has nothing to do with High Hope Farm. Brad Pfeifer was attacked on Merrilark property. It must have something to do with the camp or Brad's opposition to the mine. He's made some people pretty mad. The people who want the mine to come in, who want jobs at the mine."

Mike took an appreciative sip of coffee, reached for the sugar bowl, and ladled in three heaping teaspoons. "Need to keep my energy level up. But you're wrong, Julia. High Hope Farm isn't in the clear. Your property was the launching pad. Brad left the cookout to drive to Merrilark. Prearranged. He had a date to talk at eight-thirty to the parents of this kid who's in the infirmary."

"So you think he was trailed by someone down at the cookout at Crawfish Pond?" said Sarah.

"Someone who could run a four-minute mile. Because Brad didn't go on foot, he drove. Everyone heard his truck start up. Actually, it wasn't his truck. It was a pickup belonging to High-feather because the Merrilark vehicles were blocked on that dirt road. No turnaround in the woods. Brad asked Neil if could borrow the truck and got the go-ahead. Of course, he could have been followed by someone in another vehicle, but so far no one has remembered hearing a second motor start."

Sarah looked up. "Are you saying almost everyone knew Brad was leaving and heard him leave?"

Mike nodded. "It was no secret. Everyone at the cookout knew, and back at Merrilark the kitchen staff, a couple of counselors holding the fort, the camp nurse, they knew, too. Well, Brad made it to the infirmary okay. Parked the pickup, went down to the camp, talked to the parents. Not a long call, ten minutes maybe. Started back but never got past the parking lot. Probably knocked down where he was found. About twenty feet from the pickup. It was just luck that a counselor coming back from her day off saw him. In fact, she almost ran over him. She raced down to Merrilark for help, called the ambulance, and sent Lisa to give the alert. As you know, Mrs. Pfeifer had started to get antsy because Brad was supposed to be back before nine to hand out the awards. Camp people hate it when something fouls up their schedule, and it was time for the kiddies to be tucked into their cots."

"But it's still a camp affair," said Julia stoutly. "He was attacked on Merrilark property."

"Almost on the property line," said Mike. "Either he was ambushed by someone who knew he was going to be at the camp or he was followed on foot from the cookout—which would be tough on that rough road. It was getting pretty dark. Sun sets by eight-twenty. Anyway, we'll have to time a runner on the distance. One-way and roundtrip."

"Perhaps," put in Julia, ever hopeful, "he was followed on his way back from the infirmary by someone on Merrilark staff. But," she added, looking puzzled, "why was he attacked in that lighted parking lot? Brad could see someone coming at him."

"Maybe he knew the attacker," put in Sarah, "so he didn't defend himself."

"Or," said Mike, "if it was an ambush, the attacker knew that Brad was coming back to the truck. The path from the camp to the parking lot isn't lighted. Everyone carries flashlights. Brad, too. But it's dark around the edges. The attacker could have taken advantage of Brad's going from a dark path to a lighted area. Brad would be temporarily blinded. Just long enough to be nailed on the head. Brad left the infirmary about eight forty-five. Ten minutes for the phone call, five minutes talking to the camp nurse. A few minutes to the parking lot."

"Let's get this over with," said Julia. "When we saw Brad. When we didn't. The last time we did."

Mike nodded to Katie Waters, who poised her pencil, and then he proceeded to drag Julia and Sarah through the afternoon, the orienteering, the arrival at Crawfish Pond, the barbecue, and Sarah's final look at Brad after the s'mores had been distributed.

"He led the camps in three cheers for Aunt Julia for providing her land for the games, then each camp sang some special song and afterward Brad said he was sorry to miss the rest of the singing but he had a phone call to catch. And he left."

"Okay," said Mike. "The people we've talked to so far agree on that. But how about the others? Did you keep an eye on the Wentworths? On Colonel Dodge? On your favorite spy, Jim Shale?"

"I saw the Wentworths before supper," said Sarah. "They were going around with score sheets. After that they popped up during the barbecue business. Later I didn't pay attention. I saw Neil just before Brad left because he started juggling three apples during the singing and I thought that he was quite good at it."

"That," said Mike, "puts Neil in place a little after eight. He says he okayed Brad's use of the pickup and came back to the group. Any later sightings?"

But Sarah and Julia denied later sightings of anyone but each other and Leah Pfeifer.

"It was getting dark," said Sarah. "And we were staring into the fire, so I really couldn't identify anyone."

"How about the good colonel?" asked Mike.

"I saw Harvey before the singing," said Julia. "We ate together. I think he was jealous about Jim Shale having given the campers a lecture on the compass. I don't know where he was during the singing. But I could hear him. After Brad Pfeifer left. Harvey has this great bass voice and he was bellowing."

"And when did you stop hearing him bellow?"

"After some song from one of the Disney films. He probably didn't know the words. I don't know what time it was; I just knew I was tired and wanted to go home."

"And Jim Shale?"

Here was agreement. Jim Shale had left immediately after supper, before the cake and before the singing. He had thanked Julia and nodded briefly to Sarah. And disappeared into the woods. No, he didn't use a flashlight, it was still light enough. No, he didn't say where he was going. But here Sarah pointed out that Jim Shale had left his truck parked by Tri-County Road.

"Which gives him wheels," said Mike. "He could watch, wait, and then follow."

Sarah, suddenly weighed by fatigue, nodded without speaking. And replaced Jim Shale's name on her list. How easy for the geologist to sit quietly in his truck, wait until Brad emerged from the farm road, and then track him to the Merrilark parking lot.

"Wake up, Sarah," said Mike. "How about Mrs. Pfeifer?"

Sarah shook herself and said Mrs. Eff had spent most of the evening in their campfire circle. "She told me she was upset about Aunt Julia getting those threatening nursery rhymes."

"I thought," said Mike to Julia, "that you weren't going to talk about those poems. To anyone."

"Well, it was just Leah Pfeifer. An old friend. A while back when I saw her at the post office. After all, everyone knows I've been getting peculiar messages."

"You told them originally that you'd had threatening poetry. Not nursery rhymes. That's the one fact that wasn't let out."

A long silence. Julia stirred her coffee. Reached down for a black and white cat that had been winding about under the table, lifted him up and settled him on her lap. "This one I call Domino. Because of his spots."

"Julia," said Mike. "Did you tell that very talkative female, Mrs. Pfeifer, that you received threatening nursery rhymes? As well as other types?"

Julia stroked Domino, ruffling the fur around his neck, tickling him under the chin.

"Julia, help me," said Mike.

Julia pushed an indignant Domino from her lap and stood up. "Damn you, Mike Laaka. I don't work for the CIA. I'm not under a sworn oath to never tell anyone what's on my mind. So I told Leah about them. Who has probably told everyone in Knox County. Including Tilly and Jane. And Harvey Dodge, because he's an old gossip and can nose out anything like that in ten minutes. So Mike go back to snooping somewhere else and leave my kitchen in peace."

Mike signaled to Katie Waters, who closed her notebook and stuck her pen in a shirt pocket. "It's okay, Julia," said Mike. "So you're human. Don't worry. It would have probably leaked sometime." He stood up, made it to the door, opened it for Katie Waters, and then turned. "So the question is whether those Harvey Dodge imitations will still come in. Or the 'Abou Ben Adhem' stuff. I'm betting it'll be 'Little Miss Muffet' from now on. And Julia, if it makes you happy, go on thinking that smashing Brad Pfeifer on the head has nothing to do with High Hope Farm. Good night."

"There are times when I feel like knocking Mike Laaka over his skull, putting a bridle around his head, and then shooting him," said Julia as she and Sarah cleared the cups from the table.

"A kind heart," murmured Sarah. "And easier to deal with than George Fitts. George goes at you with an ice pick."

"Why, oh why," groaned Julia, "why can't I keep my big mouth closed? I saw Leah at the post office—what is it about post offices? You see a friend and you start to chat. And with Leah—someone of my own generation—it seemed so easy to let my hair down, babble on about the trials of Julia Clancy. Oh hell."

"It will be interesting to see if you really do start getting nursery rhymes again."

At which the kitchen door opened and Alex walked in. Disheveled, face lined. Shoulders drooping. He looked at the two women. "You two look the way I feel."

"Brad?" said Julia and Sarah in one voice.

"Critical but stable. He's being taken to Maine Medical Center in Portland. Leah Pfeifer's shaken. She thinks it's either Norminco in action or some camp parent who's gone berserk. George Fitts is letting her believe that for the time being."

"Well, why not?" demanded Julia.

"Because," said Alex, taking Sarah by the arm and pointing her toward the stairs, "because it's so obviously a part of the whole. The Rise and Fall of High Hope Farm."

"Thank you," said Julia. "You're as consoling as Mike Laaka."

"Julia," said Alex. "You will overcome. I tell everyone you're as tough as leather. This affair of Brad brings the whole mess that much closer to being solved. Believe me. Someone is trying too hard."

Sarah turned, leaned over, and kissed her aunt's cheek. "Not a bit like leather," she said. "Soft as silk. And Alex is right. This whole business is shifting around, and I think those two camps are moving front and center. I mean, now that we know that High Hope Farm isn't nesting on valuable minerals."

Aunt Julia spun around. "What do you mean? How do you know? Have you been testing my soil?"

"Or getting Jim Shale to do it," put in Alex. He stretched, made a face at Sarah. "It's too late at night to allow you more than a single paragraph. Speak."

"In a way Aunt Julia's land has been tested. Ever since the orienteering games went haywire on the camp properties fifteen years ago but worked out just fine at High Hope. Compasses give false readings over certain magnetic mineral deposits, true readings over everyday dirt and rock. Conclusion—and Jim Shale confirmed this, though not in so many words—Aunt Julia's farm has no nickel, copper, cobalt, nor magnetite or pyrrhotite—but the two camps probably do."

Julia shook her head slowly, as if the movement itself was painful. "Then why on earth? I don't understand."

"Someone wants your scalp. Or your land as just land," said Alex. "If what Sarah says is true. Maybe someone like Harvey Dodge, who wants to have his cake and eat it too."

Julia looked fiercely at Alex. "I'm not someone's cake, but you may drive me right into Harvey's arms if you go on like that. Harvey Dodge is basically a total custard. Except on a horse. As I said, the army knew what it was doing when it kept him in warehouses. Why, I've had to give his horses their shots because he goes to pieces with a syringe. And tonight I'm sure he didn't follow Brad Pfeifer. Harvey couldn't have run after a pickup truck. He's too old and too fat. So there. Scratch Harvey Dodge."

"Okay," said Sarah. "Let's think about scratching him. At least if there's a connection between your farm attacks and Brad. And the police may have to scratch Brad himself as a suspect."

"And," continued Julia, "since you're scratching people, what about Jane and Tilly? They weren't at the cookout."

"But that doesn't mean they—or one or the other—couldn't have found out that Brad was going to make a phone call. Or saw him on his way to the camp and took the opportunity."

"Sarah, no," barked Julia. "Tilly and Jane hardly know Brad Pfeifer. Tilly wants my farm, not Camp Merrilark. You want suspects. Try Neil and Winka Wentworth, who may think they can destroy competition from Merrilark and grab my farmland for their own miserable camp. Mark my words. So go to bed."

And by mutual agreement Alex and Sarah and Julia moved toward the staircase and began the climb to the upper regions. As they reached the top of the stairs, Julia turned, kissed Alex, kissed Sarah, and gave a deep sigh. "Of course, I'm just being a pig-headed, contrary old woman, but," she added, "I'm probably right."

That night Sarah dreamt of a large band of goblins on horseback, each with a face exactly that of Aunt Julia. Strangely it was a rather satisfying experience, bringing the whole High Hope Farm business directly onto the back of its owner.

Sometime after seven on the following Saturday, the twenty-fifth of June, Alex, having finished breakfast, discovered Sarah in the stable dealing with wheelbarrows, manure, and shavings. Patsy lay as usual close at hand, chewing on an equine unmentionable, which Alex thought might be some part of a hoof left over from the recent farrier visit. He then turned his attention to Sarah and told her she was wielding her barn fork in quite an expert manner and complimented her style.

"I've been forcefully instructed by forceful people," said Sarah. She leaned against a stall door and wiped her forehead. Although it was early, the day promised heat and humidity. "I'm working off a bad dream—well, a peculiar dream. Aunt Julia turned up as a suspect, a sort of multiple goblin. It's my evil self wanting to get this affair over and pinned on someone. Even poor Aunt Julia. It's left me with this poisoned feeling. As if everything we breathe is noxious and everyone we know is tainted."

"I feel a little toxic myself," admitted Alex. "And before the morning's over I'll feel worse. I'm meeting Mike at George Fitts's office, and then I'll check on how Brad Pfeifer's doing."

"While I—" began Sarah.

"While you," said Alex, "do wholesome things like sift and fork manure and toss hay. Bucolic joys. Rural recreation."

"In a setting of homicide and general destruction. But there is something about rinsing water buckets and mucking out stalls and putting in fresh shavings. I feel I'm doing the Lord's work—or at least something to do with nurture. But I want to know about tonight. Jim Shale. Shall we pursue our cocktail chitchat idea or do we know enough about Aunt Julia's worthless land?"

"See what develops. Jim Shale will probably be spending part of the day on George's hot seat. He had opportunity and means. And motive. Brad Pfeifer was fighting the mine from the word go."

Sarah turned and picked up a leather halter hanging from a rack. "See you later. I have a date to turn out a handsome gelding named Plum Duff. Called Duffie. Sixteen hands, tall, dark, and splendid, and not a cross word unless you try to put shoes on him."

"In which case you have to twitch him with a murder weapon. Or rather," said Alex, "a murder accessory. I forgot to tell you. The lab microscopic report confirms that the twitch was used on Farney's head. Hair, bits of skin, blood cells, all match."

Sarah was silent for a moment, remembering the heft and length of the twitch she had held so tightly in her hands. A murder accessory picked up in the stable. A common bludgeon just waiting to be used. "You know," she said slowly, "these incidents, shotgun blasts, bashing and banging people, it's all a bit crude."

"You want the grace of a bullet? The subtle potion of poison in the stirrup cup? The elegant twist of a dagger? The English teacher wants finesse, not brute strength? Don't be so fussy; that snaffle bit in poor Farney's mouth showed a certain pathological sophistication."

"Come on, Alex. You know what I mean. When I said crude I meant that there's no sense of planning shown in any of these incidents. Look at the weapons. Whatever's close at hand. It's someone not used to doing in people—doing in farms and old ladies. Someone without a serious weapon inventory. A shotgun, a twitch, reins, maybe some stone dropped on Brad Pfeifer's head."

But Alex merely shrugged, waved a hand, and left, leaving Sarah to consider the implications of an untutored murderer.

However, by a coincidence, the matter of head-bashing was being given serious consideration by the forces of law and order: by Sergeant George Fitts in conference at his Thomaston state police office with Deputy Investigator Michael Laaka.

The office, a dingy rectangle with utility gray metal desk, gray metal file cabinets, gray metal office chairs, and dusty venetian blinds, had all the usual ambience of a state-supported facility. It was a room that always irritated Mike, making him feel he was trapped inside a vacuum cleaner. However, the office fitted the persona of George Fitts to a T. No external distractions, no interfering aesthetics. Plain and to the point.

"What I'm saying," said Mike, choosing Sarah's very adjective, "is that this guy is plenty crude. Right from the beginning. Like fixing that board in the hayloft, bonking Conners in the pasture."

"The pasture incident may have been an accident," George reminded him. "Too bad Patrick burned the branch. But stick to known facts, Mike." George was a man who never speculated unless he had a large stash of known facts on his desk.

"Okay," said Mike. "But Farney was hit with the twitch before he was strangled, and Brad Pfeifer was slammed with something. And even the gunshot thing. A spray of shot at the farm. Lighting those fires. It all seems kind of amateur."

"Midcoast Maine isn't Mafia central," George reminded him. "Nothing organized. We usually have domestic violence, small-time drug doings. Vehicular manslaughter. Crude, as you say."

"Don't know as Julia's farm business is what you'd call domestic," said Mike. "Too wide a scope. And the Norminco mine may figure in somehow in a sort of back-ass way. And Merrilark and Highfeather. Those are well-known institutions. Kids from all over the country. And Sarah mentioned motivation . . ."

George interrupted. "Don't mess with motivation unless it's in plain sight. Changed wills, revenge, jealous boyfriends, drug deals. Or mineral deposits, of which there are none on High Hope Farm."

Mike stared. "How'd you know that? Sarah just squeezed it out of Jim Shale last night. Because of the compass deviation on one side of Tri-County Road and none on Julia's property."

George allowed his thin lips an upward curve. "It's been obvious that a sizable mineral deposit on High Hope Farm might be attractive to someone."

"So you had state geologists skulking around on Julia's land in the middle of the night? Taking core samples, drilling? Your guys were probably the ghosts that everyone's been seeing."

"No drilling. No point in spending state money and upsetting Mrs. Clancy. But she told us that she'd had wells dug in various parts of her pastures for supplying the watering troughs, so we did some checking. The tailings from the well diggings are still mounded up near the drilling sites and we had the residue tested. Since the drilling went down almost two hundred feet we had a fair sample of the rock layers at quite a depth. No sign that any mineral anomalies were present. Then we looked up old geodetic surveys and found that no compass deviations had ever been noted."

"And you didn't share any of this with your buddy in the sheriff's department?"

"I would have," said George pleasantly. "In time. However, you've found out on your own. So back to motivation. Nothing satisfactory emerges." George looked at his watch and scowled. "Go back to this business of how. Crude, you said."

"Yeah, crude," said Mike. "Rough and ready. No neat handgun stuff. No high-powered rifle or automatic weapon. Common buckshot from some everyday twenty-two-gauge shotgun. Dime a dozen around here. No fancy business for our ballistics people. What we've got is amateur hour. Take a guess. Who does that point to?"

"I told you, I don't guess. Stick to what we have. It's someone local who knows horses, is very familiar with the whole High Hope Farm setup, and wants to injure or destroy it."

"Damn it, George, let me guess if you won't. I say everything points to a female. A nonexpert equals female. A woman."

The door banged open and Alex walked in. "Is that a sexist remark, Mike? Nonexpert equals female?"

"Sit down, Alex," said George, indicating a metal chair beside the wall. "Mike here thinks the pattern of attack suggests female. Wrong. Statistics show that men are more apt to use certain methods to kill someone, women another. Women, even in these enlightened days, don't often choose physical confrontation. Fists, sticks, head bashing. But there may be a pattern."

"Sarah thinks so," said Alex. He sat down and pulled the chair closer to the desk. "I don't know about male or female, but she thinks these attacks suggest that the murderer took what came to hand or grabbed an opportunity and acted. Loosen the board in the hayloft, hang up a rocking horse when everyone's watching the race, find a twitch and Farney alone in the stable when the rice is being thrown at a wedding, know Brad Pfeifer will be alone at night and just do it. With what's available."

"Contradictions," said George. He picked up another folder, leafed through it, and pulled out a sheet. "Nursery rhymes, poetry threats. Lots of planning. Cutting out little letters, pasting them on. Wearing gloves. Delivering or posting them."

"Are you saying you've got two assault people? Or three? The poetry-clippers and the head-basher?" said Mike.

"I'm not saying anything yet," said George. "We're still sorting out last night. Looking for the so-called weapon."

And as if in answer to this statement, the telephone rang, George picked up the receiver, listened, nodded, made a note, listened again, and hung up. He looked up at Mike and Alex. "I take it back. They've found the weapon. A shovel."

"Shovel!" exclaimed Mike and Alex together.

"What the hell," said Mike. "What was a shovel doing in the parking lot? Someone starting a garden?"

"Simple," said George. "The shovel was left there from last winter. The camp caretaker always leaves a barrel of sand and a heavy shovel to use on the camp hill when it's icy. Apparently he just left the shovel there behind the Merrilark parking lot."

"So someone from Merrilark knew it was there," said Mike. "Special knowledge. That narrows the thing down."

"No," said George. "The same caretaker works for Highfeather and leaves a similar shovel there. That one is still in place. And in the winter, with no leaves on the bushes, the shovel's right out in plain sight. Not an aluminum snow shovel. A long-handled ditch-digging shovel. Lots of heft. Nice weapon."

"And you're saying," put in Alex, "that both the Merrilark people and the Highfeather tribe would know about the shovel."

"So would the whole neighborhood. Out of season both camps lend their facilities to the local public schools for teach-ins and to the Audubon Society for meetings."

"Great," said Mike. "Great. Another frigging universal weapon. Shovels, twitches, limbs of trees. Well, shit."

George ignored Mike and returned to the earlier subject. "A pattern. The weapon of choice is what comes to hand."

"When the opportunity comes up," repeated Mike.

"So our job now," said George, "is to limit opportunity and keep up surveillance. That cookout was a natural. I had ordered our men to keep track of all the High Hope people. But I never once considered that the camp personnel were at risk. I didn't have Brad Pfeifer watched. My fault. But it won't happen again."

Alex grimaced. "Talking of opportunity, that combined training affair of Julia's is going to be an open door."

"No," said George. "We'll cover that horse show like a rug. For us it's a perfect opportunity."

"Right," said Mike. "Sure. Fingerprint the horses, bug the horse trailers. Perfect opportunity, hell. Perfect to put the final whammy on the farm."

"Wrong," said George. "It's a setup for the murderer. He or she will be there. But so will we. We'll be there with a team that knows what it's doing. We're the professionals. This person is an amateur. Shovels, twitches, tree branches, soaked rags, shotgun blasts. Professionals beat amateurs. Every time."

"The hell they do," said Mike, but George was standing up, walking to his file drawer, and yanking it open.

"He won't listen," said Mike, on his way out to the state police parking lot with Alex.

"He hears you," said Alex, "but he can't give you the satisfaction. He's right about the horse show. It is a great opportunity. For catching someone. Or for someone catching it. The old window of opportunity. A two-way window."

"I never think of George as a gambler, but I'm changing my mind. Me, I bet on horse races. Get all hot and passionate. I fall in love with some beautiful Thoroughbred and I forget logic and record and bet my shirt. George, ice-water George, maybe that's the way to be. A Cool Hand Luke. Who doesn't get riled up because he doesn't care about the people. As people. He just wants to be right and nail his man. Into battle without a quiver. Take what comes and devil take the hindmost."

Alex stopped at his car door. "And the devil may do just that next weekend."

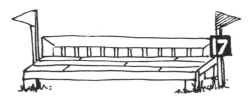

THE PICNIC BENCH

SEVENTEEN

SATURDAY morning's promise of heat was fulfilled well before noon. Sarah, toiling with wheelbarrow, fork, and water bucket, felt as if she was being smothered in a hot wet blanket. In fact, she almost envied Alex his visit to George's office, which she supposed—erroneously—to be air-conditioned. The arrival of Cousin Jessica Jacoby to spur her into greater action, to point out errors of omission in stall care, did nothing to make the morning seem shorter. There was some strange physical principle at work that allowed sawdust and shavings to work their way into socks, underpants, down the bra, in the nose, between the toes, indeed, into every body crevice.

Finally, just before noon, Sarah put down her fork and rebelled.

"Jessica, you're not even human. You should run a country, not waste your time on a little job like this. Haiti or even Eastern Europe could use you."

"I've thought about politics," said Jessica, putting down the empty wheelbarrow, "but it wouldn't leave much time for riding. Okay, let's have a break for lunch. The beginners' riding lesson is at two o'clock and that's you, isn't it? You and all the campers."

"They're having lessons today?" said Sarah, surprised. "I thought after last night . . . Bradley Pfeifer."

Jessica pushed the wheelbarrow out of the stall aisle into an alcove. "You kidding?" she said over her shoulder. "You think camp stops? Just like that. Be real. Neil Wentworth did a jump class this morning and Winka was here working out a schedule." Jessica returned to Sarah, shoulders braced, her head high and held aslant in a fair imitation of Winka's usual posture. "High Feathah campahs never let down the side," she said in a lisping version of Winka's voice and accent. "Campahs know that they will please Brad Pfeifer and Merrilark best by going on. Keeping camp spirit high."

Sarah grinned. She could almost hear Winka Wentworth. "Well, how about Mrs. Eff? Does she want the show to go on?"

"Oh sure. It's part of the camp thing. The mystique. When anything goes wrong they have a bunch of meetings and everyone is told to be especially caring and thoughtful. I mean, there wouldn't be summer camps if every little emergency knocked them flat."

"I'd call Brad Pfeifer's accident more than just a little emergency," said Sarah.

"Merrilark will get a handle on it. The kids will make get-well cards in the craft hut, and at evening campfire there'll be a talk about Brad and kids will get up and say something nice. Okay, let's find some shade and eat. I'll go up to the house and pick up our sandwiches and a Thermos of cool stuff. I told Aunt Julia it would be too hot to eat inside today."

So, thought Sarah as she watched Jessica start up toward the farmhouse, I wonder when she last saw Brad. I'll bet she didn't open up all the way with the police. Kids don't."

Jessica returned, and with these ideas at front and center, Sarah brought up the subject of last night's campfire. They were sitting, together with Patsy, under an oak tree behind the stable.

Her cousin was forthcoming. "Mr. Shale left first and then

after a while Brad left. Neil Wentworth was all over the place. Calling out songs. Juggling apples. I didn't see Mrs. Eff much but I suppose she was sitting down."

"And Winka Wentworth."

"I saw her at the beginning of the singing and then later on. I know she was at the campfire when the news came about Brad."

"You're sure?"

"Sure I'm sure. She jumped up when the news came and knocked over a big thing of cocoa. I didn't see Colonel Dodge but I heard him. He's got a big voice and he's off-key a lot."

"And Tilly and Jane never showed up?"

"They went to this Friday night bean supper thing in Union. I know because I clean for them. Once a week. Housework or help in the barn. To make some extra money."

"You work there?" This was a new idea. Jessica had access to Appleyard Farm.

"Yeah, and the place is really falling apart. Plaster sagging and paint chipping. Porch steps are loose, too."

"I don't think they have much extra money. Besides, Tilly hasn't been well. Upset. Not herself."

"Yeah, she's kind of crazy sometimes. And Jane watches her like some sort of guard dog. What I'm trying to tell you is that the other day I was cleaning out Tilly's workroom—she does pottery and quilts and stuff. It hadn't been cleaned in ages because Tilly's usually in it. Well, I was dumping the wastebasket junk into a garbage bag and Jane came in and grabbed the garbage bag and says I'm disturbing Tilly's room. And Tilly wasn't even home. She was off shopping somewhere."

Sarah nodded silently, not being particularly interested in the Appleyard cleaning arrangements.

"Well, you know what?"

"What?" said Sarah automatically. The sun was almost directly overhead, it was getting hotter by the minute, and even the shade of the oak tree gave little comfort. In fact, her chicken salad sandwich, even as it was being swallowed, was probably heating itself into a dangerous condition of salmonella.

Jessica, on the other hand, seemed relatively fresh and cool. Youth, thought Sarah with resentment.

Jessica tossed her sandwich crust to a waiting Patsy. "I mean," she said, "that I didn't know about those funny notes Aunt Julia has been getting. I sort of knew in general but not really, until Aunt Julia told Mrs. Eff, and she told everybody. About their being nursery rhymes at first and then other kinds. Made with cut-out letters. So you know what happened?"

"No," said Sarah, sitting up and taking notice, "but you're going to tell me."

"It was funny, because Jane doesn't usually bust a gut trying to empty wastebaskets. She doesn't like housework and she's usually outside or doing something in the barn. But she grabbed that garbage bag and left the room and went charging out to the back of the house like some sort of giant bumblebee was after her."

"And you followed," said Sarah helpfully.

"Wouldn't you? I mean, I didn't want to spy or anything, but I was really curious, so I followed and saw Jane go on out past the trash shed and all the way out to the manure pile—it's behind the barn. Then Jane took this fork and dug a hole and dumped the whole garbage bag stuff in and looked around as if she thought someone might see her and then she came back. I beat her back to Tilly's room and she didn't know I'd seen her."

"End of story?" said Sarah.

Jessica picked out a small plum and squeezed it thoughtfully between forefinger and thumb and then took a moist, dripping bite. "End of story," she said. "Because I didn't want to go digging around in that smelly old manure pile. I mean, I wasn't that curious. Tilly's weird. And sometimes Jane is, too. Weird about Tilly. So I just forgot about it."

"Until now?"

"Yeah, I guess so. Now that I know about these cut-out poems, I thought I'd tell someone and you're right here, and if I told the police they'd make a big deal out of it, and if I told Aunt

Julia she'd say I was snooping around where it was none of my business."

"But you don't know why Jane took the garbage bag away?"

"No, but I sure know what was in it."

Sarah restrained an impulse to shake her cousin until her teeth rattled. "Okay, Jessie. Put me out of my misery. What *was* in the garbage bag?"

Jessica smiled the smile of someone who has been playing a fish on a line and now sees that the hook is nicely snagged into its lip. "Paper," she said with satisfaction. "Little itty bits of paper. Letters cut out. From chopped-up magazines."

There was a long unbroken silence. Jessica savoring her dramatic moment, Sarah pushing her brain into gear—no mean feat on an airless day with the temperature climbing into the nineties. Tilly's wastebasket that hadn't been cleaned in ages. Tilly's workroom. Tilly the scissor poet. Or one of them. Of course the possibility had been suggested, but suddenly, faced with genuine evidence, Sarah felt rather ill. Tilly, despite her quirks and cranks, her general battiness, was such an old friend of Julia's.

"Tilly," repeated Sarah, trying to get used to the idea, "Tilly's been cutting out letters."

"Well, I suppose it was Tilly," said Jessica. "Unless it was Jane, because Jane uses Tilly's room sometimes. They sort of share it when Jane has some project. The room's always a mess."

Sarah closed her eyes. Jane? Tilly? Tilly and Jane together in a sort of destructive partnership? Or Jane covering for Tilly? Or—unlikely thought—Tilly assuming dottiness to cover Jane's determination to take over High Hope Farm.

"Hey," said Jessica, "what's the matter? I didn't mean to shake you up or anything. I just thought I should tell someone."

"You should," said Sarah firmly. "You should tell the police and as soon as possible. But first, is that manure pile still there? Jane hasn't bulldozed it, has she?"

"I don't know. Sometimes she spreads manure on the field."

"When did this all happen?" demanded Sarah.

"Day before yesterday," said Jessica promptly. "Thursday. I clean for Tilly and Jane then because it's my day off at the farm."

"And Tilly and Jane went to the bean supper Friday," said Sarah. "Do you know if they had plans for Friday during the day?"

"There was a church food sale in Union on Friday. I know because Tilly was making a pie Thursday. Then Tilly went out and that's when Jane grabbed the garbage bag away from me."

"So Jane may have been too busy Friday to move the manure."

"Maybe," said Jessica. "Maybe not."

"Are Tilly and Jane home now?" demanded Sarah.

Jessica frowned, trying to think. "I heard there's a horse show in Belfast this Saturday and that Jane's niece is riding. Tilly usually goes along with her to all of the local shows."

Sarah thought out loud. "Okay, so no one's home." Suddenly she flung herself into action. "Come on, Jessica. If what you say is true we'll tell the police this afternoon. But let's check your story out. It's perfectly possible that Jane or Tilly was working on some project that has nothing to do with Aunt Julia. I don't want to have the police go charging over there scaring them half to death over nothing." Sarah looked at her watch. "It's only twelve-thirty; you can take me over to that manure pile right now."

"In broad daylight, with all these policemen around?"

"We won't make a big production of it," said Sarah. "I'll tie Patsy up here in the shade with water and we'll just walk through the south paddock, keeping the horses between us and the farm. Then cross over, slip into the woods, cut north across the camp road, and go through the old orchard. Come into Appleyard Farm from the back."

"You mean sneak in," said Jessie.

"Nothing of the kind," said Sarah. "It won't hurt to check a manure pile privately. We'll be doing our duty as good neighbors because we care about Tilly's and Jane's peace of mind. Which I agree may be about to come to a crashing end." Sarah stood up, dusted the sandwich crumbs from her jeans, wiped a perspiring forehead, shook a few pieces of sawdust from her hair, and together the two moved purposefully toward the south paddock.

Arrived by stealth, through woods, apple orchard, and pasture, at the back side of their destination, Sarah and Jessica confronted the Appleyard Farm's manure collection. It lay steaming behind the barn—four malodorous heaps of manure and shavings.

"Oh lord," said Sarah, sniffing, "this is going to be awful. And it's all from only one horse." She braced herself. "Which pile?"

"Well," said Jessica doubtfully, "I think it's that one over by the outhouse."

"Go into the barn and grab a couple of pitchforks," commanded Sarah. "We haven't got all day and we're going to sweat like pigs."

"Pigs have sweat glands near their snouts," said Jessica. "In science last month we did sweat glands and . . ."

"Just get the forks," said Sarah. "I'll keep an eye out for cars. I think we're okay; the driveway is empty."

But it wasn't the pile over by the outhouse. Nor the large pile beyond. Nor the pile next to a roll of wire fencing.

"Damn," said Sarah. She brought her sleeve across a dripping face, leaving an unwholesome streak, put down her fork, and looked at her watch. "We've got twenty minutes to dig and then it's time for my riding lesson. Though I suppose I could call in sick."

But Jessica wasn't listening. She had stuck her fork into a small mound by her left foot and now she stared down at it. One of the fork tines had impaled a small square of stained paper. A piece of paper with irregularly sized letters still sticking to their surface. Letters making five words. Jessica gestured downward and Sarah walked over, reached down, and slid the fragile paper down the tine of the fork.

Five words. CLANCY SAT IN A HALL and a floating W.

"Wow," said Jessica. And then, triumphant, "I told you."

Sarah held the paper away from her body as if it somehow

was impregnated with a deadly poison. "This must have been a reject. The poem Aunt Julia got started 'Julia Clancy sat on a wall.' Oh lord," she said sadly, "I wish you hadn't. When we couldn't find anything, I was saying thank heavens to myself."

"So you'll keep this a secret. Just between us. Bury the paper?" asked Jessica in a hopeful voice.

"No," said Sarah. "I'll do exactly what I don't want to do. I'll go on back to the farm and put a call in to the police." She reached in her pocket and came up with a tissue, which she folded carefully around the stained scrap of paper. "Okay, come on. Let's get back. Time to bite the bullet."

"Do what?"

"Just an old expression. And it's not us who'll be biting bullets, it's Jane and Tilly."

But bullet-biting was put on momentary hold. Sarah and Jessica, straggling back in an overheated condition, met Mike himself and Julia marching down upon the stable, and before Sarah could speak Julia uncorked a sharp lecture on the necessity of staff (Jessica) and those posing as staff (Sarah) to keep themselves, regardless of temperature, in a state of cleanliness and order.

And Sarah lost it. "Aunt Julia, be quiet. Jessica and I have had it. We've been working our butts off. In the interest of finding out the truth of something. Which we found. And we're both sorry about it. So please, dear Aunt, back off. Right off."

And Julia subsided. "I'm sorry. But you both do look awful. Besides, it's hellishly hot, which always affects my temper, and Mike here has been ruining my morning. Another letter. Cut-out rhymes."

Sarah and Jessica stared, Sarah reaching in her pocket.

"Yeah," said Mike. "I've got the copy right here."

"Stevenson? James Leigh Hunt? Tennyson?" asked Sarah without much hope.

"Nursery rhyme," said Mike, handing Sarah a sheet of paper. "Came by mail. A takeoff from 'Sing a Song of Sixpence.'"

"But Julia's already had that one," said Sarah.

"This is the second verse," said Mike. "The part about the king in the counting house. Same old message."

"Let me see it," demanded Sarah. She reached her hand out, took the paper, and slowly read aloud:

Julia is in her parlour eating bitter gall;
Harvey is in his counting house planning Julia's fall.

She handed the paper back to Mike saying at the same time, "That's a little different. A direct accusation of Harvey."

"Could be a red herring," said Mike. "Harvey pointing to himself so's to look like another victim. But God-a-mighty I'd like to get a handle on this foolishness. The police have enough to do without spending time on Mother Goose."

"Mike, Aunt Julia," said Sarah slowly, "Jessica and I have something to tell you."

Julia Clancy had a very difficult few minutes. It was never hard for her to believe ill of another person—but only to a point. The point marked the difference between them and us. Tilly and Jane were us. Tilly's flights into the never-land of the psyche and the hinterlands of the occult, despite their irritant effects, were at the bottom almost endearing. Even Tilly's vision of rotating into High Hope Farm was part of the tolerable Tilly package. Julia, once friendship had been firmly established, took that friendship warts and all. Now, suddenly, it was as if this particular friendship was composed entirely of warts.

"I can't believe it," said Julia. "Tilly. Tilly and Jane. Oh, I know Tilly has been driving me up the wall all summer, but she wouldn't, I mean she couldn't do something like this. I know you suggested it, but I didn't believe you. To threaten me. Really threaten me. Try and burn down the farm. Kill Farney."

"Wait up," said Mike. "One step at a time. For now it's these nursery rhymes, nothing else. Yeah, I know Tilly's been talking like the head witch of Union and she dragged out your old rocking horse, but don't you go after them. If Tilly or Jane shows up today, act perfectly natural. I'll come back this afternoon with the lab results on the last new letter. See if it's related to the others. What kind of scissors. This afternoon we'll do another check on Tilly and Jane's activities last night. See if either or both got loose long enough to bang Brad Pfeifer over the head with a shovel. Okay, Julia?" This as Julia continued to glower in the direction of Appleyard Farm.

"And I let her bake the wedding cake," said Julia. "It might have killed us all. Arsenic or cyanide."

"But it didn't kill us," put in Sarah. "It was a wonderful cake. Listen to Mike and keep quiet. Go do something therapeutic like wash a horse."

"Come on, Sarah," said Jessica, who had been standing by unregarded but listening with great attention. "Time for your lesson, and I've got to finish three more stalls."

"Good advice," said Mike. "I'll find George and fill him in." And he turned on his heel and strode off toward the parking lot. Sarah, watching, saw that a huge triangle of wet marked the back of his shirt, a perfect testimony to the increasing heat.

"I don't think I'll survive a riding lesson," said Sarah.

"You won't have to," said Julia. "Winka is going to work with you on horse physiology, wrapping and bandaging. After all, we can't have any of the horses hit by heatstroke."

During the lesson that followed, since it didn't involve trying to balance on a horse's back, Sarah was allowed to study Winka Wentworth with greater attention than before. And Neil, too, whenever he dodged onto the scene, made a comment, identified a piece of equine anatomy, wrapped a tail, demonstrated a bandage, and then dodged out again. Sarah now put Neil and Winka definitely under the heading of a couple in trouble. Neil's interruptions irritated Winka, and once she suggested that he stay and pull his weight or leave. Was this state of affairs something growing out of? continuing? the shouting match Sarah had overheard. Out of the tensions manifest during that tea party?

However, when left to herself as the sole teacher, Winka was her usual brightly commanding self. In fact, as she brought out horses, unrolled bandages, and, pointer in hand, raced between charts depicting a horse's musculature and bone structure,

Winka acted like a one-man band. Strangely, the absent Brad Pfeifer was the presiding presence at the class. Winka referred to Brad as there in spirit, as wanting everything at Highfeather and Merrilark to go on as usual. In fact, so elevated did Winka become in a moment of remembering how Brad had supported the riding program that Sarah thought she was about to start talking of picking up the torch and have everyone break into the "Star-Spangled Banner."

The time ticked forward, the clock hands on the arena wall almost pointed to the end of the hour, and Sarah began to consider the very real possibility of a swim in the lake, or more likely a sluice with the hose followed by a gallon of Gatorade, when Neil reentered the arena, his face ashen, his lips moving soundlessly.

"Well, Neil," said Winka crossly. "What is it now? We're just finishing up." Then looking hard at her husband, her voice changed. "What is it? Is something wrong? Something at Highfeather? One of the campers?"

Neil swallowed hard and found his voice. "It's Brad Pfeifer. He never came to. He died about half an hour ago. The hospital just called."

And Winka, as if struck in the face, jerked back, brought the back of her hand to her mouth, and then slowly bowed her head.

"I suppose," said Mike meeting with Julia, Sarah, and Alex later that afternoon on the steps of the farmhouse, "we shouldn't have been so optimistic. You think everything's going along, the medical people sound cheerful, and then wham, down the tubes."

Alex nodded soberly. "Head injuries are the devil. I thought there was a fair chance for recovery. So now what?"

Mike jerked his head toward Tri-County Road, where a very large horse van was lumbering into sight, slowing, and laboriously making the turn into High Hope Farm. "That's what," he said. "Field office. George has decided to crank the whole investigation up a notch after hearing about Brad. The state police used this van as a mobile unit and a stake-out point two summers ago when the Union Fair was being vandalized and one of the barkers was strangled. It's all wired and ready to go. George has been dying to get the state police's money's worth out of the thing. Now it will just be part of the woodwork during Julia's two-day event."

Julia, who would have normally protested the invasion of a foreign vehicle on her soil, was silent. Only the biting of her lower lip showed her displeasure.

The little group watched the parking of the van, the opening of the door, the emergence of George Fitts from the passenger seat. He was almost jovial.

"I knew we'd have a use for this van someday," he said. "I've been blocking its sale for months. In the meantime, Mrs. Clancy, Sarah, Alex, come aboard. You too, Mike."

And like animals boarding some metallic ark, one by one the passengers loaded. Through what was ostensibly a dressing room door into a small but well-designed office in the space that normally held six horses.

George shook five folding chairs loose from a stack, settled them about a small desk, and opened a notebook.

"Windows," complained Mike. "We'll suffocate."

"Air-conditioning's on," said George. "Give it a minute. This was a very fancy horse van. Stolen in Florida. It was headed for Canada when we seized it. Horses and heroin. Heroin hidden in capsules in hay bales. Very tricky outfit."

"Okay, George," said Mike. "What have you got for us?"

"I'm going to bring you all—especially Mrs. Clancy—up to date, so that she'll have a full sense of what's going on with her farm."

"You have our message about letters in the manure pile," put in Julia. "Tilly and Jane. Or just Tilly. I can't believe, I mean it must have started as a joke. And then it got out of control . . ." Here Julia stumbled to a stop and simply shook her head.

"We have a search warrant and a team working nonstop on their land," said George. "Fortunately Tilly Martin and Jane Zimmer will be at the Belfast horse show until at least five and then are expected at an art gallery opening in Searsport. That gives us leeway. So far the results are satisfactory."

"So it's true," said Julia faintly. "It's been Tilly or both of them the whole time. Everything? Even killing Farney and hitting Brad Pfeifer?"

"Killing Brad Pfeifer," corrected George. "Brad Pfeifer is now a homicide."

"George, for Chrissake, get on with it," said Mike irritably. "You're leaving Julia hanging out to dry."

"By satisfaction I meant shreds of cut paper," said George, "shreds of glossy print from coated magazines—probably *Newsweek*—some found in the older manure heaps. They should have burned them, destroyed the scissors," he added in a voice of disapproval, confirming again Sarah's long-standing suspicion that George would have made as efficient a criminal as he did a policeman.

"But they didn't," said Mike unnecessarily.

"No," said George, "and the paper pieces found so far seem to match those used in the four early nursery rhymes sent to Mrs. Clancy. No scraps so far matching the new nursery rhyme verse that came in this morning. And no matching paper for the poetry of James Leigh Hunt, Robert Louis Stevenson, Andrew Marvell, or Alfred Lord Tennyson. We guess that these came to Julia from another source. Copycat work. We've had the lab working overtime on this, but we won't get a final report until tomorrow at the earliest."

"Hell," said Julia to no one in particular.

George pulled a large blue ring-binder notebook from his briefcase. "So we're adding to the case file a confirmed homicide just off Mrs. Clancy's property, homicide of a person closely connected with High Hope Farm."

"Not closely connected," protested Julia. "Just there for one cookout."

"Closely connected," repeated George. "Both Merrilark and Highfeather send their riding students here for lessons along with Mr. and Mrs. Wentworth. Both camps have camped out on your lake in past years and both camp directors were guests at

Sarah and Alex's wedding. They are part of the neighborhood dynamics."

"The mine," said Sarah, "what about the mine?"

"Norminco," said George, "was interesting when we thought that Mrs. Clancy's land might have the same mineral deposits that showed under the properties across on the east side of the Tri-County Road. Norminco remains in the picture now only as a possible purchaser of Appleyard Farm or either of the two camps. And because Brad Pfeifer was working to prevent the mine from being developed. However, Colonel Dodge is another matter."

"He's changed his mind?" said Sarah, eyes widening.

"Sarah," snapped Julia, "you're always hinting about Harvey. He wouldn't sell to Norminco. He just wouldn't. Never."

"Never say never," threw in Mike. "Okay, George, go on."

George paused, a judicious pause. Then looking directly at Julia, he said, "We've heard today that Colonel Dodge has made an arrangement with Norminco for them to lease his Quartermaster Farm if indeed the mine plan goes forward."

"Oh my God in heaven," exclaimed Julia.

"I'm sorry, Mrs. Clancy," said George, "but it's true. I had it from Jim Shale himself, and a phone call this noon confirms it."

"I don't, I won't, believe it," said Julia piteously. "Not Harvey. Not Harvey selling out . . ." She reached over and clutched Sarah's shirt as if for support.

"Leasing," said George. "Not selling."

Sarah took her aunt's hand. "Maybe it's not true. There's probably a misunderstanding. Wait until you talk to Harvey."

But Julia's face, first crumpled with shock, now turned to stone. "I'll never talk to Harvey again. The . . . the bastard."

"Maybe he was desperate for money," said Alex. "You don't know what sort of financial mess he may be in."

"He could have come to me," said Julia through a clenched jaw. "Harvey could always come to me."

"But," said Sarah, "you've been going on about cutting expenditures, saying the farm was eating up all your cash."

"The bastard," was Julia's only response.

"This is off the record," said George, "but we've had certain intimations that lately Harvey Dodge had shown an interest in the Merrilark operation and has mentioned to one of the senior counselors that he might be a part of the staff next year."

"Harvey!" exclaimed Julia. "Harvey! Harvey Dodge. A counselor! At his age. He's crazy. Crazy, stark-raving mad."

"Not exactly as a counselor," said George softly. "More as an investor. Part owner."

Alex looked up. "I thought it was a foregone conclusion that Brad Pfeifer was going to inherit the camp when Mrs. Eff retired."

"Not so foregone as you think," said George. "Brad had been asking about a wilderness camp near the Allagash. That was his specialty. Wilderness camping. Apparently he wanted to work in that area and was becoming restless as Mrs. Pfeifer's second fiddle. He wanted to save Merrilark for his aunt and then move on."

"Treason, treachery," growled Julia. "Treason, treachery, all around us. Tilly, Jane, now Harvey. And Bradley Pfeifer. Damn, damn. Oh I give up. It's like some awful play. Sarah, what's the play with that dreadful king with the humped back?"

"*Richard the Third,*" said Sarah, "but I don't think . . ."

"That's it," said Julia. "The War of the Roses and everyone with a knife out for everyone else and greed and mendacity knee-deep. All we need is two little princes smothered by pillows. And they probably will be," she added grimly. She stood up. "I'm going to feed my horses. Thank God I have my horses. And my dogs and my cats. Loyal, honest, and true. And Patrick. Because if I find that Patrick is out to get me I will commit . . . what is it I'll commit . . . that thing with a snickersnee in the stomach?"

"Hari-kari," said Sarah. "Do you want me to come with you? A trustworthy consoling niece with no ax to grind?"

"No," said Julia. "I need time to digest this. Alone. I think I'll ride this evening. Ride Duffie. Have Patrick set up some jumps for me. I need wholesome honest action."

"So you can break your neck and be rid of this cruel world?"

said Sarah. "Come on, Aunt Julia, let's go out. Just you and me and Alex. Take in an old movie."

"No," said Julia. "I know what I should do and it will be done. On the back of a horse."

And Julia moved to the door, glared at George and Mike, and departed, slamming the metal door of the trailer hard behind her.

"George," said Sarah angrily, "that was fairly brutal. Harvey is her oldest friend. Her suitor. He wants to marry her."

"He may still want to marry her, but I gather she's said no a dozen times and he's very, very short of cash. Two mortgages on that farm of his. And a lifelong interest in camping. If he can't have Julia and High Hope he may settle for Merrilark. And Mrs. Pfeifer."

"My God," said Sarah, "Mrs. Eff!"

"Mrs. Pfeifer," said Mike, "has known Harvey Dodge just as long as Julia has. They have a lot in common."

Sarah subsided, her ears ringing, her mind's eye picturing Julia's world in total disorder.

"To come back to subject one," said George, "we are dealing with two murders and a number of unexplained incidents. Sarah, I don't want you to go anyplace alone. The same for Julia. We're giving Julia protection from tonight on, putting a tail on Tilly Martin and Jane Zimmer and Harvey Dodge, and watching the personnel of both camps very closely. Until the two-day event is over, until this affair is cleared-up, you can look at High Hope Farm as an armed camp. Good night, Sarah. Alex. Don't let Mrs. Clancy do anything foolish."

"Can we stop Julia from jumping?" said Sarah to Alex as they walked slowly across to the stable.

"I'd as soon stop a diesel engine," said Alex. "But we can hover nearby to pick up the pieces and take what's left out for a movie as you suggested. Or dinner. A drive."

"Poor Aunt Julia," mourned Sarah. "It's one thing to keep saying no to a suitor; it's another to find out that he's located someone else across the street."

"As Julia pointed out," said Alex, "she has her horses. Ever loyal and true. Now let's go and see if we can persuade Patrick to keep those jumps under eleven feet high."

Julia Clancy, in a frenzy of activity, followed a demanding round of jumping on Plum Duff by vigorous hosing of her horse, a saddle-soaping of her tack, and a refresher obedience session with her two dogs, Tucker and Belle. Then, after a brief disappearance into the shower, she repaired, double scotch in hand, to the front parlor and began assaulting the piano keyboard with Chopin.

Sarah, who with Alex had watched and followed and now listened from the parlor door, stepped forward.

"Aunt Julia, stop it. Right now. You're driving us mad, and yourself into an early grave."

Julia brought her fingers down on the keys, thumped out several noisy chords, lifted her hands, and turned on the piano stool. "A timely grave, I'd say. But I need to keep moving. Doing. If I don't I will drive myself into something. Into a psychosis. I'll turn into Tilly and start seeing things."

"Come on out with us," said Sarah soothingly. "We'll find dinner somewhere. Easily digestible food. Baked potato and rice pudding. No Chopin military marches."

Julia ignored her. "I hate not doing something. I can't sit around and ponder life the way you and Alex can. I wish I were one of those elderly creatures who loll by the fireplace awash in memories of the good old days."

"No you don't," said Alex firmly. "You're not made for lolling. But Sarah's right. We'll go for a summer night drive."

But Julia was still not listening. "Everyone thinks I should cancel the event. The riders, Patrick, Leah Pfeifer. Poor dear, she called me this afternoon. Heartbroken about Brad, but even then thinking of me. But I can't cancel it. George Fitts won't let me. He isn't interested in the good of High Hope Farm. He's hoping the event is going to be a better mousetrap."

"You want action," said Sarah. "Okay, that two-day event spells action. The police can take care of the nasty stuff and you can worry about the lawn and the parking facilities and dust the tack room, fuss about the entries, and not go about trying to kill yourself jumping Duffie and destroying your piano."

Julia turned back to the piano and hammered out two resounding major chords. Then stood up. "I am surrounded by traitors," she said. "You ask me to go out and enjoy myself when Tilly and Jane and Harvey Dodge are still on the loose. At least, I haven't heard that they've been locked up."

"Aunt Julia," said Sarah patiently. "It's still not against the law to lease your property to a mine and to visit a camp director, and I'm sure that Tilly and Jane have an appointment to spend quality time with George Fitts."

"Traduced," said Julia. "Friendship sold for a mess of potage. Thieves in the night. Thieves breaking in and stealing."

"Yes, I know Grandma Douglas gave you a good biblical upbringing," said Sarah. "We can exchange quotations during dinner. How do you like 'O tiger's heart wrapped in a woman's hide'? Do you think that describes Tilly or Jane? Or even you?"

And Julia allowed herself to be led out into the night. Led out followed at a discreet distance by one of George Fitts's watchers of the night.

Restored by good food and safe company to something like equilibrium, Julia repaired to her bedroom, slipped her nightgown over her head, turned off her bedside light, and then, on an impulse, went to the window. The half moon had risen and this gave a faint blush to the landscape. She stood for a moment looking over the vista of stable and barn, whose outlines could just be made out from the night lights that bordered the big arena and the pasture and paddock entrances. There was the black rectangle of her horse trailer and there beyond, like a visiting scourge, the blacker outlines of the state police trailer-cum-office, a single light showing through one of its small windows. Then closer, below her own bedroom window, the police sedan with its occupant sitting in the front seat, the crackling of a two-way radio just audible to the upstairs watcher.

Julia, as if reluctant to trust her present peace of mind to bed and a possible nightmare, stood fixed at the window. Somewhere a barred owl hooted its four-note double bark; beyond a car horn sounded and a truck with a faulty muffler rumbled down the Tri-County Road. And then, as she turned toward the sound and watched the truck headlights approach and disappear, she saw against the single street lamp that stood at the end of her driveway a figure. A long shadowy figure. A figure that moved from the light, ducked below the sloping ground to the parking lot, twisted itself around a guardian oak tree, and vanished. Vanished and then reemerged and headed for the side of the stable.

Julia, about to leap into action, to seize the telephone, to raise the alarm, stopped dead. There was something about that figure. Slowly she lowered the arm stretched for the telephone and moved again to the window. To the side of the window, shrouding herself in the light curtain. Listening. Yes, there it came. The metallic click-and-roll. The soft drink machine in action.

Julia waited and was rewarded. The figure appeared, hesitated by the door, apparently checking out the surroundings. Then, with speed and grace, it gathered its garments—garments, which although details were unseen, somehow suggested tatters—and sped around the side of the stable and toward pasture, woods, and lake.

"So," said Julia. "You're back. No," she corrected herself, "you never left." She nodded with a certain grim satisfaction and made her way to bed.

THE WHISKEY BARRELS

EIGHTEEN

THE week following the death by shovel of Bradley Pfeifer found some of those concerned with the future of High Hope Farm afflicted with a sense that nothing was real. Sarah pointed this out to Alex on the Sunday morning after Brad's death. They were making their way on foot to Camp Merrilark, where a memorial service was being inserted into the usual service-in-the-pines.

"It's as if the things we touch will melt or wither on the vine," she said. "Nothing seems genuinely alive." She reached over for a moment to touch the dog stalking by her side. "Not even Patsy. At any moment he may vanish or turn into a frog or an ax murderer. Everything seems damaged."

Alex nodded. "And daily business is just so much trivia."

"Except medicine," said Sarah. "At least you're always trying to fend off calamity."

"I haven't fended off much lately. Sore throats and a viral pneumonia or two. High blood pressure. Nothing to compare with sitting around a campfire while Brad Pfeifer was getting his."

"Which we couldn't even begin to guess would happen."

"I'm beginning to think we should have guessed."

"That's taking blame after the fact. George himself doesn't know if Brad's death is connected to Aunt Julia's troubles. And it may not be. But it puts the Norminco people back into the picture."

Alex nodded sober agreement to this and then added, "Speaking of Julia, she seems to have settled down. No more manic activity. No more violent Chopin. Quite civil and relaxed at breakfast."

"Actually," said Sarah, "it was hymns this morning. At the piano playing 'Faith of our Fathers,' 'Love Divine'—all the peaceful ones. And she tapered off with a Mozart minuet. She hasn't gone near Mozart in ages. It's all been Sturm und Drang."

"Well, that's something positive," said Alex. He pointed ahead to where two cars and a van were making a turn into the Merrilark entrance road. "Word's gotten out. A packed congregation today."

"Everyone knows the Pfeifers," explained Sarah. She returned to her subject. "I don't trust Julia. Last night, the betrayed woman in a state of fury, this morning 'Joy of heaven to earth come down.' She knows something. Or has found something, and I don't think it's God or her Redeemer. She reminds me of a cat who has located a misplaced mouse."

Meanwhile the subject of these speculations, joined by her niece Jessica and Mike Laaka, was trekking along a few paces ahead of Sarah and Alex.

"Slow up, Julia," said Mike as Julia hurried up the road toward the Merrilark entrance. "You're tiring Jessica here, and I've been up all night with the homicide people. We put a patrol car right under your window, so I hope you felt safe."

"I saw him," said Julia. "And a number of other things."

"And what's that supposed to mean?" said Mike

"Just Aunt Julia being mysterious," said Jessica. "She acts like that so you won't know what she's really been doing."

"Jessica," said Julia coming to a halt and facing her niece. "I suggest that if you're to go to this service and not disgrace the

High Hope staff you use my comb and do something about your hair." Here Julia turned on Sarah. "You're going to have to tie Patsy up somewhere. He will not be welcome at a memorial service."

"*Did* you see something last night?" persisted Mike.

"Nothing that in the end was unusual. Or surprising." And Julia clamped her jaw closed, fished out a comb from the pocket of her navy denim skirt—worn in deference to the coming service—passed the comb to Jessica, and strode ahead with resolute steps.

"Julia," said Mike in a threatening voice. "Remember the police are your friends."

"Yeah," said Jessica. "Like they hassle you for hanging out in the mall and think you're smoking pot."

"Do you?" asked Mike.

"I don't do drugs," said Jessica in a lofty tone.

"Hurry up you two," said Julia. "It's important to arrive on time. Poor Leah Pfeifer. I called her this morning and she told me the counselors were so supportive and that Harvey Dodge was spending the whole day." For a moment Julia's serene brow creased. "I'm very glad I found out about that man now and not later."

Jessica came to a halt. "Aunt Julia, were you sort of engaged to Colonel Dodge or going to marry him? Everyone said you were."

Julia inhaled, held her breath, and slowly released it. "Never listen to gossip, Jessica. For your information, I have no intention whatsoever of marrying Colonel Dodge."

"Then you don't mind that everyone says he's been making slimy eyes at Mrs. Eff," said Jessica. "Like this I mean," and she made her face droop into spaniel-like configuration.

"Mrs. Pfeifer should beware of Colonel Traitor," said Julia. "I hope he doesn't give her inappropriate ideas. Or false hopes." And Julia broke into a trot and joined a group of neighbors making the turn into the entrance.

"Aunt Julia kinda scares me sometimes," said Jessica.

"Kid," said Mike, "you ain't alone."

* * *

The usual service-in-the-pines at Camp Merrilark had been enlarged to include the fact of Brad Pfeifer's death. Or rather, his life. "A celebration of his life," said the senior counselor, smiling what Sarah supposed was a seraphic smile. More love divine. Joy of heaven to earth come down.

It was, thought Alex, remembering the battered head, the trickle of blood from Bradley's ears, from his nose, from the corners of his mouth, as if it had all happened to another person. As if the remains of Bradley Pfeifer, now waiting for autopsy, had nothing to do with the Bradley who was being hailed as the guiding light of Camp Merrilark—or at least as the co-guiding light along with Mrs. Eff—she, in her Sunday campshirt of white blouse and white tie, sitting soberly in the forefront of the congregation. Was she celebrating? Like Julia, she had no children, so Bradley must have filled, at least in part, the role of a son. Here young voices were lifted in "Amazing Grace" and Alex told himself, Sarah's right, nothing's real. We're all being rafted along on this uplifting current, a pink cloud of celestial joy.

And so it went. Praise for Bradley. His care for children, his love of the wilderness, his protecting arm—a veiled reference perhaps to Brad's threatened confrontation with Norminco. Neil Wentworth then reminded listeners that "One short sleep past we wake eternally, and Death shall be no more . . ." and Winka spoke of brotherhood and sisterhood and said there would always be a Merrilark and a Highfeather. Then the children, a blur of white shorts and shirts, rose and sang "We Will Gather by the River."

"I feel less real than I did before the service, and that's going some," said Sarah as they left the grove of pine trees. "Of course, listening to children sing, it always makes me cry."

"Parades, too," said Julia crossly, wiping a tear that had dared to travel down her cheek. "Children in uniforms. Marching and singing. Makes me think of the Civil War somehow, though I suppose it should remind me of the Hitler Youth."

"Were Tilly and Jane there?" asked Alex. "I didn't see them."

"In the back," said Sarah. "Tilly was smiling. Radiant. I suppose she sees Brad's face somewhere up there in the stars."

"And Jane," said Mike, who had joined the party, "looked like she wanted to bite someone."

"So would you if the police had taken over your manure pile, not to say your entire house," said Julia.

At which point Jessica rejoined the homeward-bound group. "Talked with some of my friends at Merrilark. They're really shook-up about Brad." She turned to Mike. "Aren't you going to tell us about what Sarah and I found in the manure pile?"

"Jessica," said Mike, "you are a complication no one needed, but yes, the lab called me last night. The prelims are all finished on the new poem Julia got as well as finals on the old stuff. And on the scraps found at Appleyard Farm. Interesting."

"Meaning what?" said Sarah.

Mike turned around and indicated a small stand of pines that stood to one side of the pathway. "Come on, all of you. There's a picnic place for visiting parents in here. I'll explain what we've found. Yes, Jessica, you can come. After all, you're an accessory to something, aren't you? Breaking and entering a manure pile."

Mike led the little group to the clearing and pointed to one of the picnic tables. "Listen carefully," he said. "It's important because we have more than one cut-out poet loose in the neighborhood. Two, maybe three. First, as you know, the paper scraps from Tilly and Jane's manure pile match the first four nursery rhymes received. The first came at the end of March, the next three in April. Call them the Appleyard Farm collection. The Ladybird one, the Humpty-Dumpty variation—Julia on a wall—the Ding dong bell one, and last, 'Sing a Song of Sixpence'—first verse. The paper used in the very last nursery rhyme, 'Sing a Song of Sixpence,' *second* verse, about Julia eating bitter gall and Harvey Dodge planning Julia's fall, does not, repeat does not, match any paper shreds in the Appleyard manure pile. Okay, got that?"

"Got it," said Jessica. Of all the listeners Jessica was the one in a state of pleased and happy expectation. Julia, looking increasingly miserable, twisted her hands; Sarah, restless, fidgeted on her picnic bench, and Alex paced beside them.

"Right," said Mike. "So we have the Appleyard collection and the others coming later, which we'll call the copycat collection. Next we have the scissors. Further confirmation of the Tilly-Jane complicity. Two pairs of scissors found in Tilly's workroom—a room that Jane sometimes uses—match the scissor work on the first four nursery rhymes. But that ain't all."

"Spit it out," said Sarah.

"Except for the first one Julia received—the one that began 'Ladybird, ladybird / Fly away home'—the three following Appleyard entries were cut out by the same hand."

"I don't follow," said Julia crossly.

"Listen," said Mike. "The very first rhyme you got, the Ladybird one, was cut out with small curved scissors—which we found in Tilly's desk. The other three were from a pair of long-bladed scissors we found in a toolbox in that same room. Now get this. That first Ladybird poem was cut out by a left-handed person with the curved scissors; the other three by a right-handed person using the long-bladed ones."

"What!" said Sarah and Julia together. Then, Sarah, "How can you tell that?"

"Labs are wonderful," said Mike. "Under a microscope you can measure and tell the angle of the cut. Right-handed people cut down on a slant, right to left; left-handed left to right. The cutting edge shows the slant. Only machines make straight cuts."

"And," said Julia, "Tilly is left-handed, Jane is right. My God, both of them. A conspiracy."

"Tilly did the first poem, Jane the other three. Jane says she didn't tell Tilly that she was following up on the idea. We have their statements, although a statement by Tilly may not hold much water. She went on about witches. Seems *Ladybird* refers to some kind of a witch in old folklore stuff."

"Then why did Jane stop sending them?" asked Sarah. "She was just getting warmed-up."

"Jane says the murder of Farney frightened her. Claims it made her realize she was getting in too deep."

"Well then, what about the other cutouts?" demanded Sarah.

"The lab has a report on the oddballs, the copycats," said Mike. "The Stevenson poem—it's called *Requiem*—'Abou Ben Adehm,' *The Charge of the Light Brigade*. And the second verse of 'Sing a Song of Sixpence,' about the queen eating bread and gall—this last crap inspired no doubt by Julia telling the whole world she'd been getting nursery rhymes."

"Which you weren't going to hold against me," said Julia.

"I'm not," said Mike cheerfully, "but George might. It's relevant information. Anyway, the copycat stuff didn't match the manure-pile paper and Tilly-Jane scissor inventory. All the copycat stuff was done by a right-handed person using a different pair of scissors entirely."

Alex stopped his pacing and confronted Mike. "And the murders? Isn't that what we're getting at?"

"Poems and the murders are still two items. Separate and not equal. No connection yet. But, for what it's worth, the strangulation of Farney is probably the work of a right-hander. The marks from the reins suggest a twisting from left to right. The way a right-handed person would twist something."

Sarah stood up, reached over, and grabbed Alex's necktie—a formality worn for the camp service. She twisted. Left to right. And switched hands and awkwardly twisted it. Right to left.

Alex detached Sarah's hands and rubbed his neck.

"That was neat," said Jessica. "But if the two murders are connected, then we're looking for a right-handed killer."

"The police are, not you, Jessica," said Mike. "You've had your day as an investigator. And the shovel injury on Brad doesn't indicate right or left hand. It was brought down pretty squarely."

"Any other left-handers around besides Tilly?" asked Sarah.

"Yeah," said Mike. "Bradley Pfeifer, but he's dead."

"Patrick's left-handed," put in Julia. "So is Tim Fournier, our farrier. You notice these things when you watch people work with horses."

254

"Wentworths?" said Sarah. "Neil? Winka? Rafe Posner?"

"Right-handed. Along with Jane, Julia, and Harvey Dodge. And Sarah and Alex and yours truly. And Jim Shale."

"I'm right-handed," said Jessica. "So am I a suspect?"

Julia ignored her younger niece. Instead she got stiffly to her feet, extricated herself from the space between the picnic bench and the table, and headed back to the Merrilark pathway. Mike and the rest followed at her heels.

"Hey there, Julia," called Mike, "I've set up a meeting for you. By special request. With Jane. Maybe Tilly."

"No," shouted Julia over her shoulder. She moved ahead at almost a run. "I'm finished with Jane. And Tilly."

At the top of the road that led to the two camps, Mike Laaka caught up to Julia and grabbed her by the elbow, and wheeled her around. "Whoa up. You're not finished with Tilly and Jane. This is my own idea. In the interests of neighborhood peace. Jane pleaded. She wants to confess, to ask for pardon, to go on about guilt. The whole bit. You don't have to do anything but listen, okay? Those two ladies are going through hell right now—"

"Well-deserved hell," interrupted Julia.

"Hell nevertheless," said Mike. "And more hell to come. The special George Fitts brand of hell. And they'll probably be charged with something pretty damn soon."

Julia hesitated, brow creased, mouth in a downward position.

"You could just listen to them," put in Sarah. "Never mind the olive branch. Just listen."

"This is no excuse," continued Mike, "but Appleyard Farm was about to go under. In worse trouble than Harvey's place. Those two ladies don't have enough income to pay off debts, a big home equity loan. I guess Jane was frantic. Grabbing at straws. You just happened to be a straw."

For a moment Julia stood irresolute, then she stamped a foot and grimaced. "All right, Mike Laaka. Just for you. I'll listen, but I'm not going to be sentimental about this. And I'll go alone. But to threaten me, my farm. My good Lord. So where are they now?"

"They'll come to your farmhouse. I told them about noon."

"You knew I'd give in?"

"Yep," said Mike grinning. "Old stone-heart Clancy would need about five minutes of my chipping away and then she'd give in."

"Go to blazes, Mike Laaka," said Julia, and she marched off across the road and into the entrance of High Hope Farm.

Alex, who had been quietly watching the scene, now turned to Mike. "You're asking a lot of Julia. And, since Jane is right-handed, you may be asking Julia to entertain a murderer."

"Not to worry," said Mike. "We'll have a police watchdog keeping tabs on the proceedings." And with this Sarah and Alex had to be content.

Julia did not surface until midafternoon. Sarah and Alex after a pit stop at a nearby diner plunged into the business of stall care and general maintenance. The big cross-country event loomed and extra efforts were being made in the matter of neatness. By the time Julia appeared in the stable, Sarah and Alex, dripping with perspiration, had decided that whatever the future held, a horse farm was not going to be part of it.

Julia commended their efforts. "You're getting quite a sense of how a well-run stable should look," she said. "But please hang the forks and the brooms separately. Don't mix them up."

"To hell with the brooms," said Sarah. "What about Jane? Jane and Tilly?"

Julia collapsed on a bale of hay in the stable aisle. "What can I say? I suppose we have what's known as an entente. Not an *entente cordiale*, but something workable. Jane even cried. I was embarrassed for her. It seems she caught Tilly cutting out that first Ladybird effort, so Tilly told her about the rotation idea, how I'd be moving in with Harvey Dodge. And Jane bought it."

"Jane bought that rotation nonsense!" exclaimed Sarah.

"No, of course not, but she did think I'd give in to Harvey

sooner or later, and why not sooner? So Jane decided to give me a nudge. She counted on my thinking the messages came from Tilly, and, since she was mad as the March Hare, I wouldn't blame Tilly. And that I'd never dream they came from Jane because Jane is sensible. Or, if I thought the verses came from someone else in the neighborhood, I'd be frightened into accepting Harvey."

"Did she really encourage Tilly?" demanded Alex. "In the whole rotation, blood on the new-mown hay business?"

"She didn't discourage her, but then that's Jane's style. Tilly is always going off the deep end and Jane swims with the current and checks her into psychiatric care when things go too far. As she did after the rocking horse affair. But, as Mike told us, Jane claims to have become frightened after Farney's murder and stopped cutting out nursery rhymes."

Alex nodded. "Then the copycats—or cat—cranked up. Julia had gone public about the messages and so she began receiving the new series—several of which sounded like Harvey Dodge."

"All clipped out by a right-handed someone," said Sarah. "Who may or may not be the murderer."

Julia, looking rather ill, leaned back against a rack of halters. "It's bad enough having Tilly and Jane caught doing something so despicable, but what's worse is that the poems are only the tip of the iceberg." She paused and then shook herself. "Never mind. Full speed ahead. Let's bring in the horses. Let's find Patrick and tell him how glad I am that he's left-handed."

In such a fashion did the week go. Sarah absorbed in helping in barn and stable rarely lifted her head to speculate on killers, dexter or sinister; Alex retreated to the peace of medicine and an outbreak of gastrointestinal flu; George Fitts appeared on the horizon from time to time, had Jane Zimmer and Tilly as visitors to the mobile horse-trailer office, and was seen several times with Mike Laaka heading toward camps Merrilark and Highfeather. As for Jim Shale, he appeared at nearby towns and spoke of the wonders of today's mining technology and was once seen in the company of Colonel Harvey Dodge—aka traitor—at the Union Diner.

Two people appeared to have gained some sort of inner peace and went about their day with a new serenity. One was Tilly Martin, who seemed to have found Jane's guilt in the matter of sinister nursery rhymes wonderfully supportive of her plan to rotate over to High Hope Farm. The other was Julia Clancy who, apparently recovered from her confrontation with Jane Zimmer, occasionally smiled, was strangely complimentary to awkward beginning riders, and was espied one night by her niece, Sarah, carrying a freshly baked apple pie into the lower stable.

"I have two theories about Aunt Julia," said Sarah on Thursday night to Alex. They were sitting on the porch looking over the moonlit pastures. It was the last night of tranquility before the arrival of the multiple horse trailers, riders, grooms, and spectators on Friday for the weekend event. "The first theory has it that Julia has finally gone over the edge. I mean, a whole apple pie. To eat alone in the stable at eleven o'clock at night."

"Maybe Patrick was there. They shared it," said Alex. He tilted back in his rocking chair, rocked once, and then planted his feet. "Bedtime. And I've heard Julia say that she loves to be down in the stable listening to the horses breathe and stomp. So why not take an apple pie with you?"

"Besides the apple pie," Sarah persisted, "there was that bag of old clothes for the Salvation Army."

"So?"

"It's been sitting in the hall all spring and then I saw Aunt Julia haul it down to the stable."

"Probably for a pickup. The Salvation Army does that."

"They could have picked it up at the farmhouse. Why the stable? So my second theory holds that she's up to no damn good."

Alex stood up, reached out a hand, and pulled Sarah to her feet. "I like theory one. Benign madness is easier to live with than Julia on the rampage. She's probably in a free fall after being dumped by Harvey Dodge."

"No way," said Sarah. "I think she's relieved. Feelings a little bruised, but still relieved. And she's in no free fall. I prefer theory two. I think she's doing planned things."

"Probably bringing sacrificial offerings—food and clothing—to the god of horse. She probably believes in the god of horse."

"That's Saint Equus, isn't it?" said Sarah, moving to the porch door. "Come on and be quiet. She's in the parlor playing. I don't feel like a scrimmage tonight."

Together they tiptoed along the hall, past the parlor door, paused for a minute to listen to several passages, and then made it safely upstairs.

"What was she playing?" asked Alex.

Sarah shook her head. *The Ride of the Valkyries.* Wagner. She never plays Wagner."

"Well," said Alex, "she does now."

THE IN AND OUT

NINETEEN

SARAH sat bolt upright in bed. Wide awake. As if she'd never been sleepy in her life. Of course. The whole business—murder, cut-up verses, vandalism—all perfectly simple. It was entirely a matter of organization. Eliminate, reshuffle, and lay out the cards. And behold, solution. Or something close to a solution. But first, deal with the obvious. Then, as the night the day, the less obvious would fall in place.

She reached over and jolted Alex awake.

"Christ, Sarah. What time is it? It's still dark."

"Almost morning," said Sarah untruthfully. She hadn't looked at the clock.

"The hell it is." Alex rolled over, grabbed a pillow, and pulled it over his head.

Sarah snatched the pillow. "You've got to listen. I need a sounding board."

"Thanks a lot. Go to sleep. You're worse than Patsy."

"No. Listen. You might be able to contribute."

"Thanks again." But Alex struggled to a semirecumbent position.

Sarah reached over and dragged a blanket around her shoulders. "First," she said.

"You're always saying *first* and nothing comes of it," grumbled Alex.

"First," repeated Sarah. "Julia is definitely not bonkers. Scratch theory number one completely. She's feeding apple pie and taking old clothes to someone no one is supposed to know about and that someone is obviously Rafe Posner."

"The thought had occurred to me," said Alex. "But it might be our other long-lost friend, Sean Conners."

"Wrong. Aunt Julia would not succor Sean. She has no great love for him even if he is Patrick's nephew. But she has very strong mother-hen feelings for Rafe."

"Okay," said Alex, now fully awake and regretting it. "Okay, but what does that prove except that Julia's as devious as the rest of us? Maybe she's afraid Rafe's the murderer—he's right-handed—and she wants to protect him. But unless we get our hands on the man we can't be sure it's Rafe."

"Stop being reasonable. Of course it's Rafe. He's running around in horse blankets, hiding out in the woods, and eating apple pie. Never mind why Julia's doing it; just take it as a something we know and move on. Those copycat poetry messages, for instance."

"From right-handed scissor people," said Alex.

"Right. Three are from Harvey Dodge's repertoire. The Stevenson, the Marvell, the Tennyson. But would Harvey Dodge have sent them to frighten Julia into his arms? Possible. Not probable. I don't think Harvey has a creative bone in his body. He recites poetry, he doesn't write variations on it."

"Okay, so it's the Wentworths at work."

"I think so. But why are they trying to put the blame on Harvey? Well, if it's just Neil, maybe for the hell of it. If it's Winka—with or without Neil—it's to move Julia out. Highfeather can relocate on Crawfish Pond. Everyone happy."

"Except Julia."

"Except Julia. As Winka said yesterday, there'll always be a Merrilark and a Highfeather. But she didn't say *where* they'll be. For the cut-out poet, I'll bet my shirt on Neil. He's the literary one. Not that those examples show high literary merit, but they're not as bad as the Jane and Tilly entries. Winka may know the poems—they're old chesnuts—but Neil could do a better job re-writing them. I don't think Winka could write much more than the copy for camp catalogs and horse-care manuals."

"Guesswork. Based on the Sarah Deane school of character analysis. But, okay, say you've solved the riddle of the copycats—have you an arsonist and a shotgun owner up your sleeve? Not to mention a murderer or two. A head-basher and a strangler."

"A few people in mind, but nothing's jelled yet. The Brad Pfeifer killing doesn't jibe with the Farney Thompson murder. Take Jim Shale. He fits the Bradley Pfeifer sequence, but why attack Julia's farm? No minerals there. Why kill Farney? He didn't even know the man. And he isn't familiar with Julia's stable setup, where the twitch was kept. Where the curb reins were hung."

"Unless he prowled around at night?"

"Unlikely. There's something missing. What did George say? We all know something we haven't remembered. But here's something no one has pointed out. With all the goings-on, even with the threats in the cut-out poems, not a hair of Julia's head has been harmed. Nor have there been any attempts. Julia would be easier to do in than either Farney or Brad. They were strong, athletic men. So why has Julia been left untouched?"

"Too well guarded?" suggested Alex.

"Not in the beginning. She was loose and fancy-free. Easy to find alone. If someone wanted High Hope Farm, why not eliminate the owner? Kill Julia."

"So the murderer is not only a horse lover, he—or she—is a Julia lover."

"Harvey Dodge."

"But you said he wasn't up to writing variations of poems," Alex reminded her.

"Maybe we have a troika in which none of the three units

knew what the others were doing. Number one: Tilly and Jane. Number two: the Wentworths—preferably Neil carrying on the cut-out poetry tradition. Number three—alias the strangler and head-basher—Colonel Harvey Dickerson Dodge."

For a minute Alex considered this statement. Then, "No, that's wrong. I can't picture Harvey strangling his old friend Farney. Let alone decorating him with a bridle."

Sarah nodded soberly. "That bothers me, too. Aunt Julia said Harvey had trouble with physical violence."

"Although strangling is more or less bloodless."

"But nailing someone with a shovel isn't. Brad was a mess."

"Okay," said Alex. "Let it go for now. Time to face the day. Hospital this A.M. then back for the grand finale. You try to think of what it is that you should remember and can't."

"The problem is that I can't really believe in more than one murderer and perhaps an accessory. In the old English mysteries you only had one murderer. The butler or the gardener. Or the groom. Shall we consider Patrick? He's been neglected."

"Patrick is left-handed, and if you touch a single hair on Patrick's head, Julia will hit you with more than a shovel. But ask yourself this: Why has no one attacked Patrick? He's Julia's real rod and staff. Without whom . . ."

Sarah gave Patsy, who occupied the foot of the bed, a shove with her feet, pulled away the bedclothes, and stood up, bare of foot and rumpled as to nightgown. "You're right. Why not Patrick? Well, I think it's time for a bit of library research."

Alex gathered his toothbrush and bath towel. "Forget it. Today and this entire unholy weekend is dedicated to the event. When, according to George, all shall be revealed. And you will be under Julia's thumb doing your bit for God, country, and stable."

"Wrong," said Sarah. "Today the experts gather. I'll help out with early chores and then sneak off. I'm just a bit of fluff and no one will know whether I'm here or not."

Sarah's prediction proved correct. It was a day for the dyed-in-the-wool horse types. Members of the Maine Combined Training Association showed themselves early, Patrick produced a phalanx of men to work with the stalls erected in an oversized tent, and the Wentworths and Jane Zimmer—a very subdued Jane—went over the course fixing fence numbers and checking the footing. Harvey Dodge, apparently not realizing he was persona non grata, stalked about in a tattersall vest and gaiters and gave advice to whoever would stop and listen. Julia, however, steered clear of her former suitor, even at one point ducking behind a portable toilet.

Sarah, as planned, and now dressed for summertime research in clean blue cotton trousers and a white shirt, drove to the Rockland Public Library, where at ten o'clock she settled herself at a table in the children's section with a large collection of the works of Mother Goose. Small editions, large brightly colored editions, contemporary pop-up models, and at the bottom of the pile the *Oxford Nursery Rhyme Book* as edited by those two great scholars of the nursery world, Iona and Peter Opie.

An hour and a half later Sarah returned the books to the librarian with many thanks. "Just what I wanted," she announced and made her way blinking into the bright sunlight.

"So there, George Fitts," she said aloud as she climbed into her parked car. Then to herself she added, One theory down and two to go. And now I need space and quiet and no horses tramping anywhere near me. Which means avoiding High Hope Farm for a while.

With this idea in mind, Sarah drove slowly north until she came by a series of winding and rising secondary roads to a ridge overlooking a fine spread of the county and offering a distant view of the tip of a placid Crawfish Pond. Pulling the car off the road, she cut the motor, snapped on Patsy's leash, climbed out, and walked up a dirt path to a large granite outcropping, where she sat down in a circle of shade, Patsy's large rough gray head in her lap.

Time to think. To remember. She leaned back against the rock and let memories of place, voice, of people, events, of incidents float up, be acknowledged, float away. Or be questioned and be put on display in the forefront of her mind.

The first to float—who else—was Rafe Posner. Rafe imitating a ghoulie or ghostie. Why did Rafe run away when most needed? Answer: He's someone who does run away. From trouble, from a demanding boss. Rafe's run away before. Is he scared, did he do or see something, or does he just enjoy flitting about in a horse blanket?

And then out of nowhere came Neil Wentworth's Aunt Cecily. An admired and gutsy lady found squashed under a ladder. Julia reminded Neil of Aunt Cecily. Twice he mentioned her. Does Neil admire Julia as he did his aunt? What did that say about Neil? Is Neil a murderer who's an old softie about Julia? As Sarah had remarked, no one had laid a glove on Julia herself. Not yet.

Neil teaches the advanced riders. Neil is the local funnyman. Was the bridle around Farney's head funny? Showing a sense of humor. Or a sick mind. Neil has quarreled with Winka.

Winka Wentworth teaches the beginning riders. She cares about their progress; they are to be examples. She does Uncle Horace proud. Who said that? Winka has, to quote one young observer, "Highfeather on the brain." Winka looks like a dream on a horse and she drives a mean tractor. Winka has quarreled with Neil.

And Jane Zimmer. Who also drives a mean tractor. Who wanted to sell the hardscrabble Appleyard Farm and move into High Hope Farm. Wanted to do this badly enough to send threatening cut-out poems to Julia. Jane is fond of Julia. But fonder of Tilly. Will watch over Tilly until death doth them part. And Tilly? Method in her madness? Fluctuating between psychosis and cold, hard logic.

And then Harvey Dodge marched into Sarah's head and displaced Jane, whose figure had begun to fade and turn misty at the edges. Harvey Dodge, who handed his beloved assistant, Farney Thompson, over to Julia. A generous act from a suitor who is also busy arranging for Norminco to lease his land. A man who is now cozy with Mrs. Eff? Duplicitous double-dealing Colonel Dodge. Was Farney some sort of undercover agent sent to create chaos at High Hope Farm? If so, did someone catch him at it?

Then Patrick. Left-handed Patrick. Why hasn't Patrick been slugged with a twitch? Banged with a shovel? Remember, the murderer seems to act when opportunity strikes, so has Patrick never been in the wrong place at the right time?

Then there's Jim Shale, who looks like Jimmy Stewart and acts contrariwise. Did he sit by the side of the road in his truck last Friday evening on or around eight-fifteen and watch Bradley Pfeifer drive the Highfeather pickup to Camp Merrilark? Did he follow Bradley and avail himself of a waiting shovel?

So now Bradley Pfeifer moves front and center. A terrible Bradley with a cracked and bloody skull, a gasping mouth. Bradley, who was going to save Merrilark. Bradley, who was out to get—take to court—ruin—Norminco. Bradley, who is dead. A solid fact if there ever was one.

And the police love facts. Like mother's milk to them. Here Sarah gave herself a mental kick. Go on, more facts needed. Drop everything into the hopper and stir vigorously. Shake, rattle, and roll. And bake. Keep going.

Okay. The pony bridle fitted Farney's head. A horse bridle would have been too big. The twitch was available. So were those thin curb reins. So was the shovel. And the kerosene. And the rocking horse, Brandy Boy, after Tilly had dragged it out of the house. Was hanging Brandy Boy funny? Is Sean Conners dead? Or just gone. Disappeared before? during? after the Preakness? Sean Conners liked practical jokes. Was fitting Farney with a bridle his idea of a practical joke? Sean was sick, but he left the party. Leaving his—Aunt Julia's—cane.

The cane! Uncle Tom's blackthorn cane. As good a weapon as a shovel or a twitch. A heavy club of a cane. So where in hell is that cane? Last seen leaning against the side of the farmhouse. Put there by Patrick. As George Fitts said—O wise George Fitts—you all know something you haven't remembered.

And just as Sarah pictured the cane she heard Patrick's voice as he caught sight of the hanging rocking horse. "Jesus Glory be to heaven, what in hell is that?" And then other voices crowding in, demanding to be heard. Tilly going on about the horse incarnate, in the parlor telling Julia to buy a Rottweiler, and Neil Wentworth saying Harvey Dodge was an old pussycat, reminding her that pussycats can be stealthy. And Jane and Harvey lamenting the Wentworth lack of "openness," saying that they played their cards close to the chest. And Tilly—again—in her prophetic mode—saying she had warned. "Sarah, you know I warned." And then the farrier, Tim Fournier, remembering that Farney was "a pretty square guy." That it was "hard to think someone'd come along and do that to him." And then . . . and then another voice. A voice expressing regret about Farney's death, a voice going on and handing Sarah—and Alex, if he had been listening—the proof of murder. Just like that. On a platter. One small word underlining what she had found that morning in the Rockland library. And it wasn't a Troika as she had suggested. Just a two-headed monster. And motivation right there front and center.

Hadn't Jane Zimmer said start with motivation? Motivation without facts is just so much quicksand. But tie it to facts and you have something.

Sarah scrambled to her feet. To work. First eliminate. Make sureness sure. Then alert . . . whom? Mike? George? Julia? Especially Julia, because her aunt had to be dragged back once more to the moment of finding Farney, of seeing him slumped in the annex room, the bridle around his head. Then find that cane. Get it to the lab. Fast. And then, and then try to make the police sit on the murderer. Which they might do if—and it was an enormous if—the police believed Sarah's memory of one word spoken too soon. Spoken when only one person—besides the police themselves—could have known that word. If—another if—Sarah could make them believe that her library efforts had borne fruit. Were not simply a piece of minutia beloved of a nit-picking student of English literature.

"Come on, Patsy, move it," shouted Sarah, grabbing the leash and plummeting down the hill.

And into the arms of Katie Waters, deputy sheriff of Knox

County. Katie, a sardonic look on her face, her arms folded tight against her uniformed shirt. She stood there next to Sarah's car, Sarah's car keys dangling from one hand, a sheriff's department squad car parked just ahead of Sarah's rental Subaru, blocking it.

"Okay," said Katie. "I gave you fifteen minutes to meditate up there. Which was very generous of me and probably worth my job. You're to go right back. Didn't you know everyone at High Hope Farm is under surveillance? George Fitts will be chewing nails."

Sarah, her mind racing, saw her plans in jeopardy. Distraction was needed.

"I've remembered something," she said. "Very important. Uncle Tom's cane. It's a great big heavy thing. I haven't seen it since Sean Conners disappeared."

"A cane? A disappearing cane? Or a cane that disappeared with Sean Conners?"

"No, Sean left it. Which was peculiar, because he could hardly walk. Patrick put it up against the house, but I haven't seen it since that day. I think we should look for it and test it."

A puzzled look came over Katie's face. "Test it for what?"

Sarah opened her car door, pushed Patsy in, and turned. "For fingerprints and blood. For hair. For bits of flesh. Belonging to Sean Conners. You tested the twitch, now test the cane."

"Okay," said Katie. "So a cane is missing. That's something no one told me. Which isn't surprising because I spend most of my time hiding in the bushes by the mailbox. Or maybe no one knows it's missing but you. I'll report it and if it turns up we can check for Rafe Posner's prints and blood type, too. But maybe it was lifted by some light-fingered guest of Mrs. Clancy's."

"Okay, look for Rafe Posner's blood, too," said Sarah. She was determined not to share her conviction that Rafe was the blanket ghost. Not yet anyway. Not until she had confronted Aunt Julia on what must be a tender subject.

"I'll follow you back," said Katie. "And then stick with me until I hand you over to another team. High Hope Farm's a regular circus with all those horse trailers arriving. We're checking every arrival, and George Fitts has got a roof camera set up on his office trailer that looks like a ventilator."

"Great," said Sarah. She climbed in the car and, followed closely by Deputy Waters, drove toward the turnoff to Tri-County Road, her mind busy with ways of getting rid of her watchful companion. But then as she turned her car into Tri-County Road she looked into the rearview mirror at the figure of Deputy Sheriff Waters. There was something about that woman. The set of her shoulders, the determined look on her small square face with its small square chin. Mike Laaka had better look over his shoulder and see who was waiting in the wings. Katie Waters, Sarah decided, wouldn't be spending the rest of her law-enforcement career hiding in bushes watching mailboxes.

All at once Sarah made a decision. What she had planned as a solo could be better done in double harness, particularly if the partner was as solid and assured as Katie Waters. Also, it was quite possible that Katie might enjoy some time off Mike Laaka's leash, pointed toward some independent work.

Sarah slowed, pushed her turn indicator, and made an abrupt sweep into the entrance of the county fairgrounds and came to a halt under a spreading maple. Time for a private talk.

Katie was at first annoyed. She looked at her watch and frowned. But Sarah hooked her. Took her aside and opened up. The whole thing from start to finish. "Of course," she ended, "I'd like to eliminate Jim Shale first and then go for broke. Because I'm as sure as if I'd seen one or the other do it."

"Let's get one thing straight," said Katie. "Jim Shale isn't in the picture for the Farney murder. He was fishing with two friends the day of your wedding. Verification by both, who've been out of town until last night. And he claims he spent the period of Brad Pfeifer's attack at home in his cabin watching a ballgame. No proof, but there's nothing we can do right now about it. George is working full-time on Jim Shale, so butt out of that one."

"Okay," said Sarah. "So I want to stick my neck out on the other idea. Yours too, if you're with me."

Katie hesitated. "I really value my neck, and if we're going to the Wentworth house, well, won't someone be around?"

"Winka and Neil'll be over at High Hope Farm all day. Or down at Highfeather. I think we'll be safe."

"If George Fitts finds out," said Katie, "he would have me— well, not by the balls, of course, but by something serious."

"He's a very busy man today and all weekend, and as a deputy sheriff you have every right to make a friendly call. The trip is to eliminate. To clear the decks. Okay?"

"I can make a friendly call, but I haven't a search warrant."

"In the course of this call all you have to do is glance around. Not search."

"And if we find what you think we'll find—or won't find . . ."

"I'll put my knee against Mike Laaka's throat and see you get credit. Cheer up, Katie."

Here Katie Waters stopped, took a deep breath, and reached out and shook Sarah's hand. "If I'm court-martialed for breaking and entering, I hope you can get me a job at Bowmouth College. Lawn care. Taking out the trash. And," she added, "I hope to hell you're right, because I can't believe one of your so-called proofs is a misspelled word."

Sarah demurred. "Not exactly misspelled. Depends on how you look at it. But first, before the Wentworths, Aunt Julia. A very important question. Let's hope we can find her alone."

And Katie Waters with a new light in her eye returned to the squad car and started the engine.

Julia Clancy was, by a stroke of luck, alone. Sitting in the parlor with a small bowl of salad and a glass of iced tea.

"I'm in hiding," announced Julia. "Too many people, too many police. Patrick and Jessica and some of my traitorous neighbors are helping with the arrivals. So what are you up to?"

"A question," said Sarah. "Farney Thompson."

"Are you trying to ruin my lunch?"

"We're serious, Mrs. Clancy," put in Katie Waters.

"That's no excuse," said Julia tartly. "I assume that you're usually serious. Shouldn't you be out at my mailbox?"

"Not today," said Katie. "A new deputy is on that job."

"Listen, Aunt Julia," said Sarah. "It may be very important. Tell us exactly what you saw when you found Farney. Exactly how he looked. What you did. How long you stayed in the annex with him."

"You *are* trying to ruin my lunch," said Julia. "Go away. I've given my statement five hundred times and I'm not doing it again."

"Aunt Julia, please. Once more."

"Please, Mrs. Clancy," said Katie. "I'm sorry about your having to describe a dead body, but try."

"Oh damn it to hell," said Julia. Then, "All right. You're a pair of ghouls, and that was one of the worst mornings of my life." And Julia took them back with her to that early-Sunday-morning visit to the barn. The discovery that neither Rafe Posner nor Farney Thompson had started morning chores. That neither man was around. Looking, calling. Remembering that Patrick had gone to early mass. Measuring the grain, filling the water buckets. Throwing each horse a flake of hay. Deciding to take an inventory of saddle pads with an eye to ordering new ones. To the annex room. "And I found him," she finished. "In the corner."

"Go on," encouraged Sarah.

"That's it. I found him. I saw he was dead. I left and called the police. The ambulance. Everyone."

"Go back," said Katie. "You're a camera. What did you see?"

"You all know," grumbled Julia. But she tried again. Farney in the corner. As if he'd been propped up. His skin blue. Slate blue. His lips blue. Both arms hanging down. In his shirt sleeves. His jacket on the floor beside him. The bridle around his head.

"The bridle," repeated Sarah. "Did you recognize it?"

"Of course. I know a bridle when I see one."

"Which bridle?" said Katie softly.

"Great heavens, I don't know. I mean, I do know now, but I didn't then."

"You didn't say to yourself, Good Lord, it's Duffie's bridle? Or Lollipop's? Or Whiskers'?" persisted Sarah.

"No. I told you, I just saw a bridle. The poor man was dead. A good kind friend. Do you think I stood there wondering which bridle Farney was wearing? What do you take me for?"

"You didn't go close, touch him?" asked Katie.

"I reached over and touched one hand. It was cold. Stone cold. It was horrible. I got out fast and went to the telephone. The stable telephone. I don't suppose I was in the room with Farney more than two minutes."

For a moment Sarah and Katie sat there not speaking, Julia frowning at them. Then Sarah said, "Sorry, Aunt Julia. That's all. We'll leave you in peace to finish lunch."

"You have finished my lunch," snapped Julia. "Now get out. I have ten minutes left and I'm going to hit the piano. It's the only thing left to me."

"She gets dramatic, doesn't she?" said Katie as they headed out of the farmhouse.

Sarah nodded. "You don't know the half of it, but we found out what we had to. One stop more and then . . ."

"And then it's curtains?"

"Delayed curtains. George has to buy the idea. Check it out. He wouldn't dream of taking my word for something so . . . well, so skimpy. And then there's the cane. And even if we've pinned Farney Thompson's killer, there's Bradley Pfeifer's."

"What we say in the department is one murder at a time. Now let's get to the Wentworths'," said Katie. "I think we should walk. The squad car is too conspicuous. Do you think the house will be open?"

"If it isn't we can probably get in through the sun porch. If either Winka or Neil is around . . ."

"If they are," finished Katie, "I'll ask for the clothes. As part of our ongoing investigation. If they refuse . . . but I don't think they will. Cooperation has been their game from the start."

"Too cooperative," muttered Sarah.

"Don't jump the gun," warned Katie. "Wait and see. Come on, we'll walk along the opposite side of the road. Stay behind trees."

Breaking and entering the Wentworth establishment proved

the day's easiest task. No Wentworths in sight. No campers or counselors about. The front door open.

"Because they have nothing to hide," suggested Katie.

"Wait and see," said Sarah. And followed by Katie, she poked into a downstairs clothes closet, drew a blank, and then, treading lightly, went upstairs. Two closets later the only information gained was that Winka and Neil were occupying separate bedrooms—pajamas in one, nightgown in another.

"I don't see them," said Sarah. "Certainly not the blazer."

"If it's stuff only worn at weddings and for special occasions, maybe it would be somewhere else. How about the guest room clothes closet?"

"Right," said Sarah, heading into the hall, down the hall, reaching a door at the end of the passage. She opened it. Guest room. Chintz chair, floral curtains. Luggage stand. Water carafe and glass on the bedside table. Box of tissues.

"This it?" said Katie, already in the closet. She held out a man's navy blue blazer with a heraldic crest on the breast pocket. Gold and red thread. A motto. Something about magna est veritas.

"Search it," commanded Sarah.

"Wait up," said Katie. "I don't want to foul up evidence." She walked over to the bed—a four-poster—and took a tissue from the box on the table, wrapped it around two fingers, and gingerly fished in the blazer's pockets.

She hit pay dirt in the left-hand bottom pocket. "Rice," she announced. "And something else. Sort of round."

Sarah peered at the tissue. Two grains of rice and a pearl. "Tapioca," she announced. "Tilly handed out tapioca. Almost put my eyes out. There was a real rice and tapioca storm."

"So we impound this," said Katie, waving the blazer on its hanger. "For the owner's own good. And for the record."

Sarah nodded. "Let's get out of here."

The rest of the day had a schizophrenic quality. On the one hand the High Hope Farm two-day combined training event gathered numbers and steam. More trailers arrived. Horses were everywhere, being taken to their stalls in the tent, being walked, lunged, ridden, washed, curried, braided. Tim the farrier dealt in shoes lost or loose, and among the whole ordered confusion moved Julia, with Patrick and Jessica, greeting friends, pointing out stalls, giving out riders' numbers and course maps. And on the fringes, Jane, Tilly, and Harvey Dodge circled, the latter apparently still unaware of his outcast status.

At the same time the George Fitts surveillance machine was oiled and ready to go. Two rented horse trailers manned by three equestrian state troopers appeared and the occupants, complete with horses, moved among the competitors.

And in the field-office-cum-trailer sat George Fitts and Mike Laaka, reviewing the ad hoc activities of Katie Waters and Sarah. George expressed himself in frosty terms and Mike scowled at Katie and talked about suspension. Then both men started in on Sarah.

And Sarah, who had expected no great welcome, defended herself as simply a compiler of memories coupled with a little harmless footwork and then spread out the day's gleanings.

"Did you say 'skimpy'?" said Mike. "Call it feeble. Two little words. Two miserable words and some rice and tapioca. We'd be laughed out of court. And if you don't get that navy blazer back, you two will be charged with theft."

At which Sarah played her last card. Not exactly a trump but at least a face card. "The cane," she said. "Uncle Tom's cane. Find that cane and check for prints. For blood. For hair."

George sat silent for a minute. Then he reached for a phone, barked a few words, and rose to his feet. "Okay, Mike. Take some men and go over the farmhouse. Start where Sarah saw it last. Sarah, you go with them. Katie, you take a crew and do the stable area. Don't be conspicuous. And get rid of that uniform. Find some jeans. Look like someone's groom."

"The cane's probably six feet under somewhere," said Mike.

But it wasn't. The cane was discovered amongst a motley collection of walking sticks, umbrellas, ski poles, hunting crops, together with one crutch, a Victorian sunshade, a yardstick, and a flyswatter, all crammed into an ancient bronze umbrella stand in an alcove by the front parlor.

Queried by Mike in the midst of a drink and hors d'oeuvres affair held for the riders and their friends on the terrace, Julia had brushed the question away. "The cane? I put it back. Where it belonged. No, I didn't tell anyone. Why should I? It was Tom's cane. I keep it for sentiment and when my arthritis kicks up. You can't have it. You'll be wanting my rocking horse next."

This objection was overruled, and the cane and the rocking horse—"a welcome idea," said George, "we've neglected the rocking horse"—were carried off by Deputy Waters and taken to the long-suffering forensic laboratory crew in Augusta with the note that a speedy examination would be appreciated.

"You can't expect miracles," said Mike, who was walking with George and Sarah back to the trailer-office. "They're working full tilt on that Highfeather pickup that Bradley used to drive to the camp parking lot."

"I have a prelim on that," said George. He produced his notebook and flipped pages. "Evidence that both Winka and Neil Wentworth or Highfeather campers have driven or been passengers in the truck. Front seat or the open back. Fibers match the Highfeather uniform. Gray shorts, red and gray T-shirt, gray sweats."

"What do you expect?" said Mike. "The truck belongs to Highfeather, for God's sake. Neil loaned it to Brad."

"And charcoal," added George. "Bits from the soles of shoes."

"What?" exclaimed Mike and Sarah together.

"Charcoal in the truck back. From burned twigs. Pine. And particles from briquets. They used briquets for cookouts."

"But," objected Sarah, "camps are always having cookouts. And evening campfires. It doesn't mean that someone from last Friday's cookout climbed into the truck."

"It doesn't mean they didn't," said George.

Sarah's eyes widened. "You mean that someone besides Bradley might have been in that pickup? A passenger? Who went along?"

"More like a stowaway," said Mike.

"But a one-way stowaway," explained Sarah. "Because there wasn't time for anyone to follow Brad on foot, hit him, and then make it back to the campfire on foot. But hiding in the truck for the ride up might make it possible."

"Sarah," said George, "we've been planning a trial. You can be the guinea pig. Can you run?"

"Like a deer?" put in Mike.

Sarah made a face. "I'm not in top training condition, but if it's not too far."

"Not far. Maybe less than three quarters of a mile. From the Merrilark parking lot to the campfire on Crawfish Pond. After dark but before the moon comes up. We'll do a timed test. Tonight."

"You mean an enactment?"

"Except not hitting Mike with a shovel. He'll take the part of Brad and you'll jump into the back of the truck. There was a tarp back there, so someone could have hidden successfully. Be here at quarter to eight. Alex can come and hold a stopwatch. My men are tied up keeping track of this event mob so he'll be useful."

Sarah, her evening now planned, turned to the subject of the event. "Who in the neighborhood is competing?"

"The mounted suspects, you mean," said Mike. "I've got the list. As follows: Jane Zimmer, the two Wentworths, and Harvey Dodge ride the training-level course—higher jumps, longer course, more complicated dressage than the novice-level stuff."

George nodded. "As I've said, the stadium jumping and dressage are easy to watch. They're contained, inside marked areas. The cross-country is Sunday, so I'll walk the course before then."

"Better do it plenty early," said Mike. "All the riders walk the course, figure out approaches, how many strides, whether to take a shortcut, things like that."

"You mean they can't practice on a horse?" asked Sarah.

"No way," said Mike. "Riding the course ahead of time is unfair. Unlawful. Not done. No one can ride the course six weeks before the event. So the competitors walk it. Sometimes twice. Even three times."

"Sunrise Sunday morning, then," said George. "Mrs. Clancy can come with me and explain the layout." He turned to Sarah. "We are very interested in your and Katie's ideas, the evidence from Neil Wentworth's blazer, and your library work. Now I'd skip dinner if I were you. You don't want to run on a full stomach."

Sarah sighed. "I skipped lunch."

"Everyone eats too much," said George in a disapproving voice.

Sarah gave in because as she told Alex later, "George probably doesn't need real food. He's made of turnip greens and roots. Just a little water every now and then."

The Bradley head-bashing rerun, as Mike Laaka called it, took place at eight-fifteen. George, being a stickler for detail, had borrowed a pickup similar to the impounded Highfeather model, and this stood in place on the end of the dirt track leading to Crawfish Pond and the campfire site. Mike playing Bradley received permission from an imaginary Neil Wentworth to use the truck. Sarah, lurking in the dark behind a spruce tree waited for Mike/Brad to climb aboard and slam the truck door. Then, bent low, she ran for the back of the truck and hauled herself over the tailgate flattening herself on the metal floor. The truck started, bumped up the dirt track, across and along Tri-County Road, into the joint camp entrance, and, more slowly, down the left turnoff to Camp Merrilark.

Mike/Brad climbed out and, using a flashlight, made for the infirmary as Sarah jumped to the ground. Alex was waiting, stopwatch in hand. "Okay," he said. "He'll be fifteen minutes max in the infirmary. Get your shovel and wait."

Sarah, feeling almost as guilty as if she were indeed about to commit murder, found the shovel by the side of the parking lot next to a mound of sand. The original? she wondered. No, the original was still in laboratory hands. But original or not, this shovel was a nasty item. Long-handled and heavy-headed. How should she use it? Bring it down directly or try a sidewise swipe? But then she remembered she did not actually have to brain Mike.

Mike returned, whistling, up the path. "Eight forty-five," called out Alex. Sarah, in the shadows, waited until Mike was full in the glare of the parking lot lamp. "Mike," she called softly. He whirled, blinking, and Sarah raised the shovel.

"God, you scared the bejeezus out of me," said Mike. He stopped, dropped to one knee, and then arranged himself on the ground. "Okay, stash the shovel in the bushes and get going."

"Eight forty-nine," called Alex. "Four minutes for the attack and shovel disposal. Hit it."

And Sarah hit it. Although her brain urged caution she found that a surge of adrenaline was sending her at top speed. Up the path, to the dimly lit Tri-County Road. Across, she plunged into a drainage ditch. Got to her feet and hurled herself through the fence and down the pasture toward the woods. But now darkness hid the swales and rises of the field and she stumbled, fell, got up, fell again. Once she plummeted into a heavy mix of juniper and then ricocheted into an alder clump. Twice she lost the dirt track, twice she found it again. And then guided by a small fire lit by George Fitts in the interest of verisimilitude, she staggered into the beach area.

"Fourteen minutes," announced George. "If you started at eight fifty."

"Eight forty-nine," gasped Sarah.

"Not bad. Not bad at all. So it is possible," said George. "I wouldn't have thought it. And it clears up one more messy area."

"That must eliminate someone," said Sarah. "Harvey Dodge can't run, can he? So what are you going to do? Make the arrest?"

"The arrest?" It was Mike, returned with Alex in the pickup. "You civilians think all you do is run a test, go to the library, look in a man's jacket pocket, and make an arrest. Be patient. Give the murderer a loose rein. Let him show his hand."

"For once," said George, "Mike is right. I'm looking for a move on Sunday. Something untoward. During or at the end of the cross-country. Then we might have something we can take to court."

And with that Sarah and Alex had to be content.

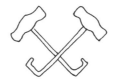

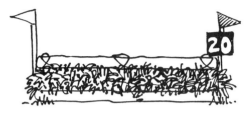

THE BRUSH

TWENTY

SATURDAY, July the second, was another hot one. Warm by six in the morning and into the eighties by seven. "Hot as a Tophet," announced Julia, who was rounding up Tucker and Belle preparatory to locking them in the dog run for the duration.

"God knows," she said, "I keep my animals under control. I tell everyone to leave theirs at home, that a horse show is no place for dogs, who will probably get into a fight or get loose and spook someone's horse. And since no one listens I've put up notices saying that dogs must be on leashes. But there's always someone's dear little golden or Jack Russell or Lab running wild."

"I get the point," Sarah said. "Patsy will be jailed. But won't it be too hot to have the stadium jumping? The dressage? All those poor people in black coats and black velvet helmets."

Julia looked at her niece in astonishment. "Cancel because the people are too hot? Nonsense. As long as the horses are cooled out properly, there's no problem. Heat is the least of my worries. I keep saying what if today is the day my farm is finally destroyed."

"You're being guarded like Buckingham Palace," said Sarah. "And the police seem to have melted into the scenery. All they had to do is wear smelly blue jeans and carry a water bucket. But," she added, "George says that today will probably be a dud."

"You sound disappointed," snapped Julia. "I can live with a dud today. And tomorrow. And I think George and Mike are part of the problem. They're just going around with their tongues hanging out. Practically inviting someone to louse up my event."

"Semper paratus," said Sarah. "Our murderer—or murderers—has shown a certain affinity for events, for parties—the Preakness, our wedding, the camp cookout. Now I'm going to put poor Patsy away and check out the whole scene."

With this Sarah turned, escorted Patsy to the dog run, and retreated to Julia's terrace. Here she could observe all the hustle and bustle of a big horse show and here she was joined by a sweltering Jessica in her white stock, white britches, black velvet hat, gleaming boots.

"I don't really understand dressage," said Sarah. "Or combined training events for that matter."

"Oh God," said Jessica. "I can't explain it in one minute. It's complicated."

"Try it," suggested Sarah. "As to a small child."

"Okay," said Jessica, sighing. "Just a minute, because I've got to be ready to ride soon. Dressage is sort of like doing school figures in skating. Except you do it on a horse. You ride different tests and some are hard and some are pretty easy. Circles, diagonals, walking, trotting, cantering. Everything's supposed to be balanced and under control. If your horse is very good—which mine isn't because he's green—then there's all sorts of fancy stuff like flying changes and piaffes and passage. You know, like the Viennese Riding School. But today all the tests are pretty simple."

"So what's combined about it?" asked Sarah.

"You do three things. Besides the dressage test you ride over a bunch of jumps in the stadium and then tomorrow you do the cross-country course. That's supposed to be the endurance part of the event. You get penalty points when your horse does something stupid like refuses a jump or if you forget the order of the jumps. Now I've got to check Cinnamon's braids. This is her first event and I'm kind of nervous."

"Of course you're not, Jessica," said a familiar voice. "Go to it; keep your chin up and your heels down and think."

Aunt Julia. She turned on Sarah. "Whatever are you doing?" Without waiting for an answer she pointed toward the stable area. "We need you to mark up the dressage scores and to help at the food tent at lunchtime. I know the show is exciting, but you're indispensable for the jobs that don't need people who know anything."

And Sarah sighed. Not the time for an argument, for repair of her self-image. She turned her back on the stadium and departed for a day of servitude in humid air and under a smoldering sun—a day so busy, so full of bodily discomfort she had little time to speculate on what Sunday might bring.

Not until Mike pulled her behind a large lilac bush after dinner. It was seven-thirty, still light and still warm with a muggy, thick feel to the air.

"Okay," said Mike, "tomorrow at five A.M. George is walking the course with Julia. You're to come along so it won't look like a police expedition. You've been noted by now as part of the stable staff."

"And tonight?" queried Sarah.

"Tonight George has a man at every fence. No one is going to get away with nothin'. Batman himself couldn't fly in. Don't get yourself in a stew."

And curiously enough, Sarah didn't. She and Alex went quietly to bed at ten-thirty.

"Still almost a full moon," said Alex, leaning out the bedroom window. "But I think we'll have rain before tomorrow night."

Sarah joined him. "It's as if the whole farm is holding its breath. Waiting. As if we should have some sort of vigil."

"George is taking care of the vigil. Accept a night of peace when it's offered. Tomorrow is coming all too soon."

It did. No sooner had Sarah put her head to the pillow than Alex was shaking her awake. "Four-thirty. We're walking the cross-country course. Put rubber boots on; it'll be wet."

Sarah sat up as if she'd been stung. "What? What about the cross-country? Did something happen? That moon."

"Calm down. Nothing happened. And moonlight may interest howling dogs but not skulking felons. What they want is the dark of night. We're meeting at the cross-country starting box."

With the exception of George Fitts, to whom time of day seemed to have no meaning, it was a heavy-eyed group that gathered at five A.M. and began the hike toward the first fence. The day promised more heat, but even now a distant grumble of thunder sounded beyond Crawfish Pond and a small wind stirred along the edge of the woods.

Sarah, stumping along next to her aunt, grabbed her elbow. "I haven't got this part straight. Do the riders race each other?"

Julia, for once, was patient. "A cross-country isn't a race; it's a timed ride over a series of natural fences. If you ride too slowly or too fast you're penalized. We have timers and jump judges at every fence to check for rule violations."

Mike turned to Sarah. "George has posted police at every fence of the cross-country; they'll sit next to the jump judge."

Julia pointed to a long brush-filled obstacle flagged with a white Number 1 on a black background. "That's the first fence of the Training Level course. The Novice course is set up through the northern fields."

"Right," said Mike. "The Novice course is being watched by the sheriff's department. But all of our favorite people are riding this course. Training Level. Okay, where next?"

"The Log is Number two and then comes the Stone Wall," said Julia. "Next, turn and splash through the Old Mill, turn back and head straight for the Hay Wagon. Number five."

"Old Mill? Hay wagon?" said Sarah. "You're not serious."

"Of course," said Julia. "Makes the course more interesting to have a theme. We're trying for a summer-on-the-farm motif."

"Not murder-on-the-farm?" said Mike, grinning. "You could

have gibbets dangling from the trees, crossed-bludgeons for fences."

Sarah gave Mike a quick jab with her elbow. "Shut up, Mike, Aunt Julia's hanging on by her teeth as it is."

At which George held up a cautionary hand. He walked up to the narrow hay wagon, got down on his hands and knees, and peered underneath. "Good place for someone to hide," he observed, rising and dusting off his trousers. "I'll make a note."

"No," said Julia loudly. "I can't have you police crawling around under my jumps. Upsetting things, knocking the flags down."

George paused, a puzzled expression on his face. "But I want to make extra sure. You don't want a fence booby-trapped. A wire stretched. One of the structural parts loosened."

"I," said Julia, "have checked myself. Patrick and I walked the course yesterday. Everything's in order."

But George's expression of puzzlement had given away to one faintly tainted with suspicion. He regarded Julia with a darkened brow and then pointed the way ahead. "Let's go on. And Mrs. Clancy, I have to do my job. I'd feel like a fool if someone was found in ambush under one of these things. Now, according to my map of the course, after the Hay Wagon you have the Snake followed by the Drop, and then the Hedge. Numbers six, seven, and eight."

"Good Lord," said Sarah. "It's like miniature golf on horseback. All these tricky little units." Then, noticing her aunt lagging behind, her face troubled, Sarah slowed her steps. "Okay, Wonder Woman," she said. "You can fool the police and me and Alex part of the time. Don't try for one hundred percent. You've got Rafe Posner stashed away under some jump, haven't you? No?" as Julia began a violent head-shaking. "Come clean. George's men will ferret him out. He's wanted for questioning and God knows what you'll be wanted for."

Julia paused, obviously struggling. "I think," she began.

But Sarah took pity. "No confessions now. But Rafe Posner loose in the middle of a cross-country event is not what you need."

Julia came to a halt and shook her head. "This is the truth. I have never seen anyone in the daytime. If someone, someone like Rafe, is hiding out in my woods by night, he's not here in the daytime. I've looked. And called. Believe me. I just don't want anyone threatened by police and their bloodhounds."

"You're saying Rafe wouldn't surface today?"

Julia closed her eyes and sighed. "I'm saying the reason the police haven't found anyone by day is because there isn't anyone to find. And they may not have searched that carefully at night."

"Hey. Hey there." It was Mike shouting from the top of a rise. "Get a move on, you two."

And Sarah and Julia hurried forward, Sarah holding Julia's hand and steadying her over the rough ground and up to a flat-topped hill.

George consulted his map. "Here's the Table, Number nine. A wide-open area, not much of an opportunity for trouble. I'll only need one man here. It's the woods I'm worried about."

And so it went. The Table, followed by a double-log obstacle called the Big Oxer, then into the woods through an enclosure named the Pig Stye, and next a steep decline and over the Coop, this a triangular affair resembling an old fashioned chicken house.

"For variety we went back to the old course this year," said Julia as the party slid and slithered down the path that led from the Coop to Crawfish Pond. "From the Coop it's an open run near the shore and then into and out of the Coffin."

"Coffin!" exclaimed Sarah.

"Just a rectangular ditch. Twenty-four-feet wide. Two-feet deep. The rider jumps in, gallops one stride, and jumps out. It's a common obstacle. Part of the old course Patrick refurbished this year to give a challenging waterfront run."

For a moment the group solemnly surveyed the Coffin—smooth of side, firm and sandy as to footing—and then turned for home, Julia increasingly winded.

"My bones," she complained, "are not made for jogging an entire cross-country course. Let's get this over with. From the

Coffin the riders head out of the woods, turn and go over the Hay Bales, then to the Wagon Wheel, gallop uphill, turn left and take the Garden Gate. Then it's straight on for the Picnic Bench, a right turn and over the Whiskey Barrels—that was Tom's favorite—then the In-and-Out, turn left and take the easy Brush, and head to the finish line. Twenty jumps in all."

"Good God," said Sarah. "People survive this?"

"Love it," said Julia. "As my students say, it's a total trip. You have no idea the feeling you get galloping through the woods, hearing your horse's feet pounding, seeing his neck stretch out, getting set for the next fence, up and over, and galloping on."

"I have," said Sarah, "a clear idea of the feeling *I'd* get."

"Forget the thrill of the chase," said Mike. "Let's finish up. Those woods are the devil. Our men will have to have eyes in the back of their heads."

Julia stood still, apparently sniffing the air. "Rain," she announced. "I can smell it. Let's hope it holds off until tonight. Now I'm off. I have to start cracking a whip. Figuratively speaking. And George, tell your men to be perfectly quiet when a rider is going by."

"Mike," said Sarah as Julia marched off to the center of her operations—to a cluster of figures standing about the starting box, "Mike, has George really looked at every jump? All those boxes and tables and coops and things?"

Mike grimaced. "For the last few days he's been busy as a bird dog. There are signs that someone—or several someones—has been sneaking around. But that's all. Not to worry. He'll have his men poking around again this morning."

"You know, that ghost or whatever it is has only been seen at night. You may not find it in daylight." There, Sarah told herself. I haven't exactly given Rafe away, but I've brought up the subject. Which, if Rafe's into murder, won't be enough, and if he's innocent, will be too much. Oh hell.

At which Mike laughed. "Sarah, you sure can complicate something beyond human belief. Don't worry about that frigging ghost. We're dealing with flesh and blood, and if it shows itself we'll nail him good. Now go along and be a spectator."

But a spectator at a cross-country event, even if possessed of seven-league boots, sees at the most only about a fifth of a single rider's performance. Most watchers either fix themselves at a single vantage point, say, on a hill, or stand between the thousand feet that separates the finish line from the starting box. Or, if restless, the enthusiast can traipse from one area to the next to catch glimpses of riders going over distant fences.

Sarah spent the morning watching the Novice Level riders take off from the starting box with the plan to become one of the peripatetic spectators during the afternoon, when the Training Level riders would be in motion.

The morning went smoothly. Sarah had the pleasure of seeing several of the older Merrilark and Highfeather children finish the novice course in one piece and still atop their mounts. Among the finishers was cousin Jessica Jacoby on Cinnamon, who clinched the white fourth-place ribbon.

"Piece of cake," said Jessica, pausing by Sarah and Alex—he back from hospital rounds.

"My very words," said Sarah, watching the pair trot off, Cinnamon's flanks heaving, her coat soaked with sweat. She turned and Alex handed her a hot dog.

"Peace and quiet so far," he observed.

"What if nothing, absolutely nothing happens?" said Sarah.

"I'd say *good.* The police machinery will continue to grind and chew and sooner or later will spit someone out. Even the someone you have fingered. And do it less colorfully than the scenario you're hoping for."

Sarah took a bite of the hot dog and then shook her head. "I'm not hoping for anything dramatic. I don't want anyone hurt."

"You lie. Deep down, the lover of fiction wants a stirring finale. Keystone Cops, *High Noon*, Birnam wood to Dunsinane. A bang not a whimper. Don't deny it. Now we've a half-hour lunch break and then it's Harvey Dodge riding Tippecanoe."

"I do deny it, and what a godawful name for a horse."

"Harvey likes battle names."

"You know," said Sarah, "if Harvey's riding in this thing, he isn't in such lousy shape as Aunt Julia seems to think. It's just possible that he could have stowed away in the pickup, brained Brad, and, walking fast, knowing the ground, made it back to the campfire sometime after nine. No one remembered him singing after a certain point."

"But he was singing after Brad had left," Alex reminded her.

"A bicycle," said Sarah. "Maybe he bicycled. Or walked back to the farmhouse, picked up his car, drove to Merrilark, drove back. After all, we know Harvey wants to muscle into the Merrilark operation. Brad Pfeifer was an obstacle. And Brad's murder is still up for grabs even if we have a handle on who killed Farney."

"You're reaching again. Besides, Brad Pfeifer was planning to leave Merrilark."

"Which Harvey may not have known. Never mind; as I said, my reach always exceeds my grasp. Then there's Neil and Winka."

"Live and kicking suspects."

"Agreed. But what about Rafe Posner? Sean Conners?"

"The ghost entry?"

"Right. Oh look, speak of the devil, there's Harvey now." Sarah pointed to a stout figure dressed jockey-style with a brown-and-tan striped shirt and matching cover to his helmet. Atop a large dark bay gelding, he trotted up to the starting box.

"I suppose," said Sarah, "his colors are a tribute to the army. His horse looks just like a moose. And I think he's crazy to jump at his age."

"My thoughts exactly," said Julia, joining them. "He's not in shape for anything but gentle hacking. But since I don't care anymore about Harvey, let him break his foolish neck."

"Which you don't mean," said Sarah.

"Well, not his neck. Perhaps a wrist."

Harvey Dodge did not break his neck. Or his wrist. But Tippecanoe—true to his name—upended his rider at the picturesque Whiskey Barrels, and Harvey twisted an ankle and bruised a shoulder landing. While the ambulance crew collected him, Julia bit her lip and went to get ice.

"That puts Harvey out of the picture, for now anyway," said Sarah. "He won't be mobile enough for any terrorist action."

But Alex had turned and was watching a rider in green and yellow colors on a gray mare sail smoothly over the first fence, and they both saw the following rider in cherry and blue on a big roan gelding deal with two hard bucks and a refusal before horse and rider lurched over the Stone Wall.

"What a sport," said Sarah, watching the rider disappear. "They call this fun?"

"You prefer skydiving? Bungee-jumping?" said Alex.

But Sarah was now listening to the countdown at the starting box. "It's Jane Zimmer next. On her old black mare."

Alex checked his list. "Lily Glendower. Safe as a church. Thump, thump, up and over." And they both watched Jane and Lily heave themselves safely over the first obstacle.

"Let's move it," said Sarah. "Keep an eye on Jane. We can head for the woods, because if something's going to happen today, it won't happen out here in broad daylight." For a second she watched Jane and Lily Glendower pound their way toward the Log jump, lift over, and gallop on.

"Jane is one pretty tough character," she told Alex.

Alex nodded agreement, and they began a hike along the side of the course, Sarah leaping nervously every time someone called "Heads up, rider coming." Pausing at the Table, Number 9, they watched five riders, wearing all colors of the rainbow, thunder past, take the Big Oxer, Fence 10, with ease and grace, gallop downhill, and disappear into the woods toward Number 11, the Pig Stye.

And then Neil Wentworth. Neil, wearing the red and gray of Highfeather, riding a handsome dark chestnut animal called Nether Wallop. Named, Alex suggested, for some English village with fond associations.

"Another weird name," muttered Sarah, watching Neil turn his horse and gallop away toward the distant Big Oxer.

"Lot of weird names," said Alex. "I was looking over the entries. You like Hungarian Stew or Sultan Goof Bah any better?"

But Sarah had turned away and was staring across the field. "Oh my God, look over there."

Alex looked. "Goddamn. Who did that?"

The two setters, Tucker and Belle, released from durance vile and now in full hunt, ran across the opening and along the brow of the hill. Behind them, moving closer to the woods, one very large hairy canine. Patsy.

Sarah went into action. "I'll go after Patsy. You try for the setters. Aunt Julia will have a stroke. And so may one of the riders."

The appearance of the dogs set up a hue and cry, and in a matter of minutes spectators and a clutch of George Fitts's surveillance corps were running fore and aft, calling and whistling. An announcer's voice blared from the starting box warning riders of loose dogs. Sarah, running and calling after Patsy, had the experience of seeing Neil Wentworth's Nether Wallop at the Big Oxer execute a sensational refusal almost in the act of lifting off—upon the appearance almost under his hooves of a busy English setter. Neil lost both stirrups, whirled his horse in a circle, slapped it hard with his jumping bat, headed for the oxer, and, stirrups still banging, cleared the logs, landed, and vanished at a gallop in the direction of the Pig Stye.

Patsy was cornered almost an hour later in a paddock holding Julia's Plum Duff and Pecos Bill, both horses being in a state of agitation due to the coming and going of galloping horses on the cross-country course. And Sarah suffered the fate of a person caught between two large excited horses and an exuberant Irish wolfhound. First she was knocked to the ground by Patsy, then in rising her left foot was firmly squashed by the weight of Duffie's left front hoof. A hoof the size of a saucepan, with the impact of a dropped bowling ball. Flames and fire, agony and shock, took hold of Sarah, and if at that moment murder had been executed on Julia Clancy and her entire stable of horses, she would have cheered.

For a few minutes she hopped about, then loosened her sneaker, fingered what she was sure was raw hamburger, stood up, and thought about something cold. The closest form of relief was the brook. Or Crawfish Pond. To hell with watching anyone do anything. To hell with loose dogs. A plague on horses and cross-country madness. Sarah limped and shuffled her way through the woods, pausing once to dip a foot in the brook, but the water was muddy, shallow, and warm. So she stumbled on toward Crawfish Pond, toward the Coop and the Coffin, her nose dripping, tears of pain tracking down her cheeks. For the moment all was peace, someone having fallen at the Snake and the next competitor held up until the unfortunate rider could catch his horse and remount.

Reaching the Pigsty, she heard the familiar cry, "Heads up, rider on the course," and turned back to see a rider galloping toward the Big Oxer. Winka Wentworth. But she wasn't galloping. What was faster than a gallop? Neophyte as Sarah was, she had seen rider after rider approach, steady his horse, set it for the fence. And, for the most part, a safe clean jump followed.

But Winka was riding the Grand National. Hell-bent for leather. She and her big bay horse—what was its name?—Highfeather's Folly—came at the double-log fence as if ten thousand guineas were riding on the result. Up, over, down and away, down toward the Pigsty—Folly at one point almost going to his knees on the steep slope. Then in and out the Pigsty like an express, and now hurtling toward the Coop, Folly's neck and shoulders lathered, foam flying from his mouth.

Sarah, heart pounding, forgetting pain and a mashed foot, took a shortcut straight down, ran forward, and joined the group of persons standing by the Coop. Joined in time to hear a man with a clipboard to say in a loud voice, "Good Christ, what in the hell is she doing?" To see a woman stand up and yell—probably in defiance of all cross-country rules—"Slow down, slow down, you damn fool." Then hearing her add, "Great God, she'll kill her horse and herself."

Sarah, rigid, found herself holding her breath, watching Winka stand in her stirrups, lean forward on Folly's neck, and take the Coop in one wide-open steeplechase stride.

"Good Christ," said the man a second time. "She'll try and

jump the whole Goddamn Coffin. Take it without the middle stride."

Sarah swallowed, clenched her fists. It seemed as if that was exactly what Winka was going to try. No sensible descent into the Coffin, but a huge leap, leaving out a stride entirely. Which of course was impossible. Wasn't it? She turned to the man, but he stood with binoculars hanging from one hand, apparently hypnotized by the approaching calamity.

Afterward Sarah was never able to put the sequence together. She played it in slow motion and then at fast forward, but it still came out a jumble. Winka galloping, leaning forward, her mouth like a red slash across her face; Folly, wild-eyed, foam-flecked, his dark coat shining with sweat—and then. And then, two English setters, one after the other, streaking across the Coffin at the very moment of Folly's taking off. Folly, in an aerial-borne curve, landing askew, coming down. Folly falling on his side, Winka almost under Folly's thrashing legs. Folly, snorting in fright, the reins broken and caught around a foreleg. A thin disheveled figure appearing from nowhere, leaping forward, pulling the rider free of those hooves. Dragging Winka to the side of the Coffin, her head in its red and gray helmet bobbing along the sandy bottom. Winka scrambling to her feet, blood coming from her mouth, pouring from her nose. Winka screaming. And screaming. A jump judge running forward. The thin figure gone. Gone before anyone even knew he was there. And Winka gone. Gone as if she'd never happened.

Leaving only Folly. Now struggling to his feet, frantic, rearing, pawing, whirling. A woman rushing forward, reaching for the broken rein. Folly held, dancing and snorting. Eyes rolling.

Sarah hobbling forward. Later she could never answer why, since all her instincts told her to leave. To get out. Get away from that maddened animal. But, pushed by some unknown force, she made it to the edge of the Coffin. And looked down. The once-smooth sand bottom was dented and marked by the passage of many hooves, but Folly's wild thrashings had torn more than the surface. His hooves had slashed down to a lower layer. A layer of moldering leaves, earth, and one arm. One arm and one hand. One disintegrating arm and hand.

THE FINISH

TWENTY-ONE

SARAH let out a yelp, backed up, stumbled, and fell heavily against the sides of the Coffin. For the space of five whole seconds she remained absolutely still, fixed by the spectral arm and hand. An arm that seemed to be rising as a separate and awful entity from a bed of choppy sand, a hand that appeared by the bending of its skeleton fingers to beckon her forward, to come and take a closer look.

This Sarah resisted. But hoisting herself to her feet, aware now that her recent exertions had aggravated the hideous throbbing in her injured foot, she turned for help and found that Folly's rearings and plungings were still occupying center stage. But then as she inched forward, Folly suddenly stood still, and trembling, sweating, was mercifully led away.

And now the arm and hand took center stage. After all, there is little more compelling than the discovery of a body where one is not supposed to be. Calls, cries, and radio action by a woman in green denim shorts—obviously one of the police plants—all brought a crowd of persons: riders already finished with their course, spectators, jump judges, and a battalion of plainclothes police. And, in a matter of minutes, George Fitts and Mike Laaka. And Alex with the two English setters yoked together by a belt, the trio followed by Patsy.

George took one look at what was now Exhibit A, shouted an order, and then whirled on the watching crowd. "Where's the rider? Where's Mrs. Wentworth?"

Looks of surprise. Heads turning. Puzzlement. Why, where was she? Then signs of concern. She must have been injured. She had fallen when her horse spooked. Spooked by those dogs. Who let dogs on the course? Absolutely criminal. The rider might have been killed. Ditto the horse. Terrible. Irresponsible. And a body. At least part of a body. Good God.

But Sarah, grabbing Mike, jabbed a hand in the direction of the waterfront. "Winka got up. She could walk. I didn't see where exactly, but I think toward the lake."

"Come on then," shouted Mike, already in motion toward the beach. And Sarah hobbled after, and with Alex just behind, the three made it to the edge of the water together.

And looked left, right, into the woods, across the pond.

"She was bleeding," said Sarah. "Her mouth and nose."

"There," shouted Alex. "Look out there. Someone's head. Swimming." He pointed at a spot some three hundred yards offshore, where a dark blob undulated and bobbed along the water.

"I can't see," said Sarah. And she couldn't because as she spoke the rain came. A few great heavy drops. Then, with no further warning, a sheet of gray rain driving down, splattering off rocks and denting the ruffled water.

"Damn, I can't see either," yelled Mike. Then, shielding his eyes from the rain, "Okay, there it is. Yes, it's someone out there. Where's a boat?"

But there was no boat. Not to speak of. Just an old skiff with long unpainted oars.

"Tell George we need a water rescue," called Mike to a man who had appeared behind him on the shore. Then Mike, not waiting for an answer, began shoving the boat toward the water's edge.

Alex, impatient, handed the dogs to the same man, stripped himself of shirt, shoes, and trousers, and was wading into the water.

"Wait up," called Mike.

"Follow me in the boat," shouted Alex, and he plunged into the deeper water and began a rhythmic forward stroke.

And Mike and Sarah pushed the skiff into the water, scrambled aboard, and Mike grabbed the oars and began pulling away. The rain beat down, the thunder began a heavy mutter, the wind rose, and small waves began breaking over the low bow of the skiff.

Sarah searched the water, aware of Alex off to starboard, swimming steadily. Beyond Alex—nothing. The dark blob had vanished into the rain-swept water. If it was Winka, thought Sarah, then she's wearing her riding boots. Wearing them because she couldn't possibly have pulled them off. Not without a bootjack. Sarah had seen Winka with the bootjack, working her feet out of her close-fitting black boots. And riding the cross-country course she would hardly have been carrying a bootjack. And the boots must by now be weighing down her lower limbs. Dragging her slowly under. A wounded woman, just fallen from a horse could not—no matter what sort of shape she was in—maintain a steady swim across a broad lake wearing riding boots.

And why was Winka swimming? To escape from what was to come? Was she disoriented, the result of a head injury? Or was it fear, shame? Desperation?

Or was it really Winka? Sarah asked herself. Or Aunt Julia's resident ghost swimming out there. Rafe Posner, rising out of the bushes to pull the rider free of the frightened horse and then vanishing again. Had he let the dogs out to put the final touch to the cross-country competition? Rafe, all along. Rafe, Aunt Julia's pet refugee, who was putting the final bite on the hand that made the apple pie.

Did that beckoning hand from the Coffin belong to Sean Conners? Sean murdered by Rafe? Or was Sean alive and well and exacting full vengeance for the injuries done him?

But at that exact moment one answer to her questions came floating by. A hat. Or to be more exact, a helmet. The sort of helmet worn by those who risk their necks jumping large animals over difficult obstacles. A helmet, floating like some sort of coconut. A coconut—or half a coconut—covered in scarlet and gray—the colors of Camp Highfeather.

It bobbled past Sarah, low in the water, almost filled from the beating rain. She reached out an arm for it and found an oar in her way.

"Got it," yelled Mike. "I'll lift it in. It's Winka's," he added unnecessarily. And then, "We'll take Alex aboard. This is pretty hopeless; the visibility is about two feet."

The addition of Alex to the skiff lowered the freeboard, but the flat-bottomed skiff, if old, was sturdy.

"Aunt Julia keeps it on the shore as a rescue boat," Sarah explained. Sometimes she goes fishing. I think Rafe used to row her out."

"Rafe," said Mike, "is something else."

"I think he just turned up," said Sarah. "Took hold of Winka before Folly could trample her. But whose body was it in there? That awful hand. The fingers were bent so it looked just as if it was calling me over. Or asking for alms . . ." She shivered. The temperature had dropped; the rain was now blowing almost sideways.

Mike stopped his oars. "We're not doing any good, and if this wind keeps up we'll swamp for sure."

Alex held up a hand. "Listen. It's a boat."

It was two boats. Two motorboats. Commandeered from two nearby summer cottages and manned by the police. The first, a sleek white fiberglass affair, churned up alongside the skiff and cut the motor. "Go on in to shore," called the man at the wheel. "You're a hazard rowing around like that. More boats are coming out. And we've called for a chopper. And a diver."

Mike nodded briefly, turned the skiff about in one swift pull of his port oar. Then, with head bent into the rain, he began the return trip. "Keep your eyes peeled," he commanded Sarah and Alex. "I'll row a zigzag course."

So Alex in the stern turning left and right, Sarah in the bow, searched the surface of the roiled water as the little boat rocked and yawed its way back to shore. And Sarah, as she squinted through the rain at the little gray waves, thought of Winka Wentworth, could almost imagine her, the lovely long blond hair unfastened from its net, flowing behind her as she turned and turned in the water, her long legs in their black riding boots weighting down her drowned body.

The need for a lifeline must be long gone. And if a line had been thrown to the swimming woman, if a hand or an oar had been held out to her, none, thought Sarah, would have been welcome. Or made use of.

Sunday night. Eight o'clock. The horse trailers, the host of riders, grooms, their friends, had departed, and the temporary stabling tent had come down. Now the parking lot, muddy and pockmarked by the rain and the trampings of many horses, held only family vehicles and the police-car collection, which included the trailer-office of Sergeant George Fitts. George himself was absent, having chosen to escort the ambulance bearing the body-in-the-Coffin to autopsy central—the forensic laboratory in Augusta.

Sarah sat at one end of a sofa, her purpled foot elevated and wrapped in flannel, a cup of tea in one hand, the returned Patsy at her feet. The rain still slanted against the window, but hot baths had been taken, a scrambled-together dinner was over, and from the parlor the dismal notes of some dirge played in a minor key sounded from the piano. Lacking the energy to ride, Julia was seeking relief from her second favorite pastime.

I've done this all before, Sarah thought, but I never remember feeling quite this dreary, this depressed. I suppose George will come bounding in with some wonderful details of a postmortem or the news that he's found a few more bodies. And Alex will arrive and tell me how efficient the divers and draggers are being even though they haven't found Winka. And Mike will show up with Rafe Posner in handcuffs.

Instead, Mike and Alex walked in at almost the same time wearing sober expressions and by the condition of their clothes proving that no truly waterproof rain gear exists.

Both carried large steaming mugs of coffee and Mike held out a large paper sack marked Dunkin' Doughnuts.

"Glad Julia keeps the coffee machine lit," said Mike. "We need to keep our juices flowing." Then, "Is that Julia playing? Sounds like a hound in pain. Alex's been down to Crawfish Pond but nothing doing, it's such a lousy night." Mike pushed his wet forelock out of his eyes and lowered himself onto the other end of Julia's sofa. Alex followed and folded himself into an armchair.

"Go on, what else?" said Sarah.

"The body in the Coffin. It's Sean Conners, all right. Even if the condition of the corpse leaves a lot to be desired."

Sarah sighed. "I supposed it had to be Sean or Rafe."

"Dead for quite a while," said Alex. "I stayed while the ambulance team dug him out. The scene-of-crime people have marked off the place and set up a watch."

"A little late for that," said Sarah.

"Have to go by the book," said Mike. "Besides, Sean hasn't been there the whole time. He was moved into place about four or five weeks ago. From the manure pile."

"Tilly and Jane's manure pile!" exclaimed Sarah.

"No," said Mike. "There are manure piles and manure piles. The body was probably from under Julia's garden manure pile because the horse stall shavings look like Julia's. She has most of her manure hauled away, but keeps some for spreading and garden use."

Sarah bit her lip and tried to think back. Back to the Preakness. A hundred years ago, wasn't it? "Has he been dead since Aunt Julia's Preakness party?" asked Sarah.

"Could be," said Mike. "Seems likely. Cranial injury. Uncle Tom's cane. Bits of hair and blood cells found on the cane. Lab will try for a match with Sean's sometime tonight."

"And Rafe Posner?" said Alex.

"AWOL," said Mike. "Still a missing person. Playing games with us. But we're betting he'll show."

"And so am I." It was Julia, stumping in from the front parlor. She looked rather like the victim of a small but efficient tornado—hair still damp and disheveled, her shirt rumpled, her trousers stained. Her face lined, pale, and creased with more than her sixty-eight years. "Rafe," said Julia, "is just being irresponsible. I'll have to lay down the law to that man."

"The law," said Mike, "can hardly wait to get its hooks on Rafe. You'll have to stand in line. And sit down, Julia, you're making us nervous. We're trying for a quick wrap-up and then I've got to make it over to Highfeather and see if Neil's come back."

"He's disappeared?" said Alex.

"After Winka took the plunge—so to speak—Neil went off to borrow a boat to help look for her. He hasn't come in so far as we know, but the police are waiting."

"Help me out," pleaded Julia. "Because I began to think it was Neil all along. Strangling Farney. If it wasn't Sean doing it, then I thought it was Neil. Though I couldn't see how he could have killed Brad Pfeifer, since he didn't leave the campfire area for more than ten minutes."

"Back up, Julia," said Mike. "Have a doughnut. I have six kinds. I'll bring you coffee or Ovaltine—whatever you drink."

"Scotch," said Julia. "Scotch on the rocks with a twist of lemon. And a plain doughnut. And then tell me about Neil."

Alex turned from the window, put down his coffee, went to the cupboard, and in short order produced drinks all round. "Nothing goes better with murder," he said, lining up a variety of bottles on a small table covered with horse periodicals, "than coffee, doughnuts, and a good snort."

"Aunt Julia's half right," said Sarah. "Neil was involved. Not exactly an accessory, because I'd guess he didn't know in advance about the murders, or even the details afterward. Judging from an argument I overheard in the stable, Neil was out of sync with Winka's master plan. He had a bit part, probably cutting out the copycat poems. I guessed Friday morning and woke Alex to tell him. Then went to the library to confirm. And told Mike and George, who said it was flimflam. No substance. What Katie Waters called a misspelled word."

"Sarah, for Lord's sake, just say what you mean," said Julia.

"Put Julia out of her misery," said Mike. "It wasn't a misspelled word. It was that everlasting British pride."

"Not exactly," said Sarah. "But some things you don't change even if you move to another country where people speak English—or a variety of it. You go on spelling words like *plow* and *honor* and *check* the British way: *plough, honour, cheque.* And say *bonnet* and *windscreen* instead of *hood* and *windshield.* And *lorry* instead of *truck.* Winka and Neil used British terms for everyday items. And they didn't change the UK spelling. When the second verse of 'Sing a Song of Sixpence' began 'Julia's in the *parlour* eating bitter gall,' the word *parlor* was spelled *parlour.* The British way."

"Maybe a British edition was used," suggested Julia.

"It might have been, although I thought that no one needs to look up the very common nursery rhymes because we all know them by heart. But if we write a word, we use the spelling we're familiar with, the way we were taught in school, and American nursery rhyme books and dictionaries as least as far back as 1930 use *parlor.* Only British Mother Goose books like the *Oxford Nursery Rhyme Book* use *parlour.*"

Mike made a face. "That's an English teacher's clue."

"It's still a clue," said Sarah. "I decided that the second verse of 'Sing a Song of Sixpence' was Neil or Winka's work. As well as the rest of the copycat stuff, which was all done by the same pair of scissors. I'm betting it was Neil. Because he can handle poetry and would have enjoyed trying to put the blame on Harvey Dodge with the Marvell and Stevenson and Tennyson imitations. A joke more in his style. Like Harvey, Winka has no imagination."

"All right, all right," said Julia impatiently. "I'll grant the second series of cutouts was a Wentworth project. But the bridle on poor Farney. Why wasn't that Neil's work? A hideous joke."

Sarah nodded. She reached to the table for a glass, added two cubes of ice, a finger of rum, and a heavy dose of lemon soda to the mix. "Agreed. It looked like Neil. And maybe that's what Winka wanted. To give it Neil's touch. But the trouble is that Neil didn't do it. He didn't have time. He was seen coming out of the lavatory by you after Alex and I had left for Nova Scotia, and before that he was present at our getaway. His blazer pocket had rice and tapioca in it. I'm still shaking it out of some of my clothes. Alex's suit jacket, too."

"Which leaves Winka," said Alex. "Of all the people who went down to the stable, only Winka had the time, and, I should add, the good right arm with which to strangle Farney. Jane Zimmer has been a possibility since no one remembered her at the rice throwing, but she's been spotted in one of the just developed photographs taken by my mother, at the time that Sarah and I drove off. My Cousin Giddy and Patrick—who is left-handed—came back to the reception. Tilly was lurking by the south paddock, but she's left-handed, too. Tim Fournier arrived well after seven-thirty to shoe Lollipop with Tilly's help. But I don't see them—both left-handers—as joint murderers of a man they both liked."

"I believe," said Julia with a certain grim satisfaction, "that I predicted Winka and Neil. If anyone had listened we might have been spared a great deal of distress."

"A prophet without honor," murmured Alex. "Go on, Sarah."

"George's telling us to remember something we already knew kept banging in my head. I went off by myself on Friday after the library visit and tried to think. It worked. I remembered Uncle Tom's cane and I remembered sitting down with Alex in Winka and Neil's living room and listening to them both say how sorry they were about Farney. And hearing Winka say, 'Imagine, he was wearing a pony bridle.' How obscene it was. Now everyone for miles around knew that Farney had on a bridle because Julia had told them when she telephoned about finding Farney in the annex. But just Winka mentioned a 'pony bridle.' That was a detail only the police knew then. Friday before the horse show I asked Aunt Julia if she remembered what kind of a bridle was around Farney's head, which horse did it belong to, and she was insulted. Said that was the least important detail of finding him. That she had no idea. So she couldn't have told Winka. In fact, until the police released the details, we only knew that *some* kind of bridle was used."

"And," added Mike, "Winka knows that barn like her own face."

"More important," said Sarah, "Winka teaches the beginners. Neil teaches the advanced kids. Winka uses the pony Gingersnap for beginners and Julia keeps Gingersnap's bridle in the grain room for that pony. Only that one little pony. The twitch, of course, is nearby, hung up with the halters. Ready and waiting."

Alex, restless as usual, stood up and began to circle the room. Then stopped in front of Sarah. "As you said, the murderer always seemed to take what came to hand."

"That's what I thought, too," said Mike. "Crude and rude. Almost random. Shotguns and broken branches. Cleaning rags."

Julia, who had been sipping her scotch, suddenly choked. "I know," she shouted. "That damn Winka. She's the one who found the kerosene-soaked rags because she started the fires."

"They were going to be found by the arson squad anyway," said Alex. "So why not divert attention from yourself by being the helpful finder? Tell your husband and let him tell the police. Nice touch."

"Nice, my eyeball," said Julia, reaching for the scotch.

"That's Winka the opportunist again," said Sarah. "Everyone was racing and chasing after Tilly's corgis, so Winka was free to plant her rags around the cross-country jumps in peace. She probably opened Jane's truck and let the dogs out herself."

"And to think," spluttered Julia, "that I allowed that female to teach children, to take her tractor all over my property."

"Easy, Aunt Julia," said Sarah. "The scotch is going to your brain. But you're right, Winka's tractor is important. She must have moved Sean Conners' body. She and Jane were all over the cross-country course in their tractors. I think Sean, after being hit with the cane, was first hauled off to the manure pile

Julia keeps for the garden. It had to be a quickie job because the Preakness would only hold everyone for a short time."

"Ten minutes at the most for some," said Alex. "Twenty minutes, an hour, for the die-hard race fans."

"All she had to do was get Sean alone," said Sarah. "He was reluctant to mix it up with the race crowd, so it would be easy to ask him to step out. Perhaps a job offer. Who knows? Say it goes like this. Sean props the cane against a tree or lets it drop while he talks to Winka. She picks it up, takes him by surprise—he was sick, feeble, possibly had been drinking. Anyway, she does it. Whacks him with the cane. Uses the same system she'd use later with Farney. Hit, stun the victim, then strangle. Drag him behind the stable perhaps. Strangle him with a lead rope. Then off to the manure pile. Cover him in a hurry. Return to the farmhouse."

"And," put in Mike, "find Julia's old rocking horse, Brandy Boy, sitting on the lawn. Another chance for a diversion."

"Absolutely. Winka has the lead rope—which she must have still been carrying because, after all, this is her first murder; she's not careful about evidence. She strings up Brandy Boy—using the release knot because it's second nature for a horse person to use that knot. Two diversions. First the Preakness gives her time for the murder, then hanging Brandy Boy gives her more time to go back to the manure pile and finish covering it."

"But," added Mike, helping himself to a third chocolate doughnut, "being an amateur, she drops the cane. Can't retrieve it because of the rocking horse crowd. Later can't find it, or if she does, never has a chance to snake it out of Julia's umbrella stand. Also, still the amateur, she uses the lead line she'd strangled Sean with for hanging Brandy Boy. Leaves an A-1 clue in broad daylight. Trouble is, we never found the lead line after the rocking horse had been put back."

Sarah flushed. "Another amateur got into the act. I picked up the lead line—Alex asked if I was stealing it—and I hung it back with all the others in the stable. Sorry about that."

"Wait until I tell George," said Mike, grinning. "He's afraid you're going to get ideas above your station. Think you could be a state trooper or something."

"George has nothing to fear," said Sarah. "But go back to the days after the Preakness. At some time Winka must have moved Sean Conners' body. The tractor again. She couldn't have left it in that manure pile because Julia regularly spreads the stuff or has it hauled away. So Winka moves the body to the Coffin. Probably thinks it's a clever place. Tamps down the footing but doesn't do a deep-down job because—and this is crucial—at that point she doesn't know Julia has changed the cross-country course. For the last few years the Coop and the Coffin and the lakefront run haven't been used. So the Coffin seems like a safe stash until there's time to bury the body in a better location."

Julia looked thoughtful. "I remember how helpful Winka was. Particularly after the fire, when we began rebuilding the jumps. That's when everyone found out about the course changes. But Winka probably couldn't shake Jane Zimmer, who was working with her. As well as Patrick and all those Maine Combined Training Association volunteers. The place was swarming and she couldn't get loose."

"Okay, Sarah, move on," said Alex. "Next it's Bradley Pfeifer. Tell Julia about your reenactment of the shovel business."

And Sarah, compressing the whole into a single paragraph, described her effort, ending, "Winka probably runs like the wind; she's built for it. She'd make better time than I did. She took advantage of everyone busy at the campfire. Jump in the truck, hide in the bushes with the shovel—the shovel she'd have seen every day all year—bash Brad, and run back."

"Run back in time," Alex said, "to plant herself at the campfire and spill her cocoa so that everyone would remember that she was down at the campfire exactly where she was supposed to be. Same pattern. Find a period of confusioh—in this case the campfire, the singing, and the fact it was getting dark. Which all brings us right back to today. Letting out the dogs. Of course, anyone could have done it. The gate wasn't locked. But it was a proven way of creating confusion—remember the corgis. Sarah said it best: Winka has no imagination. She does the same thing over and over. But there's one thing I don't understand. Nothing happened to the farm this afternoon. Not a damn thing."

"Good God," said Julia. "What do you want? Winka happened. Maybe letting the dogs out was her idea of a climax. What she was working for. Let the dogs out, ruin the cross-country, unseat riders, scare horses, and then go swimming."

"Yeah," said Mike, "letting those dogs out seems like some sort of crazy, desperate measure. No real purpose or plan."

"Winka's never had a real plan," said Sarah. "The situation's ripe and Winka responds. I think Alex is right. Just as she must have done with the corgis, she used dogs to create a diversion."

"Why!" demanded Julia. "A diversion from what? For falling off a horse? For riding too fast? So no one would notice that she'd broken her neck by turning her ride into a steeplechase?"

"Maybe she rode like that for a reason," said Mike. "She knew that a lot of horses pounding through the Coffin might turn up Sean's body. Especially since many horses wear special shoes for jumping. Shoes with studs that really chew up a footing."

"Go back to letting out Patsy and the setters," said Sarah. "I said it was a diversion. When her cross-country ride time came we'd all be busy chasing them. It was a desperation measure, but if a lot of people were tied up pursuing dogs, she might be able to finish the course—she was the last rider, remember—then come back and fix the sand over the body—in case it'd been uncovered. She must have been worried out of her mind, so she rode like a maniac. To get the ride over with. Ironic that it was her horse that uncovered the body. Ironic that it was the dogs she let loose—if she did—that spooked the horse . . ."

Mike grinned ". . . that spooked the horse that fell in the jump that dumped the rider that uncovered the body that frightened the woman . . . all on the farm that Julia built. I tell you, those nursery rhymes are mighty contagious."

"Mike," said Julia severely, "hold your tongue. This isn't a joking matter. How George Fitts puts up with you . . ."

"I'm good for George," said Mike. "Otherwise he'd be completely plastic. A police robot."

"Back to Winka," said Alex. "After she was thrown, I think she just wanted out. And took the nearest way. Crawfish Pond."

Sarah nodded soberly. "Total panic. Injured, bleeding. She may have had a concussion—that helmet notwithstanding. Helmets aren't miracle workers. I think Alex is right. She escaped. Got out. Not necessarily with suicide in mind, but in the end she ran out of options." Sarah paused, fingered a lemon-filled doughnut, pinched it so that a yellow goo oozed from its sugary hide, frowned, and put it back on top of a magazine. "Now," she said, "we can talk about motivation, because Winka Wentworth had it in spades."

"Highfeather forever," said Alex.

"Right," said Mike. "And now that George—with Sarah and Katie Waters as assistants—has zeroed in on Winka, he'll let you talk about motivation. Highfeather was threatened. Norminco was nibbling at its edge. Making offers all round town. Tilly and Jane showed signs of considering a lease. Or a sell. Harvey Dodge, ditto. But Julia's land was mineral-free. Winka and Neil knew this because of the orienteering games. Sell Highfeather's land on Fallen Tree Pond. Move Julia out, move Highfeather in. Great campsite, lake, land, stable, and arena for riding. I'd say Winka and Neil, at some point, agreed to work on the project, but Winka went in deeper. Went into murder."

"It was quite a campaign," said Mike. "If Julia won't be sensible and marry Harvey, then force the issue. Have Neil start in on the cut-out messages—Julia having gone public about the early ones. Attack her where she's vulnerable. Her farm, her helpers. Get rid of Sean Conners. Which she finally did the third time round. But then Farney turns up, so get rid of him. It's like stamping out ants. Try anything. What comes to hand. Start a fire, shoot up the place with Neil's shotgun—yes, we've gotten our search warrant and found the thing. Then eliminate Brad Pfeifer."

"Yes, Brad had to go," said Sarah, her voice rising. "Merrilark was the competition for a new campsite. Brad was determined to keep Merrilark going for his aunt, Mrs. Eff. Winka saw that the Pfeifers might sell out to Norminco and buy Julia's land—if Julia ever decided to sell. And if she did decide, she'd sell to her old buddy, Leah Pfeifer. Not to the Wentworths, who were fairly new to the area. Besides which Julia had never shown any great fondness for the two. So Winka had to get rid of Brad. Perhaps later on eliminate Leah Pfeifer if she proved troublesome."

"A question," said Julia. "Because your explanations leak like a sieve. Why not kill or maim me? Or Patrick? A couple of old geezers, easy targets. Often alone."

"I wondered about that," said Sarah. "But maybe I have an answer. A dead Julia means someone else inherits the farm. A lot of someones. You've told me you'll leave the farm to your relatives. All of us. Winka wouldn't want to deal with a set of ten or twelve heirs. Better to leave you intact and get you to move."

"And I have a possible answer to the Patrick question," said Alex unexpectedly. "Sundays, if I'm on call, I go into the hospital. See patients. Do rounds. And I often go through town. Pick up breakfast, a cup of coffee."

"Yes, yes," said Julia impatiently.

Alex raised his hand in a sort of blessing. "Peace, Julia. I pass Our Lady of Good Hope on my way and from time to time I've seen Patrick going in and coming out. And I have also seen Winka Wentworth doing the same."

"Well, yes," said Julia. "She drives the Catholic campers to mass in the camp van. I knew that. What are you trying to say?"

"That Winka Wentworth not only takes the campers, she stays with them. Goes to mass. Winka's not a true-blue Anglican. She's RC. I did a little of my own research after Sarah and I visited Highfeather and were given a catalog. There's a short bio of Winka and Neil. Winka's Anglo-Irish. Born in Dublin. Moved to England when she was about twelve. Later met Neil. Apparently didn't change her religion, but does keep her Uncle

Horace's non-denominational church-in-the-pines service going at Highfeather."

"Why didn't I know this?" demanded Julia.

"Because, dear Aunt," said Sarah, "why should you? You've never been crazy about the Wentworths. Why should you want to know where one of them goes to church?"

"So," continued Alex, "I began thinking about Patrick, why he—the number-one man at High Hope Farm—wasn't attacked, and it struck me. Patrick and Winka are both Catholic, both Irish. Perhaps she couldn't bring herself to kill him."

"Or she never got the chance," added Sarah, "but it goes to show that you shouldn't simply ask, Why was one person killed, but why was this other person *not* killed?"

Mike Laaka rose from the sofa and stretched, the tip of his hands touching Julia's low farmhouse ceiling. "Okay, buddies. Shall we move on to Rafe Posner?"

"No," shouted Sarah and Alex in one voice.

"No," said Julia. She rose in her turn and switched off a wrought-iron lamp with a tipsy lampshade. "There's a time for talking and a time for going to bed. Enough is enough. Be off. Get out. What's the expression—'Sufficient unto the day is the evil thereof.' Well, this day we've had evil by the yard. Up to our necks in it. Sticking in our craw. Down our hatch."

"I think," said Mike, "your Aunt Julia is trying to tell us something."

THE PICNIC

TWENTY-TWO

THE rain had stopped sometime in the night, yielding to a July dawn of promised brightness and warmth. Sarah had slept without moving, her dreams dodging away from recent events and centering on an early hospital experience when she had undergone an appendectomy. But in the dream the surgery was taking place on her left foot. She tried to leave the operating table, but the surgeon persisted, taking his scalpel and slicing across her instep. She sat up suddenly. Wide awake. Her foot pounding.

Of course. That damned hoof. Fifteen hundred pounds of Duffie landing on her sneaker. Gingerly she moved her foot from under the covers and slid out of bed. Alex, she saw, was still sleeping, one arm curled around the bedpost, the other across her now empty pillow. But for Sarah the night was over, and the act of dressing pointed her to the first necessity of the day. A pair of shoes. Or to be exact, one shoe. A shoe to accommodate a swollen and purpled left foot. A shoe from her own house on Sawmill Road.

Dressed and followed by Patsy, she crept downstairs, an unlaced sneaker on her injured extremity. Arriving in the kitchen, she saw by the clock that it was just five-thirty. Early enough so that even Aunt Julia was abed, the two setters still curled on rugs, the cats circled on chair seats.

Suddenly, as had happened before in the last few weeks, Sarah wanted out. Away. Away from police, the dragging of pond, the exhuming of bodies, the probing of manure piles. Limping, she made her way to the umbrella stand and selected the ski pole. Something to help forward locomotion. And in no time she and Patsy were driving the rental Subaru down through the stable parking lot, past George Fitts's theater of operations, past the pasture and paddocks of High Hope Farm.

It was good to have a purpose completely separate from homicide, even if that purpose was only the location of an oversized left shoe. But reaching the town of Union hunger overtook her and Sarah pulled up next to a local eatery, Hannibal's Café. Thank heaven it was open for business. Thinking of scrambled eggs and toast—something truly fortifying—she made her way into the diner and opted for takeout. The little town boasted several picnic tables and the idea of breakfast on the village green seemed a pleasant one.

Very pleasant indeed. A tranquil moment of hometown summer surrounded by white clapboard houses with dark green blinds, the American flag hanging from second-story windows, the spire of the Methodist church beyond the houses, the small brick post office, a matching brick bank, the town library and a somewhat battered-looking IGA supermarket.

Sarah fastened Patsy's leash to the picnic table, inserted a straw into her paper container of orange juice, and drank deeply. Then steaming-hot scrambled eggs taken from a plastic fork, buttered toast and tea. Peace at last. Well, not entirely peace, because there seemed on the fringes of the greensward a sort of well-ordered bustle. A woman with balloons, a girl carrying a French horn, two cub scouts in uniform. Someone dressed as a clown. Was something going on?

But before Sarah could puzzle out the moving scene, she was

joined. Joined by a man climbing over the picnic bench and sitting himself opposite.

Neil Wentworth.

For a moment Sarah was too astonished to speak. And then, furious. Undesirable persons forever inserting themselves into private domestic life. Even a solo breakfast impossible.

Neil produced a carton of eggs, the twin of her own, and a large paper cup of coffee. "I'm famished," he explained to Sarah.

She glared at him without speaking. Neil Wentworth. Wanted person. Homicide adjunct. And, quite likely, a new-made widower—not that this fact weighed in his favor. And what a mess. His face grimy, his red hair ruffled. Unshaven. Uncouth. And still dressed in his riding clothes. Filthy breeches, his red and gray polo shirt streaked with dirt and patches of damp, its collar torn.

"Relax, Sarah, I don't want to ruin your breakfast. Just about ten minutes of it. Sorry about the way I look. Spent the whole blessed night on Crawfish Pond looking for Winka. Gave it up this morning. Time to regroup and make a few decisions. Get something to eat. I was hoping to find you. Or Alex. And now you've saved me the trouble."

"Make it quick," answered Sarah through tight lips, "and then I'm going to call the police." She reached down to the grass and picked up her ski pole. Patsy, however, was slumbering noisily at her feet. A failed watchdog.

Neil gave a slight smile. "You can put that thing down; I'm not going to attack you. I saw you limping over here so I suppose some horse stepped on your foot. It's an occupational hazard. We all get stepped on. And you can't rile up Patsy. He's an old friend. You can call the police when I'm finished. But I think I can get loose and be elsewhere by the time they turn up. Far away, driving through those charming little backwater Maine towns with Indian names I can't pronounce, like Norridgewock, and Passadumkeag. And yes, you could shout for help to that boy riding his bike, but think what you'd miss. Neil Wentworth's story. Told in Neil's own words." He paused, looked at Sarah quizzically. "All right? I may proceed?"

Sarah studied her scrambled eggs, then lifted her head and met Neil's face. "Okay. Okay. But I don't see why. Why me?"

"Look at the options. The police? I want to talk to someone more human than George Fitts and his merry men. And not Julia, though I do admire the woman. Lots of grit. I did say, didn't I, that she closely resembles my Aunt Cecily of sacred memory who died with her boots on. Climbing a ladder. Anyway, I don't think Julia has the patience to hear me out. She's too much the victim to listen quietly without trying to do something violent, and we've already had too much of that. Haven't we?"

"Yes," said Sarah shortly. And then. "Ten minutes."

"Here goes. And eat your eggs before they cool. First, Winka. Gone. No chance she'd have made it across Crawfish Pond. Not after being thrown off Folly. Injured."

"And trying to swim in riding boots," put in Sarah, who had planned to remain entirely silent. She bit her lip and took a large bite of eggs as a way of keeping to her resolution.

Neil took a long sip of coffee, then seemed to brace himself for recitation. "So I'm alone. No Winka, no Highfeather. Colonel Dodge is nursemaiding the camp along with the senior counselors. If the camp survives, it'll be because Harvey and Leah Pfeifer take charge. Solid senior citizens. Poor Winka and her Highfeather. Always Highfeather. You think Tilly Martin is obsessed? Tilly is a rank beginner. Winka lived and breathed that camp. Day and night. Come hell, high water, or Norminco. You know, she had her eye on High Hope Farm from the minute Norminco and Jim Shale turned up."

"Because High Hope property would make a great campsite," said Sarah, giving up on the idea of being a silent listener.

"Right," said Neil. "But how to manage the removal of Julia? Those first cut-out messages that Julia announced gave us the hint and Winka ordered me to follow up with them. Winka was good at ordering. I didn't know at first that Mother Goose was involved, so I decided to implicate Harvey. His favorites: Marvell, Tennyson, Stevenson. 'Abou Ben Adhem' was a departure. I got carried away."

Sarah took a large bite of toast, chewed, and nodded to herself. So she was right about Neil as the poet. Then, "You'd given up on Harvey marrying Julia and moving her to his farm?"

"I tried to tell you about Harvey that morning when I came to the kitchen. I wasn't lying when I said he was a stealthy old pussycat. I knew he'd been visiting Leah Pfeifer, helping with some of the waterfront programs. Highfeather and Merrilark have adjacent properties, adjacent docks—as you know. One waterfront overlooks the other. The boys love the view. So, I suppose do the girls. Anyway, Harvey Dodge was at Merrilark a lot."

"Double-dealing Harvey Dodge," said Sarah.

"Courting Julia and courting Leah. And planning to make Norminco happy by leasing Quartermaster Farm to them and putting cash in his own pocket. Harvey no doubt found Leah Pfeifer an easier article to deal with than Julia. Though that's beside the point, which is that Winka saw Brad as the obstacle. And she didn't know Brad was temporary, only staying on at Merrilark to fight Norminco. No one knew about that until the police tipped their hand when they questioned us after Brad died."

"So Winka killed Bradley Pfeifer. With the shovel."

"Could be. She's one of the people who had an opportunity, but I have no proof. And I don't want proof. I thought if it wasn't Winka or Jim Shale it might be one of Julia's missing helpers—Rafe or Sean Conners. Well, no matter who killed Brad, it seemed a pretty fair solution to our problem."

"And you didn't kill anyone? Or try to? You want me to believe it's all Winka. Because it's easy to blame her now."

"But the police know very well I never had the time or opportunity. Not for Farney Thompson, not for Brad. And believe it or not, I didn't do in Rafe or Sean Conners—I'm assuming that spectral character in the Coffin is one or the other of them. And, for what it's worth, I'm not much good at bashing people.

I'm a coward. I lack focus. That essential single-mindedness. Obsession."

"Which Winka had."

"Correct. Winka never really told me what she was up to. Said she'd found Farney dead in the annex room. Not that she'd done it herself. I suppose she hung a bridle on him to throw the police off the track. She must have had the idea from last year's Halloween party, when one of the kids wanted to go as a horse wearing a real bridle and Gingersnap's was the only one that fitted the human head. But, between you and me, in case the police started pointing at her, I think the bridle was an effort to move a little blame in my direction. Share the load. I'm the joker. The fun person, and Winka must have wanted me in the plot."

"So even now you're not absolutely sure Winka killed anyone. Brad, Farney, Sean Conners. It was his body in the Coffin."

Neil paused, looked out over Sarah's head toward the bandstand that stood in the middle of the green. "Nice little town, Union," he said. "Cozy. But probably a caldron of jealousy, rage, and human mendacity." He sighed deeply. "So that's three murders. Anyway, I did begin to suspect. There was that shooting affair, after which I found my shotgun in the wrong place, and Winka telling me how a branch must have fallen on Sean Conners' head when he was sleeping in Julia's north pasture. And Winka, when she told me how she'd strung up the rocking horse to scare Julia, as part of the plan to nudge Julia out, well, she seemed entirely too nervy, too anxious about what was a pretty simple prank. And later on she was jumpy when the talk turned to Sean Conners disappearing. Then, after she found the rags that started the fire, I began to think I had a lethal wife. What Winka wanted, Winka usually got. Like one of those very dangerous Roman women. But I didn't know what to do about her because I couldn't turn her in. I mean, she *was* my wife. Not that we've been getting along that well, but I still felt a certain attachment. And I really did want to move Highfeather to High Hope Farm and make the little lady happy. Feed her obsession and make it go away."

Sarah drank the last of her tea and closed the carton over the dried mass of scrambled eggs. "So what's next?" she asked.

"There's a public telephone over by the post office. You can call the police. But by then I'll be on my way." Neil looked over at the other picnic table, where an elderly couple was unwrapping a take-out package. Beyond, two old men shared a park bench. He smiled. "Golden oldies having breakfast. Old duffers chatting it up. I don't think you could make them hold me. But it's certainly the right day for a good clean getaway."

"What do you mean?" demanded Sarah.

"Where are your eyes? Murder must have gone to your brain. It's the Fourth of July. The Glorious Fourth. Look at the bunting on the little bandstand. The flags. Every house is hanging up Old Glory. All over America, all over Maine, little towns like Union are making ready to have a parade. A celebration. Floats, hot dogs, games. Fireworks. Hurrah for Lexington and Bunker Hill. Down with the redcoats. As a true-blue British citizen I usually regret the occasion, but today I'm grateful to General Washington."

Sarah found herself increasingly irritated. "I don't see how the Fourth of July helps." She fumbled in her pocket for a quarter for her telephone call.

Neil handed her several coins. "Be my guest. And think about it. Every little town will be chockablock full of parade goings-on. The police will be part of the parade. As will the firemen and the fire engines. And the Boy Scouts, the Girl Scouts, and the chambers of commerce. The candidates for selectman. I can disappear into the crowd. And out of it. No squad car can fight its way through a Fourth of July traffic jam. Later I'll hit the secondary, the farm roads, and by afternoon be long, long gone."

Neil took a last gulp of coffee and put down his cup. "And so, Sarah, it's been a good life while it lasted. I enjoyed working with the Highfeather kids, the whole camp scene. And I'm very sorry about Winka, but I'm not staying around to identify her body. Tell Julia she can have our horses. Wallop and Folly. They'll work out nicely as school jumpers and be a lot safer to handle than that big beast Duffie." And with this Neil rose swiftly to his feet, climbed over the picnic bench, and moved out of reach. And before Sarah could protest or think about shouting "Stop, thief," he was striding fast toward the street. Then, as she stood up, holding her paper napkin, he climbed into a small blue utility truck. The engine started and the truck turned out from the curb, swung onto the road, and disappeared in a northerly direction.

Full of zeal, Sarah marched over to the telephone. And then faltered. What did she have in mind? Neil Wentworth, however deplorable, wasn't public enemy number one. Probably nothing more sinister than a material witness and the sender of threatening poems. Could he even be called an accessory? Or just a rather unprincipled dupe of a dangerous wife? And she, Sarah, was not a member of any known police force. Should she butt out? Let matters take their course? For a minute she stood irresolute. Then she reached for the quarter and dialed.

Not the police. She called High Hope Farm and Alex answered.

"For what it's worth—and I don't know if I'm being a snitch or a useful citizen—Neil Wentworth is right now heading out of Union in a small blue pickup truck."

There was a pause and then Alex told her that her news was interesting, he would tell Mike, and to come back. And that Rafe Posner had surfaced, alive and well, the police were talking to him that very moment and Julia was being protective. And that Tilly and Jane in the interest of fellowship and forgiveness had invited the neighborhood to a Fourth of July picnic that evening. And also that Colonel Harvey Dickerson Dodge had announced his engagement to Mrs. Leah Pfeifer of Camp Merrilark.

"Good Lord," Sarah exclaimed. "Poor Aunt Julia."

"Julia's making out just fine. Rafe is taking up the slack."

"And Winka Wentworth?"

"Nothing yet."

* * *

Sarah's trip to Sawmill Road and to her own farmhouse, now in the midst of renovation, was doubly useful. She found a hiking shoe with a boxy toe for her ruined foot, and, standing in the kitchen in the midst of plaster, lathes, planks, and plumbing, was reminded that sometime in the near future, she and Alex might enjoy married life under their own roof.

But on returning to High Hope Farm she was also reminded that the present, not the future, was on the table. Winka Wentworth's body had been found. Sarah arrived in time to see a plastic-shrouded something being loaded into a police ambulance; to see the ambulance depart quietly at a moderate pace—this because for the vehicle's chief passenger neither sirens nor speed was necessary.

Julia, Alex, together with Sarah, silently watched the ambulance disappear down Tri-County Road and were then joined by Mike Laaka coming from the field office-trailer with Rafe Posner in tow. Rafe, long fair hair newly brushed and tied back, dressed in clean khaki trousers and a fresh blue checked shirt, garments Sarah recognized as belonging to Alex. Aunt Julia, she told herself, must have helped herself to Alex's wardrobe. As a consequence, Rafe did not in the least resemble the ghost-in-the-blanket or the disheveled man who had sprung into the Coffin, pulling Winka Wentworth to safety.

"Okay, Julia," said Mike. "Here's Rafe. You can hire or fire him. We'll be wanting to talk with him again, probably charge him with something. Vagrancy, stealing blankets, hiding out on private property. You can have a talk with him. He can fill in some gaps for you, especially since we won't be getting anything out of Winka Wentworth. Alex, come on back to the trailer. You've got to sign a death certificate. Death by drowning."

"Rafe," said Julia. "You remember Sarah, don't you?"

"Of course," said Rafe, smiling. "I played at the wedding."

"For heaven's sake, Aunt Julia," said Sarah. "I know Rafe, and this isn't a jolly little social occasion. Rafe, aren't you going to tell us what's been going on? Everyone's been looking for you. For ages. I've just had a dose from Neil Wentworth and he doesn't seem entirely sure that Winka actually killed anyone."

"But she did," said Rafe. "Let's sit down somewhere. I'm not supposed to take off again."

"Which is something you seem to do best," said Julia tartly.

"Yeah, I know. I'll try to hang around this time because I guess I'm something called a material witness."

"Over there," said Julia. She pointed to a stone wall that wandered along the edge of the cross-country course.

And with Sarah and Julia settled on the warm ground, rocks as backrests, Rafe told his story. First, Sean Conners.

"I didn't know why Sean was having those accidents. Okay, falling through the loft wasn't that strange except the floor was pretty new. But being hit by a branch. That didn't make sense. Sean wasn't up to riding bareback like Patrick said he might have done. He was more likely sleeping. Then after the Preakness he disappeared, and I thought it was someone who had it in for him, because Sean had a helluva temper. I just didn't figure out anything until later on, I found Farney Thompson."

Julia exploded. "You, you found Farney!"

"Yeah. The night of the wedding. I left the reception just as they were throwing the rice around. Went out to check on the mares and foals and found Tilly Martin wandering around by the south paddock. She seemed sort of excited so I hung in and let her talk about the stars and the royal family and then took a walk."

"Did you see Tim Fournier, the farrier, come?" demanded Sarah.

"Yeah, I saw him drive in later. After seven-thirty. But I thought, hell, I've worked hard enough for one day, let him find someone else to twitch Lollipop. So after I saw him grab Tilly I hiked on out to the south pastures for a change of scene. But after a while the fog started rolling in, it was getting dark and chilly, so I went back to the stable thinking I'd clean some tack. Went into the annex to find some cleaning cloths and there was Farney. Godawful sight with that bridle on. Got out of there and just took off. Sort of in a panic, I guess."

"I can't think," said Julia severely, "why you aren't being charged with his murder today. You were right there."

"The police had me over the barrel about that. But I found him late. After Tim Fournier had left."

"And you never saw anyone go near Farney?"

Rafe rubbed his chin. "No. But I saw Winka Wentworth. Just before I met up with Tilly, after the rice throwing, I went by the stable door and saw Winka Wentworth with a twitch in her hand. She was wiping the thing off and I thought, What in hell is she doing with a twitch? I mean, she was all dressed up in party clothes. Pink dress that sort of floated. So why was she trying to twitch a horse? But then I thought maybe one of the horses needed medication and she had to use the twitch to keep it quiet. And I wondered who helped her. She didn't see me and I didn't think much more about it until the police told me this morning the twitch was involved in the murder. That Farney was hit in the head with it."

Sarah stopped him. "Wait up. Did Tilly verify your being out there talking to her?"

"Sure. They brought her over early this A.M. for a statement." Rafe grinned suddenly. "Tilly was in her bathrobe and looked like a witch. I mean the real thing. She said she certainly did talk to me down by the paddock fence after the rice throwing and that I didn't seem to take the planet rotations seriously. That I wasn't a believer but I was a nice guy. I had something called an aura. Anyway, I guess she got me off the hook for Farney's murder."

Sarah frowned, picked up a long piece of grass, put it in her mouth, and chewed it thoughtfully. Then shook her head. "Why for God's sake didn't you just call the police when you found the body? Why take off? Why do anything so dumb?"

Rafe nodded. "I know it looks dumb. Now. But jeezus, I was in a real sweat. Look, Sean Conners was gone. He'd been attacked twice. People were sending Julia messages, stringing up her rocking horse, shooting at her farm. And now Farney was dead. I had a damn good idea who was next on the list. Me or

Patrick. Or Julia herself. And Winka Wentworth was loose. No one would suspect her."

"But you didn't know the twitch was involved. And you said you didn't know who killed Farney." Sarah protested.

"I didn't. But Farney had on the pony bridle. I really looked at Farney. I couldn't believe he was dead. Such a neat guy. Anyway, I knew that bridle. It's kept in the grain room away from the others. It's for Gingersnap and only Winka uses Gingersnap. So I began to put two and two together."

"And you decided to hide," said Julia. "That night."

"Yeah. In the woods. Took some of the woolen coolers and rain sheets. And a shovel. A bucket. Some food from the house. Got in through the cellar door at night because I know the combination to the lock. I moved into the Coop, which makes a good shelter. Later on, when everyone began working on the cross-country course and the police started looking under jumps, I dug a hole under the Coop. Like a foxhole and slept there. Then, a while back, what with all the police around, I moved myself to an old turned-over canoe on Patrick's waterfront strip. But hiding out was worth it."

"Why?" said Julia in a dangerous voice, and Sarah could see that she was becoming impatient with her favorite helper. The prodigal was perhaps losing favor. "Why was it worth it?"

"I could keep an eye on the farm. And you. Watch over you. Keep an eye on Patrick. On Winka Wentworth. I saw her set those fires. With the kerosene. And later on I saw her move someone's body with her tractor with the front-loader. From the manure pile to the Coffin. Round about evening. I followed her. Watched her dig the body in. I suppose it was Sean's body."

"And you never went to the police?" Sarah said, incredulous.

"Like I said, I was scared. And involved. And I was afraid no one would believe me when I admitted I'd found Farney. I mean, Winka Wentworth was one powerful lady and I'm just the stable hand. I could see myself going public and accusing her and having her come around and slaughter me. Because she's a very tricky female."

"Then why," persisted Sarah, "after all the hiding, did you go public in the middle of her cross-country ride?"

Rafe looked embarrassed. "What could I do? That horse of hers was on the ground, and sure as anything she was going to get kicked. I didn't want to save her. In fact, I'd been trying to think of ways of getting rid of the woman. Like disable her. Like scare her horse during the cross-country. So I was hiding out again behind a mess of bushes and then I saw her come crashing along out of control and thought, Goddammit, that bitch is going to kill her horse. Then the dogs came out of nowhere, Folly fell, and I just dragged Winka out of trouble. Knee-jerk reaction. But I'm sure as hell not sorry about Winka Wentworth swimming off into space." Here Rafe drew a deep breath, spread his hands out in a gesture of appeal, and said, "That's it. Sorry, Mrs. Clancy. I guess I've been a hell of a nuisance and you sure don't have to keep me on anymore. Or maybe you can't because I'll be sitting in the Knox County Jail."

Julia studied Rafe Posner for a full minute and Sarah could almost see a melting process at work. Then Julia pulled herself to her feet, nodded at Rafe. "We shall see," she said. "I'll have to talk to Patrick. But for tonight . . ." here she paused, then, "for tonight, will you please help Jessica and Patrick bring the horses in and assist with the evening chores?"

The Fourth of July picnic held that evening at Appleyard Farm was, in Sarah's opinion, one of the strangest events of a very strange summer. Except for the absence of the two Wentworths, all the principal players in the recent happenings were there. Yet by constantly shifting positions each warring or contentious party managed to avoid the other. Jane did not look Julia Clancy in the eye; Harvey Dodge, one arm in a sling as a result of his fall, the other given to Leah Pfeifer, circled wide of Julia; Jim Shale avoided Mike Laaka but courted Harvey Dodge and several other farm owners; Mike Laaka dodged Jim Shale and sidestepped Tilly Martin; and Sarah moved away from Tilly, Jane, and Jim Shale, and confined herself to Alex, Jessica, and Patrick.

But all this dodging and circling was made easier by the combined forces of Camp Merrilark and Camp Highfeather (the latter greatly reduced in numbers because some anxious parents, on the news of the Wentworth defection, had removed their sons). Games had been prepared as were foot races and water balloon contests, so that the adults had plenty of cover for their avoidance maneuvers.

All the adults except Tilly Martin. She, dressed in patriotic red, white, and blue with streamers in her yellow hair, bounced happily from one group to the next. And then, just before the fireworks—courtesy of Colonel Dodge—Tilly appeared behind Sarah and tugged at her sleeve.

"Sarah, I can't wait to tell you."

"Tell me what?" said Sarah warily.

"It's so exciting. I won't be able to move to High Hope Farm after all. The planets have spoken again. Everything has changed."

"Well," said Sarah, smiling. "That sounds hopeful."

"Challenging," said Tilly. "I'm going back to school."

"School?"

"Graduate school. I'm going to study queens. Through history and through literature. I'll be in your department, I hope. I'm applying tomorrow. Bowmouth College."

"Queens?" said Sarah. "How do you mean, queens?"

"The spirit of the queen. The natural queen and the anointed queen. I feel the spirit of a queen moving within me. Ever since poor Winka Wentworth left us. But she was anti-queen, of course."

"Of course," said Sarah. She took one step back from Tilly.

"I feel moving within in me the presence of Zenobia. Her power, her majesty. Asia Minor, Syria, Mesopotamia, Egypt. I will start with Zenobia. It will make a wonderful dissertation. Women who are queens. Women who should be queens, who will metamorphose into queens. Like bees. Or moths."

"Yes," said Sarah, taking another step back. "I suppose there are a lot of them out there. Queens, I mean."

"And Sarah, I need a recommendation from you. To back up my application to graduate school."

"The firecrackers are starting," said Sarah. "Let's sit and watch." And she pulled Tilly down and gestured to Jane.

"Zenobia," she said to Jane.

"Quite sensible, I think," said Jane. "Graduate school will keep Tilly busy. We're counting on you and your friends in the English department. Tilly will need a fellowship or grant because we're absolutely out of money."

Later, on the way home, limping along with her ski pole, together with Alex and Julia, Sarah brought up the subject of Tilly's newest interest.

"Splendid," said Julia. "Takes Tilly right off my back. No more rotation nonsense."

"I don't know if the English department is ready for Queen Zenobia," said Sarah. "Perhaps the Women's Studies program has funds. But with Tilly around I'll probably start talking to planets, too. And seeing stars and casting entrails."

"And if you do," said Alex, slipping his arm under Sarah's, "please concentrate on a prophecy that forces us to rotate into our own house by the harvest moon." He turned to Julia. "Not that we're not extremely grateful—"

But Julia cut him short. "You know, Alex, when you and Sarah do leave the farm, I will, of course, miss you both, but I will also be vastly relieved. I think that the two of you seem to have a terrible capacity for attracting trouble."